GW00771665

THE KING'S QUEEN

THE KING'S QUEEN SERIES
BOOK ONE

HAYDN HUBBARD

Copyright © 2023 by Haydn Hubbard

All rights reserved.

Book Cover Design by ebooklaunch.com

No part of this book may be reproduced in any form or by any electronic or mechanical means, including information storage and retrieval systems, without written permission from the author, except for the use of brief quotations in a book review.

To everyone who searches for themselves between the lines of these pages.
Welcome home.

KRYCOLIS

A FALLS

M

THE COMPOUND

CHAPTER 1
PROLOGUE

The boy and the girl entered the woods about an hour ago as the church bells rang. The girl came first, sprinting in with her skirts in hand right while the third toll chimed. Her cheeks were painted red, and she panted from the exertion, her clear blue eyes scanning her surroundings. She couldn't have been older than ten years. The trees were dense, and the sweet scent of bread wafted through the air from a nearby bakery. Her stomach gave an audible rumble.

"Vera!" The boy followed momentarily, a breathy whine escaping his thin lips. He was much tanner than her, with a mop of dark curly hair crowning his head. He stood regally compared to her slouch, though he was a few inches shorter than her.

The girl, Vera, popped out her hip and crossed her arms, an organic and amusing dynamic threading between the two.

"You've gotten slow," she said, still breathing heavily. The smug smirk imprinted upon her lips never faltered, even as the boy began to blush.

"Or maybe you've gotten faster," he countered quickly, like a skilled swordsman parrying a blow.

"Maybe." She puffed out her chest proudly. "How will you ever become captain of the guard when you can't even beat me at a small race, Blaine?"

He mumbled something unintelligible, and Vera giggled. The two ran through the trees again, straying further and further from the palace. A third child set forward, tiny hands outstretched to join them, when his mother caught his shoulder to pull him back. He sighed as the dying sunlight ceased to warm his face, and he was forced back into the cool shade.

"Why can't I go play with them, just this once?" His large green eyes pleaded, breaking his mother's heart. Kneeling in the soft summer grass, she took both his hands in one of hers and brushed blonde hair from his face.

"Because we are shadows. Shadows mustn't enter the light or else bad things happen. Come along now, my little *Noiterón*. We've lingered too long." He nodded and allowed his mother to lead him away. The echo of Vera and Blaine's laughter was cut short by the clattering of armor and the steady pounding of hoofbeats.

"By Laei, not today." The woman prayed, swooping her son into her arms and beginning to run. He was quite old to be carried now, nearing twelve in the fall. His eyebrows furrowed in confusion, but one look at his mother's panic-stricken face told him it was best not to ask.

He'd seen that look only once before, on a day not unlike today nearly a year ago. He barely remembered what happened, but he knew that must have been the worst day of his life. Sunlight picnics and playing with other children were normal before then, and he thought he had a father. No face came to mind whenever he tried to remember, but he could recall a husky and warm voice soothing him to sleep almost every night.

His mother wouldn't speak of the time before, nor that day. She simply said, "That was then, we must focus on now." She wouldn't say what happened, but he knew. That was the day that they became shadows.

CHAPTER 2
VEROSA

Through ragged breaths, I can hear the palace guard closing in behind me, but I won't let them take me back. Not today.

My bare feet slap against the cold stone floor as I sprint down one of the castle's many hallways, billowy skirt in hand. My lungs burn as I gulp down the dank morning air with greedy breaths, but I don't dare stop for a second. I will my legs to move faster when I hear the clattering of armor grow closer.

"She went this way!" a man shouts. He sounds too close for comfort. Quickly, I turn around another corner, scanning for an exit. In such a large and grand palace, one would think there'd be more windows or stairwells rather than hallways with dead ends. And I was so sure I had seen something earlier...

"Found you."

The open window at the end of the hallway promises freedom, and the pale light of the day seeps into the darkened hallway. Five paces away, only five small paces, and freedom is mine. I check to find no one else in the hallways. They've made this too easy today. Laughing, I hoist myself onto the windowsill, letting the wind dance through my hair. The inner city lays in the distance, just beyond the palace walls.

I let myself dream of what might happen if I finally escape past those walls into the inner city. Leaning a bit further out, I can smell the fresh bread wafting from the bakery and hear the clacking of hooves below. Looking down, I can see a small procession making its way towards the palace entrance. The carriage bears the crest of the Tesslari empire. Strange, considering they aren't due for another few months.

"Oh, Laei!"

My grip slips as a servant cries out, her hands immediately clasping over her quivering lips. My heart rises to my throat as I grab hold of the sill at the last moment, but not before the maid's shrieking alerts the guards of my whereabouts.

So much for that escape plan.

With a heavy sigh, I turn to face the young men who stand at the end of the hall. They begin to advance slowly, that is, until I threateningly swing further out, my torso exposed to the wind.

"*Mei Reinhavich!*" The one in the front shouts warningly but doesn't rush forward like the others.

"One more step, gentlemen," I coo with sickening sweetness, "and I go out this window."

"Mei Reinhavich, please reconsider." a younger one in the back says, his flaming red hair poking out slightly from under his helmet. He squeaks slightly as I squint at him.

"You have a new one, Raiko?"

"Yes, after *you* caused the other one to quit." I bat my eyes coyly as if to say 'who, me?'

"I'm just helping you weed out the weak-willed ones, commander." Commander Raiko groans and presses two fingers over that lump on his nose like he always does when I'm involved.

"The king requests your return."

"Request denied." A few of them gasp, but I only catch the older commander's eye and wink. "Have a good day, gentlemen." He barely has time to grumble a 'not again' as I let go of my grip on the windowsill and fall backwards out the window with a mocking salute.

The wind howls as I fall, drowning out the startled shouts of the guards above. Some rush to the window, as if to see whether their princess finally meets her death on the rocks below. And as much as I'd hate to disappoint them, I have better things to do today than die. The ground rushes up to meet me now, the sun clouded by willowy branches, a few of which scrape my arms. Any second now...

At the last second, I reach out and grip onto one of those tree branches, sturdier and longer than the rest of them. My muscles grunt in response to the force, and my shoulders threaten to pop from their sockets. Somehow everything stays intact and uninjured. I hang about ten feet from the ground, the bark biting into my palms as I hold myself up. Laughing victoriously, I spare a glance upward. None of the faces stare back at me; they're already on the move. Soon, I would be too. It had been luck, really, that I had spotted this tree when I slipped earlier, or else I would be holed back up in that study right now. Now just to get down...

Kicking my frilly skirts away from my ankles, I swing slightly. I must get closer to the trunk of that tree to plant my feet and find my way down. I'm almost there when I hear the first crack, and then the second.

Snap.

"Oh, no." My saving branch gives way beneath my weight, leaving me to fall to the into the mercy of the hard ground below. The wind whistles in my ear, a taunting melody as I screw my eyes shut and brace for the impact. A few seconds pass. I land lightly with a thud, though it's not against the ground. Rather, I fall against something much more forgiving. Forcing my eyes open, they meet a pair of steely gray and murderous anger. Okay, so maybe not as forgiving.

I can feel Captain Blaine's shoulders rise and fall heavily as he huffs. His jaw clicks as he tightens it. He's gnawing at his lip, a habit he's kept since childhood. A habit that usually comes right before he chews me out. And luckily enough, judging by his pursed lips and furrowed brow, he's having a bad day.

"Good catch." The metal of his armor tings as I pat his solid chest and attempt to push off of it. His grip tightens and holds me in place firmly against him. The mere pressure of it forces me to meet his eye.

"On my list of things to do today, catching you as you fell out of a tree was not one of them, *Mei Reinhavich*."

"Variety is the spice of life, they say." If Blaine could cross his arms right now, I'm sure he would, and he'd also give me that same 'you're lucky you're royalty or I'd give you a smackdown' look. "I can walk myself, you know."

"And risk you running off again? I think not. At least one person in this castle has got to keep their guard up around you." I look forward and pretend those words don't sting, that they don't mean something more.

"Is carrying me bad for your leg?"

No answer.

"Can you at least tell me where we are going?"

"Where do you think? Back to the palace." He grunts in effort, though I know it's from trying not to snap at me rather than carrying my extra weight. I'm certain at this point Blaine could carry an ox without breaking a sweat, just to prove a point to all those stuck-up nobles and generals.

"Why don't you just throw me under one of those carriages instead?" I grumble. His grip tenses on my waist as a group of merchants pass us, and he moves to shift his shielding arm in front of me. Yet another old habit. An old reminder. With a small cough and a nod to the passing men, he finally sets me down, but not without a stern look that tells me better than to run.

"Don't tempt me," he almost jokes, but his voice sounds... tired.

My gaze lands on his face, to the dark skin under his eyes where two dark circles reside. His jaw is still tight, and his curly dark hair is tousled as if he keeps running his hand through it. His hand is always within reach of his sword.

"You look tired. Ophelus keeping you up late these days?"

"No more than usual." His response is terse.

"You should go rest."

"I could rest if you stopped jumping out of windows, Verosa," he snaps, though his features immediately soften in regret as I step away. My name feels so heavy on his tongue. It sounded like he was spitting a curse rather than the name of someone who meant... well, whatever I meant to him.

"Verosa, I-" His voice is softer now, softer than it's been in months, when his eyes suddenly widen. "Look out!"

Spinning around, I find myself facing dark black eyes, so close I can see the two brown orbs residing in their pupils. Pure black hair coats powerful muscles, shiny dapples rippling across its barrel and flank. Beautiful. The stallion is both beautiful and deadly as it pauses only moments from crashing into me. I'm about to reach out my hand when it wheels into a rear, shaking out its mane, its nostrils flaring with rage. An ornate leather saddle decorates its back, but the loose, leather reins hang torn from the bridle. Blaine dives into me right as it strikes out with its front hooves, its muscles rippling with power. We both roll to the side, his body covering my own, his hands cradling my head. A young squire dives for the reins but is knocked aside as if he weighs nothing. Just then, a familiar mop of blonde hair appears before us.

"Easy, friend. I'd hate to put down a stunning creature like yourself," he soothes, slowly inching towards the raging beast. It lets out a shrill whinny, and I can see white in the corner of its eyes.

"Hurry up and grab it already, Torin!" Blaine hisses, still shielding me with his own body. I want to get up and help, but the oaf won't budge.

"Patience," Torin hums, approaching the stunning creature. He goes completely still before, in one fluid motion, he grabs the reins. The stallion tosses his neck once, but no further protest is made.

"See, that wasn't so hard now, was it… *Vestíg.*"

Shadow. What an appropriate name. Torin turns to smile at us with his signature loopy grin. He was always like that, cunning, alarmingly patient, and he might have a few screws loose as well. He's Blaine's secondhand man, an assistant, but Blaine would never accept someone calling him that. I did once, and he didn't speak to me until I threw myself into the moat. I found leeches in places no one should find leeches.

Torin hands Vestíg to another stable hand, who apologizes profusely for the blunder. Our friend simply laughs it off. "No harm no foul," he says.

"Well, looks like the horse wasn't the only one who slipped loose today. What are you doing out here, *Mei Reinhavich?*" Torin teases, poking my side with a long finger.

"Oh, you know, just taking an afternoon stroll."

"She jumped out of a window."

"Captain!" I hiss, elbowing him once.

"Then fell out of a tree." Torin clutches his belly when he laughs, and I feel my cheeks heat up in embarrassment. It's almost nice seeing Blaine crack even the smallest smiles. Torin, with his loopy grins and dazzling charm, seems to bring that side out in everyone he meets. Rumor has it he once charmed the Vari prince for his hand in marriage after one night, though he ultimately refused. I have yet to ask him if that certain rumor is true or as ridiculous as the rest of them.

The Vari man jogs to keep up with us and Blaine's powerful stride. His blonde hair bounces with almost the same amount of life he possesses and stands stark in contrast to his tan skin. Blaine nearly choked when he saw it, but I think it suits him.

Blaine only commented on how the dye must have rotten his brain, and that was that.

A few of the palace guard have caught up now, standing in the entryway to the palace, unsure of whether or not to approach.

"You lot!" Blaine makes the decision for them. I can hear the clinking of their chainmail as they collectively jump, then move forward in uniformed rows. Torin moves to attention on my free side, casting me a frivolous wink when Blaine isn't looking.

"That's the third time this week. You block the windows first. Those were my orders, and yet none of you followed them." He glowers down at them all, suddenly making these large men seem very small. The air hangs dead in silence, the boisterous sounds of the busy palace fading into the background. "This was your last strike. If a raid were to happen right now, the princess would be dead. All of you will go report to the barracks. Due punishment will be issued there." They all salute their captain in silence before marching back to where they came from in perfect unison.

"Everyone except you," Blaine growls, pointing a finger at the redheaded boy from earlier. He emits a sound that sounds like an 'eep' before bowing his head in regard for his senior officer. A pink blush paints his cheeks and ears, hiding most of his freckles. "Escort the princess back to the study, if you think yourself capable. If not, you are more than welcome to hand in your resignation now."

His words douse me in a cold shock. His voice is cruel and unfal-

8

tering and still so foreign even after all these years. Sure, they should've kept their heads and remembered orders, but there's never any real danger in the palace. Surely this was all too great of a punishment, the public humiliation. And yet I found guilt gnawing away in the pits of my stomach, soon masked by anger.

"That's enough, captain." I attempt to make my voice as stern and commanding as his had been. "You only caught me because you had the advantage of knowing me better."

"One must make use of any knowledge given to them, *Mei Reinhavich.*"

"Oh yeah?" I scoff. "Well, here's some knowledge for you. You'd fight a lot better if you took your sword and pulled it out of your-"

"Ah *Mei Reinhavich!*" Torin interrupts with an uncomfortably charming laugh. "Maybe it would be best if followed the young gentleman here. If not for your own reputation, then his... hmm?" he whispers the last bit with a slight inclination of the head towards the crowd forming on the outskirts of our small circle. A few of the Tesslari representatives are staring among the onlookers, but only one catches my eye.

"Who wears a hood in this heat?" I whisper to Torin as I reach for the younger knight's arm. My friend looks over his shoulder and only shrugs. "Southerners?"

"Funny."

The stranger seems to notice and nods his head with a serpentine smile. I shiver despite the heat wave flooding our borders.

"You were going somewhere?"

"Of course. You may escort me back to my studies now. Good day, *captain.*" I bite back my response to Blaine, who offers only a gruff nod and kisses the top of my extended hand. His lips send a soft shiver through my arm to my frantically beating heart. Sweat suddenly slicks itself against my forehead, and I fight the urge to fan myself.

"See you later, Vera." Torin smiles into the back of my hand before once again whispering, "such an interesting relationship you both have."

He's gone with a wink before I can risk my reputation more by flipping him a vulgar gesture.

Torin is right, though, about our relationship. Blaine, my best friend in this whole world, hates my guts now, I think. I'd love to know where it all went wrong.

The walk back to my studies is pleasant enough, and I savor every moment before I have to return to that room. The poor boy attached to my arm shakes in his armored boots every step of the way. He answers all my questions with "no, *Mei Reinhavich*" or "*a su sonjí (as you wish)*."

The halls are bustling with activity today, bakers rush with their precious ingredients in hand, and maids dust off the older tapestries. I sigh in admiration at the sight of those golden threads sparkling in the daylight. The finery and the marvelous stories lining them... I'd much rather help them dust than go back to this lesson.

"Did you have a good 'walk', your Highness?" Ms. Eida asks through her clenched teeth upon my return to the study. She's a mousey old woman with silver hair pinned tightly atop her head. Her thin lips are pressed into a courteous smile, and I can tell that her patience is running thin.

"Oh yes, it was quite refreshing." I smile with feigned innocence, though I know my cheeks are still flushed with the exertion of my failed escape. Ms. Eida nods curtly, that vein bulging from her forehead again.

"Very good. You're dismissed." She waves her shaking hands at the young guard, whose face blushes crimson again once the attention is turned to him. He squeaks and offers a hasty bow before stumbling out from the room. The door is left slightly ajar upon his departure. The clacking of Eida's heels sounds like chickens strutting as she takes small, hurried steps to shut the door. The thought makes me giggle.

"That boy won't last," the elderly woman groans while she lowers herself back into her chair.

"Who is he?" I ask. "I haven't seen him before."

"No one of consequence."

I frown, but Ms. Eida doesn't seem to care too much for my displeasure, as per usual.

"Your Highness!" My tutor's shrill voice and the aggressive tapping of her foot brings makes my head spin. "Who established the Raonkin Mage ban of 1428?"

"My great-great-great-great-uncle, King Alguird the Fourth." Eida smiles satisfactorily.

"Excellent, now tell me..."

I answer all of her questions with the same dull, monotone voice I always use with her, trying to slip away mentally if I can't physically escape today. It's never anything exciting or useful. Just facts about people who are too dead for me to care about.

I rest my head on my arms and think back to that horse from earlier, Vestíg. He must have come with the Tesslari delegates, seeing as Torin didn't know him. My friend spends most, if not all, of his free time in the stables, grooming, riding, and flirting with the stable hands.

But then what of the Tesslari? It is customary for delegates to visit every few years, as we also send our own party to their empire to ensure our alliance is still strong. However, the delegates weren't supposed to arrive with such a grand procession for a few more months, let alone today. Then there was that man from earlier. Something about him unsettled me. Maybe it was the way I couldn't see his eyes from under that hood or how unnaturally white his teeth were. I'll have to ply Blaine for information later; if Father were to tell anyone, he would be among those told.

"I can't keep working like this!" someone hisses in the distance, though it all sounds like I'm under water, the words floating just out of reach. I must have dozed off.

"I understand, take the afternoon, Ms. Eida. I will call for Tanja to come deal with the princess."

"Thank you. She needs you to keep her head on her shoulders."

"Good day, madam."

Those scuttling footsteps recede, and I screw my eyes shut even tighter once I hear the faltering steps coming towards me. The footsteps stop a few inches away, and then a warm breath is fanning my face. So close, this person is so close now. A gloved hand reaches up and gently brushes a stray hair from my face. My breath hitches, and the hand falls as if it has been burned.

"I know you're awake, Verosa," Blaine says coldly, that warmth disappearing immediately. He takes a few steps back, but I keep my eyes shut and force my breathing to be even. He waits a minute, and I debate dropping this act when he begins to walk away.

"Fetch Tanja. The princess has been requested for dinner by His Majesty," he says before adding quietly, "they'll have company."

The maid he stopped agrees in a hushed whisper before darting off down the hall to find my lady in waiting. Blaine pauses before his off-beat footsteps echo down the hallway, going the opposite way. Like he was never really here at all. My cheek and tip of my ear burns red hot where he had touched it. What had he been thinking?

I don't have time to consider it when Tanja enters the room. I can tell it's her by her bouncy and graceful footsteps.

"Mai Reinhavich." Her voice is a saccharine song, a lilting croon. Then, when she confirms no one can hear her, she shouts, "VERA!" She smacks my arm.

"Ow! What the-"

"Oh, good, you're up." She laughs, tugging me unceremoniously to my feet. Her deep brown eyes are sparkling with mischief. Her chestnut curls bounce on her shoulders with every step as she drags me towards the door.

"His Majesty has requested a royal dinner tonight, so we've got to get started early if we want you to be ready in time."

I scoff. "It can hardly be called a 'royal dinner' when there's only two of us and that grand dining hall."

"Well." Tanja bites her lip and looks down at her feet before staring back up at me. I'm caught off-guard when I fully blink sleep from my eyes and take in her appearance. Her shoulders are slumped, rather than pinned back with that regal dignity Tanja usually carries herself with, and her skirts are rumpled as if she's been clutching at them all day. I pull us to a stop.

"What is it?" I demand. My beloved maid begins fiddling with a loose curl.

"You just have company tonight, that's all!" she says suddenly, all of that exuberant joy once more highlighting her feminine features. She takes to humming a tune as she drags me to the bathing chambers, as if having forgotten all that troubled her before.

"Who?" I ask as she and the maids begin stripping my worn skirts and gown from my body. Royalty has long since left me without a scrap of modesty...around my maids, at least. I let them guide me towards the luxurious tub while Tanja pulls out an engraved box.

"A Tesslari delegate. Your father will explain more at dinner." She plucks a single comb from the box before setting it down beside the rest of her kit. The maids begin scrubbing the dirt from my arms, and one has taken to plucking the splinters from earlier out of my palms.

"Can't you tell me who? Or what it's about?" Tanja freezes before shaking her head.

"I don't know any of the details, just what I'm to prepare you for. And as much as I love you, Vera, I'm not going to risk my head to satiate your curiosity."

"I suppose you do have too pretty of a head," I muse, and she affectionately taps my nose with a smile on her face. I'm not sure what to consider Tanja. She is definitely a friend, or something of the sort, but a friendship between a maid and the heir to the throne is imbalanced. I could never take her to the villages just for an afternoon off or to the bathhouses in the inner circles of the palace. Anything we do together, she would be bound to wait on me and protect me. Some days even I question if our friendship is real or bought by the crown. But I love her dearly, and if I were allowed to have one, I would call her my friend.

"Don't frown, it causes wrinkles." Tanja's willowy fingers find my face, pressing and massaging some rich lotion into it. She pulls the corners of my lips back into a smile, and I swat her hands away.

"Tonight I think we do away with that braid and pin your hair up in curls like mine." The maids giggle as she lathers a thick shampoo into my hair and piles all of it atop my head. I pucker my lips in a pose before shaking my head, spraying her with bubbles. "Do what you'd like so long as you promise not to stab my scalp with those pins this time."

"Hmm, I can't promise that." Tanja considers before shoving my head underwater. I come up sputtering and glare at her, surely resembling a wet rat. She gently pats my head like a puppy before the maids yank me to my feet and roughly scrub me dry.

"The king has requested you wear this gown tonight. He had it tailored for the occasion."

"Laei, who is this delegate?" I gasp, gazing at the long black gown. It has a modest sweetheart neckline that fades into a sleek angel sleeve. The silk thing hangs sultry across every hollow and curve, with a long, thin golden belt hanging loosely around my waist. The lustrous fabric shimmers between shades of silver and emerald when it catches in the light, the colors of the Tesslari empire.

"Not what I would've picked," Tanja tuts instead of answering my question, "but it will do."

She begins to set out bejeweled jars of ointments, paints, and oils, carefully examining each one under the torchlight. Once satisfied with her selection, she dismisses the other maids, leaving us alone. She slowly uncaps the first jar.

"Do we have to do all the paints and powders tonight?" I groan, noticing the pouf in her hand. She pats my hand sympathetically with a small grimace and nod. Sighing, I resign myself to sulking in my chair as she begins her work.

The tapping of the pouf against my forehead drops the downfall of powder across my cheeks and eyelids. I scrunch my nose in distaste. It's so itchy. Tanja hums while she works, ignoring my complaints.

Outside, the sun has begun to set, tinges of pink and gold fighting for dominance over the auburn sky. The sun herself rests atop the lake outside my window, the last of its golden rays catching on the lithe branches of the weeping willow. The heat is unfaltering despite the dying sun. The last of the summer days are the hottest here in Krycolis.

Tanja dips her paintbrush into the only black oil now and ever so carefully darkens my lashes, then my eyebrows. I've always found this part ridiculous, considering my hair is already black, but trying to argue with Tanja is like trying to argue with my father. They both are always right.

"Stop sighing like this is the end of the world. It's one dinner." Tanja roughly smears the rough across my cheekbones and the bridge of my nose.

"It feels like the end of the world." I groan as she slaps more cosmetics across my cheeks. She frowns.

"Your face gets red so easily."

"Shut up. I know."

"Just be grateful the king is letting you socialize after the last incident. How is Duke Gadsden doing anyway?"

"I haven't received any more marriage proposals, so I would say he's doing well. Finally," I grumble as Tanja runs her hands through my hair, plucking pieces to pin back into place. She hums contently while she works, careful not to pinch my scalp.

"I'm going out tonight while you're at dinner with that other maid, Ruby."

"Aren't you supposed to ask me these things first?" I laugh. Tanja places her hands on my shoulders and leans forward, locking my eyes through the mirror.

"May I go on a date with a beautiful maid while you languish in a political dinner?" I roll my eyes. "Thought so."

"And who will keep me company when I have to complain about said dinner?"

"You could always call in that captain of yours." She spins away from me, striking a dramatic pose in the doorway, her hand pressed to her heart. "Oh, Blaine, I simply cannot bear my royal duties any longer. Let's run away together and start a farm. We can have some cows and chickens, and you could do all the work because I couldn't bear to get dirt under my fingernails-"

"Enough!" Tanja giggles as she dodges my expertly thrown pillow. It nearly knocks a poor maid over as she enters the doorway, all the color draining from her face.

"Pardon me, the king requests the princess."

Tanja blushes and straightens her skirts. "Of course. I will send her out in a moment. You may leave us."

"By the Laei, was that Ruby?" I wiggle my eyebrows suggestively, and know I have my answer when color blooms in her high cheeks. "She's pretty."

"I know. Now get dressed so I can go." She points a well-manicured finger towards the beautiful gown from earlier. I oblige and slip into it, noting the way the silk fits my every curve like a glove. The fabric is soft, but by no means is the gown comfortable. I put on my slippers and make to leave when Tanja rushes forward, a tiara in hand.

"Just know I love you very much, and that I will be back in the morning." She kisses my cheek after fastening the tiara in place and flings open the door before I have the opportunity to ask any questions.

"Have fun!" Tanja drawls out the word 'fun' before turning away as a heavy hand lands on my shoulder.

"Hello, Blaine."

"Mei Reinhavich." He nods curtly and extends his arm. I ignore the thrum of energy that shocks through my core as I accept it, draping my own across his. He clears his throat, and we begin our walk to the dining hall, where my father and this mysterious delegate await.

"So, do you know what this meeting is about?"

"Perhaps."

"And I'm guessing you can't tell me what it's about?"

"You'll find out soon enough." Typical. We continue in silence, our echoing footsteps the only sound in the hallway. The occasional servant offers a passing nod or bow, but other than that, there is nothing. It's suffocating. That is until Torin appears on my other side.

"By the Laei, try not to look like you're going to a funeral," he tuts, pushing my chin up with his thumb. "Though the black isn't helping the atmosphere."

"Father picked it out."

"Of course, he did."

"I gather you know what this is about as well?" Torin nods. "And I guess you won't tell me either."

"More like can't tell you," he amends, linking his arm through my spare one, "but don't worry, you'll find out soon enough." We pause before two grand doors, mahogany inlaid with pure gold with carved ivory handles. Extravagant and showy. My companions let go of my arms, Blaine leaves first with a tight face. Torin stays an extra moment.

"Ready to go face the wolves?" I offer a weak smile, and he kisses the back of my hand before he gestures to the guard to announce my arrival. He takes a step back, bows, and then those two grand doors open.

CHAPTER 3
VEROSA

The table is already piled high with an exquisite array of meats and fruits. Multiple servants rush about to fill goblets with wine or to offer their services. It's a perfect picture of regal elegance and gluttony.

The sounds of chairs scraping on the floor fills the room as our guest stands, while the head of the table remains seated. My gaze tracks to my father first, where he sits in his golden chair at the end of the table, his polished crown sparkling atop his head in the firelight. I curtsy and approach him first, offering a kiss on the cheek before I find my own seat.

"Verosa." His voice is dry gravel on a dirt road. Thick and withered. "We have a guest tonight." As if I couldn't see that. I turn my gaze to the visitor to greet them, but my words die in my throat.

"It is a pleasure to make the acquaintance of such a renowned beauty." The man with the hood from earlier smiles again, no less eerily than the first time. Now that he wears no hood, I can see how truly handsome he is. He has fair skin without a blemish in sight, along with inky black hair that is perfectly combed to the side of his head. He has the eyes of the Tesslari empire: slightly upturned and dark pools of an iris.

His teeth shine unnaturally white as he smiles, and he has a fine physique.

Our delegate wears a deep emerald tunic with black pants and a matching elegant black coat so finely tailored it looks as if it is a second skin. Every inch of him oozes with glamour and confidence.

"Lucius." He extends his hand. Mechanically, I give him mine, and he presses a soft kiss atop my glove.

"The pleasure is mine." I say all to unconvincingly.

"Verosa." My father flashes a warning glance at my curt tone.

"The pleasure is mine." I repeat with a bit more warmth to my tone. No further pleasantries are exchanged nor does my father spare me a second glance.

I take note that there is no one else in the enormous dining hall, and the far expanse of the table sits empty except for our end. Ophelus, my father, motions for Lucius to sit, and calls for the dinner to begin.

My plate remains relatively untouched as I study the man across from me. The servants seem on edge, just as everyone else in this palace has been all day, but nonetheless, he flashes that stunning smile and thanks them personally every time they attend to him. He eats with his left hand and cuts his food with the utmost precision. He is clearly skilled with other forms of blades. He discusses casual politics with my father, mainly regarding the longstanding alliance between Krycolis and Tesslari. Then there is the casual mention of Irene.

"Father, forgive me, but may I ask the nature of this dinner?" I interrupt.

A maid drops a tray, causing meats and wine to spill across the cold marble floor. She apologizes profusely while Ophelus clears his throat. His stony gaze captures mine. The deep worry lines that crease his features seemingly more prominent in this light.

"As you know, Verosa, my marriage to Irene was a part of stabilizing the alliance between our two empires. I married a noble as there was no princess at the time." Lucius takes a long and slow drink. "Therefore, you will marry Prince Lucius of the Tesslari Empire to finally solidify our alliance and merge the kingdoms."

The sounds of my knife hitting the table and my chair scraping backward fill the room as I stand in one fluid motion.

"Verosa," Ophelus snaps. "Sit down."

"No." My hands are shaking at my sides. I can't remember how to stand, walk, or think. How did I hold my hands before this? What did I do with my feet when idle? "No I think I need to be alone."

And yet, I stand still, so utterly still when I should be moving, should be running for the door. Air evades my lungs no matter how much I gulp down. Lucius' handsome face begins to blur when my feet finally begin to move. The king reaches out to grab my arm when my apparent fiancé reaches out to stop him.

"I am sure it is quite the shock. Perhaps it would be best..."

I can't hear him finish before I'm out of the dining hall, the hallways before me forming an elaborate maze. Where was my room, where was the exit?

"Woah, Vera." Torin reaches out and takes ahold of my arms as I fall forward, steadying me against his shoulder. His usually jovial face is grim as he takes me in and barks for the surrounding servants to leave us. "He told you."

"Hmm." He half carries, half drags me back to my room, passing me off to a maid with the promise to come back later.

I had been foolish to hope to marry for love, or even the occasional wish to never marry at all. I should have known my father had planned something already. He is always scheming, always plotting something five steps ahead of where I am.

A part of my treacherous heart feels awful for Lucius, his fiancé running out the moment their engagement is revealed. But the greater portion feels nothing but a boiling pit of rage in my gut. He knew and was perfectly calm. I am alone in my rage.

They all knew, and I had played the part of their pretty little fool.

The moonlight filters in through the open window, dancing across all the edges of my chambers. At some point, Torin comes back and tells me that Lucius and my father dined for many hours into a drunken stupor, before the servants showed both men to their rooms, praying the cold walk there might sober them up. I thank him before dismissing him for the night, feeling an overwhelming need to be alone. Now I lay alone, shivering in my bed despite the intense heat in the dead of night.

My gaze is locked at the foot of my bed, where a dark shadow snorts in the night.

There is Vestíg, his gaze wild and bright. The look of an animal cornered and afraid, lacking restraint. I am sure that my eyes shine with the same terrifying glint. How sad it is to understand a beast without words better than a father with a slit tongue.

Propping myself up, I let my legs dangle over the edge of the bed. Vestíg stands still in the moonlight.

"Do what I can't," he seems to say. And I do.

The wind rustles through my cloak as I toss it over my shoulders and begin to pack. Warm trousers, an extra blouse, money, some bandages and ointment, and a few rations to last me until I'm out of the kingdom. The cloth sack falls heavy upon my back, and memories flood my mind. I'm quick to shove them down. It's been years since I last ran away, and even then, it had only been for a night.

Pausing, I look back into my room one last time. Tanja won't be back for a few hours, and she will be the first to notice I am missing. I debate leaving her a note but decide against it. Time is of the essence. I turn to find Vestíg gone, if he had ever been there in the first place.

I still remember which stones click when they're stepped on and the guards' nightly patrol patterns. Take the path to the left, and only to the left. Stay close to the walls, cling to the shadows. The shadows are my friends for once. With the wind to my back, I sprint down these familiar corridors, maybe for the last time. I don't dare pause for sentiment, but the images remain all the same.

Down that hall is where I tripped and skinned my knee. Irene had the maid give me the switch for getting blood on my new spring gown. There, at the end of the other corridor, is the kitchen, where Blaine and Torin had snuck jelly tarts and other sweets to my room that night. Outside the window is the well that Torin fell in when we were seven, and there's the rose garden where Miss Eida gave me my first dance lesson. I stepped on her toes.

I only pause to think when my fingers find that one loose stone I used last time. One pull and the wall opens just enough to slide through. Blaine and I had found it together, but why had he not patched it up? Could he have so easily forgotten? No, he has a memory like that of a raven. I almost laugh at my next thought. There's no way he would have purposely left me an out. Oh well, it doesn't matter now.

The light of the castle begins to fade as I squeeze through the cracks, then I am submerged in the darkness. The passage hasn't changed much; it still drips and creaks the same as it did when I was younger. The black walls stink of rotting sewage, mold, and something metallic that I know is not iron. I dare not think of what I might be stepping in that would make such a noise.

I reach into my pocket as soon as I replace the stone, seeking a light grey powder.

"*Illumis*," I whisper to the dust before scattering it across my path. Immediately, it begins to glow, a dim golden hue surrounding the dingy passageway now. *Deun:* light. The gift of my ancestors.

My mother, the Queen, never cared much for stories and myths unless they validated her own power. Her favorite was the tale of *Ricor*, the dark angel who ate the tongue of children who disrespected their mothers. Despite her tale of *Ricor*, I grew to love myths all the more. They were my own little rebellion against Queen Irene's iron fist. Torin used to tell me the stories I craved, he always has had such a way with words. My favorite was always that of the two Great Ones. Raonkin and Deungrid, darkness and light.

The story goes that in the beginning there were two beings, the Laeis. They were genderless and purely ethereal. It was said that even the heavens bowed down to them. Some variations say they both were timeless, but others say Deungrid was wrought from pure stardust, and Raonkin was born from their shadow. Everything was peaceful for a while, then Raonkin wanted too much. They attempted to smother Deungrid and keep the earth for themselves. As a punishment for their crimes, Deungrid made them both mortal, a balance to each other. Raonkin was now a woman, and Deungrid a man.

They say their blood courses through everyone's veins even now, some Raonkin and others Deungrid. As a descendent of Deungrid, I am considered to be blessed. I'm not sure I feel blessed, but my heart swells and I stand a bit taller when someone discusses my heritage. Everyone I know is blessed; they have to be to work within the palace. In the kingdom, those who are descendants of Deungrid are the nobles and royalty, the palace staff and the royal guard. Those who descend from Raonkin are the lower class, the prostitutes and bartenders, criminals and cannon fodder of the army. Occasionally, a Raonkin will make it to middle class, but they keep to themselves lest they draw too much negative attention. Like a tick burrows itself under the fur of a dog to hide its back while it sucks the innocent's blood.

"Did you hear that the princess is engaged?" I jump when the voice comes booming from my right. I must be in-between walls; the knights' quarters should be nearby. If I'm where I think I am, freedom should only be a few paces ahead. I wonder if I'll meet a Raonkin out there, and what will they look like? Presumably nothing like myself. Maybe they'll have dusty grey hair and black eyes with ashy skin and purple veins that spider up their elongated arms. I shudder. This narrow passage suddenly feels colder.

"We aren't discussing this."

My heart lurches into my throat.

"Come on, Blaine. Maybe she'll take you as a personal guard or something." The same voice from earlier comes again. It's pitchy and unfamiliar, presumably a younger recruit.

Fighting against every fiber of my being, I pause to press my ear to the stone, ignoring how it feels moist and squishy.

"Hey, piss off," Torin chides, followed by a heavy thunk.

Some grumbling later, Blaine raises his voice. "And do what? Have me escort her to his chambers every night, watch her in the arms of a loving husband? Pretend that whatever friendship we had never existed to save his pride? No, a soldier knows when to cut his losses."

I don't pretend that the word 'friendship' doesn't sting. Was that all I ever was to him? All I am? What other *friends* had he ran with to our safe house in the forest, read poetry, and snuck out of Ms. Eida's lessons with? When night fell, did he kiss them too? Tender, slow and cautious, afraid they might break beneath his touch? Sure, we were young, and I know that it all happened so long ago. But a part of me hoped, a foolish and naive part of me, that it had been something more to him too.

"No," I whisper a promise, my throat raw, "no more tears tonight." It takes the taste of blood to bring me back. I've bitten my cheek. *Take* *things one step at a tim*e. His voice rings clear in the back of my mind. I don't look back.

The night clings to me like a damp cloth the moment I emerge from the palace walls. The cool air is invigorating as it whips against my face. To the West, twinkling lights scatter across the horizon, the distant sound of music carried by the wind. No doubt it comes from some lavish party being thrown by a noble. It's been a while since I've gone to one. The last time was nearly a year ago. That was back before the rebel attacks became more and more frequent.

I hum contently and allow myself to sway to the music. When the night began, I had worn a stunning crimson gown embroidered with pure gold thread, my hair up and hanging in perfectly coiled ringlets about my face. As the event drew on, my neck became damp with sweat, and my long silk gloves began to wrinkle from the constant hand kisses and exchange of dance partners. I miss the luxury of drinking *Tyjn* with the other nobles. Its sultry, sweet taste still fresh upon my lips as I listened to the gossip of the older noblewomen. And secretly, I miss sneaking off to admire the tapestries in the decadent halls, to trace the details of the oil paintings with my gaze. Such subtle luxuries of a previous life I never thought I would miss. If I turn back now, could I still attend these parties? Would I be allowed as a married woman, one day a queen?

No. No man will make that choice for me. I am a woman, would have been a queen, but never a pet.

Then again, I think to myself, *if I take this next step, I won't be queen.*

I look to the East, where only a few very dim lights dot the sky. Irene warned me once that all that is foul originates in the East. Walking sirens that eat men's hearts right from their chest, giants that snatch women from their beds. No one dares ask what happens to the children. It's the kind of place no featherbedded princess would tread.

But I will be free. I step forward, my toes pointing eastward.

"Come back, claim your birthright," the palace calls. "Stay."

One foot forward at a time.

"Please." The voice is warm and sounds like rendezvouses outside the palace walls, diving in front of the switch for each other. Bloody knees, loose teeth, and stolen jelly tarts. Summer laughter and midnight stolen kisses.

I raise my chin and ignore the call.

"May Deungrid guide me," I pray aloud. One step at a time. And if I dare to hope, I might pray for Father's forgiveness too.

The buildings creak with weariness as a forlorn breeze blows through the square, a slight drizzle of rain smattering against the unpaved road. Each face I pass is the same, etched with weariness and worn heavy by time. The lights flicker from rowdy taverns as the boisterous expletives seep through open windows into the road. Women lean their backs against the walls, skirts held up to their waists, eager patrons panting like dogs at their heels. And somewhere in the distance, a low bellow resounds deep from the heart of the town. Something longing for blood.

That's what I had expected, at least, judging from the stories I heard from Irene, but this place is alive. Shops and taverns leave their doors and windows open, bright lights pouring out to illuminate the streets where the vendors peddle. They sell jeweled hair pins, painted flags, sweet bread, and savory *leeche*. The women wear bright colors and even tighter corsets, but no one seems to eye them with lust or disgust. The men tip their worn hats at them as if they are fine ladies, and they respond with a giggle and a curtsy, occasionally a kiss upon the head if the man is handsome enough. Instead of the sounds of brawling leaking out from the taverns, it's loud and beautiful music; the sound of people laughing and dancing.

Sure, the roads are a little cracked, and the windowpanes are dirty, but this place is nothing like how Irene described it to me when I was a child. Why would she have lied? The more I look around, the more evident the answer to my own question becomes. Had I known such a place like this exists, I never would have wanted to return to the palace, with its rigid rules and forced niceties.

My eyes linger upon a specific tavern, the door painted a gaudy emerald green. The sign above reads "Ryson's Beer and Bread." Seems simple enough, but through the open windows, I can hear the beautiful strum of a lyre, and see elegant women sashaying in their skirts. My mind tells me it's time to move on, but the lost child in me, well, she tells me one second to look couldn't hurt. Right?

I'm hit with the stench of beer and *leeche* the minute I step into Ryson's and stifle a gag. The rest of the patrons don't seem to mind as they down their drinks, dancing and laughing amongst each other. Slowly, I lower my hood and step forward, bumping right into someone.

"Hey-"

"Oh, my Laei, I am so sorry," I apologize immediately, glancing up to see warm amber eyes staring back at me. His face softens once he sees me, and he steps back, allowing me space.

"No, I apologize. I should have looked where I was going. Bit disorienting in here, isn't it?" he asks, flashing a charming grin. I feel my cheeks heat up immediately. Was this flirting? I've never been flirted with before, unless you count Blaine's occasional glares in the hallway.

"Ha, yeah it's my first time." I nervously rub my arms, taking in my surroundings. Time seems to have stopped, though I know the music is still playing, and the dancers are still whirling in the center. Their skirts seem to flit in slow motion, flashing brazen colors like the most extravagant of silk butterflies. I take time to notice him too. He's young and probably my age, with a tall stature and athletic physique. He has dark chestnut tresses that reach his shoulder and a golden olive complexion that matches his hazel eyes perfectly. If I hadn't known better, I'd assume he was some deity or foreign prince. But his clothes, though being clean and neat, are still worn and the type accustomed to the lower-class citizens. And despite his good charm, he stinks of *leeche*.

"That makes sense now," he says with a smile. "I would've recognized you if you'd been here before."

"Oh?" My heart rate quickens, and I slowly reach for the hood of my cloak, preparing to dart out the door. If he recognizes me, the guard will be here in under an hour, and the borders will be locked down. I won't be able to make it out in time.

"Of course, it's not every day you see such a beauty." He takes my hand and presses a chaste kiss to the back of it, then laughs.

"You blush easily."

"Sorry," I mumble, "I'm not quite used to this kind of attention."

"Really?" His eyes widen, and his shock seems genuine. I restrain a snort. If any man dared to look at me too long, he'd soon become either Blaine or Tanja's problem, and if the poor chap was unlucky enough, the king's. Though, with Ophelus, it was always about setting an example, commanding respect. He didn't care enough to be bothered if I had an affair. So long as I don't get caught, that is.

"Well, then, Woden Ryson. Pleasure to make your acquaintance."

"Ryson? Like the sign outside the door?" He laughs again, running his hand through his hair and pushing it out of his face. The old wooden floors creak as Woden steps back, stretching his arms out to the side.

"The one and only." His grin resembles that of a clever fox, but he has the kind eyes of a puppy. Come to think of it, he reminds me of this old lapdog Irene used to bring with her everywhere. It was an old Spaniel, with a silky caramel coat and wide almond eyes. I used to give it kisses when Irene wasn't looking, and it would respond by snuffling its wet nose against my hair.

"Vera." I shake his clammy hand.

"No last name?" I shake my head. "Alright then, Vera No Last Name, I think you owe me a dance."

"I don't owe you anything."

"No, but I'd like one." He stares at me again with that kind, hopeful face, and I feel my resolve crumble again. A few moments couldn't hurt. He takes my cloak and hangs it off the back of a chair, and suddenly I feel a bit silly. All the other girls wear silk skirts of beautiful flashing colors, their arms decorated with golden circlets; jewels crowning the hair that they've piled atop their head. Yet here I am, wearing my weather-beaten trousers and cotton blouse, the hem of my pants tucked into thick leather boots. For the first time in my life, I feel out of place amidst the luxury. The other girls seem to notice too, giggling behind their silks. Woden pays them no mind as he grabs my hand and pulls me into the thick of it, the men whooping and clapping him on the back as we make our way into the center. He shouts something I don't understand to the band, and an even quicker tune begins, the fiddler shredding the strings of his beautiful instrument. The other patrons cheer and stomp their feet, pairing up for the dance.

"Come on!" Woden shouts over the music, taking my hand again.

"What are we doing?"

"Just follow my lead, and don't step on my toes. I like these shoes." I find myself laughing despite myself. We trip over the swirling silks and satin slippers of the other dancers, much to their ire and Woden's delight. He takes to muttering something along the lines of "pretentious bastards" among other expletives. The tips of my ears burn hot and red at this, but he just keeps grinning as if he didn't just curse everyone in this room and their mother.

"You're stiff as my aví!" I cock my head in confusion. "It's Nevan for grandmother." He explains. That makes more sense now. Neva is our neighbor to the South, a small country wedged just between Krycolis and Varium. Known for their extravagant wealth despite their size and love of luxury, Neva is mostly comprised of wealthy merchants and vacation homes. It's where Blaine's father was born, before he fell in love with Blaine's mother, a Vari immigrant, and moved to Krycolis. He was a fun-loving man, his hair always neatly coiffed to the side of his head, and golden circlets weighed down his every limb. Even his casket was marble inlaid with gold and jewels, an extravagant resting place for an extravagant man. *The apple clearly falls far from the tree*, I think as Blaine's stern set face comes to mind.

Woden, however? The perfect image of Nevan stereotype.

His hand finds my waist and pulls me closer, showing me which motions to mimic with my feet for each new song. It takes a few tries, but years of royal dance lessons pay off as I pick up the jig rather quickly. I only step on his toes once. I had to buy him a drink for it, which I claimed was ridiculous since he owned the place and could just take whatever he wanted. He responded with that stupid grin as he took my money.

It's almost like a fever dream. The blaring music, the myriad of exotic colors encompassing the room, the feather light touch of bodies passing each other. Woden darts in and out now, begrudgingly switching partners as the dance requires. I find myself in the arms of a burly man with a ruddy face and equally red mustache. I'm sure he told me his name, but I've long since forgotten it now.

I drink *leeche*, it's warm yet cheap taste searing against my tongue. I say nothing. They consider it a luxury. A few of the dancing girls, *dansarinas* Woden had called them, stopped by to offer me tips and take a sip of my *leeche*. I happily let them and secretly swipe the red lipstick left behind on the glass upon my own lips.

Then it's back to dancing in a drunken stupor, a frenzy of swirling limbs and bodies all in too close of quarters. A large hand closes around my shoulder, and I toss my head back...right back into Woden's nose.

"I am so sorry!" He tilts his head forward, blood dripping from his face. I reach my hand out to help when I spot it and freeze where I stand. Mingling amongst the crimson dripping from his fingers is silver. The blood of the cursed. My eyes widen as I trail the length of him, his seemingly normal clothes and charming smile. His kind hands now coated in silver-flecked blood. Hands that had held mine.

If Woden notices my alarm, he doesn't say anything, just offers me a slanted look from the corner of his eye. My heart pounds in my chest. Surely he can hear it. Silently, I curse myself. I should have never come here. If he knows I'm blessed...I don't want to think of what will happen.

A glint of rusting copper catches my eye. Woden's nose has stopped bleeding now, and he wipes the rest of his tainted blood on his trousers.

"Are you okay?" he asks like I wasn't the one who just hit him. As if he cares.

"I'm fine, I think I just need some air."

"Okay, the exit is right there, I can come with-"

"No!" I say a little too eagerly. He eyes me warily. Were his eyes that perturbing orange shade before? I raise my shoulders back and force myself to look upon his deceptive face. "No, I can handle it myself, thank you."

"Okay. I'll be waiting." He kisses my hand again in mock chivalry.

I'm sure you will be, I think bitterly to myself. And to think I fell right into his trap. How long was he going to string me along for before he slit my throat? How many women in here hid silver blood behind those extravagant costumes? I'd rather not stay to find out. My pouch and cloak are nowhere to be found; I'll have to get new provisions wherever I go. Forcing myself to walk slowly and not look back, I reach the door. It creaks as I open it, and it feels like every eye in the room is on me.

With a chill I realize, *they've known I was prey all along.*

Swallowing hard, I throw open the door and step out into the cool night air, allowing myself my first deep breath in what feels like forever.

The stars are brilliant diamonds carefully placed against an indigo canvas. They twinkle in shades of pinks, blues, greens, and purples. Silvers and golds. I can see the constellations of Deungrid and the warrior Heila, drawing back her bowstring and pointing her arrow tip south even now. Even from my window at the palace, I have never seen such a clear night sky.

Taking a moment to survey my surroundings, I notice I've stepped into an alleyway behind the bar. Broken cobblestones worn in by years of use and neglect pave the road. Broken beer bottles, *leeche* cups, and other crimson stained objects I'd sooner forget litter along the walls.

Crash.

The sound of glass breaking and swearing. A younger voice piques up above the rest. More glass breaking. It's coming from further down the alley. The dark part. I take a step in the opposite direction when I hear that voice again. Its words are mumbled and intelligible, but sound desperate.

My conscience shoves against my mind as I flit between morals and safety. *Don't intervene* my mind screams. *Stick to the shadows.*

For whatever reason still unknown to me, I turn and run into the dark of the alleyway, towards the sounds of shattering glass.

CHAPTER 4

ROWAN

I was doing fine until she showed up, stepping out into the moonlight with her blue-black hair, shimmering and iridescent. She is beautiful, but I've seen plenty of beautiful women before. No, what struck me is how completely and utterly stupid she must be.

She wears simple green trousers, the color of the sage that Mother burns sometimes, and an ivory-colored blouse unbuttoned just to below her collarbones. No armor. No weaponry. No defense.

Tonight started off well enough. Kya found our target quickly and effectively silenced the defenses while I went after the mark. A newer merchant from Varium. I pretended not to see the burning hatred masking the usually gentle slopes of her face and turned my back when she put him down. What you don't know can't come back to haunt you.

Then, somewhere between there and our third hit, it all went wrong. An ambush, no doubt from Mavis' cronies. My assassin was injured, I had to get her out. One thing led to another, and now here I am, bleeding in a dark alleyway with these two oafs bearing down on me.

To an outsider the situation looks bleak, but I have the cards ordered just how I like them. I've always preferred the odds to be against me, it's familiar territory. I have my handle on the hilt of my knife when they relent, and lo and behold there she is.

"Unhand him," she orders, her voice possessing the commanding power that she herself does not. Idiot Number One and Idiot Number Two look at each other for a moment, then to me, and back to her before bursting out with raucous laughter. It sounds like gravel against gravel.

"I thought we stabbed his bitch already?" the bigger one says, his fist still wrapped in my hair, blood melting among the golden tresses. White hot anger bubbles in my gut. Kya better have gotten out, or I swear, I will tear them apart limb by limb.

"No, you moron." The weevil looking one smacks Big Guy upside the head with a look of contempt. "That one was different. This one is light." The third moron in the alley stiffens, her hands already clenching fists at her side. She takes a step forward just as the Weevil does, narrowly dodging the needle he flings from his sleeve. Her pretty blue eyes widen in shock when she sees it sticking out of the stone wall beside her, and I hope that fear is enough for her to leave. The last thing I need is civilian blood on my hands.

"Slippery little..." He doesn't get the chance to finish his sentence as she throws a quick right hook, the hit landing on his nose with a sickening crunch. The Weevil throws his head back, howling in pain as silver-flecked blood spews from between his fingertips. Pulling his hand back, he stares at the blood, eyes wide, pupils dilated. It forms a streaky path from his nose to between his thin and cracked lips.

"Lupo, deal with him," He hisses to the goon still holding my head, bloody spittle flying from his mouth, and he speaks, "You're gonna regret that, bitch."

"Make me." Her voice wavers as she speaks, but her feet stand firm, toes facing towards her opponent. She's going to get herself killed.

Weevil lunges forward, fingers reaching deep into his cloak. I take this as my cue to strike a distracted Lupo, kicking my free leg up directly into his groin. He drops my head on instinct to grip his damaged crotch, and I use the momentum to slam my head into his with a resounding CRACK! Stumbling back against the wall, the large man looks up at me, utterly dumbfounded, as I twirl a glass bottle in my hand.

The glass cascade to the ground, rippling like a miniature waterfall as it shatters over his head. That final look of pure, wide-eyed confusion satiates my pride. Until I hear her.

Spinning hot on my heels, I turn to find Weevil standing a few feet away, the young woman from earlier pressed against his chest. His rusted blade pricks the soft flesh of her neck, but not deep enough to draw blood. Not yet. He wants me without having to shed a woman's blood. He'd lose a considerable number of fingers if Mavis learned he harmed an innocent woman, the risk has to be worth bringing in the prize. Me.

"She's not mine," I speak slowly, lowering the remnant of the broken bottle, my hands up for emphasis. "You know my crew. She's just some random girl."

"Maybe, but do you want her blood on your hands, *Noiteron?*" Weevil digs his filthy weapon deeper into her pale skin. She cries out in pain as the blade draws blood. I suck in a deep breath at what I see. Pure, golden blood. Not gold mingling with red, but pure gold. Her face pales as she notices the golden stream staining her blouse, and she fights to get loose. This only drives the blade deeper. "Well, look here, I've found myself a pureblood." His cackle sends chills up my spine. Purebloods are rare. There are very few of them left. A few hundred years ago, they were hunted to near extinction. Blockheaded nobles believed their blood had medicinal properties. Those that are left stay in hiding or seek protection from the king if they're blessed. Finding a blessed pureblood like this is like stumbling upon a gold mine, with all the gold already waiting in neat rows for the taking.

But she's a woman, a frightened human who, in the end, tried to help. Mavis has sunk low, but not low enough for a job like this. Weevil on the other hand? He wouldn't need Mavis anymore after tonight if he gets away.

"Okay, what do you want. Me? Trade me for her, Mavis will probably promote you," I coax him, slowly reaching for that one vial in my breast pocket. I know he'll never take the bait; he has the look in his eyes of a rich man already. Ravenous greed coats his gaze as he watches the gold blood drip from her strained neck. The look of a man who knows he'll never starve or beg again. No, I just need more time.

"Are you kidding me?" He barks his ugly laughter again. Cocky bastard, basking in his victory early. "You're worthless compared to her. You know how much just one vial of her blood goes for, right?"

Her blouse is nearly completely soaked to the point of being see through, his hungry gaze soaking in every fearful breath she takes. He pulls back her dark hair from her neck, offering himself a better view of his prize as it drips. he whispers something in her ear that makes her freeze, even her erratic breathing pauses.

"You know you should probably move that blade and staunch the bleeding. You're losing your wealth by the second," I point out, biding my time. If I can just get him to lower that damn knife...

"Why should I?" he says, thinking he knows my game. "I can just slit her throat now and collect the blood here. I'm not picky." His yellow teeth graze her earlobe, and she has to stop herself from yanking her head the opposite way. I secretly hope Mavis has more spies here, then she can gut him like the pig he is when he inevitably goes groveling back.

"True, or you could keep her alive and have a steady source of income for the rest of your miserable life." I raise one hand to my chin as if pondering the possibilities. Just enough to distract him as I reach across my heart and snag the pouch. It slips easily enough into my dark sleeve without him noticing. Weevil considers this for a second, lowering the knife only slightly. Just enough so that it's not bearing into her anymore. I can see her swallow for the first time, fresh tears leaking from the corner of those pretty eyes.

"Or you could kill her now, slit her throat, and hang her up to bleed like a doe."

A small noise comes from her throat as I step closer, her mouth dropping open in a silent plea.

"Please-"

"But you know, there's something most people don't know about purebloods." I cut her off, giving her a look that I hope Weevil doesn't catch. His face contorts into ugly greed and lust as he leans closer. I can smell it now, the blood. Tangy and metallic, haunting the already dank air as I step even closer. Weevil allows it.

"There's a place they bleed from where the blood is purer than the rest of the body. A gift from Deungrid himself." I fold my hands in mocking prayer, Weevil's eyes roam her body, searching for any place purer than the other. He runs a finger from her neck, down her arm, and to her hand. Pressing the back of her wrist to his ear, searching for a stronger pulse.

"Where?"

"Here." I take his hand holding the blade, and though he stiffens, he allows me to guide his hand down to the back of her knee. He digs the blade in slightly, as if to test, and that's when I strike. Gripping his wrist still, I bring my knee up to his head, a gruesome cracking noise filling the alley as I make contact with his jaw. A few of his teeth fall and land in the silver and red blood pooling on the ground already. He looks up at me with anger etched across his ugly and narrow features.

"Send Mavis my regards while you still have a tongue," I hiss as I bring my foot down on his hand, his disgusting dagger dropping from his grip with an anguished cry.

"Run!" I shout to the young woman, and for once, she listens. Then Weevil begins to laugh, and before I can slip the pouch from my fingers, he grabs something from within his sleeve with his unbroken hand.

"I don't need a tongue for this." The green dart flies from his wrist before I have a chance to stop it, and lands home less than a second later. I watch in horror as she falls, the needle sticking out from the back of her leg. She hits the ground heavily and silently, dust rising around her. Not even a whimper of pain to say she's still alive escapes her lips.

The villain keeps laughing deliriously, blood pouring from between his lips.

"She'll be dead within the hour. She'll be dead-" A swift kick to the head shuts him up. I should've known Mavis wouldn't have sent them out without Etherbane. I could scream out of frustration. She's always one step ahead of me. And I know it's my fault.

Light begins to filter into the alley as the door down the road opens. Ryson's.

"Vera?" a man calls out, still too far to see us, but too close for comfort. I move to leave when her soft breathing reaches my ears. It's shallow, too shallow. She should have never started a fight she couldn't finish. If she dies tonight that's between her and the Laei. I need to get to Kya, to protect my own.

To ignore a crime is the same as to commit it.

The words enter my mind before I can stop them, her clear voice flooding my senses. A saying she told me as a boy. It's almost funny, in a sad and sadistic way, how her voice is the one I hear now if I have a morally sound thought.

I look back at her, crumpled on broken and dirty stone, blood pooling from under her indigo tresses. Her face is concealed by the darkness, making it so much easier to just slip away. Forget about her. Forget tonight happened.

I know as I move that I am going to regret this.

"You'd better be worth it," I grumble as I toss the cotton pouch on the ground, deep gray so damp it's almost blue exploding over the whole alley, covering us and any sign of a fight. My muscles and the lacerations coating my arms groan in complaint as I scoop her into my arms, keeping the needle in her leg. Aiko will need it if she's to make the antidote. Her head hits my chest softly, and I can see her chest rising and falling too quickly through her soaked shirt. I swear I can hear her mumble a 'thank you' as I start away. The darkness clings to me as it always has, lending me its cover as I jump from rooftop to rooftop, making my way West. It's nearly forty minutes on foot, and I hope that her pure blood saves her from some of the poison.

I can see the palace in the distance, its hulking figure still noticeable along the deep purple sky. As we get closer, I can see that nearly all the lights are on, despite it being well past midnight now. God forbid a king let his oil lamp run dry for one night while his people starve. I spit a curse at him and that monstrosity as I pass. May he rot early.

The lights are off when I arrive, but nevertheless, I pound on the back door of the Iales manor until the door swings open, revealing an incredibly small and equally angry woman. Aiko stands before me, her eyes still heavy lidded with sleep, fluffy white slippers adorning her feet.

"You'd better start praying right now, Rowan or I-" Her voice dies in her throat as she stares at the barely moving girl in my arms, bearing the same black hair and blue eyes as her.

"I don't pray." Is all I can say before she's ushering me into the room, not even bothering to lock the door as she swipes all contents from her lounge room table. A few of the plates and cups shatter, leaving a hazardous mosaic across the floor. Aiko doesn't seem to mind as she sets the girl on the table, inspecting her wounds. Her eyes drift to that needle, and she sucks in a sharp breath. "Etherbane," she breathes. Her eyes widen. She looks to me.

"How long?"

"Maybe forty minutes. I got here as quick as I could." Her face hardens to the point of ice. If I touch it, I'm sure it will be cold. A single nod is my sign, I will have to hold her steady while she removes the needle.

Etherbane is tricky, it's not designed like normal poisons. Since it only affects those who are blessed, it slows their quickened healing abilities. We have to let it flow until they're on the brink of death because the antidote is poison too. The second poison shouldn't even give a pureblood so much as a fever, but we can't risk the body trying to fight off the antidote instead of the poison. It needs to be occupied.

It is difficult to kill someone who is blessed, but not impossible. That's just how Deungrid designed it to be. The cost, in the end, is far too great, making it undesirable. But not for Mavis.

Aiko flicks the needle aside into an empty ceramic bowl. It tinkles a merry tune against the wind as it falls, clearly out of place. The girl's face has gone clammy now, her already pale skin a deathly white, black skeins of poison working their way through her veins towards her slowly beating heart. With every beat it seems to drag, as if it can't bear to go on.

"Now," Aiko commands, shoving the antidote into my hands while she tips the girl's head back. Her pale purple lips fall open slightly, wide enough that I can slip the liquid through. Aiko's short hair flips into her face, and she hisses as a bit of the precious antidote dribbles onto the girl's chin. I proceed with excessive caution after catching her glare.

Aiko can't possibly even reach my shoulders, but I don't mention that to her. Last time I did she threatened me saying she might not be able to reach my shoulders, but she could reach something much more important. A chill caresses my spine at the thought.

"She'll be fine," she finally deduces, gently plopping a wet rag against her forehead with such a motherly tender that I know what thoughts are crossing her mind. "Where did you find her?"

"The hit went south. She intervened of her own accord."

"Where was it?"

Silence.

"Where was it?" she asks again, her blue eyes blazing with the ferocity of a tigress. Her tiny hands pause from their work as she turns to face me.

"Belam. We started in Adil and worked our way to Belam."

I don't have time to duck as a dirty wet rag slaps against my face. It's tempting to leave it plastered across my face just so I don't have to face Aiko. However, not tempting enough when I recall what it's used for. I peel it from my face and drop it in that same ceramic pot, Aiko now only a few feet away. Despite standing at a solid five feet tall and all of her soft features, Aiko is probably the most terrifying woman I know. No - person I know. She grips a fistful of my torn shirt and uses it to drag me to her eye level. I wince the whole way.

"Have you lost your mind?" She seethes. Her hot breath fans my face, warming it as if to say, 'have the dignity to be ashamed.'

"Belam. That's Mavis' territory, and before it was hers, it was her father's. And his father's. There is nothing for you in Belam, why don't you-"

"I learned who my father is tonight."

Aiko stills, her face draining of color. "Oh."

Oh? So she knew too. After all these years of watching us, letting me watch my mother struggle, she has the nerve to show she's known.

"You won't find him in Belam." Is all she says as she moves to wet another rag. Her nimble fingers begin unbuttoning the blouse of the girl. I pay no mind. Golden blood seeps through the cream rag as she presses it to her neck. The older woman's eyes widen, but she says nothing.

"No, but my informant was there with a way in. Until we were ambushed." Her throat visibly constricts at my words, but I don't bother to rein in the sharp anger whetting my tongue. "Why didn't you tell me?"

"It wasn't mine to tell."

"But Mother-"

"It was your mother who told me not to tell you," she snaps, tossing the bloody rag into the pot while grabbing yet another. That wound on her neck won't stop bleeding, it'll need stitches or a healer. I don't bother to answer again, my head spinning.

My father. Those words send a chill through my body, the hot type that comes with fever. All this time, he should've been there. None of this would happen, Mother would've never-

Cold and concrete resolution stiffens my features. The very beat of my heart is lead inside of my chest. I'll kill him. I will kill him for all he's done to us, to her.

"Clean yourself up before she wakes up. Finneas should be here any second with the needle and salve." I hadn't noticed she'd left the room until she lay her petite hand across my shoulder. In her other hand is a clean rag, her eyes probing the deep cut near my shoulder. When did they get me?

Wordlessly, I accept it, hissing as soon as the towel makes contact with my open flesh. I note thankfully that she chose a black cloth, perfect for hiding my blood. The last thing I need is for tonight to blow up in my face even more.

Finneas enters the room as if on cue. The burly man's shadow coats most of the basement as he lumbers down to meet us. The stairs creak under his weight, but he pays no mind. The light glints off of his squared jaw and the faint semblance of an auburn mustache above his lip. He places the needle and ointment container in Aiko's hand with a gentleness that no one ever expects from the large man.

Aiko only steps closer to me, beckoning for me to push the collar of my shirt down to expose the wound.

"Shouldn't you tend to her first?" She shakes her head.

"I need her body to fight off the poison first, it'll start leaking from the wound soon enough." *Leaking*? I stifle a gag at the thought.

"Oh, how delightful," I say with a grimace. Aiko only rolls her eyes before dabbing the alcohol and ointment-soaked rag directly onto my wound. Finneas whistles while I grit my teeth, Weevil's cruel dagger sliced deeper than I had expected.

"Quit whining, it's just a scratch," he jokes, his broad chest rumbling with laughter. I make to retort when another dab from Aiko sends me hissing.

"Your wife has cold fingers."

"Then do it yourself." The damp and bloody rag squelches as it slides against my leather pants, causing Finneas to cringe. His wife pays no mind as she saunters back over to the girl from earlier. What once was a pinprick of golden blood on her calf is now a large and raised lump, mottled in hues of purple and red. It is indeed oozing something unnaturally green. Aiko cleans it away with the utmost care and gentleness, her gaze lingering on the girl's face.

"Where was that carefulness when you were helping me?"

"You'd better start stitching yourself up before I give you something to whine about." She doesn't bother to tear her gaze from her new patient, and Finneas only pats my shoulder in sympathy. I jolt from the brute strength of the man, and he mumbles a sheepish apology. So our relationship always goes, Aiko and I mouthing off at each other, and Finneas watching amused from the background. To be fair, he gets his own jabs in there on occasion.

At the first pierce of the needle, my eyes water, blurring the dimly lit room. The girl's face becomes a swirl of peach, purple, and pure gold. She looks like an oil painting that Mother has hanging in the kitchen, Raon incarnate. How ironic.

If there's any beauty in her, it's impossible to tell beneath the blood and bruising. Her lip is swollen, a hint of purple peeking out from underneath her curtain bangs. A slight trickle of golden blood dribbles from her nose, no doubt from the strain of the poison. That begs my next question.

"What's a pureblood doing in Belam?" Finneas muses, leaning against the doorframe. His eyes trace her thin frame, her round face. He bites his lip in worry. A father without a child, as he's always been.

"That's what I was wondering." The needle slides through my flesh again, and I begin to feel nauseous. Give me a knife, an arrow, a sword. Anything but a needle. "Don't they normally stay in the palace? Under protection, right?"

"If they choose, but yes, normally," Finneas confirms.

"She's on the run," Aiko muses, bandaging up the girl's leg and tipping water between her lips. "Clearly noble, well fed, and groomed."

"You make her sound like a pet." I attempt a joke, but Aiko turns to me with a face of stone.

"Why do you think she's running? She's clearly desperate or else she wouldn't have picked Belam. That place is teeming with criminals, no pureblood in their right mind would go there unless they wanted to be strung up to bleed out like a pig."

"Or if the alternative is much worse," Finneas agrees, and I nod. The way she had blindly stepped in to save me, she either has no self-regard or no knowledge of the outside world and its workings.

"Soft hands," I note.

"And look at her shoes," Aiko continues, the bandage now tied neatly. I look and notice what she has. They're made for travel and of fine leather, but the soles are barely worn.

"The style is one that was popular years ago so they're not new," Finneas muses, causing Aiko and I to stare at him incredulously.

"What? I bought them for Aiko."

"She is very clearly running from something," Aiko continues our conversation, shaking her head slightly, "or someone."

"Who would want to run from life in a palace?" I turn on Finneas. "Besides the security is insanely tight knit, no one gets in or out without the captain of the king's personal guard allowing it."

"Maybe she's the exception."

"Or he allowed it," Aiko counters her husband with a quick remark. He pauses to consider it before shrugging his large shoulders.

"Whatever the reason, she's here now. We need to decide what we are going to do with her."

"I say she's not our problem," I say, glancing again to where she lay still on the table. I hadn't even wanted her help, and in the end, she had been more of a hinderance. She saved me, and I saved her right back. Twice. We are beyond equal; she can pay me back by getting out of my hair.

"She won't get far with that leg. Not without assistance." Aiko brushes her own short indigo hair back from her face and rubbing her temples.

"Then send for an escort from the palace. You have the connections."

"I won't send her back to where she's clearly running from!" The shorter woman gasps, clutching the girl's hand. I run my own hand through my hair in exasperation. I knew she would respond this way. She did when she met Kya, anyway. I can't blame her, not after all she's done for me, but I can't save everyone. Neither can she, the only difference is I don't pretend I can.

I'm about to respond when a rustling noise startles us all. The girl shifts restlessly, her eyelids barely open.

"Mom?"

Aiko goes still, as if someone had dumped a bucket of ice water over her head. The room is silent, with only the faint sigh of the wind swishing through the heavily embroidered curtains. Finneas turns, ever so silently, to look out the window. His wife sniffs slightly before placing a pale hand delicately upon the girl's cheek. In response, she brings her own hand up to cover Aiko's, whimpering into the warmth.

"You're safe, darling," Aiko murmurs, so soft and kind.

The girl's eyes shoot open at this, vibrant and electric blue, so much brighter in the candlelight than they had been in Belam. They widen with the same fear she had carefully kept concealed back in that alley. In a swift motion, she grabs a butter knife from the corner of the table, pointing it threateningly towards Aiko, pain highlighting my friend's features.

"Who are you?" she hisses through gritted teeth, golden blood still dripping from her pert nose.

"We mean you no harm." The older woman speaks slowly as if attempting to soothe a startled animal. Placating and amicable.

"Who. Are. You," the girl repeats. Finneas has moved from his spot by the window, shifting himself between Aiko and the girl. She looks at him wildly, her small hand trembling around the smooth and blunt blade.

"They're the people who saved you from Etherbane when you so foolishly stepped into that fight," I croon now, smiling wickedly as I step out from the shadows. Her attention turns to me, her lips parting slightly and eyebrows shooting up in recognition. I pretend to pay her no mind as I finish the last stitch on my arm. "Think you could put the knife down, sweetheart? Not that it'll do you much good."

"If it won't do much then why insist I put it away?" Her voice a saccharine crow that matches my own. I nearly jump in shock. Such a clever tongue from a sweet thing.

"Because you're being rude, and I don't negotiate with people while they're holding any form of weaponry."

She seems to consider this while I consider her. She has a kind, round face, and a slim figure with no muscle whatsoever on her body. A pampered princess, it would seem. Her hair is inky and long like Aiko's, her eyes sweet and round. She must be of faded Tesslarian descent, having the same soft and contrasting facial features they're often marked by.

I extend my hand for the cutlery and just as I think she is going to hand it over she rears the weapon back and drives it straight into my palm. The crude and dull blade slides in easily, her panic reinforcing what little strength she has left. I swear vehemently and pull my hand away before she can pull the blade out.

"Some thanks for the people who saved your life." Finneas remarks, his arms crossed and cutting an imposing figure in the small room. The woman's face blanches and she raises her shaking fists, her eyes darting around the room for an escape.

Aiko watches with feline curiosity before shooting a glance in my direction. I have the wound bandaged already. Her eyes narrow and I take that as my cue to intervene. My neck pops as I loll it around leisurely.

The blade entered the fleshy bit of my palm, thankfully not hitting any bone or anything that could have proven to be a problem. No, her assault is more of an annoyance compared to the other injuries I've garnered over the years.

"Did making me bleed make you feel better?"

The woman raises her shaking chin in defiance. "Maybe."

I release a mirthless chuckle, my eyes darkening. Much to her credit she doesn't shrink back any further. "Ready to have an adult conversation now?"

She hesitates for only a moment before nodding. The nobles visibly relax. They are no strangers to my usual and unorthodox methods. I know Aiko would prefer it if I do not lead anymore trouble to her door.

"Who are you running from?" I ask. No sign of shock registers on the young woman's face as she calmly crosses one dainty ankle over the other.

"A man with a name and no face." She's smug about her own response while I bristle.

"Why Belam?"

"Why not?"

"I could give you a hundred reasons or so."

"Then please do." She smiles sweetly.

"Do you always speak in circles?"

"Do you always act like an ass?" Finneas snorts at this before excusing himself with a small apology. Aiko just barely conceals her own smile before moving to follow her husband.

"I thought I was supposed to be asking the questions here, *Vera*." I smirk coyly and watch as that smooth facade crumbles completely. Her lower lip quivers, and her shoulders stiffen. Aiko and Finneas turn again, once more observing the scene silently. Vera leaps to her feet... only to collapse on the ground in pain, her leg not supporting her weight just yet. Aiko is there in a second but steps back when Vera raises her fists.

"How do you know who I am?" Her courtier's voice has lowered to a strained snarl as she bares her teeth with each word. How interesting. To be honest, I had been guessing it was her that the man from Ryson's was looking for, but I hadn't fully expected to be right.

"A friend of yours came looking when you were knocked out." I watch as the little color left in her face begins to drain to a pale milky white hue. "You wouldn't happen to know him, would you?"

"You didn't... You didn't tell him where I was?" She leans forward on her knees, dropping the knife to clasp those dainty hands around my knee. "Please..."

"What would it matter if I did?"

"He'll kill me," she rasps. Her nails bite through the leather of my pants, her blood starting to soak through Aiko's bandage again. "He's cursed."

The older couple eyes me warily now, waiting for a flinch or telltale sign. I don't give them the satisfaction. Instead, I shake Vera's grip from my knee and crouch down to her level, hooking my thumb under her chin and bringing her gaze to mine. Her left eye has begun to puff up, but luckily for her, there's no bruising. She bites her lip anxiously, wincing at the painful and swollen flesh before lowering her gaze to the floor. A sharp tug to her chin has her raising it again.

"And why would he do that?" I murmur, flicking that thumb over her lip to brush away the blood. Up close, there was no denying her beauty, even despite the grime and gore. Her face is fair with a slight shower of freckles across her nose and cheekbones, her eyebrows rounded in a neutral soft look, her lips perfectly rosy and plump. Her indigo locks fall in loose waves about her shoulders, not straight enough for the nobles' preferred look, but freer. Untamed. She has this unbroken spirit about her. The type of spirit that allowed her to walk into a fight to save a stranger and wield a butterknife against a wanted criminal.

"He knows what I am. He could *smell* it."

I blink in shock before bursting into laughter. She looks at me in confusion and frowns, yanking her chin from my grip. She's also very naïve, I suppose.

"What's so funny?" she demands, crossing her arms across her chest and rocking back on her heels. I note that some color has returned to her face, no doubt a haze of embarrassment.

"I thought purebloods were supposed to be educated?" I chuckle softly. "But clearly someone has purposely kept you under a rock. No, he couldn't *smell* it. He has human senses just like you. Besides, he couldn't harm you, let alone kill you. Not without dark magic."

"What? How was that other man able to cut me then?" she asks, her eyebrow furrowed in a confused frown. Her fingertips ghost the laceration across her neck, now expertly bandaged.

"That blade was enchanted with dark magic by a very powerful sorceress. But without it, he couldn't have killed you."

"Why not?" She leans forward now, her shoulders trembling slightly. Aiko edges closer, eyeing her with warm concern.

"Eager for the sweet kiss of death?" I laugh, then yelp as Aiko elbows my gut with the precision of a scorpion.

"Those who are blessed cannot be killed by most mortal means," the woman explains. "Except for by age, illness, another blessed one, or dark magic. Dark magic is the only way for one who is cursed to kill someone who is blessed, but the cost is very steep."

"What is it?"

Aiko pauses and looks towards me for a moment with pain in her eyes. A silent caress of pity for something I am yet to be aware of.

"Their mind," she says slowly. "It was Deungrid's way to protect his descendants from those of Raonkin. Cursed kin are clever. Their wits are the strongest weapon in their arsenal. It is beyond precious to them, and if they were to raise hands against those blessed by the light..."

"They would lose that which they valued most," I finish for her. Aiko swallows deeply, her throat bobbing with the effort and she nods in appreciation. I'll be sure to ask her about that later.

"And what of you all? What are you?" The question is worded bluntly, and I pretend not to notice her hand snaking backwards. Not to mention the way her eyes drift towards the window, the stairs, the door behind her. Eyeing every exit.

"We are blessed," Aiko answers as I open my mouth, before continuing softly. "All of us."

Her hands clasp together in front of her, and she smiles, her voice sweet and low. The hum of a mother. Vera nods but misses that one nervous tell. Aiko fiddles with her hands when she lies.

"Can I trust you?" Vera whispers, almost inaudible.

"Yes." From me it would've been a lie, but Aiko takes both her hands in her own and squeezes them firmly. A promise, and only once in all my time of knowing her has this woman broken a promise.

"I'm engaged." Vera lowers her chin in shame, her bangs forming a curtain between her and the rest of us. "That's why I'm running. My- the king arranged it as a prosperous treaty between us and another land. I don't want- I can't... I can't be tied down to a man I don't know. Not yet."

Aiko nods her head in understanding. The new boots, the fight in Belam. We are dealing with a guilty runaway who has been preened her whole life for this once alliance. Who has the guts to turn away from it all, or the selfishness. I haven't decided how I feel about this yet.

"How do we help you?" Aiko brushes the young woman's hair from her eyes and tucks it gingerly behind her ear. I have to look away when she leans into the touch, it feels too personal.

"I can't go back."

"Well, you're not capable of living on your own, and you're sure as hell not staying here," I scoff, rising to my feet. Finneas steps forward and offers Vera his hand and arm to lean on as she tries to get up again. She obliges and opens her mouth in protest when Finneas cuts her off.

"He's right. If you stayed here, we would harbor you, but you'd be a fugitive and they'd find you easily. We are only a half hour walk from the outer circle of the palace. And you have clearly shown you have no survival skills on your own... sorry." He apologizes when her glare shifts to him. "I'm not saying you can't stay; the choice is yours completely. But you must be prepared to survive on your own, or else you'll get caught, killed, or worse."

Vera's shoulders slump in defeat, and a spark of pity lights in my chest. I am quick to smother that ember. I won't get involved, not when I have so much riding on my shoulders already. And Kya...

Her gaze drifts to me, and I can practically see the gears shifting in her head.

"You can train me."

"Ha!" I gasp out a laugh. "And why would I help a good for nothing brat who can't even clean up her own messes?"

"Why not? You clearly know how to survive on your own, and I'm a noble with access to the palace. Surely there must be something I can offer you."

Unabashed bribery. I smirk at that. If she were less of mollycoddled brat, she might've fit in well with us.

But then a thought crosses my mind. A fleeting and potentially foolish thought, but it might work out well for me in the end. And for my mother. Aiko stirs beside me as if she knows what has passed into my head, as if she plans to speak out against it. I speak first.

"One second thought, an alliance could prove to be advantageous to me." I take a step forward, and then another. Vera, much to her credit, doesn't balk. "But I have some conditions."

"Name them." Oh, sweet desperation, what blindsided fools it makes of us all.

"One, you must never speak to anyone about what happened tonight. Must never mention whose faces you saw, what stories you might've heard. My friends here took you into their home and tended to you despite being high in power. One slip up could cost them... Dearly." She nods vigorously, making eye contact with Finneas and Aiko as if silently promising this to them. "And second, we meet in the palace."

"W-what?" she sputters, her jaw dropping slightly.

"Well, where else would you suggest? I doubt you'll be able to escape twice so soon after the first, let alone multiple times. And I have some business to take care of that can't be done outside the palace walls."

Tendrils of mist begin to seep from the floor, heating with the coming day. Outside the window, lighter hues of blues and purples contrast against the deep navy sky. Slowly, the stars begin to wink out. Finneas stifles a yawn.

I watch as she scrunches her nose in distaste and fight the urge to shake an answer out of her. It has been a long night. The least she can do is answer before daybreak, so I still have the cover of shadow to return home in. I needed to get to Kya first and see to it that her wound has been tended to. No doubt Amír has been all over it already, but still. The way we left things unsettles me.

"Deal," she finally says, extending that bloody and scraped hand. I glance downwards at it before shaking it with a stone face. Her grip is soft, yet firm. She shakes hard, as if she has something to prove. We hold each other's gaze a grip for a moment before Finneas interrupts with a cough.

"Would you like some help getting home?" he offers to Vera, having produced a new cloak from a nearby closet. Vera drops my hand to gratefully take it, and I notice that in her wake she's left a print of gold across the skeins of my palm.

"Thank you," I can vaguely hear her whisper to Aiko, as she probably shoots a glare at me, and then the slam of the door as Finneas leads her home. No sweet goodbyes or gratitude. Not for me, anyway. My attention is fixed on my hand, where hers had been moments ago. I never knew that there were so many shades of gold.

"Of all the stupid, reckless things you could've done." Aiko sets upon me the moment the door swings shut. She runs a hand through her hair while I merely walk over to the table and pour myself a glass of some random colored liquor. I down the amber colored liquid in one gulp.

"What, should I have spit on it?"

"I know what you're doing this for," she whispers, and I pour another glass.

"Oh?"

"You're going after him," she clarifies. "You're going after your father."

"Congratulations, you've figured it out. Would you like a medal?"

"You can watch your tone with me, young man. After everything we've done for you, some respect would be a welcome change," she snarls and snatches my third glass from my hands right as I go to tip it between my lips, and downs it herself. "Your mother and I have done everything in our power to keep you safe from him, and you're about to go charging into the lion's den to... to what? Settle some score? He's not just any other noble, people will notice."

The glass shatters against the table as she drops it, her hands falling heavy at her side. Dawn has begun to stretch her willowy fingers across the sky now. Tinges of bronze, fuchsias, and skeins of lilac mingle together. One by one, the oil lamps are lit in each window, the restless servants begin to emerge from their masters' homes to set about their morning tasks. Those said masters are still asleep in their cushy beds, unaware of the life blossoming around them.

I nudge away a piece of broken glass with my toe, clearing a path to my cloak. I pause at the door to turn back and look at Aiko, her frail frame encapsulated in weak golden light. She could fool any man for an angel, if it were not for the deep sadness time has etched into her features.

"The problem is," I say as a way of goodbye, "you focused on protecting me from him when all along you should've been worried about keeping him safe from me."

CHAPTER 5

VEROSA

F inneas, I learn, is a curious and kind man. He knows the best paths to take to avoid the bustle of the early morning crowds and where the wild blackberries grow along said path. And what he doesn't know, he isn't afraid to ask about.

"Do you wear your hair braided like that often?" he questions, motioning to the crown braided across the top of my head. It had fallen out in the scuffle, and I had redone it as we walked. Finneas had watched, fascinated the whole time.

"Most of the time, unless it's a special occasion," I explain with a heavy sigh. "My mother always braided it like this, and after her passing, I kept doing it myself. Creature of habit."

"I'm sorry for your loss."

"Don't be, she was a terrible person." For the first time this whole walk, Finneas shuts his mouth. Not that I really mind talking to him; for the most part, he seems harmless. No, it's the woman I'd have to worry about between the two of them. Aiko, that silver fox. When I was under, I could hear bits and pieces of what she was saying, how quickly she knew my motives. How to get me to talk... All it took was one friendly face, and I crumbled. Her wit is unparalleled, and I must be on my guard if I am ever to encounter her again.

And that boy. When I saw him in that alleyway, I had assumed he was on the losing side. It wasn't until after I had intervened that I realized that they didn't have him. He had them. He was ruthless, in both hand and mind. I had been completely convinced that a part of my body was purer than the rest and that I just never knew about it. If that woman was a fox, then he was a serpent.

The only thing I can't figure out is why he saved me. Why risk it? I couldn't get a read on him, and it still irks me.

"So, that guy back there..." I groan, realizing I never even got his name. "What's his deal?"

"Ah. Rowan is an interesting case, we will say. He's got motives for his motives, that's for sure, but he's a good kid at heart, I think. He won't come to the palace just to murder you in cold blood if that's what you're worried about. That would be too inconvenient for him."

"Oh. How comforting."

Rowan. The name is familiar. It takes a minute before I remember where I've seen it before. Rowan was the prince in a book Tanja read for me as a child. He came and saved the kingdom from ruin and married 'goodness and truth' rather than a woman. Whatever the hell that means. But it was my favorite story. Whenever Tanja finished, I would take its worn cover between my hands and trace every ridge and stitch with my tiny fingers. I'd smell the pages and hold it for a minute; imagine a world where I could live a life like that.

Goodness and truth were just about as far away from the boy from last night as they could get. That murderous expression on his face as he brought his knee into my captor's jaw pops into my mind. I shiver.

"Are you cold?" Finneas asks, already removing his own woolen cloak to drape atop my own.

"No, no, just thinking."

"About that fiancé you're running away from?"

"Sure," I lie.

"You could just have another man or lover challenge him to a duel for your hand. That's how I married Aiko," he says it so nonchalantly I almost miss it.

"Wh-what?" I sputter, staring up at him. At those fine lines crinkling in the corner of his eyes, his soft mouth and sun kissed freckles. He looks nearly identical to a teddy bear Blaine gave me one birthday.

"Well, it's a long story..." he trails off, scratching at the back of his neck.

I smile. "We have time."

He looks at me and stumbles, his face reading pure surprise before he offers a lazy smile, seemingly having forgotten whatever he had seen in me that had caused such a shock.

"We met at her Ball of Deun when she came of age," he began explaining, and I nodded along expectantly. I remember my own ball when I turned 16, a blessed lady's entrance into society. Suitors generally come pouring in afterwards.

"She was the most radiant woman I had ever seen. She wore a flowing lilac gown, embroidered with golden thread and millions of tiny diamonds. She looked like dawn herself, that one hour before the sun rises when they sky is purple and the stars still glimmer? That was her. She was short in stature, that clearly hasn't changed, but she held the room's attention like no one I'd ever seen before. She was a force to be reckoned with. Every eligible bachelor in the room sought her hand for a dance, and one by one, she rejected them. She contented herself by standing by the band and swirling to the music by herself. I was immediately in love with her." He sighs dreamily, his eyes glazed with the fond memory.

"And then what happened?" I lean forward, feeling once more like a child listening to Tanja read to me.

"I went to try my luck when the music slowed, but someone beat me there. She rejected him like all the others, like she probably would've done with me, but instead of leaving, he reached out to grab her by the wrist and demanded she dance with him." He growls. "Well, I saw red, and next thing I knew, I had broken his entitled little nose. He was on the floor, screaming and bloody, but I didn't care. I turned around, expecting her to thank me or be awed. But she had walked away! I sulked by the refreshments the rest of the night until the bartender came over and slipped me a note. I was requested by the lake behind the manor.

"I was drunk at this point, and it probably wasn't my best idea to go alone in a strange building as the son of a duke, but I went anyway. And there she was, splendid in the moonlight. I swear, she was glowing, her eyes, that dress, her very skin. All of it. And we continued to meet like that, in secret. She didn't want the world to know we were courting yet, and it wasn't until it was announced in the paper that she was engaged that I knew why."

Something stirred deep in my chest. This story is too familiar, as I walk the lines of it even now.

"Well, I went to her in a fit, how could she use me like that and such nonsense. That's when she begged me to run away, said it was the man whose nose I had broken all those years ago. That he had bought her out from her family. I would've left for her, but that's when a maid caught us and told her father. Our meetings stopped, she was never there anymore, and I could only imagine in torment what was going on behind those closed doors. The wedding date encroached closer and closer, so I did the only thing I could think of. I challenged him to a duel to the death for her hand."

"You can do that?" I inquire. My mind starts racing with possibilities, if Blaine knew that there was a way out of my marriage, why hadn't he done anything? But then again, why would he, and why am I still holding onto what he's clearly already let go of.

The large man chuckles. "Medieval, isn't it? But yes, it's ancient Krycolian tradition that any man of noble birth equal to or greater than in power to the bride can challenge her fiancé to a duel to the death. Whoever is left gets to marry her. And I won. We married a month later, then moved here. We've been here ever since."

The golden green glow of the forest lulls us into an easy silence now, the weight of his declaration settling heavily on my chest. Then I think of Aiko, wondering what she would've looked like that night. I can picture it as clearly as if woven into one of those exquisite tapestries I study, her dancing with her hair unbound encapsulated by glowing moonlight. A goddess born in human flesh.

"Do you ever regret it? Killing him, I mean?"

Finneas stops to think about it, rubbing that stubbly ghost of a mustache above his lip pensively before he shakes his head.

"For her, I would do it a million times over again," he says before he holds his hand out to stop us both. I pause and listen, only to hear nothing.

"What is it?"

"Guards nearby. I can't get you in closer, you know the rotations better than I do probably. Anything past this point, I'll be a hinderance." He motions forward to the path before us. "Keep straight on this path, and you'll reach the southern wall."

I nod, hearing the clatter of armor and hooves faintly in the distance now and know he's right. It's only a few moments past dawn. The darkness provides just enough cover for me to slip back through the wall undetected, but not with the larger man attached to my hip.

"How will I find Rowan again?" I stop after a few steps, and he stops to think about it for a minute before a large grin splits across his face.

"You won't find him, he finds you!" He laughs heartily. The jovial man moves to take another step before he pauses and spins around again to face me. "Oh, and Vera? Pleasure meeting you."

I can't stop the matching grin that grows on my own features.

"Likewise."

The clamoring of the guard grows closer, and in a blink, Finneas is gone. I'm left staring for at the spot where he used to be but find no trace of the unusual man. The sly fox and her loyal brute, indeed.

Flipping my cloak up over my head, I take a deep breath to steel myself against the foreboding presence of home and the monsters that lay slumbering within it. One step at a time, I make my way to the palace wall.

"Good morning!" I say cheerfully upon entering the kitchen through the back door. I had left my gifted cloak tucked into a crevice in my hidden passageway and was careful to pull my pant legs down to cover any wounds I had sustained. Miraculously, they never tore during the events of last night.

"*Mai Reinhavich*." The cook curtsies deeply. "What are you doing here so early in the morning?"

The kitchen wallpaper is peeling from the heat of the stone stoves, and what is left of it is charred black. The stones along the floor are smooth and worn with the hurried footsteps of the kitchen staff, all who wear matching ivory aprons and silk slippers embroidered in golden thread with the family crest. Busy as always, they scurry along, their arms weighted down with heavy golden platters of fruits and tarts. Never is anything silver.

"I went for a walk early this morning to clear my head," I answer, snatching an apple from the tray of a passing maid. "But between you and me, I couldn't sleep."

The diminutive woman nods curtly, understanding clearly written across her pinched and ruddy features. Something over my shoulder catches her eye, and she leans in closer to whisper in my ear.

"Well, I don't think someone else could either." I trace her gaze to where Blaine stands in the entryway, his powerful frame leaning hard against the wall. His eyes are downcast and his shoulders bunched tight. It tells me enough.

"Excuse me for a moment." She bows her head, and I brush past her without a second thought. Ten paces have me standing before Blaine, my arms crossed tightly across my chest.

"Were you ever going to say something or were you going to sulk in the shadows all morning?" My voice is colder than I had expected and laced with fatigue. Blaine's mouth sets a hard line, and he jerks his chin towards the now empty kitchen.

"Point taken." I sigh, leaning heavy against the wall across from him. "What did you want?"

"What are you planning?" I quirked an eyebrow.

"What ever could you mean?"

Then those shoulders are back, his hands flexing at his side before bunching into fists. I feel a guilty twinge of satisfaction at that. That even though his walls are up again, they're there because of me, and he still cares enough to give a reaction, no matter how negative it is.

But then he looks at me, and his gaze levels on my face. Before I can blink he's there, his calloused hand brushing back my carefully placed bangs to reveal that nasty gash and the mottled flesh around it. I wince as he gently prods, and he withdraws his hand immediately.

"Who did this to you?"

I glanced between us then, at the space between us. Even in his protective fury, he bears more weight on his bad leg, careful that no part of him touches any part of me. A low boil of fury pools in my gut, and I shove him hard in the chest.

"What's it to you?" I hiss through clenched teeth as I stalk towards him now. "You knew the whole time anyway."

He stumbles a bit before righting himself, his eyes hardened again. "Did he-"

I laugh, a sick sardonic sound even to my own ears. "No, but gods, you knew this whole time. And you didn't even bother to tell me I was going to be sold off like cattle, married to the highest bidder."

"It's for the kingdom."

Wrong words. Those are the wrong words for him to say.

"Oh, and you'd know wouldn't you? That's all that matters to you, anyway. My whole life, I've made decisions for the good of the kingdom, and what about me? What about what happens to me in the end? Does that matter to you after everything? By the gods, if you weren't going to fight, I thought you might as well have given me the chance to!"

My throat burns as I swallow the sob rising and blink back my traitorous tears. I won't give him the satisfaction of seeing me cry. Never again.

"Conveniently, there were no guards outside your room last night, were there?"

There's silence, and then the offbeat echo of his footsteps as he melds into the darkness of the hallway, leaving me to be fanned by the flames of the bridges I just burned. Despite the heat of the kitchen, I find myself shivering again.

The stables are undoubtedly the grandest part of the palace, with walls of tall white brick and trellises coated in ivy and wisteria blooms. The flooring is pure, polished cobblestone, and the stalls are of the richest grenadil wood. Horse and rider are constantly coming and going, not a single speck of dust on the fine animals. It is exactly where I need to be right now.

I find Torin flirting with a random stableboy near the east entrance, his finely clothed back turned to me. I can't help but roll my eyes as I approach. Truly no one is safe from his charms. No one but me, that is.

The young stableboy goes rigid when he spots me behind my friend and looks as though he cannot decide whether he should bow or run.

"Gaven what- By the Laei!" Torin curses when he spins to find me within a breath's width of him. "Who taught you to sneak like that?" The stableboy, Gaven, finally decides on bowing before jogging off to do whatever task he had been set to before Torin undoubtedly disrupted it.

"Isolated princess, remember? A girl's got to get around somehow."

"Noted." He coughs and rolls his shoulders.

"How's the horse from yesterday?" I ask, nodding my head in the direction of a certain stall. The beautiful stallion has his head out, his neck craned and teeth bared at anyone who comes too close.

"Ah, just as righteously pissed off as before."

As he speaks, Vestíg reaches out and grabs the collar of a stable hand who walks too close to his stall and gives a ferocious tug. The poor girl lets out a blood curdling scream as her blouse begins to tear and his large teeth graze her neck, though not deep enough to draw blood, I note. Torin rushes over with the others to try and pull her free. She lands heavily against the stone. Just as the creature is about to strike again, I throw myself between them and brace for the grinding of teeth, flesh, blood, and bone, but it doesn't come. Instead, I find myself staring into two flared nostrils, the fine animal's neck curved as to let me know he has the space to lash out if he wants to. But he doesn't. Rather, his hot breath fans my face, and I find myself reaching up to touch his muzzle when something hard slams into my abdomen.

Vestíg immediately begins to snort and kick at the stall door, pinning his ears and shaking out his midnight mane. His neck ripples with powerful corded muscle, the faint signs of dapples showing across his crest.

"What are you thinking Vera?" Torin grunts as he pushes himself off of me, brushing off some invisible dust on the lapels of his jacket before extending his hand. I brush it aside and pick myself up, staring back at the raging beast, who seems less beast-like now than he had before.

"What, so everyone else can help, but I can't?"

"Notice how everyone else stayed *away* from his mouth." Torin emphasizes the word 'away' with wild gesticulations. "But not you, you put your face right up in there."

"Whatever, no harm no foul right?"

Torin eyes me suspiciously before letting out a deep breath. "Right...

what were you here for, anyway? Just to see the horse that almost killed you?"

"I need to blow off some steam, I want you to take me for a ride."

"I'll do it." A suave voice says from behind us both, and I spin to find none other than my fiancé standing there. He wears a deep maroon tunic under a black leather vest, embroidered with copper thread. His dark trousers are tucking into tall riding boots, a man who came prepared to play the part.

"I asked Torin," I reply curtly, already walking to where Gaven has begun tacking my mare. A sweet-tempered thing, plump with a lovely dappled grey coat.

"Torin, I believe, has some more pressing matters to attend to. Right, Torin?" Lucius responds with a wink in the direction of Gaven. Torin, the lecherous traitor, straightens his collar and grins.

"I believe I do, Mei Reinhavich. Enjoy your ride, My Lieges." He sketches a bow and ignores the vulgar gesture I give him behind my back. Lucius, to his credit, does not seem bothered. Instead, he rather skillfully tacks one of the Tesslari horses that he arrived with yesterday.

"Are our horses not well suited to you, your highness?"

"On the contrary," he says in his infuriating courtier's voice. "Jacques here could go with a good hack though."

I scoff. "You named your horse Jacques?"

"It's a noble name. Besides, my mother told me that giving something a human name increases its value." He shrugs.

Did your mother teach you how to be an arrogant prick too? I want to ask, but I bite my tongue and urge my mare into a clumsy trot. The mare steps out with long and gracious strides, however, it's my riding that makes it so ungraceful. Admittedly, it has been some time since I've last ridden, and my muscles are already beginning to ache with the strain of holding myself in the saddle.

"You know," Lucius says from where he sits, poised with perfect equitation atop his own mount. "It would be easier if you let your legs lengthen and wrap around her barrel rather than shortening them and sticking your heels in the air."

"Oh, so now you're an expert equestrian as well?"

"I did lead my father's cavalry when I was 15."

Pretentious bastard. I ignore him for a moment before I feel myself begin to tip to the left and lose my balance. Begrudgingly I extend my legs and hold pressure in my thighs, and find, albeit much to my displeasure, that he had been right. The mare sighs in relief as I cease to thump on her back, and I give her a quick, apologetic pat. Lucius nods his approval, as if I ever had sought it out.

A slight cool breeze wisps by as we trot smoothly over the palace grounds. The large canopy trees stretch their willowy arms above our heads, offering shade and privacy. I let my head tip back and stare into the filtered sunlight as it dances between the emerald leaves. The earth thrums with life as hooves pound stone and dirt, and the air smells of rain. From my peripheral, I can see Lucius staring, and as he opens his mouth to say something, I urge my mount into a canter.

I can hear Jacque's thunderous steps encroaching and curse bitterly to myself. Just what would it take to shake this prince?

My mount squeals in displeasure as I give a hard yank on the reins, and she dives right onto a path less trodden. Pebbles kick up and bounce off the trees on our ever-narrowing path. Minuscule branches reach out to caress my arms with prickling scratches, but I pay them no mind as I spot a clearing that promises freedom. If I could just get there...

At the last moment, Lucius pulls up beside me and grabs my reins, pulling us both to a halt right as my mare's front hooves cross over the threshold of the clearing.

"Can we talk, instead of you nearly killing yourself and your poor horse?" he says calmly, without so much as breaking a sweat. My shoulders heave as I give him an indignant glare, ignoring the burning in my thighs and core.

"What is there to talk about?"

"You're joking right?" I raise an eyebrow, and he sighs. "No, apparently not. Why do you think so ill of me when we only met last night? A night where both of us were playing a part."

"Why do you assume I have to talk to you when we only just met last night?"

"I can at least give a straightforward answer." He dismounts in one fluid motion. "We are to be married in a few months' time, whether you like it or not, and I'd rather not marry a stranger."

He extends his hand to help me down, but I swing my leg over and dismount myself, my joints protesting the jarring motion. The reins slide over my mare's head easily, slick with sweat, as I lead her to a nearby brook to drink. I had been unfair to the poor creature.

"I'd rather marry a stranger than an enemy."

"I am not your enemy, Verosa."

The distant song of a bird in the forest is his only response, the tune light and tittering despite the tension in our clearing. I take the time to study him, to really look at him this time.

He is not unattractive, in fact, quite the opposite. His hair is a midnight black like mine, with matching dark irises. There is something brooding about his features, his finely carved nose, strong jaw, thin lips, and the slight upturn of his eyes. His extravagant clothes are tailored to his well-muscled body, fitting every hollow and curve. He is the spitting image of all he is to represent, a noble prince with fine breeding and a noble heart filled to the brim with valor. I have to turn away, but this, it seems, finally lights a dim fire in my fiancé.

"I never wanted this marriage either." He softly grabs at my sleeve, cautious, ever so cautious as not to touch my skin. I could've laughed, what a showy gentleman.

"Really? Because that's not what you told my father, the king, last night," I say as I snatch my arm back from his grasp. Lucius drops it immediately and takes a step back.

"It's called a facade, Verosa. I was simply telling the king what he wanted to hear."

"And how do I know that this isn't a 'facade' right now, Lucius?" I say, whirling on him with all the fury of my throbbing leg and bleeding heart. All of my pent-up frustration drips from my words like venom. Falling for Wooden's trap, nearly getting killed in that fight, every one of Rowan's snide remarks and cocky smirks. Blaine is in the back of my mind, and so is his self-righteous pity. "How do I know you're not just manipulating me as well?"

I don't realize I'm crying until he brings one of those gloved hands up to my cheek and brushes a single burning tear away.

"Because," Lucius speaks slowly as he pulls his hand back to his side, "you're much too smart for that."

"You're dancing with treason."

"Can't we have one pleasant conversation? Why is everything so fight or flight with you?" Something must have slipped through my guarded features, a softening of the mouth or a downward glance, for understanding shows now on Lucius' handsome face. He takes a step closer and speaks, his voice as smooth as silk. "Perhaps it is because it is all you've ever known?"

"Don't try to analyze me," I snap, but Lucius advances again, forcing me to take a step back. The hem of my pants clings to my ankles as I step into the stream.

"I was grieving the death of my mother when my father came and told me I was to marry some strange princess in a neighboring land. There was no time to fight or run. I was tired and cornered, and I understand completely how you feel." His gaze is pleading as he takes both of my hands in his own. "I am not here to fight you. I won't even ask for your love, just maybe a chance to be your friend?"

My wound stings as sweat drips from my forehead into it, and I bite my lip to avoid crying out in pain. Lucius seems to notice and raises his hand as if to check when I jump back and force a smile.

"You can try." Now I've put my foot in my mouth. "You may try until the end of our betrothal to be my friend, and at our wedding, I will decide whether or not I accept your friendship."

Lucius raises his eyebrow, as if to say 'I'm not sure you have a choice' but he doesn't have a chance to respond before I'm back on my horse.

"Come," I command. "It's well past time we get back."

His eyebrows raise, and he offers a sly grin before vaulting atop his mount in one fluid motion. He lands lightly on the creature's back before urging him into a trot.

"Your wish is my command." He winks, and I fight the bile back down my throat. Kicking my mare forward, we transition into a canter and begin the all too long ride back to the inner palace.

The trip back surprisingly isn't too bad. Lucius remains quiet most of the time. Even I have to admit that he reads me well. He knew when to push and when to stand down. If we had met under different circumstances perhaps, I would have even liked him, but now I am not so sure.

I want to spend more time at the stables and with Torin, but Tanja finds me the minute I crossed into the threshold with a message.

"What happened to her?" I ask, scanning the letter. "It's not like Eida to just leave without warning. And resignation? She's worked here for years."

"Aw, worried?" Tanja teases. "Maybe you finally drove her away, congratulations! I don't know, she was old. Maybe she just wanted to retire."

"Yeah, you're probably right," I hum.

"I thought you'd be happy about this? I mean, the old bat drove you crazy."

"Yeah, I know, just things are changing so quickly- too quickly." My friend goes quiet at this, shoving her hands back in her pockets as we walk. She wears her hair pinned back today, her loose curls bouncing atop her head as she walks. I smile softly to myself, judging by her effort, I'd say the date went well.

"Don't be too upset," she says catching my stare. "I've heard your new tutor is very attractive."

I quirk an eyebrow as we enter the library. The smell of worn leather and fresh pages greets me as soon as we step foot in the ancient room. Rows and rows of books new and old line the walls, with little desks nestled between them for secluded studying.

"Oh, really?" I ask before I can spot the figure in front of us. I hardly recognize him in all his finer garb.

"Really." Rowan smirks from where he sits perched atop a desk. "Ready for your lesson, Vera?"

CHAPTER 6
VEROSA

O f all the ways I thought Rowan would infiltrate the palace, this is not one of them. In my wildest dreams, I saw him barging in as a knight in training, disrupting practice, or posing as a cook and poisoning my meal out of spite. Maybe I had thought he would sneak through my window in the middle of the night to steal me away for training or kill me off to tidy up loose ends. In the more boring of scenarios, he didn't come at all.

And yet here he is, dressed in a fine pressed blouse, his tailored coat hanging loosely on a chair as he reads a book, sitting on a table in the royal library. He wears that Cheshire cat grin that feels so familiar already, and makes his way over to where we stand, me dumbfounded in the doorway.

"Pleasure to meet you." I force through gritted teeth, taking his hand so that he may press a kiss atop mine. Tanja watches giddy from the side, fanning her cheeks every so often in mocking.

"You are dismissed." Tanja curtsies and takes her leave. The moment those doors slam shut and I know we are alone, I snatch my hand back and cast my iciest glare his way.

"What in the Laei are you doing here?"

Rowan raises an eyebrow and dusts an invisible speck of dirt of the lapel of his jacket, making his way back to his previous seat. Ignoring my question, he picks his book up again and begins to read before pointing to a certain word on the page and bookmarking it.

"If I am not mistaken, you were the one who asked me to train you, did you not?" he says without looking up.

"I didn't think you'd come as my tutor!"

"I don't see a problem here." He sighs heavily, slamming the book shut. "I needed a way into the palace and you needed a teacher. That was our deal. This was the best way to solve both of our needs inconspicuously. Trust me, this is not enjoyable for me. You nobles wear such stuffy clothing, no wonder you all walk like there's a stick up your ass."

My face flushes at his brazen words, more so because I know he is right. Huffing, I take my seat across from him, in an actual chair rather than a table. I fiddle with my hands at my sides and cross my ankles, waiting for him to begin. He just looks at me as if I've started bleeding silver.

"Well? What's your plan?"

"Ah, well, that depends. I have my plan, but I can't exactly share that with you-"

"Of course not," I mumble under my breath.

"-but I have to shape it around your desires, or else you'll probably out me to the palace guard." He continues with a wry smile. "So it depends on what you need from me. You said training, but I still don't know what kind."

I pause to think upon that for a moment. I am classically trained, having started my royal lessons at only three years old. All my teachers have praised my intuition and skill, and yet I still fell into Woden's trap.

"Physical, mostly. I can't fight, I'm good at running but don't know how to handle any weaponry or defend myself in a fight," I admit sheepishly. Rowan nods, looking deep in thought.

"We need to work on your reflexes." He nods carefully before tossing his book at me, which I catch with ease. Before I can open my mouth, however, another one hits me square in the gut. "Your enemy won't wait for you to recover from the first attack. So that will be our first lesson before we move on to anything else."

I'm about to bark back a retort when a young maid enters the room, knocking softly and walking even softer as she pads into the library. Her footsteps don't make a sound as she crosses the room and bows slightly at the waist. Rowan's eyes rove over her figure, unreadable. She wears the usual palace uniform but has paired it with elbow-high ivory gloves, stark in contrast to her deep-toned skin. Her black curls are pinned tight to her head beneath a bonnet, a few stray hairs poking out before her striking amber eyes. She might be the most beautiful girl I've ever seen.

"You sent for me, my Lord?" She speaks lowly, her voice a melodious alto that reminds me of gospel singing in the church.

"And did you bring what I asked?"

She grits her teeth but smiles pleasantly.

"Yes, my Lord." She places a fresh stack of paper and a well of ink in his hands before he dismisses her with a nod. I can hardly blink before she's gone without a whisper to remember her by.

"Who was that?"

"A maid," he deadpans, dumping the materials in my lap. "Start copying these facts from that book in your lap." I glance down at the text, a withered biography of past kings and their most notable traditions. It looks just like any other textbook Miss Eida would make me read if she were still here.

"Why?"

"Just shut up and do it," he snaps, reading again. "Unless you want nothing to show of your studies?"

I open then close my mouth, gaping like a fish as I struggle to think of an insult to return the sharp sting of his words, but I find nothing. So I do as he says. I copy endless dates of anarchies come and gone, queens that these men married, divorced, murdered, or were unfaithful to. A shiver works its way down my spine. Rowan is quiet, until he speaks up after some time.

"Who instituted the Raonkin Purge Party?"

"Duke Rajo Kyzen." I answer with ease.

"What was his wife's name?"

"Lindietta Marcella Kyzen."

"Where is Varium?"

"South of Neva."

"Who was your first love?"

I open my mouth to respond but hesitate right before I notice the sly smirk on Rowan's face, then what I had almost said. Rising to my feet, I throw the book at his face, only for him to catch it flawlessly with one hand. That scoundrel. A furious heat crawls up the back of my neck and creeps into my cheeks.

"You-"

"Your reflexes are quick, but they need to be tuned. It isn't all physical," he explains, ducking as I throw the quill at him next. "You got comfortable in letting them take over subconsciously. That's dangerous. Your reflexes might save you, but if you don't school them, you could offer up the wrong information to the wrong person. Right now, it's just something embarrassing, but next time, it could be something that endangers you and others. Like your being a pureblood?"

I feel my rage subside ever so slightly as cold realization dawns on me. Woden flashes in my mind again, those swirling silk skirts and charming grins that lulled me into false confidence. I sit back down.

"How do I do that?" Rowan rolls up the cuffs of his sleeves to his elbows, over dramatically flexing as he checks a pocket watch and looks out at the dying sun.

"Prove I can trust you, and I'll show you how."

"You said you'd train me!" I protest.

"And this is part of it," he snaps, his chair scraping against the floor as he rises to lean across the table. "A truth for a truth, that is the game we will play, Vera. I am not going to put people in danger to satiate you without earning something in return. So prove it. Prove I can trust you."

Alarms blare in my mind, warning sirens that scream 'this man is dangerous, stay far away,' though some traitorous filth whispers, 'he can set you free.' And if I don't take this chance now, who knows when the next one will arise?

"I don't like how much I have to gamble with you." I huff, and he laughs breathlessly, rocking back to stand straight up.

"It's not a gamble if it's guaranteed to succeed."

"Is it though?"

"Is anything?"

"Look who is speaking in riddles now." I gather my books in my hands to stand and face him. He may have backed me into a corner, but I will face him with dignity regardless. "Come back tomorrow night, and you will have your proof."

"I will look forward to it." Rowan sketches a bow as he gathers his materials. "Keep studying, my faithful pupil. Also, I know your answer would have been that captain. Don't think I can't see the eye sex you two have in the halls." I fight the urge to flip an obscene gesture at his back as he walks away. His shoulders shake, as if he knows and is laughing. It does make me wonder, just how dangerous is this fox that I've led straight into the coop?

I find Lucius leaving dinner late that night and pull him into an empty room the moment no one is looking. He complies silently, not making a sound until I've locked the door behind me.

"I didn't expect to meet again so soon, let alone be yanked into a secluded room." He chuckles softly, his voice laced with light mirth. He rocks back to lean against the wall and adjusts the cuffs of his sleeves.

"You wanted to be friends, right?"

"At the least, yes." His voice is steady and patient, and I wonder just how long it will stay that way, if at all, after I reveal what I need of him. He eyes me curiously, the air of the room suddenly thicker. Reaching into the folds of my skirt, I pull out the parchment, placing it in his hands forcefully. He makes to unroll it, but I hold steadfast to his wrist.

"I need you to find this information for me and return it before nightfall tomorrow. You are to tell no one of what you're searching for or why. If you do, our deal is off, and I will not marry you, regardless of what my father says. Am I understood?" Lucius goes deathly still, my quickened breathing the only sound filling the airy room. He searches for any signs of hesitancy in my features, and when he finds none, he nods. He inhales sharply, eyeing my request.

"You know, most women ask for jewelry or precious stones from their betrothed, but this..." He swallows thickly. "I'm assuming you won't tell me why you need it, but may I ask why you think they'll give this to me?"

"You're the future king."

"And you the future queen," he quips sharply.

"I have a habit." I blush to the tips of my ears now. "A very bad habit of running away. They wouldn't give me anything that would make it easier for me to do so."

Lucius stares at me for a moment before his curious gaze melts into light laughter. He clutches the parchment tighter, squinting a bit before placing a hand on my shoulder.

"What gave it away? The horse chase in the woods or watching you be escorted by half the guard this morning?" he says, his voice dripping with sarcasm. "But if this is what it takes to earn your trust, you will have it by nightfall as you've requested."

I wouldn't go as far as to say trust, but it could be a good start for the both of us. He bends slightly as the hip in a mock bow before he slips through the door seemingly unnoticed. I wait a moment myself before leaving as well. Slowly, I pick my way back to my own room, my mind racing.

Rowan had warned me before he left to find a way from the palace grounds after nightfall tomorrow night, that our business would take place miles away. My heart stutters at the thought, and I place a hand over my chest. The minute I am capable of fending for myself, I will be rid of him, as well as my expectant fiancé. As well as Blaine.

A pang of guilt wracks my body as I think of leaving him, but he had said it himself. If he would not come for me, I will not stay for him.

Moonlight ripples through my sheer curtains and into my room, splaying across my silken pillows. Jewels adorn my dresser, my closet full to the brim with the finest of clothing and warm, sturdy shoes. My attached washroom has marble floors, and the walls are inlaid with gold and mother of pearl. Every luxury money could buy is here, and yet these canopy feelings resemble a bird cage more and more each day; the windows seemingly grow smaller.

Soon, though, I will get out there and see the world. Soon these four barred walls will be a distant memory. Soon I can choose what life I wish to live for myself without my father pulling the strings.

Burrowing deep into my covers, I feel a weight lifted from my shoulders for what feels like the first time in my life. Soon.

CHAPTER 7
VEROSA

The sun is already beginning to set, and Lucius is nowhere to be seen. Maids and servants rush about the halls per usual, dusting tapestries and polishing the floors. Each and every one of them bow as they pass, and I pray that as I smile back, they cannot see the sweat beading along my forehead or the anxious fidget of my hands.

When I saw him this morning, he was chatting with a few of the guards, Blaine standing suspiciously in the corner. Of everyone I have to look out for with this plan, it is him. Sure, Blaine had no issue letting me go the first time, back when he thought I could escape. But now, he would be able to see through me. He knows me too well. If Lucius were to accidentally let it slip that I needed this information, then it would be over.

I nearly jump out of my own skin when I feel a firm hand close around my elbow. Lucius whispers low in my ear, "Don't give them cause for suspicion."

"Do you have it?" I answer breathlessly before I feel the weight of the paper slipping back into my pocket. If not for the people around us, I would have slapped him for placing it there himself.

"Ask, and you shall receive." I nod, about to walk off, when his grip on my elbow tightens, guiding me to face him. "Don't do anything fool-ish." I snatch my arm back, eyeing him dangerously. Lucius, much to his credit, doesn't balk from my icy indignation. Rather, he stands his ground and holds my gaze.

"I wouldn't dream of it," I respond briskly before storming down the hall to the library. Once I'm sure there's nothing but me and the books here, I pull open the scroll and hiss. I had my doubts, but Lucius actually did it. Copying everything down onto a separate scroll, I tuck them into my bosom and shirk off my skirts, revealing the loose-fitting pants I've been wearing beneath all day.

Ducking between guards and hallways, I find my way through the passage to go meet Rowan at our rendezvous point. The church bells chime nine times in the distant, the sound being carried by a brisk breeze. Rowan steps out from behind some shrubbery at that moment, perfectly punctual.

"I have to admit," he drawls with that sardonic grin of his, "I am so very curious as to what you have to offer that could be worth my while."

My closed fist slams into his chest, eliciting a startled grunt. The parchment crinkles as he takes it from my grasp, and I lower my hand. His eyes scan the page before he lets out a low whistle, tucking the parchment into his satchel.

"And how do I know this information is true?"

"How do you think I got here? I followed the guard rotations as listed, everyone was where that paper said without fail, and I was able to sneak through. The castle has several weak points that allow approxi-mately thirty seconds to slip past the defenses. You'd have to be quick, but it is doable." My hands begin to shake at my sides. With this infor-mation, anyone quick and stealthy enough could break into the castle, my home, and do whatever they wish. I can spot my own room on that page, as well as Father's. The only two rooms in the whole palace where there is no opening for someone to slip through. If this information falls into the wrong hands... but then again, who is to say the wrong hands don't belong to Rowan? I might have just signed my death warrant and handed it to him, as well as damned everyone else inside.

"You must want out very badly if you're willing to give me this." He eyes me warily out from the corner of his eye.

"I trust you," I choke out, noticing now how truly dark it is. No one would see if something were to happen to me right now.

"You shouldn't." He takes my hand then and pulls me towards a dark horse. "Not until I give you cause to, anyway. But after tonight, you will have enough over me to even the playing field again."

"I just handed you my life and countless others' on a silver platter, I'm not sure there's much you could offer me that would put us in any form of even." I slide into the saddle behind him, ignoring every point of contact between us. I want to be sick, right here over his fine horse and leather-clad body.

"And I'm about to do the same." Is all he says before he urges the horse into a canter, and soon, a gallop. With a small cry, I cross two fingers across my chest in a prayer to the gods to ward off evil. Rowan is still seated before me, so clearly the gods are choosing not to listen today.

The wind draws tears from my eyes as I cling to his back, praying for everything to be over. Through bleary peaks over his shoulder, I can see Belam in the distance, and the bright lights of the West. Raucous laughter dances with sophisticated music. The swirls of scarlet silks and the satin slippers soon to be discarded in the corner of a ballroom. And Rowan in the center of it all, the shadows clinging to his body as if they are a second skin. Night bows to him, but the stars reflect in his eyes, saving him from the appearance of a monster. Perhaps an old god instead.

The chill drives me closer, and I bury my face in his back. His shoulders rumble with laughter and I'm glad that the night covers my cowering crimson face. After what feels like an eternity has passed, my guide halts our mount. The wind dies from my ears, and I am suddenly very aware to how close I am huddled to him.

"We're here."

I remain still, waiting for a moment, until Rowan clears his throat and jerks his chin towards the ground. I dismount clumsily, my legs still shaking from the long ride. Rowan smoothly leaps down from our mount, landing silently upon the rocks.

"Just this way." He brings the reins over the horse's neck and grabs my elbow with his other hand. He guides my stumbling form through the brush, and I note how deep in the woods we are. How silently stalking the night is. If Rowan notices my trepidation, he doesn't speak of it. He picks his way confidently across the rocks, appearing at home with the dark.

I nearly run into him when he stops abruptly and unlocks a door. I hadn't even seen the building before us. Blood rushes in my ears. The lock clicks then falls to the ground. Light floods from the door as it opens, temporarily blinding me. In a few quick seconds, Rowan pulls us both into the building and locks the door behind us. A low whistle blows through the room.

"And here I was thinking you got caught." A short, young woman with generous curves steps out from a doorway, dressed in nothing but a silk robe. She tuts her tongue in my direction, and I recognize her as the beautiful maid from the palace. The one who stumbled in calling Rowan 'Lord'. "Lovely to see you again Verosa."

"Go get dressed, we have business to discuss." Rowan huffs irately. "And I never get caught."

The woman rolls her lovely hazel eyes but leaves the room, only to return moments later dressed, though personally I think the robe covered more. A single sash of crimson fabric covers her breasts and exposes her midriff. A matching skirt of the same color hangs low across her hips, accentuated by a chunky gold belt. Her right hand draws my attention first, with it being covered with whorls of red ink, and I note them as traditional Vari markings. It is a tattoo of the individual's greatest desire, marked when they come of age. Only, hers looks smudged. Then I realize that it's paint, not a tattoo.

What catches my eye second is a thick bandage wrapping around her hips, poking out just above the waistband of her skirt. Those thugs' words ring back in my head from a few nights ago. The night where I met Rowan.

"You're his bitch!" I say before I can stop myself. Rowan smacks his forehead with his palm in remembrance while the woman quirks an eyebrow upward.

"Excuse me?"

"It's just something Mavis' men said, Kya." Rowan assuages the

71

woman, Kya, though she doesn't look upset. Her face is the perfect picture of amusement.

"I like you," she murmurs, stepping close enough that I can smell the vanilla and cinnamon perfume upon her neck. "But you'd do well to remember that I'm no one's bitch."

"Except Amír's." Another voice, male this time, piques from a darkened corner. A man, looking no older than Kya, sits fiddling with something in his lap. His rich and dark skin tone is accented with beads of sweat across his brow, and his eyes are of the darkest shade of gold.

My face flushes with embarrassment as Kya turns her attention to the man in the corner, her mouth gaping open before she swallows back whatever sarcastic quip she was preparing.

"Classy Derrín." She clucks her tongue. "Verosa, Derrín. My little brother."

"Twin brother. But yes, younger." Derrín corrects, not bothering to look up from his lap. Unlike Kya, he wears plain clothing, a simple linen tunic tucked into brown pants. His sock-clad feet tap impatiently against the floor.

"Pleasure." I nod, my confusion growing by the second. Who were these people, why did Rowan think I needed to meet them, and who was this Amír that they all kept referring to?

And why was Rowan looking at Kya like that?

His eyes found her supple form the moment we entered, and though it should mean nothing to me, I still felt... angry. A spark of something molten boiled deep in my gut, something that I didn't deserve to feel. Jealousy.

Rowan is an insufferable pain in the ass at best, a murderous criminal at worst. Sure, he is handsome in that roguish and somehow charming way, but nonetheless, to feel jealous? I love Blaine, and I am engaged to Lucius. I don't need to feel jealous over Rowan too. He is a small string attached to a larger picture, a single stitch in my tapestry. He means nothing to me.

And yet, this aching feeling only intensifies when the door is thrown open again. A tall and elegant figure breezes into the room. Her face is hidden by a deep burgundy cloak, but I can already tell by the fine contours of her figure that it is beautiful as well. Her long legs cover the distance between her and us in moments before she was stands before Rowan and me.

With a dramatic toss, the cloak falls, and long scarlet locks tumble free past her shoulders. A single streak of white dashes through the red, and I fight the urge to gasp when I see her beautiful face.

Her eyes are an even deeper shade of emerald than Rowan's, a shade of green that I didn't know could exist. They are framed by thick red lashes, with a perfectly placed splatter of freckles painted across her cheeks and the bridge of her nose. Her fair complexion is marbled with whorls of skin as pale as snow, and I notice the pattern continues across the visible skin along her arms as well.

She could easily be one of the loveliest women I've ever seen if it not for the deep-seated scowl that contorts her features.

Her eyes rove over my face, and I find myself wishing to shrink back, to grab Rowan's arm and beg him to take me home. But I don't, and instead settle for accepting the disgust she throws my way, feeling it in my gut as well. She raises a perfect crimson eyebrow when Kya clears her throat from across the room.

"You sure know how to make an entrance," she drawls, dragging her teeth over her lower lip. "I'm sure you had plenty of time to come up with it though considering that you're late. Again." She stands, her golden arms laying across her ample bosom, eyes narrowing to slits. The atmosphere of the room. Rowan smirks like he knows something bad is going to happen, and I find myself subconsciously inching towards the exit. Only Derrín doesn't respond, his long and nimble fingers still fiddling with whatever is in his lap.

"Laei, you're insufferable." Amír, I presume, groans and begins to storm towards the other woman. I jump back, preparing for a fight, when the redhead latches onto Kya.

"Not again." Is all Derrín mumbles, though not looking bothered at all by the fact that his sister is now pinned against the wall, Amír's tongue down her throat.

Rowan chuckles when he sees my presumably gobstopped expression, and he nods his head in their direction with pointed eyes. I grit my teeth in irritation knowing that he can read me so well already.

"It's one of my charms." He grins before clearing his throat annoyingly towards the two women in the corner. "Amír, I expect you have a reason for being late?"

"Just as I suspect you have a reason for bringing an outsider into our home," Amír snaps back, begrudgingly leaving her lover to report to Rowan. Red lipstick is smudged across the corner of her mouth. "A noble, nonetheless. So what form of demon has possessed you now, Rowan?"

The two go toe to toe, a low growl settling in the base of his throat. It's all I can do to watch as they tower over me, their power domineering as they match each other, neither of them willing to stand down.

Rowan mouths something unintelligible to her, and her features soften even just a fraction, and she nods.

"Mavis' men were found encroaching on our territory. I was investigating why. Turns out there's a rumor going on." Her eyes glance towards me now. "A rumor that Rowan has found himself a pureblood."

The color drains from Rowan's face as he curses softly under his breath.

"If Mavis knows then..."

"Then it's only a matter of time," Amír confirms, some secret, unspoken understanding passing between them. Rowan's shoulders square as he turns to face Kya.

"Her training starts tonight." The shorter woman nods curtly, stepping forward to usher me away as Amír and Rowan begin to walk towards an adjacent room to discuss whoever this Mavis threat is.

Everything begins to click now. The fight in Belam, the secret house in the woods, why he needs to meet more in the palace than here. Why he wouldn't reveal these things to me without sufficient collateral.

Rowan was the *Noiteron*, the ruthless leader of the Nightwalkers. A legend among criminals and a nightmare among nobles. And now I was one of them.

"Rowan, wait!" I grab the sleeve of his tunic before I can stop myself. He turns his face to me then, softening just slightly. "Am I in danger?" He eyes me curiously, as if noticing something he hasn't seen from me yet. He gives my hand a light squeeze and a small smirk.

"You've been in danger since you chose to leave the comforts of the palace and step into that fight. The question is, do you want to hide from it or learn to face it?"

And there it is, the question I've been longing to be asked since I was born, since I learned I was a pureblood. My father would say it is best to hide, as he's hid me away my whole life. A part of me calls to that, to go back to my cushy life with maids waiting for my beckoning call. The tug at my heart demands something greater though, to get out there and see the world I've been hidden from. Sure, that world may be dangerous, but with Rowan's help, maybe it could be beautiful too.

I should be terrified. I've heard the rumors, the silent assassin, ruthless gunslinger, and mechanical mastermind all led by the worst of them all. But maybe fear only works on those with something left to lose.

I slide my hand down from his sleeve to wrap my fingers around his wrist and smile.

"Teach me."

CHAPTER 8

VEROSA

I hit the floor with a heavy thud, the lanterns hanging from the walls rattling as I fall. Kya stands above me, the blunted tip of a wooden dagger pressed lightly against my throat. She smiles and holds out a hand to help me up.

"You're getting better at thinking on your feet. You almost got me that time."

"Yeah, right." I scoff, accepting her hand. "It's been nearly three weeks, and I still haven't been able to land a hit on you." For the past few weeks, my days have fallen into a routine: study with Rowan during the day, then sneak out at night to train with Kya, and occasionally, Derrín will come watch or offer unhelpful tips. Rowan and Amír are almost never around. They're always off plotting in that little study of his. Not that I mind all that much. Amír doesn't seem to like me. Every time I see her, she offers a sneer or a sarcastic quip on my form. If I were any better and knew my prop weapon would hit its mark, I might hurl it at her.

Honestly, I can't see how she and Kya are together. Amír is cruel and sadistic, oftentimes disappearing for long hours just to return covered in blood and a sick smile on her face, her guns still smoking. The second in command of the Nightwalkers, a villainess with a twisted lust for death.

Kya, however, is sweet and demure. She has a silver tongue of her own and dozens of small knives hidden across her scantily clad body, and yet she smiles softly every night when I arrive. She may best me in our combat training every time, but she helps me from the ground, bandages my wounds afterwards, and encourages me to try again. She's the closest thing I have to a friend in this place.

Every time Amír isn't with Rowan scheming, Kya is there to wipe the blood from her face. On the nights where Kya has a mission, which are increasing as she heals, Amír is there waiting by the door, concerned gaze sweeping over her girlfriend's form for any injuries. If there's a bruise or cut on her body, she demands a name, and if that person is not dead yet, she sets out only to come back hours later, blood on her hands. Kya pretends not to know what she's done and cleans her up again with the same love and adoration in her eyes.

No such care is saved for me as Kya knocks me flat on my ass again.

"Good to see you're embracing the dirt," Amír jibes today, stalking out the front door, her cloak swirling about her ankles. Kya offers a sympathetic look.

"Try not to take it personal."

I almost laugh. "How can I not? She hates me, and I've done nothing to her!"

"It's not you that she hates." Kya soothes, taking my weapon from my hand and guiding me to a seat. "It's what you represent. The blessed have hurt all of us in one way or another, and you're a pureblood of their kind."

"You say that like you're not blessed." I choose my words carefully. Everything is a dance these days, the steps determined by what information one is willing to reveal or hide. Kya might be kind, but she's no exception to this. Her eyes darken, and she inhales sharply as if steeling herself against what she might say.

"Because we aren't. Not Derrín and I, anyway." She notices my wide eyes and can probably hear my racing heart. But I can't run, no, she would easily overpower me. "Rowan and Amír are the only ones with any blessed blood in them."

Of course, they're the only two blessed in the building. The two people who can't stand me. I stand to leave, and Kya lets me, but I don't take a step towards the door. She raises an eyebrow.

"You're not leaving?"

"I am... confused," I admit. "I have been raised to believe that all the cursed want to kill me, and that they're born evil. But you don't seem evil." As soon as the words leave my mouth, I feel foolish. She is a Night-walker. Just like Rowan, just like Amír, and now just like me. She's killed people before; I've seen her in action and know how capable she is. But does it make her evil?

"I can understand your confusion. I used to think that of myself too." She sighs heavily, resting both weapons a healthy distance away, though I know she has more hidden on her figure.

Tentatively I make up my mind and sit back down beside her. "Why?"

"Because," she looks up at me, "you weren't the only one raised to fear the curse. Derrín and I are from Varium, and as a noble, I'm sure you know that while things are bad here for the cursed, it's nothing compared to over there."

I nod pensively. I've heard the stories. To be born cursed in Varium was to be born already dead. They host hunting festivals, where the blessed are released from work for the week to hunt down any cursed that may have escaped from prisons and work camps. Most of the time, they're found dismembered in the woods along the borders, only a few feet from freedom. The purebloods are strung up in the town centers, their blood collected as they bleed out. They give a portion of the blood to the government to use as weaponry, the rest is sold to the highest bidder. It hadn't bothered me as much before, it never fully sat right, but now I feel unsettled.

"Derrín and I escaped. But imagine being a child and told you were born evil, that you were lower than dirt and just lucky to be alive every day for years. It haunts you, even when you're free." Her gaze shifts towards her feet. "We aren't born evil, Vera. We just were born different."

She stops speaking, leaving me at a crossroads. She's given me a choice, to stay or go. Slowly I rise to my feet and extend my hand.

"Let's go again." None of that supposed evil is seen in the smile that graces Kya's face when she takes my hand and passes over my weapon. We move to our starting positions, and I shift my weight to prepare for her oncoming attack. She lunges silently, and I duck, her wooden blade just grazing my cheek. I deliver a blow of my own, and she parries it, shifting forward to place me on the defensive side. She swings a punch with her unarmed fist that collides with my ribs, but not quite enough to truly knock me off my feet. I feign a loss of balance and begin to slip forward when I hook the back of her leg with my own. She lands on her back as I roll to stand above her, my wooden dagger tip pressed above her heart.

The sounds of my panting fill the silent room, the exertion of our latest round leaving my cheeks flushed and hair falling out of my braid into my face. A slow clapping fills the room as Amír and Rowan watch, the latter with a proud smile.

Amír nods with begrudging respect, but nonetheless shoves past me to help her girlfriend to her feet. Kya stands, a wicked gleam in her eye.

"Who knew all we had to do was piss you off?" She grins widely, ignoring Amír's fussing. "Well done."

I clasp her hand firmly, sweat clinging to us both, and resolve firm in my mind. Since leaving the palace, I've learned that nearly everything I was raised to know was wrong. Someone has intentionally kept the truth from me, and I think I know who.

I wince when I rise from bed the next morning, my sore muscles aching from the constant strenuous activity. I've found myself changed in these past three weeks though. Color is returning to my cheeks, toned muscle begins to line the contours of my body, and as the cooks noticed I have been eating more as well.

"You've been eating well." Torin snorts as I shovel down another forkful of eggs and eye the platter of fruit in front of him. He sighs and pushes it my way. "You look healthier."

"Well, I've been getting out more thanks to my fiancé." I roll my eyes, remembering how yesterday Lucius insisted on teaching me archery. Between that lesson and sparring with Kya, my arms hang like lead against my side. Lucius, for all his irritating grabs for my affection, does have his perks. Somehow, he has convinced my father to let me out of the palace more often, with him as my escort, of course. We go out into the noble towns in disguises and spend the day among the villagers pretending to be normal for just an afternoon.

"How's that, by the way?" He jabs a piece of melon off my plate, ignoring the daggers Blaine is glaring into him. I roll my eyes, slowly losing my appetite.

"He's not a horrible person, I'll give him that," I grumble, fighting off his fork with my own as it comes in for a second steal. "It's just not the choice I would've made for myself."

"Suppose the downfall of royalty is you don't make the choices until you wear the crown," he says pensively, his mouth full of food. Blaine shoves him in the shoulder, causing him to choke.

"Manners."

"Apologies, Father." Torin grins and sketches a half bow, resulting in yet another withering look from Blaine. Despite my fatigue, I laugh softly under my breath. The constancy of their bickering has kept me anchored these past few weeks. "Ver, don't you have somewhere to be?"

I swear softly under my breath when I note the time. I'm late for Rowan again, and I know well enough now that I will pay for it later. I wince, remembering the last time I was late and forced to spar with Amír that night. I think I might still have some lingering bruises.

Fisting my skirts and hiking them up above my knees, I begin to sprint out the door.

"Don't you worry, Mei Reinhavich, I don't mind cleaning this up!" Torin calls after me sarcastically. I grin as I sprint out and shout a thank you.

I'm winded by the time I reach the study, but not nearly as out of breath as I would have been three weeks ago. Smoothing my gown, I step inside, doing my best to conceal my ragged breaths. Rowan is seated casually in his usual chair, a large leather seat in a secluded part of the library near a bay window. He doesn't deign to look up when I approach. I clear my throat.

"I have a request."

"Bold words coming from someone who is late." I bite my tongue when he looks up. The sunlight catches the wisps of his blonde hair, casting a golden halo about his head. His mouth is soft but set in a hard line. My gaze lingers too long there.

"I want to learn about the cursed." I don't bother with a response, but instead sit in the chair across from him. "I spoke with Kya. I know about her and Derrín."

This seems to pique his interest finally, and he leans forward, bracing his forearms against his thighs. He gesticulates casually as if to say 'well, go on then.'

"I want to know the truth. Someone's been lying to me, and I want to know who." I lower my voice as I speak now, every sound of the palace amplified in my ears. "I can't trust anyone here to give it to me. I don't know who to trust even here, this place... its secrets might run even deeper than yours."

He tilts his head to the side, and chews at his lower lip as if contemplating. I'm afraid he might reject my proposal when he fishes out a stack of papers from his knapsack.

"Kya told me. I thought you might have questions, but now I'm curious."

His little game, of course. Information for information.

"The Queen was not who people believed she was." A chill runs down my spine, as if my mother is in this room watching me now. "Many people went 'missing' after being seen visiting her chambers. Some believe the king helped cover it up. The servants won't tell the truth, many are still loyal to her or fear retribution from her spirit."

Rowan considers this, and my heart begins to race. Perhaps that was too much information, though vague, it could lead to answers about who I am if the right people are asked. It could open conversation on who my mother really was and what she did to me.

"Interesting." Is all he says, his eyes shuttering. I hate him when he does this. It's like he disappears and travels somewhere dark. Somewhere I can't follow him. He stands up and gazes out that large window, watching the noble children play in the courtyard, their hands and smiling faces outstretched in the sun.

"What is every weak man afraid of?" he asks suddenly, not turning from the window.

"I don't know."

"A woman who is stronger than him," he answers, stalking back towards me. "The blessed like to skew the origin story of our two gods in a way that is favorable for them. The truth is that Deungrid and Raonkin were friends, equal in strength and intellect. That is until Deungrid noticed Raonkin's powers were growing to be greater than his own. His were dependent on hers."

I nod, noting how stars are only visible at night, and a candle's flame is only brilliant when in contrast to shadow. Rowan continues.

"He became a tyrant, trying to restrict when she could or couldn't use her powers. She became bolder once she realized what threatened him so about her. She put him in his place, and it was his breaking point." Rowan shivers and unrolls his sleeves. "He cursed her, and the two of them became mortal. It is said he turned her into a woman as an attempt to make her weaker than him, and himself a man. However, when he saw this did nothing against her growing powers, he cursed her offspring. If one of Raonkin descent were to use magic, they would lose their minds."

"Their minds?"

"Their minds. The things that gave them power of those of light. Raonkin was clever, cleverer than him, and Deungrid knew it. He knew her descendants would carry on this trait, and so the curse was not only to protect himself, but his offspring as well. Then they could never raise hands against him again without risking what mattered to them most." Aiko's face pops into my mind now, and the information she gave me when we met.

"Why would they lie about that? Why this prejudice against the cursed when Raonkin was the victim?" I shout in a fury, and Rowan quickly clamps his hand over my mouth. Footsteps echo in the hallway outside. They pause for a moment before continuing past us, and Rowan drops his hand.

"Quiet! I could lose my head for telling you that. It's considered treason," he hisses through clenched teeth. I clamp my mouth shut. "Besides, it's not all so black and white. Raonkin's magic relies on the essence of living things, even before the curse. Sacrifices had to be made, and some of her descendants still use this form of sorcery to avoid the cost themselves."

My blood runs cold at the thought. Human sacrifices, even in these modern times. I shudder to think how lucky I was to find Rowan rather than someone more insidious. Though ironically enough, I'm not so sure things are black and white with him either.

I've seen him in a fight. He is ruthless, and I know he only kept that thug in the alley alive to pass on a message to whoever Mavis was. I've heard the statistics of the kills he and the Nightwalkers have made, have heard the stories of him sending body parts home to families for ransom.

And yet he had saved me when he didn't have to. He brought me to Aiko and Finneas to be treated rather than selling my blood for profit. And he is helping me now, albeit for his own unknown gain.

"Anyways, I really wish you would spend less time flirting with that captain and more time in our lessons. He's clearly not interested if he keeps rejecting the advances of a noblewoman."

"You can go fuck yourself, Rowan."

"A lady by title but not by tongue," he croons, his emerald eyes shuttering. "What a lovely, wicked mouth."

"You're disgusting." But he sees me flinch.

Rowan clears his throat, snapping the book in his hands shut and dropping it on the oak table in one fluid motion.

"I crossed a line." He apologizes then, bracing his forearms against his thighs. His eyes search my face for a moment before they meet mine, a twinkle of amusement dancing in them. "And for all my teasing..."

"I know." I interrupt, the conversation suddenly feeling more personal and rawer than any we'd had before. I know that it's only teasing. Playful banter. I know deep down that it's all a mask. A mask to hide something raw and vulnerable that he's not ready for anyone else to see yet. And I'm fine with that because truthfully, I'm not sure I'm ready to shirk my own facade. If he found out the truth of who I am...

"What's your favorite food?"

"What?" He stares at me for a moment, bewilderment painting his face. I almost laugh.

"What's your favorite food?" I repeat. "Is it chicken? Fish?"

"Oh, Laei not fish. Anything but fish," he groans, clutching his stomach like a toddler. I raise an incredulous eyebrow towards him as he fakes gagging over the side of the table. He sees the expectancy written across my features and moves to elaborate. "I don't do seafood. I don't know why, it's just the smell, the taste. Those beady little eyes staring back at you in most dishes." He squints his own eyes and pinches his fingers and features together, as if staring right back at the imaginary fish. As if asserting his dominance over the wooden table before us. I eye him with faint amusement as he stops and stares back at me. The corners of his lips tug upwards in a charismatic grin, and I find myself grinning back.

Until he slams a stack of paper before me.

"Finish one of these pages, and you get to ask me any question you like." I groan in response as he simply sits smug and catlike. He picks at some invisible speck of dust on his fine coat while he waits.

"And who's to say you'll answer those questions truthfully?" I ask, not bothering to tear my eyes from the paper this time. I can hear the cockiness in his voice without looking.

"I guess you'll have to find out. After you finish that page."

The word is tedious, and mostly foolish busy work such as listing dates of nobles, various laws I already know, and even a few notes on banquet etiquette. I'm nearly finished with the first page when I notice a third figure standing by our table.

Lucius has his hands in his pockets and grins when my gaze meets his, those white teeth flashing. Something predatory stirs in his features as he takes in Rowan, his casual demeanor and effortless handsomeness. Also how close the two of us are sitting.

"Verosa, I've been looking everywhere for you." He smiles again, though this time something clicks in his jaw.

"Lucius." I say slowly, praying Rowan will take a hint. He shows no sign of even hearing. "You know I have my studies at this time."

"Must have slipped my mind," he lies before turning to Rowan. "I am Lucius, Verosa's fiancé."

Rowan finally looks up from his reading now, raising his eyebrows at me in amusement. I begin to pray to the Laei when I see the wicked glint in his eyes.

"Oh? Rowan, Verosa's tutor. It's an honor to finally meet the nobleman I've heard so much about." Lucius' face lights up, and when his gaze turns to me, Rowan smirks in my direction. I kick his shin under the table.

"I would love to hear what she has said." His voice is playful, the opposite of what it had been moments before. Rowan stifles a laugh behind his book, but his face turns neutral once more when Lucius turns back to him.

"Perhaps another time. We are finishing up a lesson. She should be done soon."

"Of course. Enjoy your studies, Verosa. Rowan." Rowan nods as my fiancé leaves before letting out a low whistle.

"So that's the fiancé. Was he not tall, dark, and handsome enough for you?"

"Prick." I shove the stack of papers back towards him and stand up. "We are done for today."

"You haven't finished-" I don't wait to hear the rest of his sentence when I storm out of the library, heading straight for my room. Rowan doesn't follow.

I think it would be easier to like Rowan if I could understand him. One moment he is playful and charming, the next his guard is up, and he's pulling cruel stunts. It's enough to make me want to ram my head into a wall just trying to hold a conversation with him.

I lean against the window of my room, gazing out to find all the children have gone inside now. Despite my anger, my mind wanders back to him, watching out of his own window with something that I could mistake as longing written across his features. That is, if I didn't know better.

I need a distraction. Now. Changing into a simple tunic and loose-fitting pants, I storm through the hallways until I find the door I am searching for and knock. Lucius answers with surprise lighting up his face, and even more so when I shove my sack into his arms.

"Come on. I need to blow off some steam." Lucius obliges as we make our way down to a hidden field behind the palace, right near a large lake.

As the raven-haired man spreads out the blanket across the grass, I pick up a few rocks and chuck them as hard as I can at the still water, watching the ripples as if in a trance. He finishes laying out our lunch and comes up behind me.

"They won't skip if you throw that hard."

"I want them to sink."

"Oh." He silently watches for a moment, keeping his distance still before clearing his throat. "Would you like to talk about it?"

Huffing, I watch as the last of my rocks sinks to the bottom of the lake, and a heavy emptiness fills my chest instead.

"How is your relationship with your mother?"

Lucius' body goes rigid.

"My mother is dead."

Oh. I now remember attending the funeral a few years back. The alliance deemed it necessary. It hadn't dawned on me then that some people had loving mothers and loved them in return.

"I'm sorry. Common ground I suppose."

"Yeah." He laughs humorlessly. "I suppose it is." He motions for me to sit next to him. Guilt settles deep in my bones, and I oblige, still keeping a healthy distance between us. The wind rustles through his hair as he leans back to rest on his elbows and stares at the sky.

"I loved my mom. She was the bravest, most loving woman I've ever known, but she was also a notorious spitfire. I think you would've liked her." I can't help myself, and I blush. "She passed a few years ago. You seemed curious when I said I didn't want this marriage either. I'm going through with it because it was something she wanted for me."

The breeze grazes my flushed cheeks as I lay down next to him, the both of us facing the sky as we let the weight of his words settle in the earth between us. A few clouds dot along the blue sky, sunlight streaking through the trees above us.

"Mine's dead, but it still feels like she's fucking me over," I admit bluntly, and I hear him chuckle beside me. I feel my lips crack open in the smallest of smiles as I continue. "When my best friend went to war, she put him on the frontlines as an inexperienced soldier. He came back a ghost of himself, and I think I still blame her. Not to mention that she was never much of a mother, anyway. I have a feeling she's behind this marriage too. It all just seems such her style..." I drift off, gazing at a particularly fat and fluffy cloud above my head. I hear rustling from beside me as Lucius props up onto his elbows and stares at me curiously.

"What?"

"You may be Irene's daughter, but your beauty is entirely your own," he whispers, his jaw clenched. "You have the heart of a warrior and the spirit of a queen. It's admirable, really, how you never fail to speak your mind."

I loll my head to the side to look at him, and I really look at him this time. He has a dimple on his left cheek and a small scar on his forehead that's barely noticeable unless up close. His eyebrows are arched softly as if in perpetual worry, but his eyes are kind and welcoming. I find myself smiling at him and he gasps softly.

"I think I quite like when you smile at me like that, Verosa."

"And I think you're not quite who I thought you were, Lucius."

My fiancé grins at that and runs a hand through his hair. "I am glad to exceed your expectations." A pang of guilt stabs at my heart when I see the hopefulness he wears so clearly. When I know myself what I plan to do, who I am. And yet I hold his gaze and whisper back, "So am I."

CHAPTER 9

ROWAN

Amír is there waiting when I return from the palace, a fresh laceration still dripping with blood across her arm. I note Kya's handiwork in the stitches, but the Vari woman is nowhere to be seen.

"Did you get the information?"

"Rowan, this has got to stop," Amír fumes, clutching at her newest wound. "You are running us ragged every night. One revenge plot was bad enough, but now two? We need to stop and be sensible." Stalking over to my desk, I pull out a parchment and strike an X through a location. I will take Amír's lack of an answer to mean that she never found Mavis' newest compound.

"Earth to Rowan? Can you stop brooding so we can have a conversation?"

"I'm not brooding." The redhead laughs.

"And I can shoot with my left hand." She rolls her eyes, snatching the paper from my grasp and circling another location on the map. "My scouts reported that this is where we have the best chance of finding anyone with intel." I stare at the red circle on the map, a city just south of Belam called Ira in the heart of Mavis' territory.

"And how the hell do you suppose we get in? You and Kya will be recognized on the spot, and we sure as hell aren't sending Derrín. I'll get shot the moment I cross the line between territories." My head feels heavy as I rest it in my hands. Mavis' men have been getting bolder, with more intel on us than we have on them. With rumors of Vera's existence getting out there, the attacks on my Nightwalkers have been growing more severe and closer to home. I couldn't let them find her... or Vera.

"I think we need to consider two possibilities, the first being that we need to move your mother into this compound. It will be safer for her to hide here, even if it is closer to the palace." I nod, agreeing completely. "Second, it's time to send Vera on her first mission."

"Absolutely not." I slam my fist on the table, ignoring the splinters stabbing into it.

"Rowan, think clearly here. You said it yourself that none of us can go, and we need this information if we ever want to stop her or your father. She's ready, I've seen her fight. Kya can stay right outside the bar while I cover the exits."

"We are not debating this. She's not going, end of story." Images of the first night I met her flood my mind, specifically the ones where she almost died because of me. It may be a part of our deal, but I will not put her in that danger again. Not until she's ready and willing,

"Will you stop thinking with your dick!" Amír whirls on me in a fury as I go to leave the room. "If you hadn't so royally fucked up with your last girlfriend, I wouldn't have to send this one in to clean up the mess."

Something in me snaps, whether at the way she speaks of Vera or mentioning my past with Mavis, I don't know, but a fist of rage squeezes my heart as I advance on my second. Amír, much to her credit, doesn't balk.

"You do not speak of her like that."

"No, you do not like how I speak of her, but I will do it anyway because it's what you need to hear. You brought her here and put all of our lives in danger, so now she's going to help bring us out of it."

"And what if this was Kya?" My second in command doesn't even blink as she glares at me steely eyed and gets closer to my face.

"I would let her go. Because while she's my girlfriend, she's also a soldier and knows her duty. Just like Vera does." A fine mist of spittle hits my face as she speaks unapologetically. "You're letting your feelings for her cloud your judgement, just like they did with Mavis."

"I don't-."

"Then send her into the field."

"Fine."

The slam of the door echoes in my wake as I leave Amír to fume alone in the study. A candle snuffs out as my cape billows over it, and with a light curse I fumble in the dark for a match. The flame sizzles then sparks as a hand far gentler than mine kindles it before falling back to her side. I had nearly forgotten that Vera had followed me from the palace tonight, my mind was so muddled with other thoughts.

The noble clutches at a bruising arm, and her hair clings to her forehead, damp with sweat. Yet she carries an elegance about her even now, with a victorious smile placed firmly on her lips.

"I managed to knock Kya off her feet while you were gone. Don't worry, she got me back." She laughs softly, jutting her chin in the direction of her bruise. "Don't tell Amír. She might skin me alive."

"You and me both." I mumble under my breath.

"What was that?"

"We have to talk about something." I nod my head towards a simple couch in the center of our makeshift living room. She falls heavily against it, letting the cushions bear the weight of her fatigue. Lolling her head to the side, she elicits a low groan before covering her mouth with her hand.

"Sorry, that wasn't very ladylike."

I laugh.

"Do you think I gave a single damn about if you act like a lady?" She shakes her head fervently. "Good, because I don't. None of us do. But..." I trail off, staring at a random splinter on the wall across from us, Amír's words ringing through my head still. I hate how much it bothers me and hate even more that they were true.

None of us would be in this position if I hadn't trusted Mavis, hadn't fallen for her. Granted, we would probably be in a new sort of trouble, but none worse than this.

"You're not thinking ahead," she'd say. *"Use the brain in that pretty little head and think. If your enemy is five steps ahead, you need to be six."*

But what if your enemy is miles ahead instead and knows your deepest secrets?

"-owan. Rowan?"

Vera. She reminds me so much of her before everything went south, and yet the two couldn't be more different. Both share that fiery disposition, their desire to be greater than those around them. Neither are afraid to work or be dirty to achieve their goals. And yet if Mavis had seen me in that alley at first glance, she would've turned the other way and not lose any sleep over it. Mavis would've cut the heart out of her fiancé rather than run. She always has been the type to face her problems head on, and often with violence. Vera, though, she tried to save a stranger, naive that it may be. She is kind to the servants when we are in the palace and speaks softly to the horses.

Yes, she's an intolerable spitfire at best and a downright spoiled, prejudiced brat at worst, but there's something gentle in her soul that is missing from Mavis'. She is a paradox in and of herself, an ocean of fire, like seeing the moon in broad daylight. I've seen her sock a man in the throat then cry because she stepped on a lizard. I don't think I'll ever fully understand her.

"I'm going to need you to act like a lady for one night," I amend, pulling out the map Amír and I were just pouring over. "We have a hit that is going to take place in Ira. It's a scouting mission, gather intel and get out."

"Ira, isn't that-"

"Enemy territory? Yeah, I know. That's why I can't go, and neither can Kya or Amír."

"Will you send Derrín then?"

"I'm sending you."

Vera is on her feet in an instant, all of the color draining from her pretty face. I rise with her as she grinds the palms of her hands into her eyes and spins to face the wall.

"How do you know I'm ready?"

"I've seen you. This is a simple mission; you just need to get the information out of some guys and then get out. There will be no fighting necessary, but if it comes down to it, I know you can handle yourself." I watch as she bites her lip, nearly enough to draw blood, when I can't stand the distance anymore. Grabbing her arms, I turn her until she's facing me. "I am putting my faith in you, Ver. I believe in you."

I bend down so our eyes meet and hold in a gasp when they do. Where she was once golden, she's now blue where the light dances in her eyes. How many shades is this girl? Wisps of indigo hair fall free from her braided crown, one catching between her lips. Brushing a strand back with my hand, I look up again when she speaks, her voice breathless.

"You called me Ver." So I did. Stepping back and releasing her arms, I clear my throat and check the time. "I'll do it." She has found the strength behind her voice again, and she says it again louder now. "I'll do it."

"Great. You leave now." Amír speaks from the doorway of the study, already suited in her own armor, gun holstered at her hip. Kya steps out from behind her, clad in leather trousers, thick-soled boots, and a scarf covering everything below her eyes. The smaller woman tosses a swirl of teal silks towards her friend, who catches it with a dumbfounded expression.

"Amír and I will guard the only entrances and exits as well as patrol the area around it. I'll help you with your garments quickly." I turn my back as the two squabble, Verosa protesting loudly as Kya strips her bare then places the smooth silks in the right places.

"This is demoralizing," Vera huffs indignantly as I turn around. A blue band of silk warps around her breasts, leaving her midriff and shoulder exposed to the night breeze. A slightly darker skirt flows freely from her waist, daring slits snaking up to show a bit of her smooth legs.

"You look great."

"I look like a prostitute."

"Exactly." Amír grins wickedly. "That's what you're posing as, princess." Curiously enough, Vera stiffens at her words.

"I have to seduce the informant?" she screeches, crossing her arms across her stomach in an attempt to protect her virtue when she notices that does nothing for the modesty of her top. Huffing she jabs her index finger deep enough into my chest to hurt.

"Enjoy the show, asshole," she hisses. I cough to hide my laughter, but it's not enough for Amír to not notice how my eyes trail her out of the room. My second raises a well-groomed eyebrow before following her out. Kya lays a soft hand on my arm.

"I won't let anything happen to her."

I swallow thickly, patting the top of her hand once. "You'd better not."

The night drags on after the trio leaves, and I find myself sitting across from Derrín in his room while he fiddles with his invention.

"Are you going to stare or are you going to ask?" the male twin says without lifting his gaze from his project.

"What is it?"

"It's a communication device. It's designed to relay nearly instantaneous messages across a long range of distances," he explains, holding up the nearly complete project. "I figured it could be helpful on hits, especially when we are all in multiple places. I can check in on Kya on the longer missions."

"I think Amír might fight you for it then."

"Or you if it were Verosa," Derrín deadpans, and only then does he raise his gaze. A warm, hazy blush slowly begins to creep up the back of my neck, and a tingling sensation rushes through my limbs. I don't need to respond, Derrín already knows.

"You sure know how to pick them."

"What do you mean?"

He only shrugs. "You've got a type. Comes with strings attached, insane attitudes, unrelenting curiosity." Derrín counts off on his fingers. "Not to mention, people who have no interest in you whatsoever."

A low fire boils in my gut, and I clench my jaw. Derrín said it so bluntly and so casually, but it had been honest. Something sparks in my chest every time I look at Verosa, something that I thought had died long ago. Something that should've stayed dead.

"I can't afford to get involved. There's too much at stake," I defend, rising to my feet. "You should feel lucky you don't have to deal with this."

"I am," he mumbles but then sets to fiddling with his thumbs. "But have you ever stopped to think about what comes next? What happens after you kill your father? You'll have some powerful people coming after you."

"None more powerful than him."

"And what about Verosa?"

That awful feeling tugs at my gut again.

"She'll go off on her own, maybe even leave the country. She'll have the means to run from her fiancé forever if she needs to. And we will go our own way when the time comes."

A cruel fingernail traces from the back of my neck, dragging up to the shell of my ear. I shiver at her voice.

"You're falling behind pretty boy," Mavis croons in my ear. *"You'll run out of things to kill eventually, and then what? What will you become other than a pretty murderous thing?"* I shiver despite myself.

"She could stay, you know. You could ask her to join us." My mechanic concludes, oblivious to my inner turmoil. I can only open my mouth to fire back a sarcastic retort of some kind when we hear the front door swing open. Two sets of footsteps are followed by a long drag.

"Rowan!"

Derrín is on his feet in an instant when his twin's voice rings out through our compound, and silently, we both dash to the main entrance. There we find tears streaking down Kya's pretty face as she and Vera drag a half-conscious and bleeding Amír through the doorway.

Vera stumbles as I take my second in command from them both, laying her flat across our sofa to assess the damage.

"We were set up," she hisses through clenched teeth as she limps forward, taking the Kya's knife from her shaking hand. "She took a dagger to the thigh. Judging by the amount of blood, they got her femoral artery. We don't have much time left." She slices through Amír's trousers while Kya sobs silently into her hands, unable to move.

Amír has been in her fair share of fights, both working for me and even before we found each other. I know she can take a hit, but staring at her nearly lifeless eyes, I know Vera is right.

"Tell me what to do."

Vera looks over, her wide eyes filled with determination as she hands the knife to me. Weighing Kya's weapon in my hand, I squint in confusion when she holds her palm flat to me.

"Cut me."

CHAPTER 10

VEROSA

The rustic tavern Amír guided us to reminds me too much of Ryson's, from the swirling silk *dansarinas* and the cheap *leeche* to the keen stares of every male in my direction. For a moment, I am back to where I was a few weeks ago, scared, lost, and alone.

Except now I am not alone. Kya, my friend, is on the roof, guarding every entrance and exit. I can almost feel her eyes tracing my movements now. Even Amír's presence as she patrols the area outside fills me with comfort, for even in her dislike for me, I know she won't let any harm come my way.

In the corner of the bar, I find my target, a middle-aged man with a scruffy black beard and a long, thin scar over his left eye. A large hound dog sits by his feet, chewing on something that looks suspiciously like a finger bone.

Taking a deep breath to steel myself against my anxiety, I plaster a sultry smile on my face and put effort into sashaying my hips as I wander over to him. His eyes peer over the rim of his glass, lust glossing them as I lay a hand on his forearm.

"I know I'm not supposed to do this, but can I sit here with you for a moment? It's my first night, and my feet are killing me." I throw in a little lip quiver that used to make Blaine double over, and the man concedes.

"Please," he says, motioning to the seat next to him. "Sit."

I take the moment to survey my surroundings. If this goes south, the closest exit is the window just over his shoulder, otherwise I would have to make my way through the dancers to the back door. I don't know how fast he is. In a flight situation I have the size advantage, however, in a fight...

"You're too kind, sir." I smile and frill my skirts as I sit, ignoring the moistness of the chair. I may need a hundred baths to forget this night. "Makes me wonder what you're doing here alone."

"I'm not looking for a bed partner, miss." I quirk an eyebrow at his gruff response. His body language says differently. His eyes drift towards the door, pausing as if waiting for someone, and I trace his gaze.

"How about a friend then? You look awfully lonely sitting here," I coax, accepting two cups of *leeche* from a passing waitress. He eyes the extended drink suspiciously but takes it anyway after I take a swig of mine and choke. The large man laughs while I sputter, the cheap drink leaving a residue to coat my tongue.

"Not much of a drinker?" He chuckles, downing his in one go and extending his hand for mine. Pulling a face and shivering, I hand it over to him, grateful to not have to drink the foul liquor again. "You're an odd one, makes me wonder how you ended up here."

"If I tell you, will you answer as well?" I stall for time, watching his every motion carefully. His shoulders stiffen at first, but he relaxes with a nod.

"Very well."

I hail the waitress over for more drinks as he finishes his and hands the large hound by his feet a hunk of meat.

"My little sister is sick, and my family needs the money." I feign a whimper, and the dog whines at his feet. "This whole place scares me, honestly, but I need to help her. No one else will, and I can't imagine if she..."

It sounds fake even to my ears and I can only pray he is dumb enough to believe my poor acting skills. A gloved hand brushes a stray tear from my cheek. I flutter my eyelashes and try to focus on his scar rather than his face.

"I may be able to help." He removes his hand and scratches his dog's head. "My name is Luren, my boss sent me here to find someone. If you have any idea who this woman is, my boss would be willing to pay handsomely."

I swallow thickly and nod. Something is off. The music has grown quieter than before, and Luren's hound begins to snarl softly, his hackles raised and teeth bared. My eyes drift down towards his hip, where a dark dagger lays. A cursed blade. What's more is it is laced with a green substance I know all too well. Etherbane.

"Who is your boss?" My fingers smooth the silks around my waist, fumbling for the rough edge of the concealed blade, but I am too slow.

My suspicions are confirmed when he leaps to his feet, his meaty fist tightening around my neck. I gasp for breath and my eyes water. A trap. All of it was a trap.

"Tell Mavis we have her!" He shouts over the crowd before turning back to me. "Save your crocodile tears, *pureblood*."

I struggle against his grip, red fogging the corners of my vision. Several armed men burst through the crowd, eliciting shrieks of terror from the innocent onlookers. The dancers huddle in the corner, the elders shielding the younger girls.

Luren's hand roughly palms my hip, finding the dagger Kya had hidden there before we left. He tuts his tongue before tossing it aside with a triumphant snarl that tells me he thinks he's won.

Glass shatters as Kya breaks through the window, and gunshots ring out through the building as Amír slams open the side door, gun leveled at Luren's head. I use the momentary shock to slam my knee into his groin and my head into his own. He crumples with a string of prolific curses while I slide to the ground. Air, I need air, but there's no time. Bodies hit the floor as Kya carves her way through the crowd, and I feel my heart stop.

Gone is the smiling face that helps me back up from a spar, and now I realize that in all our training sessions, she never once used herself to her full capability. This is the feared assassin of the Nightwalkers, and she's killing for me.

She grips my hands fiercely, pulling me to my feet. "Can you walk?"

I nod, staring at the blood left behind on my hands as she whips out her daggers again.

"Careful. He has Etherbane."

"I noticed." I grimace in response.

She instructs me to stay close behind her as we make our way to the front of the building, where Amír is smashing a man's head with the butt end of her gun. Blood splatters across my face as Kya slits a man's throat, and I shriek, distracting my friends long enough for more assailants to strike.

A swarm of bodies closes Kya from my view as many make their way towards them, forgetting entirely about me. I rise to my feet only to be pulled back down again by a strong hand wrapped around my leg. My ankle gives a sickening crunch as I land, and I stifle a cry as I notice the dagger, my dagger, aimed for my chest.

"I won't kill you," Luren grunts, his scarred eye wider than the other. "Boss needs you alive, but I can still make it hurt." He raises the blade again, and I roll, though it slices my arm. Golden blood begins to flow freely from the wound, pouring onto the filthy ground. A few patrons take notice then and murmur amongst themselves. Shit, I can't let them see my face.

Just barely dodging another assault, I bring my fist up into his nose and hook my leg around his neck, effectively flipping him on his back. He drags the blade across my leg, skinning my calf. My knee nearly grazes his poisoned dagger. With a half-broken sob I fall to the floor, crawling towards the exit, where I can still hear the sounds of fighting.

At this point, I doubt that Kya and Amír are coming for me. It's too much of a risk. I am on my own. The nearest exit is the window, if I could just make it there... An all too familiar hand wraps around my exposed wound, and Luren drags my leg towards himself.

"You fucking bitch," he grits through clenched yellow teeth, clutching at his bloody nose. "Fuck Mavis. I'll kill you myself. I swear, I'll kill you. I'll-"

The grizzled man drops his knife with an agonizing scream, blood pouring fourth freely from the bullet hole in his hand. Amír stands a few feet away, Kya carving their way through the crowd towards me.

The redhead loops an arm under my arms and hauls me to my feet. "We need to go. NOW."

"You came back."

"Save your gratitude for when we make it out of here. Alive," she sneers, but I can see the cold sweat beading along her forehead. Kya points to the window, and without waiting for a command pulls out one of her espas and tosses the slender blade through the window. The glass shatters and scatters along the floor. It's a clear shot if we beat the crowd.

We are only a pace away when Amír cries out, falling to her knees. Kya screams as she sees the blood staining her lover's trousers, the gold and red blossom growing far too quickly.

"Shit." She curses softly as Mavis' cronies advance, one coming to retrieve his dagger from where it lays beneath her. "Leave me."

"Are you out of your mind?" Kya's voice is shrill with something I'm unaccustomed to hearing from her. Terror. Pure, unadulterated terror. She readies her single espa to fight, but it's one assassin against dozens of men.

I loop my arms around Amír's shoulders, carrying the brunt of her weight and run as quickly as I can to the window. It's low enough to slip out without a running start, but the jagged glass is menacing and waiting to draw blood. Then again, so are the men in the other room. I think I'll fall to the mercy of the glass.

"Hold on!" I shout and hurl the both of us through the window, doing my best to cover the other woman's body with my own. I scream for every bit of glass that bites into my bare flesh, my costume doing less for my protection than it does my modesty. Kya follows our lead and jumps through the notably less hazardous window in pursuit. After plucking her weapon from the ground, she rushes forward to take some of the burden from me.

The shouts ring out as our assailants rush through the entrance of the bar, too large to fit through the windows. We need to get out of here, now.

"Any shortcuts you could tell us about, assassin?" I groan under the weight of Amír and my wounds, trying to ignore the tears flowing down the Vari woman's cheeks. "Now would be a great time to tell us."

She snaps out of her haze just enough to point into the forest behind a large building. "There."

I grit my teeth and will my shaking legs to move in stronger and longer strides. "Okay, just hang in there, Amír."

I receive no response.

I practically fall through the door once we reach the compound, crying out for help inaudibly.

"Rowan!" Kya sobs as she looks at her partner hanging nearly life-less between us. "Please-" She breaks down into hysterics, dumping most of the gunslinger's weight onto me. My legs are buckling by the time Rowan and Derrín come running into the room.

"Please," I whisper, but the words get caught in my throat. Rowan understands and takes her from me, laying her flat across our sofa to inspect the damage.

"We were set up." I limp forward, dragging myself with sheer deter-mination despite my spinning head. "She took a dagger to the thigh. Judging by the amount of blood, they got her femoral artery. We don't have much time left." I didn't think Kya could cry anymore, but my words certainly do nothing to assuage her concerns. Neither do Amír's heavy lidded eyes or blood soaked pants. Gently, I take a dagger from my friend and slice the second's trousers off, not caring for modesty. Blood sprays outwards in a steady stream, confirming my theory.

Rowan swallows hard all while staring into the redhead's eyes.

"Tell me what to do."

I inhale sharply. I haven't done this in years and swore then I wouldn't do it again. I *couldn't* do it again.

But I couldn't let Amír die, not after she came back for me.

"Cut me."

Rowan's mouth drops open in realization then hardens in a firm line.

"No."

"Rowan, please," I beg, pleadingly searching his gaze. Amír is running out of time. "I don't know how deep I can go without it scarring or nerve damage. I need you to do it."

Perhaps it is the urgency in my voice, or Kya's now silent screaming that causes him to falter. Or maybe it's that when he traces my own gaze down, he finds a scar running the length of my palm and knows.

"I trust you." I say, pressing Kya's blade into his hand and delicately folding his fingers around it. I wait for him to respond with the usual "you shouldn't." But instead, he carefully picks up my hand, the one left unscarred, and brings it up to the blade. He looks at me one last time as if to ask permission. I nod.

"Do it."

Slowly and gracefully, he drags the blade across my skin, and I bite my tongue to avoid crying out. His hands only begin to shake when he drops the knife, and I feel tears prick the corner of my vision.

Kya and Derrín move out of my way when I approach the ever-fading redhead on the couch. Her calculating green eyes slide over to me, and even I can see they are dull and fading fast.

I hold my bleeding hand up to her and those eyes widen. She shakes her head violently.

"No."

"Amír, you need to drink." I hiss, bringing my hand to her mouth. She smacks it away, losing a few drops of precious blood.

"You're dying, you bitch," I snap, taking ahold of her wrist as Kya begins wailing again. "So shut up and drink."

Maybe it's my tone that shocks some life back into her, or seeing the usually strong Kya so unhinged, but Amír listens for once and drinks, squeezing her eyes shut.

"Don't you dare spit it out." I hiss in slight pain, but more so discomfort at the intimacy of the situation. When she's done, I move it down to her wound and spread the blood across it with a prayer to Deungrid that it works, just once more.

Slowly, the wound stitches itself closed, the blood slowing until it stops completely. Color slowly blooms in the gunslinger's cheeks, and she sighs softly. Kya rushes past me to embrace her lover, who offers the faintest nod of gratitude.

A soft sigh escapes from Rowan's lips, caressing the shell of my ear stand and sending a shiver down my spine.

"Thank you."

Spinning to face him, I look up with a smile. "You're wel...You're..." His eyebrows furrow as I trail off. "You're spin... spinning."

Someone screams my name as I go down, and I wait for the cold floor to greet me, but solid arms wrap around my midsection and hold me to a warm chest. Everything feels so far away. It's such a lovely heartbeat...

"-osa! VERA!"

Rowan's face is softer than I've ever seen it, silver tears of worry pricking the corners of his eyes. Black fuzzes out my peripheral vision as he leans closer, the fear written across his features. A hand, it might be my hand, reaches up to touch his face, to smooth out the worry lines. As the world spins to a halt, the hand drops down to my side, and darkness envelopes me.

CHAPTER II

VEROSA

A soft breeze caresses my cheek in greeting while a soft whisper of light slips into the room. The first break of dawn from an open window. *My* window. The scent of jasmine and morning dew hits the moment my eyes shoot open.

I make to leap from where I lay in my bed when firm hands grip my shoulders, effectively pinning my weakened body against the down pillows.

"Stay down," Rowan growls. "You lost too much blood too quickly."

Like hell I'll stay down. Feebly shoving his hands off, I rise to my feet, panic seeping in when I notice the blood on his hands, silver and gold. No signs of Kya or Amír. Rowan watches as a stumble to my bedroom door, something like cool amusement flickering across his features when I close the entrance. He raises an eyebrow, a silent challenge as if to say *do you really think anyone would catch us if I didn't want them to?*

Bastard. His lips quirk up slightly at my response.

"Is she... are they going to be okay?" I whisper softly into the room, though not at all as timidly as I might've been a few weeks ago. Rowan sighs heavily, those powerful forearms braced against his thighs. He looks so small sitting atop the stool next to my vanity. Like a man in a dollhouse.

"They're both fine. Amír was already leaping up to catch you as you fell, but I've told her and Kya to lay low for a while. So should you. Your injuries were nearly as bad as Amír's."

Fine. Rowan said they were fine, and I hadn't missed the soft arc of his mouth as he whispered, "Fine, *because of you.*"

Slowly, my shoulders curled in on themselves, and I wrapped my arms around my midsection. Fine. Not bleeding out or screaming or dead. Fine. I never stopped to think about what would've happened if they weren't, nor realized how much the two women meant to me. How much all of them mean to me. The first tear falls before I realize it.

Rowan takes one large step, and then he's here, holding my head to his chest. Letting me hear his heartbeat.

"We're alive. We're okay."

Those four words are all I need to hear. He mentioned no limp, no maiming scars lacing my friends. Even Amír. Amír had come back for me.

A sniffling nod later, I disentangle myself from him, though I immediately miss his warmth and the scent of citrus and leather that enveloped me just as much as he had.

"It's getting light out." I say, my voice barely above a whisper. "You should go."

His mouth hardens to a thin line, but he doesn't argue as he notices dawn's willowy fingers stretch closer to my window, slowly eliminating those shadows that cling to him. Soon the guards would rotate, the one chance Rowan would have to slip out unnoticed.

He slings a leg out the window, ever so casually, might I add, before tossing a grim look my way. "I mean it, Vera. Lay low for a bit, say you're feeling unwell today, and let no one in. Your blood should help heal your noticeable wounds by tomorrow. Kya will stop by then to check on you."

I don't have time to ask how he knew which room had been mine, though I assume Kya did some snooping of her own, before Rowan throws himself out the window. He's gone with nothing but a whisper by the time the sun warms the stones of the palace.

"What the fuck, Verosa."

No.

No this can't be happening.

The door to my bathroom creaks open as Blaine swears, his dark face paling to a sickly shade of grey. His gaze trails down to my shaking frame, still clad in my whorish silks, still bleeding, shoddily bandaged wounds on full display. My heart slows. No, I can't afford to panic. Panic will have my head on the butcher's block, regardless of whether it still wears a tiara.

So I swallow thickly and muster as much confidence I can to say, "I can't remember the last time I heard you swear."

He should turn cold with restrained rage, roll his eyes with indifference, and leave. But he bites his lip and stares hard into my eyes.

"*What* did he do to you."

"Nothing!" I say too quickly, reaching out for his arm. He jumps back as if burned. "He did nothing to me. I did this, I chose this. If you would let me explain-"

"Explain what exactly? How you've been acting strange lately? How I came to check on you because I was worried and found out you weren't here? How, when you came back, *he* was carrying you— your gods-damned tutor was carrying you unconscious and bloody in the silks of a courtesan. So explain to me what, Verosa, you have been doing. What has he done to you?"

My face burns, but I refuse to linger on the fact that he worried for me. That he came. If I could get on my knees I would, if I thought I could get up and not face the king. If Lucius never had to find out, to see the look of betrayal on his face when he knew I was running.

"Please." A tear slips down the bridge of my nose, then a second. How had it gotten so out of control so quickly? When did the silver of my friend's eyes turn into cool unflinching iron?

A heavy sigh, then shuffling as gentle hands rested on my arm. I lifted my gaze to Torin's, his usual jovial grin gone and replaced with a thin frown. The sight nearly breaks me— breaks me enough that I didn't wonder where he had appeared from.

"You two need to lower your voices before someone else comes snooping and reports back to Ophelus," he hisses, explaining his entrance. "Vera, you're going to go into that bathroom and clean yourself. Then you will give me those clothes, and I will take care of it. We are going to tell everyone you're sick and not to be seen, and then the three of us are going to figure this out."

No questions asked, no judgment evident in his voice. Just the cool and calculating voice of the captain's second, taking control of the situation. With a nod and not another word spoken, I slink off into the bathroom and gasp when I catch sight of myself in one of the many long mirrors.

No wonder Blaine has gone pale.

The already scandalous sash across my breasts is torn, blood and dirt covering the fabric where it barely covers anything anymore. My midriff is wrapped with what I recognize as Derrín's handiwork, distinguished from Amír's by the way the bandages are already falling—not that I'm ungrateful. Someone had taken great care to remove all the glass that had imbedded itself under my skin and to apply a salve on all the little lacerations. Another bandage was covering the entirety of my calf, and I wince as I remember the flash of the blade as it skinned my leg. Tiny cuts, already healing, lace my arms. My legs. I may have well just been dug up from my grave.

Limping to the tub, I draw a hot bath, grateful for the commodity of running water more now than ever. Slowly, using a carefully concealed dagger that Kya had hidden in my bosom, I cut the flimsy fabric from my form. Shivering naked in the cold bathroom, I remove all the bandages and lower myself into the tub.

The hot water elicits a hiss of pain from my lips as it makes contact with my wounds. Torin calls from the other room, and Blaine is already limping for the door when I call out that I'm fine. No, the pain is a welcome distraction. Something tells me the following conversation is going to be far worse than this. With the slowest of strokes, I drag a rag across my broken skin, languishing in the hot water mixing with my golden blood.

Torin takes the silks the moment I step out from my bathroom, clad only in a light pink robe. Blaine coughs, some of his color returning to his face as Torin hands a more modest nightgown my way. I raise an eyebrow as if to ask how he knew where to find it, but he only grins. A welcome sight.

"For the captain's sake."

My dry lip splits as I try to crack a smile, and I excuse myself to the bathroom again as both men rush forward in a panic.

By the time I return, clothed like I had been sleeping peacefully in my bed all night until I woke up feverish, Torin is sprawled himself across my bed. Blaine sits on the same stool Rowan had only an hour before. Inexplicably, the thought sends a pang through my heart.

"So, here's how this is gonna go." Torin's expression turns grim again as he pats the bed beside him. Slowly, I sit. "You're going to tell us everything. Don't bother leaving anything out, or else Blaine here is just going to assume the worst and rip your tutor to shreds the next time he sees."

I almost laugh. He can certainly try.

"And then, we are going to fix whatever mess you've gotten yourself into, okay?" His hands grasp mine so earnestly, his voice cracking with sincerity, and I know that it's not only Blaine who had assumed the worst when he saw his princess dressed in the teal garb of a courtesan covered in blood.

Quietly, I tell them everything, from running away that first night and meeting Rowan, though I leave out the names of Aiko and Finneas just in case the king does hear. I tell them how I still have bruises from Kya knocking me on my ass for weeks, the glares from Amír that live in my nightmares, and how I nearly wept when I realized they didn't abandon me tonight. They listen attentively, everyone careful not to breath too loudly as the castle comes to rise. They listen until the words stop coming, and then we sit in silence.

Torin is the first to speak.

"Well, shit."

"Such eloquence after I just spilled my heart to you." I laugh softly and nervously, my gaze darting to where Blaine now stands with his hands in his pockets. His shoulders curved inwards. "Say something. Please."

"What is there to say?" His cold indifference hits like a brick to the chest. Silently, I stare, pleading at him to look at me. To understand.

"Okay then." I hate the way my voice cracks. "I don't plan on stopping. I'm leaving this palace, when I do depends on you two. If you tell the king, then I'm leaving now. If you don't, then I'll stay until I know I can keep myself safe. Until Rowan is finished training me."

Blaine swears softly under his breath, his face a mask of cool rage. "I don't like this. He's just using you."

"And I'm using him," I reassure the irate captain. "I just need him to train me to survive on my own. I will have to cross the border, maybe even leave through the port. There's a large harbor in Varium if I could just get there first. I'll start a new life, where people have never heard of Princess Verosa of Krycolis."

"I don't like this. Not one bit." The captain, the man I loved and called a friend, spins on his heel and turns his back to me.

"Where are you going?" No response. "I didn't see you caring when my father sold me off to Lucius under the guise of a political alliance." My words come out sharper than I had intended, a sparking rage that demands to be released. "I'm not in the position to wait anymore."

That rage is smothered by a cool blanket of ice the moment I watch the captain's shoulders stiffen, and his voice comes out as a croak.

"Why do you think I didn't seal that passage?"

"Don't you dare."

My heart stops the moment I hear the click of the door, and his offbeat footsteps echoing down the hallway. Step, step, drag. A step, another...

How dare he. How dare he do one good thing and hold it over my head? Even if he had sealed that passage, he didn't do it for me. No, he knew if I really wanted to escape, I would. I'd throw myself out a window if I had to. He has seen me do it before.

Torin leans forward with a sigh.

"You know, Vera, there's a story I used to tell the squires. The story of a princess who wanted too much." Torin braces his forearms against his thighs as he glances sideways in my direction. "She was ambitious but greedy. Nothing was enough for her, and in the end, her greed left her with nothing."

"Greed?" I scoff. "Torin all I want is my freedom. To be able to go where I want when I want without someone reporting my every move back to my father... or my fiancé soon enough. Is it selfish to want what others have?"

"You assume we're all free."

"What do you presume to mean by that?"

"Have you ever considered that the walls surrounding this palace aren't to keep you in, but to keep others out? People who want to kill the monarchy, to kill you?"

"The cursed aren't all evil." I counter quickly, catching onto the edge in his voice. An edge I had recognized in my own not too long ago, before I met Rowan. Kya. Torin raises an eyebrow suspiciously but carries on nonetheless.

"Sure, it might not always be the cursed. It could be a blessed. It could be a friend, anyone, really. You trust the wrong person in this world, Vera, and you're dead."

"What about you? Can I trust you?"

Torin sighs pragmatically, then stands to ruffle my hair.

"Always. I am loyal to you Verosa, greedy princess or not."

CHAPTER 12

VEROSA

Never in my life have I seen so many flowers in one room. Word got out to the rest of the maids, and eventually, my father and Lucius that I was unwell and not taking any visitors. It was probably the most peaceful morning of my life, until the first bouquet of flowers was left outside my door.

Tanja is the only one allowed in, and I made a show of coughing and hiding under the covers every time she entered. She carried the flowers — white roses, into the room, and placed them in a vase next to my vanity. Approximately an hour later, there was another sure knock on my door and another bouquet. Lilies this time. Then, an hour later, sunflowers. Every hour until dusk flowers showed up. Soft pink roses, daisies, red carnations, and blue irises. All signed by Lucius.

The only thing that gives away Kya's entrance is her kitten-like sneeze as she steps from the shadows.

"I didn't know you were so into botany." She sniffles lightly. With expert grace, she dodges a lavishly embroidered pillow tossed her way. Her motions are fluid, a dancing flame, and my voice catches in my throat. Rowan hadn't lied, she's fine. A few bruises and small cuts litter her arms, but other than that... fine.

"I was wondering when you were going to come down from up there." I laugh, rising to a seated position.

Kya gives a long sideways glance.

"Impressive, not even Rowan can tell when I stalk him."

A soft laugh as I whisper, "It's your cinnamon perfume." Then I add, "I knew you were here all day."

"Hmm." She hums, her eyes gazing out the window. Somewhere far away from here.

Then she turns. The moonlight shimmers across her sultry hair as she takes one step forward, then another until she crashes into me, knocking us both flat against my headboard.

"Thank you for saving her," she breathes, and I note the slight tremor in her lilting voice. My sweet Kya, my friend who loves so fully.

"So you're not mad at me for messing up the mission?"

The Vari assassin shakes her head fervently, her dark hair swishing about her sweet face. A few strands stick to her sweat slick forehead. Her golden eyes stare hard into my face, the eyes of Deun, I note, not missing the irony.

"You did fine, Vera. It was a trap, and we all walked into it." She nudges my shoulder with a slight wince. "And we all walked out of it."

"I should have done something though." I burry my face in my hands. "But no matter how hard I tried, I just couldn't bring myself to stab him."

"Don't be ashamed of your pure hands, Vera, some of us wish we could wash ours clean again."

"Even you?"

Kya pauses for a moment before her shoulders slump forward in a moment of vulnerability. "Some days," she admits, "I can't tell where the blood ends and the paint begins."

We stay there like this for a moment, my head resting on her shoulder with her tracing soft shapes across my shoulders. Not a sound in the room save for the near silent susurration of the wind blowing in from the open window. The scent of jasmine and wisteria drifts in, caressing us into peace until Kya sneezes again.

"Bless you." I laugh, but she's already on her feet, daggers poised and ready. Her eyes warn me we weren't alone. I want to shout at her to hide and to put those damn daggers down.

"You're not going to skewer my maids." I hiss between clenched teeth.

"Please don't. I quite like my organs where they are." Torin drawls from his position, where he leans lazily against the door. "Kya, I presume?"

"Friends. Both of them." I whisper to her as Blaine steps into the light, his handsome face grim and set in a hard line. Kya sets her face in stone to match and sheaths her *espas*, but noticeably keeps her hand close to the hilt. Wary, but willing to listen.

Throwing off my covers to reveal a dark blouse and fitted trousers already stuffed into thick-soled leather boots, I stalk towards the entrance and my friends.

"They're coming with tonight." If Kya is surprised, she doesn't show it, much to her credit, just cocks a single eyebrow skyward.

"Rowan won't be happy."

"I'll deal with Rowan."

She sucks on her teeth, then huffs under her breath, "I'm sure you will." She nods to the window and tosses out a rope. It unravels slowly, rippling towards the ground silently. No guards startle or appear to apprehend them. Kya juts a chin towards it. "Let's make this quick, before the guards notice. There are two horses so we will have to ride double."

I try not to think about that last statement as I slip out the window with graceful skill. The rope no longer snags or burns beneath my touch. I barely make a sound as I land, and Kya lands silently beside me. Blaine and Torin then follow, albeit clumsier than the two of us. My friend motions for us to make for the horses as she cuts the rope, and I mount the sweet chestnut gelding waiting by the outer wall. Blaine mounts behind me and moves to take the reins from my hands, but I grip tight.

"I can handle it," I hiss between clenched teeth. His eyes flash with a moment of shock and hurt, then back to that cool indifference. Good, let him wonder how much he truly knows about me.

Ever since he found out where I've been spending my nights, Blaine has kept his distance. Not that he can come into my room whenever he liked, I'm supposed to be sick, but he could try. The only conversation we've had since was the one we had this afternoon where he and Torin said they were coming with tonight.

There wasn't much room for argument, not when Blaine fixed that glare on my bandaged midsection, where my wounds were healing slower than usual. I had been quick to pull the hem of my blouse down and agree quietly.

Blaine's legs hang tightly against the gelding's barrel; occasionally, his bad leg will swing forward and brush against mine. The lightest touch, and my knuckles go white against the reins. If Blaine notices, he doesn't say anything.

Neither of us mention the blush I keep blaming on the cold rather than his arms wrapped around my waist.

The moonlight slowly disappears beneath the shadows of the growing and spindly trees of the forest. My grip tightens, and Blaine silently shifts closer. His arms tense against my midsection.

There are no lights to be seen in the dense forest, not as we cross that one boundary separating the blessed towns from the cursed. And despite my growing lack of fear of the cursed, a shiver drags its icy fingers down my spine.

Normally, Rowan and I would plod along a well-lit path to reach the compound, though I understand Kya's reasoning for choosing this unfamiliar path. The darkness will conceal the way, and if Blaine or Torin were to report to the king the dwellings of the most notorious criminals in Krycolis, they wouldn't be able to lead the way back to us.

"Are you alright?" Blaine whispers, just loud enough for the two of us to hear. Torin and Kya pull ahead of us slightly, disappearing into the unnatural dark first. I straighten my spine. It's the first words he's spoken to me today, the gravely tone of his voice now slightly unfamiliar.

"I'm fine." My voice cracks as I respond, my knuckles turn white as they grip the reins tighter now. That darkness... I can't go in again.

Slowly, Blaine reaches forward, his gloved hands closing over mine to disentangle the leather reins from between my fingers. With one hand, he guides us into that unholy void, and the other, he holds flat against the plane of my stomach. A constant reminder.

"Lean back and close your eyes."

"But—"

"I'll leave a light on." His voice fogs in the air before us, the darkness soon claiming even that. Just ahead, I can barely make out the silhouette of Kya and Torin's mare.

"I'll leave a light on," he repeats, his fingers splaying across my stomach. I'll leave a light on. Our phrase since we were children. An oath he had yet to break and used so rarely. Trust. He is asking me to trust him despite my fear, despite my panic. Trust him to get us out of this safe and alive. I haven't heard him say it since... well. Since before he left me and promised to return.

Slowly, I close my eyes and lean back again his chest, feeling incredibly small and helpless. The darkness claims everything, our sight, the sounds around us, even the warmth from my body drains as panic sets in.

But Blaine's heart beats steady through his cream-colored tunic. He has forgone his usual chest plate and armor, and I can feel every rippling muscle tense beneath the cloth at my touch. A slight satisfaction simmers in my chest at this realization.

A soft wind blows past us, fanning my cheeks with the soft smell of rose buds. Innocent. Sweet. How out of place in a place like this.

A few moments pass, then Blaine uncurls his fingers from where they were fisted in the fabric of my blouse, and he halts our mount.

"We're here." Kya calls from up front as I open my eyes. The front door of the compound swings open, and out steps a furious Rowan.

CHAPTER 13

VEROSA

Kya and I have been sparring for nearly an hour, with Torin and Blaine looking on in the corner. The former nods with an appreciative whistle, while his captain remains silent. If he's surprised by everything I've learned he doesn't show it. He just grits his teeth. We still haven't spoken since we arrived at the compound.

And I haven't spoken to Rowan since he stormed off into that study, Amír close on his heels with a death glare towards me and the obviously unwanted guests. If I have to guess, she's probably in there now telling him to cut ties before it's too late, like I hadn't just saved her life a few days ago.

I suppose I should be grateful for the consistency. Amír is nothing if not loyal to her beliefs, even if those beliefs include thinking that I'm some demon spawn from Hell here to wreck her precious life. I feint left as the thought comes to mind. Maybe I should've left her in that tavern to rot.

Kya ducks to avoid my blow, a drastic measure I had made without thinking, and she uses the moment to attack my now unguarded ribs. I land heavily on the dirty stone floor, my tailbone throbbing with the impact.

"How's that stone taste?" Torin quips from his stance against the wall. I flip him a vulgar gesture in retaliation. Perhaps he and Amír would get on well, if only for the sake of taking turns to jab at me whenever I eat shit during training.

"Why don't you come show me how it's done then?" I hiss through clenched teeth. "Oh, great Master Torin."

Kya raises her wooden dagger menacingly.

"No, I think you've got it covered." The young man gulps.

"Thought so."

The young Vari woman helps me to my feet with a smug grin, then winces when she sees the budding bruise across my ribs that peaks out from under my bindings. Both of us had stripped from our blouses moments into training. The sweat had been sticking to our clothes and smothered us both. Torin, of course, hadn't cared, but Blaine has kept his eyes trained on the ground since, only turning his gaze upwards to watch when we sparred. He sits in Derrín's usual seat, his leg throbbing from the long ride here.

"Where is Derrín tonight, anyway?" I wonder aloud. Kya's twin has been nowhere to be seen since entering the compound, which I consider unusual because I've never heard of him going on any solo missions. Or any missions at all, for that matter.

"He left to go see a merchant in the North." Kya swallows a mouthful of water and extends the canteen my way. "Said he needed some more supplies that only this man could provide for whatever secret project he's working on."

"He still hasn't told you what it is yet?"

"Nope. Only Rowan knows." I return the canteen after a healthy swig and pull a face. Of course, he does. At this point, I'm convinced there's nothing this man doesn't know. Well, except for one thing.

"Okay, enough talk. Let's try again." Kya drops her weapons, and I follow suit, noticing where this is going, when the door to the study suddenly swings open.

Rowan strides out, his face a mask of cool and collected calm as he surveys the scene. He offers only a slight inclination of the head in Torin and Blaine's direction, then fixes his emerald gaze on me.

Rowan rolls his sleeves up, revealing the tan skin below all that leather. I swallow thickly as he grabs a wooden sword off the wall, the corded muscle of his arms rippling where exposed. He lifts the weapon with ease and nods to where I stand beside Kya, both of us panting with exertion from our sparring.

"I need to work off some steam."

His glare tells me that I'm the reason for said steam and that we would discuss this later.

Kya nods. "We were just about to start hand to hand combat. After that last heist, I figured it would be good for her to learn how to fight a larger enemy." The blonde mercenary only shrugs and rests the sword against the wall again before stepping up before me. His sly, emerald eyes slide up and down my frame as he raises his fists to begin the spar. He winks.

"Ladies first."

"Such a gentleman." I roll my eyes to hide the flush creeping up from the back of my neck. I rock back on my heels and throw the first punch, only for him to duck and catch my side. It stings but doesn't hurt nearly as much as it should. I let him throw the next punch and back up, lunging to the side to allow momentum to fight half my battle for me.

"Come on, Vera, you're fighting like a coward." His words spark a small fire in my gut, as does the frivolous wink and smirk he sends my way, but one look at Kya snuffs it. His taunts are to frustrate me and have me make a desperate move. If I lung forward on the assault, I lose my advantage in this fight, and he wins. I'm dead.

Stepping back, I keep an even distance before us Rowan strikes out again. This time I reciprocate with a front kick to the gut. He staggers a moment, his blonde hair falling into his eyes as he glares in my direction.

"Not bad."

"You want some more?" In my moment of gloating, he manages to land a fairly strong hit to my torso. I hiss at the small hurt when I realize what he's been doing.

"You're pulling your punches!" I cry indignantly, and he flashes that Cheshire Cat grin of his.

"I wanted to give you some sort of chance."

"I can take you."

We both know my confidence is misplaced, but I don't expect him to lung forward with the speed and drive of a madman as he dodges all my assaults and sweeps my legs out from under me. Before I have the chance to strike, he's settled his knees on either side of my hips, one of his hands pinning both of mine above my head while the other toys with a loose strand of hair. I struggle to no avail as his grip tightens, though not enough to hurt. His warm breath fans my cheeks as he lowers his face to mine, the two of us nearly nose to nose. His hair cascades around his head, a halo of gold encapsulating us both. He looks like a saint, if a saint wore all black leather and blood.

His eyes glimmer dangerously, and I find myself holding my breath as he leans closer, the scent of twilight swirling between us.

"No, you can't." His weight settles heavily over my body as he tucks that strand of hair behind my ear. "You need to be better. I can't stomach the thought of another man pinning you down like this."

Then strong furious hands are ripping him off, hauling him to his feet and pinning him against the wall and gripping his throat.

Blaine's face is a perfect portrait of righteous fury and rage. Gone is the aloof calmness I've grown accustomed to. No, I imagine this is the last face his enemies on the battlefield had seen. The face of a warrior, and perhaps a monster.

"You don't touch her," He seethes, his jaw clicking as he bares his teeth dangerously close to Rowan's throat. A part of me wonders if he'd rip it out.

"Blaine!" I cry out, scrambling to my feet.

But Rowan just smirks and raises an eyebrow with his usual suaveness.

"Or what?" His eyes flick down to Blaine's snarl then back to his eyes. "You'll bite me?"

"You'd like that wouldn't you?"

"I'd much prefer if she did it." I'm too stunned to comprehend what Rowan is saying when Blaine presses him further into the wall, only for Rowan to push back.

"I'm growing tired of this." He cracks his neck and steps forward as if he hadn't just had our best captain's hands around his throat. "Get over yourself, Vera could've had me off if she wanted to."

If it had been anyone other than him, no, probably not. But I had seen the hesitance in his eyes, the gentle caution. If I had shoved, he would've yielded.

"Unless she liked it."

And with four words, all of Blaine's restraint snaps, and he winds his fist back for a punch. I lunge to step between them both when Kya gets there first, her swift hands catching his fist where it still waits in the air, eager to probably knock Rowan's teeth out.

"Take a walk," she hisses tightening her grip. "Both of you."

A seething rage burns bright in Blaine's steely grey eyes, but a brighter fire is lit in hers. Her stare is a warning: back down or be burned. Slowly, he relents, and the assassin drops her arm. Without another word, he storms from the room, his footsteps echoing until the slam of the door rattles the walls.

"Go after him."

Torin nods and does as I ask of him, his footsteps light and quick. Surely enough, the door opens and closes again.

"Ha! And you have the nerve to whine about how he isn't in love with you," Rowan drawls, rubbing his neck where the faint beginnings of a bruise are starting to show. His sardonic laughter fills the space between us, followed by a yelp of pain as my shoe hits the back of his head.

"You're looking better than the last time I saw you." A new voice enters the room, high and lilting like a flute. The sly fox.

Aiko steps in first, her slender form clothed in a fine velvet gown of the deepest indigo hues. Her dark hair is pinned in coifs atop her head, making her look every part the regal noble I had somehow forgotten she is. Finneas follows after her, his hulking frame nearly getting caught in the doorway as he tries to catch up to his wife. But my attention isn't on him. No, my gaze traces the light streaming from the main room to the third shadow waiting in the doorway.

A diminutive blonde woman steps through, her face worn weary with time and grief. Her eyes are a piercing, emerald green that bear such sorrow, and yet she has laugh lines in the corners of her eyes. Her strides are short yet powerful, and her shoulders rest square over her hips. This is a woman who could have fooled me for a queen.

Abashedly noticing my half-nakedness, I lung for my shirt and toss it over my head before bowing lightly at the waist.

"Thanks to you." I say gratefully, softening slightly towards the woman who saved my life. Her shoulders relax, and before I know it, she has her arms wrapped around me in a brief but sure hug. Her bluebell eyes shine as she grins from ear to ear, her regal pretenses dropping in an instant.

"I am just glad to see you're okay. You had us worried."

"So this is the young woman I can keep hearing about." The blonde woman steps forward again, resting her hand on Finneas' arm for support. "Pleasure to meet you, Verosa."

"How do you know my name?"

"Your name never seems to leave my son's lips."

When I started training with the Nightwalkers, I thought that nothing could shock me anymore. Tonight, I have once again been proven wrong as Rowan responds. "Mother, please."

Rowan's tenebrous voice is filled with an unfamiliar resignation, and I find myself smiling softly.

Now that the woman is standing in the light, it is easy to see the resemblance, aside from the same hair and eye color, he has her formal posture and wild mannerisms when he's relaxed. Her voice is soft, the same voice I heard him use when I asked him to cut me.

"Emilie." She extends a slender hand. "Come, walk with me, child."

"That's not necessary, Vera."

"I'd be delighted." Ever so gently, I accept her hand and allow her to drape her arm across my own, acting the role of chivalrous courtier. That is until she turns her back, and I can stick my tongue out at Rowan. He flips me off in return.

"I've heard you're becoming a force to be reckoned with. Quite the spitfire. After that little show, I can see why my son likes you so much." Despite the cool breeze outside, I can feel a scarlet blush heat my cheeks and the tips of my ears.

"Oh, you saw that?"

Emilie laughs at the way my voice cracks and tosses her head back, letting her hair fall loose past her shoulders. I think back on Rowan's coy face and Casanova persona and wonder how he could've come from such a lovely woman.

"Don't worry too much, I was young once too." She pauses behind a tree and motions for me to join her. "But it's slipping away."

I turn my face to question her, but she merely juts her chin before her. There I can see him, sitting next to Torin deep in conversation, his fists still clenched at his side.

"A man of virtue, yes?" she hums.

"More than any I've ever known."

Emilie snorts softly, such a peculiar sound from a refined lady. She smirks, and suddenly I see Rowan's face fully in hers. It's so startling I almost stumble. That rage and sorrow I saw in her eyes may have worn her features but not her soul.

"It gets to the best of them eventually." I cock my head in confusion, eyeing the two men before us.

"What does?"

"Love, dear."

Now I do stumble, my breath hitching in my throat. I can still feel Blaine's hands brushing away my bangs, staring at my wounds with murder in his eyes. I can see him pulling Rowan off of me, the ferocity of his uncharacteristically agile movements. He rubs his crippled leg.

"Blaine doesn't love me." My voice is barely above a whisper, but it sounds like an obvious lie even to my ears. The bloodshed, the war, the healing, and the abandonment. I had thought everything was so clear, but now... Blaine left the passage open for me. He cleaned up every mess I made. He followed me here. As the realization begins to sink in, another one hits. How far is he willing to go to prove that love, and how would I feel if he went too far this time?

"Love is the cruelest killer of all. Do you know why, dear?" I shake my head. "Because it's the only devil that doesn't hide its horns. We look it in its ugly face every time and still fall for it. We destroy ourselves in the name of love."

I double over, covering my mouth with the back of my hand. Had he gone into that war for me? Had he destroyed himself for me?

"It's not an easy lesson to learn, but you'll do well to remember it," Emilie warns, but there is no sharp bite to her words, only soft sorrow and kindness. Her lips part as if she's been haunted, and the color drains from her face slightly. She grips my arm tighter. "If you don't remember it, find a reminder."

"You sound as if you speak from experience."

I don't mean to cross a line, but her mouth hardens, and her steps falter. Bracing myself, I wait for the wicked words to flay my skin, or perhaps even a whip hidden in the skirts of her gown.

Her palm presses softly against my cheek and she smiles.

"My son is my reminder every day. My reminder of why I destroyed myself."

I swallow thickly. "Was it worth it?"

"Every second of it." She steps ahead on her own for a moment, the stars shining on her long golden tresses. "The heart is a fickle thing, Verosa, I know, but you can't have them both. You need to choose before someone gets hurt."

Emilie extends that slender arm again, the limb of a wraith both haunted and haunting, and I guide her back to the house. I don't have the heart to tell her it might be too late for that.

CHAPTER 14

ROWAN

I have officially decided that Duke Gadsden might be the most obnoxious man I had ever met, and if I had my sword, I would be tempted to skewer him if only to watch that smug smirk slide from his oily face.

Vera had told me stories of his various proposals over the years one of those days when she thought I wasn't listening. His first proposal had come when she had turned fifteen, and the last about two weeks before we met in that alley. It took quite a bit of restraint for me not to laugh when she told me how she got him to back off, and it took more restraint now not to strangle him.

As if being a slimy pedophile wasn't enough, he has to have the most boorish sense of humor and nasally voice that raises the very hairs on my arms.

"You're quite a handsome gentleman, Lord Rowan. I would love to see what your mother must have looked like in her youth," he cackles, a small snort interwoven with the guttural sound.

Just as I am beginning to plan my escape route for after I strangle him with his own toupee, a firm hand rests on my shoulder.

"Rowan," Lucius says by way of greeting. "I was just looking for you."

I plaster a smile on my face, though half of it is genuine relief, as I spin to face the other man. We are both about equal in stature, though I feel the need to square my shoulders each time I look him in the eye. If only the crown prince of Tesslari knew just who was hiding under all these fine clothes. Perhaps the royal would wet himself.

"What a coincidence, I was just on my way to find you." I sketch a shallow and mocking bow. "Until next time, Duke."

The slimy older gentleman, probably well into his fifties by now, offers a yellow-toothed smile and stalks back off to the end of the hall. Only when he is out of sight do I let myself sigh, exhaling the majority of my rage.

"How'd you wind up having to deal with that deplorable man?" Lucius' voice is smooth with a soft lilt of amusement. His well-manicured nails pick at an invisible spec of lint off his finely tailored coat. The perfect picture of a cool and calculating prince, regal and kingly already.

"I was actually on my way to see you."

"Oh?"

"It's about Verosa." At the mention of his fiancé, the prince's lips form a hard line, and his eyes narrow in concern. "I know she has been feeling unwell, and I thought a trip to the sea would be helpful. I selected a location rich in history for her studies, with not enough wind for her to catch a chill."

That wasn't fully true, and I'm sure lying to the future king will come with its repercussions, but I'll deal with that later.

Vera is almost always late to her lessons, giving me more time to peruse the royal libraries. Hidden back in the far corner of a shelf laden with dust and shadow is an old leather-bound book. A book on the power of the pureblood.

I've seen it before, that power simmering beneath the surface of her gaze, though she seems unaware. A few nights ago, when she was pinned beneath me, I felt it. Felt the air get cold and the lights flicker.

"That's the Cliffs of Ialenia," Lucius notes, eying the map in my hands. "Home of the great pureblood mages."

"There's an ancient myth that wading in the shallows of the ocean will speed up the healing process of any wound of sickness." As well as increase the powers of any pureblood with magical abilities.

"But why come to me with this?"

"Well, as archaic as it might be, you're her fiancé, and I don't know who her parents are."

"You don't..." An incredulous stare.

"No. Verosa has been rather hush about it, not that I care. If she wants to keep it a secret, then it's her secret to decide when to reveal."

Lucius nods slowly, his jaw clicking as he considers what I've presented him with. His dark eyes shift under his furrowed brows. This man could have been melded from the crowns of fallen kings for all his regal mannerisms. A fitting king for this kingdom.

And yet Vera doesn't want him.

"I can get this trip approved." He speaks softly and slowly. "But I will need you to do something for me too."

My spine straightens, but I nod my head as if to ask him to continue. What could the future king need from a tutor? I've seen these cases before, powerful men needing someone insignificant to do the dirty work. Normally I am the one hired for the dirty work, but something in his shifting gaze makes me pause.

I nearly choke when he says, "I need you to keep an eye on Blaine."

"Pardon?" Vera probably would've laughed at me after punching the daylights out of her fiancé for suggesting such a thing.

Lucius' eyes darken, and his shoulders tense. Something primal— something *dark* exudes from his very being and fills the hall. A familiar shiver caresses my skin, leaving gooseflesh in its wake. It's the same sensation I had on that day nearly 10 years ago. The day my mother left my father.

"I know about them. I've seen him pacing the halls at night outside of her room when he is supposed to be stationed at the other end of the palace." So *that* is where Vera got the palace layout from. "I've seen them dining together, him staring when she's not looking. We can't have the captain of the Guard in love with my wife."

"She's not your wife."

"Not yet," Lucius amends with a small laugh, his hand firmly clasping my shoulder in an amicable gesture. "I trust you, Rowan, so let's help each other out."

- Chapter 16 -

CHAPTER 15
VEROSA

"Pack your bags, sunshine, we're going on a trip," Rowan says by way of greeting as he slams a stack of books down on my bedside table. I run my thumb over the spines, admiring the raised ridges of the titles beneath the pad of my finger. *Ialenia Falls, Touch of Light, Power of the Pureblood Mages.*

"And why, exactly, are you throwing down books on purebloods and their powers on my vanity... Hey! That's fragile," I hiss, batting a perfume bottle from his hand as he tosses it in the air. Gently, I set it atop the vanity and fix him with a glare.

"I've done my research, asked about, if you will, and the only name of any pureblood in this palace in the records is yours. The last pureblood in the palace died nearly nine years ago." He responds casually, as if that answers my question in any way. My heart races for only a moment before I remember that titles are never included in the pureblood records. I've never been able to figure out why it is done that way but today I thank Deungrid for it. How could I have thought he wouldn't try to find out more than I am willing to give? Everyone in the palace is keeping my identity a secret for now, but how long until he figures out the truth of who I am?

"Your point is?"

"Don't you find it odd, that in a kingdom that practically worships the blessed, you're the only pureblood?"

I shrug, "Purebloods are rare, whether blessed or cursed. I'm not too surprised."

Rowan rolls his eyes, but his shoulders are tense as he stands and snatches the knapsack hanging from my bathroom door. Dramatically flinging open my closet, he rummages through, much to my protest, until he finds a dress that he deems acceptable and tosses it my way along with the sack.

"Hurry up and get dressed. The carriage leaves in half an hour." Is all he says before disappearing out the door in a blink. As if he had never been here at all.

Repressing a shudder, I stare back to where he had stood moments before. Sometimes I find myself forgetting where he comes from. What he is capable of. There are moments now where I find his strength a reassurance, and his slivers of kindness a reminder. A reminder of the boy Emilie sees, trying to break through the pain of those secrets he harbors.

Then the mercenary comes back, and I'm left wondering where we stand.

Though the same could be said for the rest of the Nightwalkers. Derrín is rarely at the compound anymore; always off working on that secret project. I know Rowan knows what it is, and they just don't trust me enough to say. Or it's none of my business.

Kya is always kind and sweet, but she's keeping secrets too. I'll watch her eyes shift to avoid my gaze whenever someone brings up Varium, or the evident shame written across her face when she paints those whorls on her arms. She hasn't told me why they're painted on rather than tattooed, though, to be fair, I haven't asked. I doubt even Rowan or Amír know what they mean, if anyone knew, it would be her twin.

I am keeping my own secrets as well, I often have to remind myself. No one knows that I am the heir to the throne, and per my request, both Lucius and my father have kept it a secret from Rowan. I had pleaded under the guise of desiring normalcy, saying I didn't want special treatment from a new tutor. In reality, I wasn't ready for the hatred that he would look at me with when he found out. It's impossible to miss the obvious look of disgust on the mercenary's face when he eyes the higher-ranked nobles of the palace. A countenance that only worsens whenever we pass those large oak doors to the throne room. Rowan may have his reasons, but he hates the royal family.

The knock comes right on time just as I had expected. Blaine had stood outside the door a few moments before knocking, presumably trying to figure out how to approach. We haven't spoken since the incident at the compound, and after my talk with Emilie, I'm not sure how to face him. How pitiful. The man who was my best friend above all else is now pausing to figure out how to knock on my door. And I'm wondering whether or not to open it.

Blaine's face is taut, his eyebrows furrowed, and jaw set when I open the door. I'm about to offer a sarcastic quip when I notice the dark circles worsening below his eyes, and he offers an armored arm.

"I've been sent to escort you to your carriage." How welcoming.

Without a word, I accept his arm, a servant taking my bags despite my protests, and we walk through the weathered halls of the palace. The windows are all closed today to keep out the Autumn chill. Despite the heat wave flooding our borders only a few weeks ago, Autumn crept in silently before effectively having all the women changing from their summer dresses to fur coats. Krycolis has always been known for its extreme weather, but even this is a bit much for our kingdom. The cold kisses the back of my neck, as if death is trying to grip a spindly hand around my heart.

"Do the escorts know that Rowan doesn't know who I am?" I ask in an attempt to both shake the chill and break the unbearable silence. Something tells me they're related.

"All have been thoroughly debriefed on what they need to know." Is his terse response.

"Oh."

"Do you have something else to say, *Mei Reinhavich?*"

His steely glare is unrelenting as he eyes the gown I'm in, one that Rowan chose to prove a point, apparently. The gown is a burnt autumn color with long billowing sleeves and a low neckline. My dagger is strapped under my skirts, of course, and I'm wearing thick-soled boots just in case. None of this fools Blaine, of course.

"No, but you clearly do."

"How quickly you've turned from princess to mercenary. Is that steel on the toe of your boots, or cursed blood? He's all over you now, and you can't even see it."

It is all I can do to stare at him with wild bewilderment. What the hell does he mean by that? What does one thing have to do with the other?

"If you don't like me fighting with them, then find another way," I snap, tired of this game already. I should've been more careful. I never should've gotten Blaine involved. It only complicates things more. It would've been better to just disappear and let him wonder where I had gone, maybe then he would've realized that he had pushed me away.

His face is blank as he hands me over to the care of Rowan and Commander Raiko and walks away with not even a bow. The commander bristles at his uncharacteristic insubordination but says nothing as he turns to command his men. I wince along with them at the newfound sharpness of his tongue. Leave it to Blaine to ruin a mood in less than thirty seconds.

"Quit frowning," Rowan chides, resuming his role of tutor. "He's a captain, you're supposed to outrank him. His actions mean nothing to you, not in front of them."

I take offense to his reprimand until I trace his gaze back to where a few of the knights are watching wearily. The gossip surrounding Blaine and mine's relationship surely hasn't lessened over the years since we've grown apart. Perhaps I can pin the blame on him once again, after all, it was his sulking I heard in the knight's quarters the night of my engagement. If he had just held his tongue...

Rowan pinches my underarm. "Smile. You're supposed to be sick not dying."

I offer a weak smile then slam my heel down on the soft of his foot.

"Apologies sir," I drawl to feign innocence, "I suppose I haven't regained all my strength or balance yet."

His foot promptly juts out and knocks me forward. I bite my tongue as he grips my elbow to steady me. "It would appear so." Then he whispers with that Cheshire Cat grin, "Eat shit, princess."

The commander clears his throat right as I'm about to retort or unsheathe that hidden blade and cut that smirk from his face. Not that it would've phased him. I think the gods themselves could show up, and Rowan would flip them a vulgar gesture then carry on with his day. I'd be lying if I said a part of his cool consistency didn't excite me just a little. To know I could show the worst of me and he wouldn't even bat an eye.

The footman opens the door with a deep bow, and I notice him biting his tongue to keep from calling me Mei Reinhavich out of habit. If Rowan notices, he doesn't say anything, just follows me into the carriage. The door closes with a snick, then the echoes of hoof beats on gravel carry us onward.

I take to staring contently out the window while Rowan pulls his hat over his face as if to doze off, though I can tell he's not asleep.

Grassy emerald hills roll out before us, painted golden at their arches with the morning sunlight and dew. The blue sky boasts a few fluffy clouds that dot along the horizon and the occasional small bird. We pass a fawn and its mother at one point.

"Sometimes it's strange to think that they can go as far as their legs can take them." I remark to Rowan's fake-sleeping form. "No fathers or fiancés to tell them where their boundaries are. There's no difference between the East and West deer. No talk of assassinations and arranged marriage. They're free."

"They don't live long." Rowan peaks out from under the brim of his cap.

"But they *live*," I whisper breathlessly. My companion's eyes shutter for a moment as if considering this, then promptly close again, leaving me with only my thoughts. We have long since passed the fawn and his rolling hills. All of it for him to take.

CHAPTER 16
VEROSA

The carriage halts suddenly, and I find myself gripping the seat to keep from falling. Rowan's eyes are open and focused over my shoulder, where a gentle sea breeze whispers through the curtains of the open window.

"Come on," he says softly and nudges me with an elbow. "We're here."

Ialenia falls. It was situated on the Eastern shoreline of Krycolis and roughly a day's carriage ride from the palace. The storm clouds we had seen briefly on our ride over have completely vanished, leaving only clear blue skies that reflect evenly across the ocean at the base of the cliffs. Despite years of neglect, the grass grows evenly, with flowers that should have been out of season still blooming in full color. The trees stretch skyward, sparse enough to provide a bit of ambiance but no real shade from the unrelenting sun. However, the sea breeze wicked the sweat from my brow as soon as it formed. The place was perfect, no doubt due to the magic deeply imbued in its roots.

I'd read that back when the pureblood mages owned and cultivated the land, it had boasted temples spanning across the entirety of the cliffside with a small village nestled at the base of the cliffs. A stairway of seven thousand steps led the way from the villages to the temples, but that hadn't separated their magic and home lives. Even the children could make the trek with ease, an ability accredited to their pureblood blessings, and would oftentimes spend the days running through the temples or tinkering with magic in the gardens. That was before my great grandfather destroyed them all.

The mages had refused to follow Deungrid despite his being the source of their powers. Despite being overtly pious, the king hadn't found reason to eradicate them until they began to shelter purebloods escaping Varium. cursed purebloods. They had claimed it had been a gift given to them by the god himself and that they should be free to use its blessings as they saw fit. My grandfather decided that as king, it was his god-given right to rule as he saw fit, and he slaughtered them all.

It is said that as the pureblood mages were dying, they combined their power with the dark magic of the cursed and cast a curse upon their king. He died without an heir, and thus the line of succession shifted to his adoptive brother, his brother's son, and then my father.

"I'm surprised the king hasn't completely destroyed this place yet," Rowan remarked with a low whistle. "I can practically feel the magic and curse here. Maybe his heir will."

I suppressed a cough. "I doubt it. The princess seems completely different from her father."

"I forget that you palace prudes are allowed to know her identity. Any chance you want to let me in on that secret?"

"Ha! You'll have to wait until she makes her debut, just like every other poor suitor."

"Me, a suitor? Did you hit your head too hard getting out of the carriage?"

"Shut up," I growl as he flicks my forehead, then scampers to safety only to bump into Commander Raiko. It takes all my willpower not to laugh as I watch the mercenary's usually suave demeanor crumble into embarrassment as he apologizes profusely to his senior. Rowan never seemed to be the type to care about ranking before, albeit he kept up the pretenses of titles around Lucius, but he has shown a deep-rooted respect for the commander this trip. Perhaps one killer knows another and respects honor over coin.

"How'd you even convince the king to let me come here?"

"Oh, I didn't." I raise an eyebrow. "Lucius did."

Stumbling, I right myself just before I can hit the stony path we walk on. Lucius? He got Lucius involved in this?

"It wasn't that difficult really. All I told him was that the waters here were said to have healing properties due to the magic of mages still being present. I thought that could help your little 'sickness.' Lucius was more than happy to help," Rowan speaks softly, a slight inflection of his voice during that last part drew my attention, but before I can ask about it, he's offering me his arm and nodding towards the cliffs. Begrudgingly, I accept while the guards stay behind to keep watch. The falls are secluded, with only one way in and out of the area we are. If anyone were to come, they'd have to come through the one path my guards are stationed at, giving Rowan and me time to set off alone for whatever plan he has.

Before long, small stones appear along the side of the path. These stones gradually grow larger, until they're the size of a small boulder, then there are clumps of them together. It takes only a moment to distinguish a ruined doorway and mapped out floor of a building. We're walking through the ruins of temples.

I can sense it stronger then, the thrumming in my blood. Rowan had mentioned something similar earlier, a feeling, but this was stronger than any feeling I'd ever had before by tenfold. It's as if the magic in my blood, however faint, is alive and trying to burn its way out of my veins. I gasp and grab at my heart. Rowan's hands shoot out to steady me, but no surprise shows on his face. Concern, yes, but it is as if he expected this to happen.

"Come, let's sit down for a moment." I follow him to the edge of the cliff and am about to make a quip about him pushing me off when he rolls out a mat and helps me down to sit.

"Careful now, we wouldn't want you falling for me." He winks, earning a pebble to the forehead. His laughter chases me as I stare down the edge of the cliff. Roaring waves crash against the base of the cliffs, breaking up rock and painting the water a murky green. Any trace of the village that used to reside there is long gone now, leaving only a king and unforgiving fall.

I shudder. "Don't even joke about those things. A fall from this height would kill us. Should we sit further back?" Rowan only rolls his eyes and kicks his legs out over the edge.

"Relax, Vera. I won't let you fall." He sounds so sincere that I find myself leaning back on propped up elbows beside him, allowing concern for death to fade. Instead, I focus on the steady thrum of magic simmering just beneath the surface of my skin. It has dulled slightly, enough to be just mildly uncomfortable.

It's silent for a moment, with only the whistling wind filling the uncomfortable silence as we stare back out at the waves. Rowan just watches quietly while I fiddle with my hands, unsure how to fill the time.

"So why did we actually come here?" I finally ask, and when he doesn't answer, I assume the wind has carried my words far from his ears, so I ask again. "I assume you have one of your famous ulterior motives."

"You have been acting strange lately," he whispers with a trace of mirth lingering in his voice.

I coo. "Aw, careful, it might sound like you care about me." Rowan only scoffs and tosses a pebble over the cliffside. I can't hear it land over the roar of the waves.

"Would that be so awful?"

"Hm?"

"If I cared about you?" Rowan's gaze turns to me now, inquisitive and piercing. The image of his face as I passed out earlier this week flashes across my mind, and I'm quick to push it down.

"Well, I suppose it wouldn't be the worst thing in the world." I elbow him lightly, then dig my fingers into the dirt to keep myself from teetering forward. Rowan laughs lightly, jumping away but never losing his balance.

"But really," he says after a moment of composing himself, "are you alright? I know Blaine and Torin finding out wasn't..."

"A part of your master plan?"

"I was going to say helpful." He eyes me sideways before falling silent. I take this as my cue to speak, but nothing comes out as I open my mouth. Where can I even start? How do I breach this conversation with someone who sits attached to my hip and yet feels so distant? 'Hey Rowan, I was in love with Blaine, and now he hates me, but I don't know if I care that he does anymore?'

Was. I *was* in love with Blaine.

The realization slams hard into my chest, and I find myself reeling and swallowing bile in my throat. When had I fallen out of love with him, was it when Emilie confirmed he still loved me? Am I really so spiteful that I'd fall out of love just in retaliation, or is it that I'd met someone who understood me? Someone who doesn't judge the blood on my hands or in my veins, nor deem me selfish for wanting more than this stifling life.

Silently, Rowan's hand wraps around my wrist.

"My mother was a beautiful woman," he starts suddenly, his emerald eyes darkening. "I remember when I was younger, she was probably the most beautiful woman I'd ever seen. She was radiant and kind to everyone. We never had much money, but that didn't matter. We were happy, and I had a father who came and went."

I inhale sharply. Rowan has never mentioned his father to me before. None of the Nightwalkers ever mentioned it, so I assumed I wasn't supposed to ask.

"Then one day something happened. I was young. I don't know what happened fully, but I remember this pull of dark magic and another woman with my father. I heard screams, laughter, then silence. I saw golden blood and felt my mother's arms wrap around me and she ran. She didn't take anything other than me, not that there was much to begin with, but we never saw him again. We lived in the shadows, and mother, who thrived in the light, began to waste away." He swallows hard. "She's nothing but a shell of who she used to be. My father stole that light from her."

The wind blows the hair from his face, and I see him in a new light for once. A scared boy forced to grow up too soon in a world of kill or be killed. That carefully crafted anger and sarcasm honed to perfection is meant to defend the scared child within. I move his hand from my wrist to my hand and squeeze it lightly.

"Your mom loves you very much. I didn't know her before all this, but that love keeps her going. Maybe you're her new light." *And maybe mine,* I add silently. Rowan's mouth softens into a small smile, and he nudges me with his shoulder. A bit of lilting laughter then a comfortable silence.

CHAPTER 17

ROWAN

Vera's shoulders loosen and fall as if some invisible tension has released its grip on her. The sight brings a small relief until she asks, "And what about you, Mister Mercenary? What about your wants and longings?"

"I don't long for anything," I correct her, not bothering to turn my face from where the brisk breeze scatters flecks of sea water across it. The tiny droplets are freezing and sting, but it's a welcome distraction. "I simply don't have the time. Things change, you either adapt or get left behind." It sounds false even to my ears.

She seems to consider that for a moment, and her gaze perceivably shifts from the ocean to me. From my peripheral, I can see she looks hesitant and curious, if not a bit wary.

"Out with it."

"I hate change," Vera spews out quickly, a slight slip of tongue that has her blushing to the tips of her ears.

"Oh? I didn't take you for the traditional type," I tease. She gives me a pointed look that only says 'you've offended me and my entire bloodline. Prepare to die.'

"I'm not I just... I need the comforts of consistency, " She explains with a heavy sigh, rocking forward to brace her elbows against her thighs. Her face in her hands. "I love having more freedom. That's been a welcome change, but it's still just daunting. Like I'm treading in unfamiliar waters. Like Blaine."

"Blaine is unfamiliar waters?"

"Yes and no. He was my best friend, and I think he still is, I'm just not sure. I see him and expect a hug or a joke or a soft smile, like he used to do. Now it's all 'Yes, my lady. No, my lady. Stop jumping out of windows, my lady.' I don't know how to blur the lines between then and now."

"And you miss him," I conclude, knowing full well how that feels. To miss someone right in front of you. To know you love them and hate who they've become. To hate the shell of them while you're scrambling for the pieces, desperately trying to glue them all back together again with your own blood.

Vera goes quiet for a moment. The world around us seems to respond, the clouds beginning to form above, the last streaks of golden sunlight weakly bathing her hair and face. The ocean calms to a dangerous, glass-like state, the wind whipping through the silky fabric of her blue dress. My breath hitches in my throat when she turns back to look at me. She gives me a soft sad smile that doesn't reach her eyes.

"I long for him in every still moment. Every time things get too quiet, he's there." A shuddering sigh. "When I can't outrun time, I yearn."

Ignoring the gentle pang in my chest, I prod forward. "Why don't you just tell him you're still in love with him then?"

Verosa sighs, tensing up once more as she fiddles with a blade of grass. She lifts her chin as if bracing against the truth, then says, "Because I don't. Not that way anymore, at least. Somewhere along the line, I gave up on something that died years ago, and I think I'm better for it."

Now it is my turn to keel forward in shock, not that I haven't noticed the subtle shifts in their interactions as of late. If he had pulled that little stunt back during training only a few months ago, Vera would have been a stumbling, blushing mess. Rather, a cool rage and bewilderment had coated her mannerisms the rest of the night and the next few missions she had been sent on. All of those missions had been wildly successful, so maybe I owed Blaine a thank you card or some flowers.

"So he's not the one you'd die for," I murmur, waiting for a reaction to this new piece of wisdom. Vera's face scrunches in confusion, and she tosses her hands in the air.

"Am I supposed to know what you mean by that?"

"My mother always told me there were two types of love, the type you would kill for, and the type you would die for. See, I would kill for any of the guys back home. Kya, Amír, Derrín, even Finneas and Aiko. It takes a special person to die for."

Vera considers this for a moment. "Would you die for your mother?"

"Of course."

The young pureblood nods pensively before stating plainly, "I wouldn't. My mother was a bitch, and I'm relieved she's dead." She looks up at my undoubtedly startled expression and asks, "Am I going to Hell for that?"

"If you're going to Hell, then I am definitely going wherever you religious people say is worse than Hell." The wind whistled sounding like a distant scream, and Vera laughs a bit, some of the light returning to her.

"She was awful. I don't ever remember her telling me she loved me, but I remember every lashing I'd receive when I'd 'embarrass' her in front of high society. She once brought out a riding whip, and I bled for days, or she would just start restricting my meals before large events. Meeting your mother was like a breath of fresh air."

My jaw goes slack in horror. The fact that someone as kind and lovely as Verosa could be subjected to such villainy from such a young age... An iron fist of rage wraps around my heart and squeezed it tightly. I open my mouth to offer consolation, but Vera holds up a hand to silence me.

"I don't want your pity."

"Then I won't give it," I amend with a small smirk. "Mavis might have schooled any pity from my heart years ago."

The words slip from between my lips before I can stop them, and despite this, the coming question still stings worse than the biting wind.

"Who is this Mavis?" Vera giggles softly to herself. "I mean, I know the whole sworn nemesis plotline from the others, but who is she to you?"

I brace myself against the brutal truth. How will Vera feel to know this, how will things change between us? Perhaps she will simply turn away, and it will not be entirely unjustified.

"She's my ex-fiancé."

Vera blinks once, then twice.

And then she laughs, and even though she's laughing at me, it feels as if every fiber of my being has been lit on fire. It's the way she throws her head back and doesn't hide the silver tears dripping down her cheeks. How raw and real she feels, and how something alive begins to stir in my cold chest.

I know now that if I could only hear one sound for the rest of eternity, it would be her laugh. Clear and sweet as sunlight reflecting on the ocean, it would be a blessing to never hear anything else again.

"Shut up," I say.

This only makes Vera laugh harder, clutching my forearm as she doubles over. Then it hits me, and I fight the urge to keel over myself. For all those burning touches, those shared moments of raw vulnerability, and the constellation of freckles across her cheek, her nose, and the lightness in my chest mean something. Something I have run from, a truth that I buried to avoid further wounds. Because the truth is that I have fallen in love with Verosa, and I know she deserves someone far greater than I could ever hope to become.

I cannot even say that a woman like Vera deserves better, because there is no other like her, and there never will be. Perhaps that is what I've feared the most all along, that for her there will be better men, but for me there will be no one else.

"I'm sorry." She wipes at her eyes with the back of her hand. "It's just of all the answers I expected... Wow."

"Wow? That's all you can say?"

"I mean what did you expect me to say? I thought this was just a turf war, but that's deeper and awful."

"Thank you for pointing that out." I groan and pinch the bridge of my nose. "I thought you'd be horrified or disgusted."

Vera peers out from underneath her bangs, her head quirked in a curious gesture that reminds me unflatteringly of a parrot. She would probably hit me if she were able to hear my thoughts.

"I had a relationship with the captain of the Guard and pined after him for years, and you're currently helping me run away from my fiancé. Why would I be horrified by your one failed relationships?"

A faint heat creeps its way up my neck, and I find myself turning my head away. Of course, Verosa wouldn't be disgusted. She's not Mavis. No, she's so much braver and kinder.

A thought fleets across my mind. Perhaps Derrín was right. Maybe Vera would stay with us if I asked her. Maybe, just maybe, she could be a Nightwalker.

"Vera, would you-"

I turn to her to find her doubling over in pain, her veins glowing faint beneath her skin. Her eyes are squeezed tightly shut, and her breaths coming out in short wheezing puffs.

"Vera? Verosa!"

The pureblood doesn't respond.

CHAPTER 18
VEROSA

The pain is incomparable to any other pain I've felt in my nineteen years of living. I had attempted to ignore the growing and searing pain as I spoke with Rowan, pleased to finally be able to unearth the human beneath the killer, but my bout of laughter sent hot pain shooting from my core through my limbs. It felt as if a fire had been lit, a fire which is now trying to burn me through.

Rowan flips me onto my back and swears vehemently. His hands pull back to reveal burn marks. I *burned* him.

Regardless, I feel his arms loop under my knees and arms before we are walking, no, running away from the cliffside. The smell of smoke fills my nostrils as Rowan sprints, but he grits his teeth and continues.

"What is happening to me?" I rasp between dry and cracking lips. My eyes swell shut until I can't see the friend holding me anymore.

"Good news, my theory was correct. Bad news, you're dying."

"What theory, you asshole!" I hiss as the searing pain reaches my head. The scent of charred human flesh floods my nostrils, and a slight rumbling begins to appear.

"I'll explain in a minute." He groans. "Hold your breath!" Deciding not to argue due to both pain and fatigue, I inhale one last time right before I hear a splash and a coolness washing over my body. The swelling of my body dies down enough for me to open my eyes. Rowan and I are underwater. His chest and arms are red and bubbling with blisters from carrying me, but I watch in shock as the skin slowly knits itself back together, and his burns heal. Slowly the heat in my body rescinds, and I'm left feeling nothing but the cool water around me.

We breach the surface moments later, a wild fear and guilt plaguing Rowan's tense features. We both sputter for breath, and his wet hair splatters across his forehead.

"What fucking theory, you jerk." I shove hard against his chest, sending us both back under the water as I disentangle our limbs. His eyebrows furrow, and he jumps up immediately.

"You have magic."

I'm left blindly stuttering at that. "I don't know what you're talking about."

He snarls lowly. "Don't lie to me Vera, we're beyond that."

A retort fights its way up my throat, but I'm quick to swallow it. Any progress we had made only a few moments before is destroyed with a few simple words. I wasn't brought here for anything other than Rowan's personal motives, as per usual. I was foolish to think that anything could change.

"It's nothing more than a party trick." I wait for Rowan to nod his head before diving to the bottom of the natural pool and grabbing a handful of silt. The water smooths out the edges of my anger. Perhaps it contains both sedatives and healing properties. I stay under the water a moment more until I feel the desire to strangle Rowan subside enough to emerge back into the open.

"You were down there a while." The urge returns.

Nonetheless, I lead him to a shallow point of the lake, where I don't have to continue to tread water. The mercenary follows, shaking his hair out like some giant wet dog. The droplets platter across my face, and if he hadn't just saved my life, I would've smacked him.

Though he did put it in danger in the first place, for whatever this theory was.

Some of the silt escapes my hands as my fingers unfurl, and Rowan watches unamused as I lift my palms skyward. Taking a deep steadying breath, I feel deep into my core, reaching for the magic that threatened to burn me alive only moments before. For a moment, fear grips my heart, if I burn up again...

The gentle waves of the lake and rumble of the waterfall behind us steadies my hands, and I breathe deeply. Rowan watches intently as I latch onto the magic and siphon it into the silt.

"*Lumis.*"

Immediately, a dull glow forms, but it's not enough. I reach into myself again and push the magic to flow through my veins, enhanced by my pureblood blessings, and let it flow freely from my hands into the silt. Slowly, it is no longer silt in my hands, but glowing specs of light that float forwards into the air.

More. I push the lights higher, until they float around us of their own accord, some going as far as to stick in Rowan's hair and across his face. We wade deeper out into the water, the lights fluttering slowly. I'm sure many are stuck in my hair now and laugh to myself. Rowan's face is a mixture of horror and wonder as the lights bob gently against the water or our skin before drifting into the air again.

Slight steam begins to form around my hands as the water dries. Too much, I was using too much all at once. I rarely used this gift in the palace, Irene's warnings of what would happen if people learned that I had these powers still stark in my mind. Her deep, violet eyes stare into my heart, and the lights extinguish all at once, and the lights turn back into dirt before falling to the ground.

"Vera?"

"Does that prove your theory?" I pant, my limbs suddenly heavy and hanging by my side like lead. The fatigue seeps deep into my bones, and I swim back to shore before I drown. The thrum of power beneath my skin dulls, content with being released.

I turn to lay on my back, still in the shallow water. I can't say I'm particularly mad at Rowan. I should have expected there to be some convoluted scheme behind this trip, but a heavy disappointment still settles in my chest. I thought we'd come far enough to consider ourselves friends, and yet, I feel like no more than a stepping stone for him to achieve his own goals.

The water ripples, and I can hear a slight sloshing before Rowan settles next to me, following suit and laying sprawled out on his back.

He folds his hands across his chest and stares skywards, as if he could still see the lights floating around us in the dying daylight.

"I never thought it would hurt you." He lifts his arms to show his burns fully healed, but his white tunic is still charred from where my burning skin had scorched him. "There's so little information written on people like you that I just didn't know. I thought it didn't have any repercussions, unlike dark magic. I guess I wasn't thinking realistically."

His hair floats around his face as if in a golden halo. Compared to my dark and angular features, I think he looks more like a pureblood than I do. In this light, he is the spitting image of Emilie.

"I was trying to help you. The only thing I could find in the library on the pureblood mages is that if they went without using their magic for prolonged periods of time, the magic would burn them up from inside. When I started seeing those signs in you, like your eyes faintly glowing during training, or this raw aura of power that seems to follow you, I... I wanted to spare you from that fate. I thought this would awaken the magic enough for a release; I never would have brought you here if I had known what would happen. I would've found another way."

We don't look at each other, but I can still feel the lingering question in the air. How would things shift after today? With both this knowledge of my magic being greater than I'd thought and Rowan suddenly behaving like a decent human, it feels like the earth is being pulled out from beneath my feet. But in the end, he had been honest, something that is rare in my life these days.

I close my eyes. "You're lucky I'm too exhausted to punch you."

Rowan's laughter sends waves through the small pool that splashes up against the sides of my face. "I suppose I should be relieved."

I hum, the weariness in my bones settling deep now as I fight the urge to doze off. If this was only the surface of my power and using it drained me this much, I can't imagine how exhausting the full extent of my magic could be. Gift of the Pureblood my ass.

"So what do we do now? Where do we go from here?" I finally ask, propping myself up on my elbows. Rowan stands first before offering me a hand. He glances pointedly towards the sky, where I find storm clouds swelling on the horizon.

"We go back to the carriage, get you a change of dry clothes, and keep digging. There's got to be something on the mages that wasn't destroyed that we could use to help you. If you could harness this power, then we could save you from any future burnouts, and you wouldn't need to worry about protecting yourself on the run anymore." I wring my skirts out as we walk and dry my dagger before it rusts. Rowan was being uncharacteristically positive about this situation, considering we both just learned I was a walking weapon. Or savior. I hope the day never comes where I'm forced to choose. Will I destroy this world or be the one to save it? To kill or to die, Rowan had said.

Raiko laughs upon seeing our sorry state, both of us drenched and quite miserable looking. Rowan's excuse of the healing waters for my 'sickness' covers the true reason for our state. The last thing I need is my father or Lucius to find about my powers or burnout.

"Feeling better, my lady?" Raiko bows deeply while a squire hands me a parcel with a fresh dress in it. I nod gratefully and slip off to change. I sigh contently. nothing feels better than dry clothes after being soaked. These little luxuries are what keep me from running away from the palace permanently. That and the fact that there are now two villains rather than one.

Raiko shuts the door behind Rowan after he settles into the carriage, freshly changed as well. Thankfully, his coat covers the charred white tunic, and the falls healed any wounds I had inflicted upon him.

"Thanks, by the way," I offer into the dark of the carriage, "for helping me. And I'm sorry for burning you."

Rowan offers a crooked grin. "I had it coming. Try and get some rest."

Rest would seem impossible if I hadn't just used all my energy on a foolish light show. Rowan cracks open a book he brought, continuing to research as my eyelids begin to droop. The steady prattle of the wheels and hooves on gravel slowly lull me into a fitful sleep.

CHAPTER 19
VEROSA

The low whinny of a horse and a distant shout startle me from my sleep. The lights of our transport have been snuffed out and the curtains drawn. I slept long enough for the dark to fully settle around us, and fear wraps its fist around my heart. I'm about to beg for a light when Rowan raises a single finger to his lips. The motion sends a chill down my spine. Something is not right.

The carriage suddenly stops with a jolt, knocking me from the seat. Quick and sturdy hands find my shoulders, and I look up with a blush to find Rowan staring at me with concern.

"Fine. I'm fine," I say, but he is already looking through the curtained window. The silken drapes brush back just enough that I can just barely see the outlines of dark trees but nothing more. I lean forward to peak through, only to be met with a heavy force against my chest. Rowan throws his body over my own right as the first arrow shatters through the window, planting itself in the carriage wall I was leaning moments before. Where that arrow would have gone right through my eye.

Rowan swears. There's a slight trickle of blood running down his tricep, grazed by the arrow meant for me. I reach out for it, but he brushes off my concern, dragging out multiple hidden knives and a sword from under the cushions of the carriage. Firmly, one fine and wicked blade is pressed into my open hands. Its edge is serrated and cruel. The type of blade that lusts for blood and carnage. The rest of the arsenal of weaponry is strapped to him as he stands. Another volley of arrows slams against the carriage, rocking it.

"No matter what you hear, no matter what happens you are to stay in this carriage. Understood?" He groans, rolling out his injured shoulder. "This is a coordinated ambush. These men don't care if they have to steal, murder, or rape for what they want. You let me and the guards handle this. And stay hidden. If anyone comes at you, you slash first and ask questions later. Got it?"

"Absolutely not." I stand up, furious. "You've sent me on all these missions. I know how to fight. You need me out there."

Rowan shoves my shoulders hard, forcing me down into my seat. His gaze is unreadable as he looks me over one last time. Then I recognize it. Panic. Because if this was coordinated, then our assailants are here for me.

"I need you to stay safe. The others don't know you can fight either, it would jeopardize our whole mission. I know you can handle yourself, but sit this one out. I'll be back soon."

I can only nod dumbly, panic dulling my senses, filling my eardrums to the point where I can barely comprehend or hear his words. Barely hear them. But my fear is not for myself. It for him.

"Remember your training." Is the only form of goodbye I get before he flings himself from the hidden doors under the carriage. The sounds of fighting grow louder as I bolt the side doors shut, the lowly feeling of cowardice suddenly setting itself deep within my bones. *No*, I try to remind myself through short breaths. *I am not a coward, I am following orders. I can't risk the greater mission, and I can't risk Rowan worrying about me. I'd only be a distraction, one that could get the mercenary killed.*

So instead, I clutch that cruel dagger close to my chest, my heart pounding wildly against it. Stay in the carriage. The carriage with a broken window during an ambush. Seems an easy enough task. Just wait for the slaughter to finish, and go home. This isn't real, this is just another one of Blaine's drills. When this is all over, he's going to pop out from behind the trees and laugh at me with those flaming iron eyes watering before tearing into his men over some minuscule error. Somewhere in the near distance I can hear someone cry out, and suddenly everything becomes very real.

Rowan. It could be Rowan.

I stand suddenly, the carriage rocking. My first mistake. They had thought the carriage to be empty now. But I don't care. He could be hurt or worse. I don't notice the smoke filling the compartment until it's to my nose. Until I'm coughing and gagging and blind. Not until a large, leather-clad hand reaches up through that trap door in the bottom and pulls me down.

The scream that tears loose from my throat is cut off when my head slams against a carriage bench, and I see stars as my partially limp body is dragged from the compartment. My fingers loosened around the hilt of my blade as I fall; it clatters to the side as I begin to slip through the opening. At the last second, I manage to pull it with me, slashing blindly into the smoke. A faint and wicked chuckle is the only response I receive.

The gravel bites into my stinging palms as I grapple for any foothold, anything to hold onto. To stop this. For, in my blind terror, any semblance of training Rowan might have worked to instill evades me.

The smoke. It's the smoke, they had laced it with some sedative or drug before setting it upon me. My senses fog over more, increasing the effects of the concussion I have undoubtedly received through that fall.

If I was only at full strength. If only I hadn't burned out earlier. If only I hadn't been drugged or concussed. All of it is pointless now,

As soon as I'm free from underneath our carriage, those same rough hands hook under my arms, hauling me unceremoniously to my feet. It's then that I blindly slash one more time, my vision still dazed and doubled. A sick crunch and a cry of pain and anger confirms that I did hit something, and so does the swift punch to my jaw. My head reels once more. One arm wraps around my torso, and the other grapples for my blade, then tosses it out of my reach.

Looking up, I'm able to see a thick bearded face and black beady eyes staring in the distance. We start to move. I flinch my gaze away as he stares back.

Someone shouts my name in the distance. I spare a moment to look out at the scene through heavy lids, and we're losing. Badly. Only Rowan and the captain are still cutting through opponents as if they are nothing but smoke and mist and shadow. It was one of the younger knights who had shouted my name and paid for it with his life. I cry out at the sight of a jagged blade puncture through his sternum, then drag down to his navel. I have to force myself to look away as his entrails begin to pour from the laceration. He is still screaming as they drive the blade through his skull next. A sickening crunch of bone and iron and flesh.

Rowan's face is that of a warrior, and I had almost forgotten that beneath all his wit and charm, this is the world he grew up in. The filthy streets, fighting for his safety and his mother's. A beautiful face hiding the killer beneath, willing to do what has to be done.

That same face turns towards where the dead soldier had cried out, his cooling finger still pointing towards where I am being dragged away with a dagger to my throat. Wild fear enters his eyes before it is smothered by icy and unforgiving rage. I can still see two of him as he runs closer, sword out, slashing through opponents as if they were nothing more than clay. Despite the various wounds I see littering his body, no one touches him now. The sight brings some sense back to me. Our eyes meet in confirmation. I will fight. I know how to fight.

My head slams into my assailant's so hard I see stars, and I know I'm only worsening my injuries, but I grit my teeth. I don't waste the moment as the momentum of the swing takes him off his balance. With his knife no longer baring down on my throat, I hook my foot around the back of his knee and pull. The man falls heavily, buying just a second for my escape. I make to run as Rowan comes closer, but the man's free arm juts out and grabs my own, pulling me down with him. I spin, narrowly avoiding his waiting blade.

Too far. Rowan is still too far.

We grapple in the dirt, my damned skirts getting in the way as I try to kick and fight. My assailant notices and flips me so I'm pinned beneath him. His knees are braced on either side of my hips, dagger held high above my heart.

"Pica a rebvela!" he cries.

For the rebellion.

I brace myself for the steel to bury itself in my heart. A whisper of prayer to Deun, *make it quick.*

The sweet sting of death never comes. Something warm and sticky splatters against my bare arms. My face and my raised hands.

Daring to open my eyes, the commander stands above me now, kicking the headless corpse aside and grabbing the dagger before it can fall into me.

"*Mei Reinhavich*, are you hurt?" He grips my arms, his gaze inspecting. Vigorously, I shake my head despite the pounding in it and the shallow cuts lacing my palms and back. None of it is serious, not compared to the deep gash that runs over his own eyelid down to his jaw.

"I'll take her, Raiko." Rowan answers now, having slain the last few villains in his way. Without waiting for confirmation, he grabs my arm and pulls me to his side, setting off again towards the carriage.

"I told you to stay in the carriage."

"If you couldn't tell I didn't have much of a say in the matter." I retort, though I duck behind his arm as he reaches out to parry against another attack. They battle it out for a moment, with me pressed against his blood-soaked back. I can't tell if it's his or not. Maybe it's mine.

"It doesn't matter now." He groans as he delivers the killing blow. More blood sprays across us both. So much blood. "We need to get you out of here."

We are at the carriage now. I spy my missing blade by the front wheel and duck to pick it up, coming face to face with a rebel attacker. I scream and drive my foot into his face before I realize he's already dead. Rowan spins from where he works on one of the horses' harnesses, cutting it loose and leading it over.

"I'm not leaving without you," I protest. It is one thing to hide, another to run.

"You don't have a choice," he growls as he grabs my waist, those same steady and gentle hands lifting me up onto the bare back of that gray mare. I shriek at him to put me down, but he doesn't answer. Just slaps the mare's rump with a small smile that says, 'I'll come back for you.' Some deep tug in my heart tells me he won't.

The mare startles forward, from a dead halt to a canter, and then into a frantic gallop. I try to pull on her mane, willing her to stop, to turn around, to bring him back with me. But I've always been a mediocre rider, even with tack. Now here, riding bareback and completely exhausted... it's all I can do to stay on. My legs slide back, my rear coming off her back. I bury my fist in her mane and clamp my legs down with my sore muscles barking with pain at the effort.

We make it maybe fifty feet into the woods before I'm tackled from the back of my horse. She squeals and rears before running down the path we were on. The jagged stones and twigs stab into my bare back, tearing open flesh and stealing the air from my lungs.

"You run," he grunts, his voice younger than the other man. His deep brown hood falls back to reveal only wide eyes rimmed with hate.

"You run like a coward while foolish men stay and die for you. Are their lives worth less than yours?" He hisses through clenched teeth, his hands wrapping themselves around my neck. I gasp as he squeezes harder with each word.

"N- no." Searing tears burn my eyes and cheeks as red starts to cloud my vision. I'm going to die. I'm going to die in these woods, a hateful coward. And those soldiers. They died for nothing.

"Don't waste your tears on me," he says reaching back. I note how his hands shake. Something dark glints in his hands. I force myself to stare him in the eye, praying for some glimpse of humanity. "I will enjoy feeling your heart stop against my blade."

"Don't." I try with my last breath. A plea.

Too late. The rebel raises his blade and plunges it down.

Then his jaw slackens, his eye wide with terror as I ram my blade into his gut, his own still hovering above me. He begins to fall over, removing his other hand from my throat as he slips.

I catch him in my arms, unable to stop the tears as they flow freely now. He gasps, open mouthed as I hold him, lowering him onto the ground.

"Shh, it's alright," I murmur. "It's all going to be okay."

"F-for me. But not... not for you." He spits on my face. I don't bother to wipe it away. "You will rue the day your wicked flesh fails you. When you rot to hell, I'll be waiting. We *all* will be waiting." And as if that last curse, a promise, took all that was left of his life, he fell limp in my arms. With trembling fingers, I brush his hood back, the hair from his eyes. With a startled cry, I drop my hand as if burned. He was probably about fifteen years old. So young. So hateful. And so dead. Dead by my own blood crusted hands.

I can't find it in myself to drop him, to let him rest in the arms of the Laei. So I hold him. And weep bitterly. As if, by mourning him whole-heartedly enough, my tears can wash his blood from my hands. As if some blessing of my blood I could heal him. But I had checked, and he bled silver. I could only poison him further.

CHAPTER 20
VEROSA

I'm not sure how long I sat there and cried, nor do I know when the rain started. Only that it did. At some point, I think I hear a wolf howl in the distance, but I only held the boy closer and pray that it will kill me too. His family deserves something to bury.

One large hand rests on my shoulder, the other clamps down on my mouth. I nearly scream, but a pitiful croak emits instead.

"Don't make a sound, there could be... oh." My heart stops pounding. That voice. Devoid of any charm or clever banter, all replaced by dread and tiredness. Nevertheless, I know that voice. I look up to find Rowan staring down at me with something like the fading of fear and newfound relief in his eyes. Until sympathy overpowers them both.

"I- I killed him."

"Vera... oh, fucking hell!" Rowan jumps back as I keen over and vomit all over his shoes. I sink to my knees, retching in the filth and blood of my sin. I close my eyes, but he's there, his lifeless eyes staring back into mine. I can see his soul draining from him, all because of me. I stole his life. I murdered him.

"Murderer. Murderer!" I cry out, sobbing into my hands. My chest is tight, my face streaked with dirt and blood.

"Vera." Rowan sinks down with me, ignoring my pool of bile. "Look at me."

I can't. The metallic scent of blood hangs thick in the air. It clings to me. It knows what I did. My balled fists shake uncontrollably at my side when I feel one of Rowan's hands close over both of them. His other hand is holding me up by my shoulders, and I feel his pulse through his grip.

"Look at me," he commands, and this time I oblige. Gone is his all-knowing smirk, his eyes shrouded but soft. It's the most vulnerable I've seen him. That alone scares me.

Slowly, he brings my fists to my chest, holding them above my heart. It beats a little quicker, but it's as sure as ever. I begin to shake harder now, but Rowan won't let me fall. That boy a few feet away from me, he had a heartbeat too.

"I murdered him."

"No. You survived."

"But I still killed him!"

"And he would have killed you with no such regret." His eyebrows furrow in fervor, and I notice he grips me a bit tighter now, with newfound conviction. It's as if his own words are sinking in for him. I'd almost died. Somehow that fact had been lost on me.

"It should have-"

"Don't," he growls, gripping my shoulders so tightly I cry out. His hands immediately drop to his sides. "Don't say it should have been you. Don't you ever think for a second that it would be better that way."

He says it with such ferocity that my heart begins to slow, and by some miracle, I start to believe him. My sight begins to focus again, drifting towards that boy. That body. The mist starting to rise from it, when Rowan's fingers hook under my chin.

"Don't look." he whispers. His voice tender yet still holding that same commanding presence. So I don't. I look at him instead. I've never noticed before how green his eyes truly are, dashing emerald swirling with chartreuse eddies and whorls of shamrock. Deep golden flecks highlight in speckles along his iris, and if I look hard enough I can see tinges of deep blue warming the depths of his gaze. My gaze drops to his sturdy and straight nose, his strong jawline and chilled cheekbones. A light and faded scar grazes right below his ear down towards his neck, and I shudder to think of what could've caused it.

Incidents like tonight perhaps, I muse once I notice he's bleeding. A deep gash along his forearm drips crimson blood, tinged with gold and...

Silver.

"You... you're a..."

"Hybrid. Yes." He breathes, his smooth voice crystallizing in the air in front of us. My fingers ghost the wound where both silver and gold blood trickle forth. Hybrid. Rowan is a Hybrid.

Hybrids who are illegal due to their mostly unknown abilities. Hybrids are more powerful than the blessed and the cursed because they had the body of the blessed, the mind of the cursed, and no such boundaries that withhold them from practicing dark magic. Everything suddenly makes sense.

"Does it scare you?" he whispers.

I pause for a moment, then look up at him with a smile. "No."

Rowan's shoulders sag, and his jaw unclenches. His hands fall heavy by his sides, and he lets his eyes close. With staggering steps, he takes my hands and guides me further through the forest.

"Are the rebels..."

"Dead." Rowan grits his teeth. "But we need to keep moving, more will come along when they don't return either with you or a report."

"What did they want with me?"

Rowan eyes me sideways, as if asking if I really want to know. My firm glare and slight dip of my chin seems to convince him.

"To kill you to make a point. Couldn't you tell when they tried to stab you at every chance they got?"

"Can you stop acting like a prick for five seconds and just answer the question?" Rowan grunts and drops my hand, allowing me to lag behind. Perhaps calling the person leading me from the dark a prick isn't my wisest idea.

"Well?"

"Most of them were cursed."

"Most?"

"Some blessed choose to fight with them. They too believe our system is... outdated." He chooses his words carefully as he slowly begins to rise, dragging me with. Crunch. My ankle tweaks beneath my weight, and I slip back down to the ground.

"I must've hurt it during the fight." It seems like a trivial thing to complain about after everything. The image of that young knight pops into my mind, dead and cold upon the ground.

"Lean on me," he grunts, hauling me back to my feet with a wince. I move to protest. His arm... but he just shoots me a glare, telling me to hold my tongue. There's no use arguing with him. Not like this.

But his arm.... There's so much blood. Too much blood. It soaks through his shirt into the pale blue gossamer of my gown, dripping on the ground as we walk. His gaze traces mine to that hideous wound, and he swears softly under his breath.

"This will lead a trail." He curses again.

"We should go back to the carriage. Maybe the commander will..."

"The commander is dead, Verosa." He shrugs me off, leaving me to wobble on my own weight. My shoulder barks in pain as I stumble against a nearby tree, holding onto it as the world spins. No, the commander is fine. We just spoke back when I...

Back when I left him behind. Outnumbered in the fray of the fight. When I ran like a coward and killed the person to call me out on it.

"I shouldn't have run," Rowan says then, as if reading my thoughts perfectly as he so often does. "The minute I heard you scream, I ran. I didn't look to see if the commander or any of the men needed help. I ran right for you. Raiko might still be alive if I hadn't."

"No-"

"Yes, Vera."

"Stop interrupting me!" I finally explode, the world still spinning. "My Laei, you think you know everything, you insufferable ass! I can hardly get a word in without you correcting me, so for once, just shut the fuck up. These men didn't die because of you. They died because someone killed them. If I were in your position, you would've told me I was just following orders. You were ordered to protect me, just like I was ordered to run. So stop moping on that rock, and let me bandage that goddamn wound."

Silence. Pure and smothering silence.

Before laughter.

Raucous, unfiltered, and wild laughter. Rowan clutches his stomach, doubling over and clutching his wounded arm, but he still laughs. The rain continues to pour, streaking down his tan face, making him look like one of those men from Tanja's romance novels. His saturated hair clings to his forehead, his full brows.

Then I begin to laugh too. Maybe it's delirium or fever from the rain. I don't care. I laugh and laugh and laugh until it breaks into sobs. Hiccupping sobs between shattered breaths and spinning trees. Too fast, everything in this life moves too fast.

I make to step forward when my face is buried in a strong chest, firm arms encircling my waist, pulling me closer to him. The scent of ocean and leather and citrus floats to me, swallows me whole. Rowan's broad chin rests atop my head, encouraging me to bury my face in the soaked leather of his vest. I oblige, and we rest there for a moment. The world slows to an even halt eventually, and I spare a few seconds more before I pull back. His groans in protest but stops when I bend down and tear what's left of the bottom of my gown clean off, baring to just above my knees.

Rowan watches me with curious eyes as I wind the cloth around the wound, pulling tight with expert hands. I pause only when he winces, but a subtle nod of encouragement has me finishing the bandage. He takes a moment to inspect it before nodding his approval.

"Where'd you learn to tie a bandage like that?" He flexes his arm, and I pretend not to notice the way his firm muscles coil and strain against the cotton of his shirt.

"I'm a good for nothing brat who likes to cause trouble, remember?" Faint color blooms in those high cheeks as he recalls what he called me when we first met. "I learned quickly to clean up my messes."

"Ah, I guess I did say that." He cringes as we stomp onwards. The rain continues its onslaught, thoroughly soaking us as if we're still in that pond, though this water sends a chill through my bones. Even Rowan, who I am convinced is a human heater, begins to shiver. The one good thing I can say for the storm is that the floods cover our tracks, and the occasional lightning strike illuminates the path as it shatters against the sky.

"Where are we going?" I dare not to speak above a whisper at this point, and I cling close to Rowan as the trees thicken, blocking out any light. If he notices the way my face is practically pressed into his back, he plays the part of the gentleman for once and doesn't make a sarcastic remark.

"There's an inn nearby in my territory. Once we get there, we should be safe from Mavis and the rebels, and I will send out a clean-up crew to gather the bodies for the rebels to bury."

I ignore the way my gut churns at the word 'bodies.'

"Clean-up crew? You mean there's more Nightwalkers than just the four of you?" I ask incredulously. Rowan just turns back to me with open mouthed disbelief.

"Does the king only govern those in the palace? I have my own underlings Ver. Who the hell do you think covered your first mission as a bar fight after you came home with my dying second before you passed out yourself? Stunts like that are expensive and require manpower."

"My apologies, My Liege," I seethe between clenched teeth. Hot tears of pain and fear begin to slide their way down my face, blending in with the torrential downpour. My wounds throb, my ankle is barely supporting my weight anymore, and I rely heavily on Rowan's shaking form to keep up.

We remain silent as we walk, until a dim light starts to form up ahead. The sight causes me to pick up my pace and ignore my stabbing pains. Rowan subconsciously does as well, and we both half walk, half run towards the light and find ourselves in front of an inn in Adil.

Adil is still far enough out that no one bats an eye at Rowan and I's bloody and filthy bodies, though they do gawk at my bare calves. If I had half my strength regained, I would shake them until their tiny brains came out their nose and scream at them about priorities, but Rowan clutches my hand in his as we trudge to the inn.

"Stick close, and follow my lead," he whispers under his breath. "Not everyone here is mine, so hold your tongue."

I can only swallow thickly as the lion leads me directly into his den.

CHAPTER 21
VEROSA

Rowan stalks to the front desk, where the innkeeper sleeps. His face contorts with disgust for a moment before he announces loudly in a wail, "Please, kind soul, my wife and I were on our way here when we were robbed by merciless thugs. I barely fought them off, but she's quite shaken. Please take pity on two pour souls."

Refraining from laughing in a state of delirium is a true testament to my acting skills, and I allow my lower lip to wobble bit. A few patrons look on in pity or disgust, but the innkeeper schools his countenance of a savvy businessman once the shock of being startled awake wears off.

"I don't know, how much coin do you have to offer?"

"23 coins."

"Gold or silver?"

"17 silver, 5 gold."

"Gold might be a trouble around these parts."

"That's why I'm entrusting you with it," Rowan counters quickly.

The innkeeper sighs. "And who should I book the room under?"

"Leo and Marie."

The innkeeper scribbles all this down furiously before handing a different sheet of paper to Rowan. The young man, far too young to be an innkeeper, leans over the desk and speaks lowly. "I'll send this on to our most trusted crew. They won't say a word." He presses a key into Rowan's palm. "Usual room, I'll send for the doctor tonight and some horses in the morning. I assume you'll be out of here before they follow you."

Rowan accepts the key as if it is a mere handshake. "Good man." The innkeeper only grunts and stalks off silently through a door behind the counter without accepting any money. Rowan holds my hand tightly and guides me up the first few stairs, but when he is sure no one is watching, he takes a sharp left into a broom closet.

"Well, this is cozy," I jest while he takes to pushing aside some meager cleaning supplies. He doesn't bother with a response before he pushes a particular stone, causing the whole wall to slide and reveal a large room.

"You were saying?" Rowan responds drily.

The room is large, with two large beds on either side of the room. Each are lavishly decorated with a multitude of colorful pillows and embroidered throw blankets. The walls are coated with hand-painted designs, minuscule whorls of pearlescent gold paint that stretches like veiny webs across the entirety of the room. A plush carpet greets my feet as I remove my muddy boots, and Rowan settles on a chair seated next to a matching mahogany table.

"The bathroom is right through those doors if you'd like to wash up before the doctor arrives." Rowan winces as he bends over to untie his boots.

"Let me." I bend before him, untying his laces swiftly and helping remove the filthy boot. Rowan watches silently, his motions stiff and lagging.

I rock back on my heels, even the small motion draining all remaining energy from my body. Adil is a half day's ride from the palace. We will probably have to leave by first light to avoid attracting attention and to beat the scouts my father will undoubtedly send out once news reaches him.

Torin will probably be with them, possibly Blaine as well, but I doubt it. Blaine is needed to stay at the palace and guard my father, but no force will dare stop Torin if any of us are thought to be in danger.

"Are you alright?" Is the only slightly intelligible thing that comes to mind as I try to fill the silence. Rowan's labored breathing causes a physical pain in my chest. I know he must have gone through much worse to collect the scars I've seen him wear proudly, but still, I did this. I did this.

Rowan laughs a bit. "Never been better, sunshine."

I can't find anything to laugh about in the moment. My lower lip quivers, and my shoulders cave in on themselves. No tears fall, but dry sobs wrack my chest. Torin was right, all of this happened because of one greedy princess.

Rowan moves with a speed I didn't think he could still possess and wraps his arms around my wet and shaking frame. It is stiff, his motions not as languid as before, just another reminder of the pain I've caused him.

"Why did you come back?" I dare not say anything above a rasping whisper for fear my voice may betray me. "Why would you come for me?"

Rowan's arms fall from my shoulders to encircle my waist, his head now resting heavily on his shoulders. Why would he have done it? He could've died. He could've...

"I couldn't stop myself." He drew in a ragged breath. "I heard your screams, and I... I couldn't stop myself from running to you. Couldn't help but think that if something happened I- I'd never forgive myself."

He lifts his head from my shoulder.

"Because you make this sort of life bearable, Vera. And I want you, no, I *need* you," he brings his lips close to mine, "to stay."

To stay, with him and Kya, Amír, Derrín. To be a Nightwalker. A home, someone to stay.

But do I deserve this?

My body shudders, cold against his own- warm and slick with blood. His blood. He lowers his hand from my face, silent understanding passing between us. It's enough to make me sob again.

"I'm s-sorry," I blubber between blood-encrusted lips. The words taste metallic. "I just can't right now, not with his blood on me."

Blood-crusted hair falls loose around my face, a personal curtain between Rowan and me. I can't bear it, not the look of pity or disgust he probably wears. Not the disappointment.

But rather, a calloused hand grips my own, a second raising up to my jaw. He hooks his finger under my chin, gently raising my gaze to his own. To my shock, I find only deep and unwavering understanding.

"Don't ever apologize to me. Not for that." My throat constricts as he lowers his hand again, but he still grips mine, his thumb tracing lazy circles across the back of it.

"I will wait for you."

His gaze drops to my hand as he holds it, then slowly he raises it to his lips, stopping just close enough that his breath scatters across the top. His emerald green eyes lift up again to meet mine, a request.

"May I?"

A small smile tries to tug at the corners of my mouth as I nod my head and whisper a "yes." Rowan seems to notice because he smiles into the kiss he presses atop my hand.

His lips feel exactly how I imagined them, soft and gentle, yet a silent hunger lurks beneath them. My faces flushes a light pink as I imagine what it will feel like for those lips capture my own. I've dreamt of it, I want that so desperately, but I just can't. Not now. I hate to ask this of him, but he will wait, I know it, even if it kills him.

There's a soft knock at the door, assumably more for our comfort than announcing herself given there is no real door, not from the outside. The doctor steps in, her hair pinned tightly to her scalp in such a way that pulls all of her pretty features into a tight countenance. Her thin lips press firmly together as she lays her equipment out across the mahogany table. She begins to sanitize her tools with no glimpse of a smile or small talk.

She moves towards Rowan first, but he shakes his head and motions for me to take a seat. I oblige as she begins to assess my visible wounds.

"You will have to take that dress off."

Rowan promptly excuses himself from the room.

The doctor's skilled hands are cold as she lays them against my mottled skin. Occasionally she will tut to herself or scribble something on a scrap sheet of paper. She makes no comment on my blood.

After a while she finally deduces that my wounds are not horribly severe, mostly a few shallow cuts and deep bruises. The smoke I inhaled won't cause any issues. However, slamming my head into the carriage benches left me with a nasty concussion. She advises that I avoid any strenuous activities, jarring motions, loud noises, bright lights, and reading for a few weeks.

"Thank you."

She dismisses me to the bath with a disinterested flick of her wrist and goes to fetch Rowan from the broom closet, where he has been hiding this whole time. I scoff slightly at the slight but forget my offense as soon as I spot the pristine bathtub in the center of the room.

It is almost cathartic, watching the multicolored blood streak and run in muddy whorls from my limbs. Within moments, the once clear water is a ruddy brown, and I haven't even dunked my head under the water. I empty the basin and refill it again, and then twice more before the water runs clear, and I step out. A fluffy towel sits on the edge of the sink, and I run it across my skin and hair, frowning when it comes back clean. It doesn't feel right, to take a life and not have to be stained with his blood for life. But would he have felt the same if it was my body they would find in the morning?

For once I wouldn't mind Tanja scrubbing the skin from my bones and coating my face with paints until I can't recognize myself. The feeling of looking in the mirror now is comparable.

When I step out from the bathroom, now clean and dressed in a soft nightgown, the doctor is finishing a final stitch on the arrow wound Rowan took for me. He withholds a wince as she ties the final knot and nods her head. The mercenary king presses a few gold pieces in her hand and mumbles a thanks before she takes her leave.

Catching my stare, Rowan winks. "I'm going to bathe unless you've used all the hot water. Try not to think about me too hard, you've got to take care of that concussion, Ver."

My cheeks burn with indignation, and he laughs before closing the door with a soft snick behind him. Prick.

I claim the bed furthest from the door. Rowan may trust these people, but my nerves have been set on edge. However, it is hard to stay irritated or anxious as my skin touches the soft silk sheets.

"Seriously?" I scoff. "How filthy rich is this moron?" From an inexhaustible supply of horses, owning multiple taverns and inns, to such luxurious private rooms and free-flowing gold coins, Rowan's wealth must be comparable to the king's. I suppose he is called the King of Mercenaries for a reason.

The sounds of footsteps and dripping water emits from the bathroom as I burrow deeper into the covers. There is so much Rowan I must talk about still, his confession, my own feelings, our next move, who I am, really. Maybe that last one can wait, at least until I'm finally free of that wretched castle.

Exhaustion pulls a blanket over my shoulders and closes my eyes with gentle hands, and I drift off to sleep just as Rowan opens the door.

CHAPTER 22

VEROSA

The hallways all look the same. Where am I, and where am I even going?

The tapestries stare back at me, the same as they always have, but something has changed. The faces, those beautifully woven faces of all my childhood heroes are no longer smiling. Each one stares back, their faces twisted with horror.

"Verosa."

No.

I turn down one at random and begin to sprint, ignoring my burning lungs and aching muscles. The voices draw closer, murmuring my name as if a prayer.

"Verosa."

No. No, no, no, no, no.

Invisible hands reach out and take ahold of me. Pulling the clothes from my skin and the skin from my bones. Blood and tears mix as I cry out for someone, anyone to come save me. The cool marble floor answers my calls as they pull me down further.

I can't move. I can't think. I can't breathe. I can't-

"Vera."

This is the end. Darkness washes over me in rolling waves. A pit forms in my stomach that feels like I am falling. These hands keep pulling, stripping me away until I am nothing but a carcass. A frail open body with a gaping heart still pumping out golden blood. Slowly, the hands reach for that too.

"I told you you'd rot," one of them whispers.

"She never listens," the other agrees, more feminine and sadistic.

"Verosa." Icy fear wraps itself around, and I violently shake as I bleed out. Why won't anyone help me?

"Vera."

The howling draws closer now.

"Vera."

I take in one final breath and then scream.

"VERA!" Someone grips my shoulders firmly, shaking me awake. The silhouette of a man hovers above me in the dark, his hair brushing against my forehead. Rowan. Rowan is here, but where is here?

The inn, the room at the inn booked under Leo and Marie. The room where I fell asleep safely. I am safe.

Still, I quiver beneath him, my headboard slightly tapping the wall behind it. My eyes adjust to the dark a bit more, and I look up to see Rowan's face tightened with concern as he searches my own for any signs of pain. His knees press slightly into my sides as he leans above me, the bed still shaking. Then I realize it is not the bed that is shaking, but me.

"I-"

"Don't speak. Just breathe." He watches as I take three deep breaths, counting and breathing with me, before he rocks back on his heels and allows me to sit up. The bed creaks as I do so, but it helps to be upright.

"Do you want to talk about it?" I shake my head. "Alright."

We sit in silence, his thumb lazily tracing circles across my knee without any other form of contact. Every fiber of my being seems to focus on where his skin touches mine, where little jolts of electricity shoot through me. It is not an uncomfortable feeling.

"I get them too sometimes," he whispers. "Nightmares, that is. I suppose it wouldn't help to say it's just a dream, but it's nothing you can't handle."

From anyone else, those words would have angered me. I know I can handle it, but from him, that reassurance means everything. Even after tonight, where I failed so spectacularly, he still believes in me.

I swallow thickly. "Light."

"What?"

"I'm afraid of the dark."

Realization must have dawned on him, for within the next few seconds, an oil lamp is lit, and I can read the guilt across his features. No mockery or pity, just shame.

"I didn't know."

"I didn't tell."

"Fair enough." He chuckles, his voice laced with mirth. "Scoot over."

I raise an eyebrow at him. "What?"

Rowan sighs and rolls those emerald eyes as if the answer should be obvious, but I perch still as a sentry as he stands before me. And then he hooks one arm under my knees and the other around my shoulders and lifts me up. He walks the three paces between our two beds and plops me down with an unladylike 'oomph' before rolling me to the side closest to the wall. Silently, he slips under the covers beside me, leaving the lamp burning on the table next to us.

"And just what do you think you're doing?" I question as he burrows in deeper, grinning like a cat.

"Protecting my 'wife' from the dark," he jokes as he turns so his back is to me. "But don't worry, I'm a gentleman, and I'll keep my hands to myself."

I snort. "You and gentleman don't belong in the same sentence together."

"Ouch, I guess the honeymoon phase is over." I can feel his shoulders shake as he laughs, rattling our shared and small bed. Despite this, he is sure to leave even the tiniest sliver of space between us, and I am sure he must be half hanging off the bed. With anyone else, the situation would have felt stiff and awkward, but here with Rowan, I felt safe and known.

I think of all my dates with Lucius, the anxiety and anger wearing through my body. I had thought at the time I was just nervous. Here was this attractive man not making me fight for his attention. Here was someone who was willing to bow to me, regardless of what I said or did to try and spark something. I can no longer deny my lingering feelings for him, but neither can I continue to deny the fact that we are wrong for each other.

Lucius bows but never challenges me. He views my word as God. And yet, I feel that he still holds the reins.

And then there's Blaine. Blaine who, even when he loved me, never let me have that freedom I desired. I know he tried. He tried so hard and loved me more than I thought possible until it ended. Until he did it all for me. A pang of sorrow floods my heart for a moment, but I shake myself right. I will not allow myself to feel shame for moving on.

"Turn around."

Rowan obliges, and his chest presses against my back. He must realize it as well, and shuffles backwards so that he must be leaning half off the bed again.

"You can hold me, you know." A pause. "Can you hold me?"

The sheets rustle as Rowan shifts closer, and one arm slips under my pillow. The other lazily drapes over my waist. His breath skitters across the nape of my neck, sending shivers down my spine.

"Is this okay?" His voice is thick with sleepiness, a drowsy lull in my ears. I can discern his heartbeat through my back, a reminder that he lives. That he's here. That we are safe. I nod, allowing my eyes to drift closed for a moment.

Creak.

Rowan's arm shoots from my waist to grab the assailant's wrist in a second, twisting it with a painful crack. The masked man cries out in pain but still uses his other hand to grab for my hair. As if on instinct, my hand balls into a fist ready to aim, but Rowan is there first, wrapping his arms around the man's midsection and tackling him to the ground. He lands blow after blow, one sickening and crunching thud after the other until the assailant resembles more like a victim. Rowan stands grimly before turning back to face me, where I still lay in the bed. Utterly motionless and useless in that fight.

His lips part in questioning, worry coating his features, but before he can ask anything, the man on the ground is moving again. Something dark glints in his hand. A cursed blade. I recognized it from that night in Belam. The only way the cursed can kill me. Every soldier of the rebellion was armed with one. Then it clicked. Rowan had missed one.

And he's about to miss it again. So caught up in his worry for my well-being, he doesn't see the knife angle straight for his heart.

Without thinking, I open my palms and cry out in an ancient dialect. "Dila!" The word sounds broken on my heavy tongue, but perhaps Deungrid understands, because at that moment, a pure beam of light shoots from my hands into the man's eyes. He screams out in pain, giving me a split second to act. I leap from the bed, grabbing the oil lamp from next to the bed and smashed it over his head.

For a moment there is silence, and then Rowan's eyes drift from our assailant's unconscious form to where I stand, still clutching tightly at the lamp. Then back to the body. Then to me. He whistles lowly.

"Nice form."

A huff of laughter escapes from between my lips. "Thanks. Is he...."

"No." Rowan's eyes darken as he steps forward to assess the damage done. "No, he's just knocked out cold. He will come to in a bit." The mercenary lifts the blade from the other man's hand and swears when he notices the same thing I did.

"We must have missed one," I offer unhelpfully. Rowan's shoulders square as he tosses my torn and blood-stained gown my way. I slip into it wordlessly as he takes to binding the man's hands and feet together.

"If one got away, he probably told the others where he was going. We need to leave; our position is compromised."

"And risk more of them finding us?"

"I'll handle it. I'll send word for Amír, she will take you back to the palace and take care of you." He sighs heavily as he runs a bloody hand through his hair. Some of the blood streaks through his golden locks, painting them red and silver instead. His usually tan skin looks grey, and his eyes look heavy. Tired. He looks so tired.

I take a step forward and lay my hand gently on his shoulder. "And what about you? Who will take care of you?"

Rowan offers a sardonic grin, though it lacks his usual cocky flair.

"I'll take care of me. Don't you worry." He props the man up against the wall before slipping out of the room, presumably to go send for

Amír. Uncomfortable with the idea of being alone in a room with someone who wants me dead, I follow.

When we get to the bottom of the stairs, I catch a flash of red hair with a single white streak. Amír steps out from the shadows, her gun drawn and at the ready to greet us.

"You got here quickly."

"An armed ambush on a royal carriage?" She scoffs. "News travels quick."

I shift uncomfortably on the balls of my feet. Amír and I haven't spoken since she'd saved my life, and I hers in return. The only form of communication between us since was a singular death glare the day I'd brought Torin and Blaine to the compound. A chill curls down my spine, licking each vertebra with cold fear as she sends another withering look my way.

Rowan clears his throat. "I'm going to take care of this. I need you to escort her back to the palace."

Amír offers no verbal response, only harshly grabs my elbow to drag me out the door. I don't even have the chance to say goodbye to Rowan. A sharp pain shoots through my heart. What if he's injured while 'taking care of' this mess, or worse?

Amír only rolls her eyes at my apparently visible fear. "He'll be fine. The one you should worry about is yourself."

Her voice is colder than usual as she walks ahead, her steps stiff and shoulders squared. My tired and sore muscles groan as I jog to keep up.

"What do you mean?"

"Those rebels weren't after some random pureblood. They were after you, weren't they, Princess Verosa?"

My steps falter.

No. No, this couldn't be happening.

Amír turns around with a wicked grin on her face. Her eyebrows pinch together as if they're trying to hold the thin line between her patience and fury. My mouth sours as I fight the urge to vomit.

"It suddenly makes sense now. The naivety, the prejudice; the privilege." Rowan's second continues, stalking ever closer to me. "Does he even know what you're asking of him? Does Rowan even know who you are?"

My hands begin to shake at my sides. How dare she ask such blunt questions, and how dare she be right?

"He knows who I am." My voice shakes even at a whisper. "He just doesn't know what I am."

How did she find out? No, this isn't the question I should be asking right now. I should be wondering how it took so long for any of them to find out. They're the Nightwalkers, for the gods' sakes.

Amír stills for a moment before speaking. Her voice is a death rattle as hurt and anger lace her alto tone. "He deserves to know."

"He can't know!" I plead. How had this gone so wrong so quickly? How did everything spin so out of control? "Please, he can't."

"You're asking him to commit treason! He deserves the right to know and reevaluate whatever deal the two of you have going on, as well as whatever the hell is growing between you. You can't keep lying to him."

Brazen tears dare to stream down my face. I should have seen this coming. Whatever delusional fantasy I dreamt of is washing away with the rain streams at my feet. So I do the only thing I can think to do. I kneel before the gunslinger.

"I didn't mean to lie," I whisper. "I planned on telling him, I swear it, but only once I had left the palace for good. That way, if something happened, if we got caught, he could have deniability. He could hate me, but he could deny knowing what he was doing. It would be believable too, considering I asked my father and fiancé to not reveal who I am for the sake of normalcy. The blame would all fall on me, I am trying to protect him."

Every broken thought from my heart slips into my words, staining my pleas like the blood I've spilt. If Rowan knows who I am, his fate will be sealed. Death by my father's command. I can't let him die, I can't lose anyone else, I can't...

I can't tell him the full truth. Not yet. For lurking deeper still in my heart is a malicious spark of fear, just waiting to catch alight. It wraps its icy hand around my heart and squeezes tightly as Amír stares down at my wretched form. I await whatever brutal tongue flaying the gunslinger has prepared, but instead she kneels beside me and speaks softly.

"He wouldn't leave you."

"What?"

She dips her chin. "Back in that tavern, on your first mission, you were shocked that I came back for you. You looked to be in such disbelief that anyone would come save you."

"I thought you hated me." My lower lip wobbles slightly as I speak. None of this is missed by the redhead's assessing gaze. Tentatively, she slips her hand into mine.

"But it wasn't just me. When Kya, your friend, came for you, you were also shocked. When Blaine started that fight with Rowan at the compound, then too." She inhales sharply. "Do you really think your life is worth so little that we wouldn't come for you? That we wouldn't fight for you? Do you think of yourself as that worthless and undeserving of love?"

A fat tear plops from my cheek to my hand, where it is still encased in Amír's.

Oh.

My fingers ghost the side of my face. When had I started crying?

Amír holds my hand tighter. "You're worthy of the good in this world, Vera. You don't have to sacrifice yourself to deserve love and friendship. You're enough," then she whispers, "and Rowan would stay, even if you told him the truth. Even before whatever deal you two have going on started." Somehow I know she isn't only referring to my training and Rowan's time in the palace.

"How do you know?"

Amír breathes deeply and closes her eyes as if steeling herself against whatever she's about to say.

"Because," she murmurs, "he did it for me."

The rain settles coldly in my bones as Amír stares unabashedly at my face. She doesn't balk at my weepy eyes nor scold me for daring to feel upset. She gazes through my eyes into my heart, and for once, she lets me into her own.

The rain nearly drowns out the sound of her low voice, but she parts her lips with her chin held high. The weather slows, and the ground rumbles in response, as if the gods know better than to speak over her.

"My father's wealth could rival your own's, and my mother was considered the most beautiful woman in our city. My three older sisters inherited her beauty and his greed, but I was born... different." I trace her gaze to the pale patterns of skin across her exposed arms and face, and she nods in confirmation. "We were blessed with our money, our looks, and our wealth. My parents had been praying for a pureblood as a reward for their 'virtue', and instead, they received me. I was considered a bad omen, a curse from Raonkin meant to taint our pure family lineage. I was treated no better than a cursed criminal.

"My parents wanted to be rid of me as soon as possible, but Krycolian law prohibits slavery, so they found an alternate solution. I suppose you of all people understand to what I am referring."

"An arranged marriage."

Amír nods. "On my fifteenth birthday, they held a secret auction in Adil for my hand in marriage. They must have only sent out invitations to the slimiest old men in Krycolis, or those were the only ones with low enough morals to show up."

My gut churns, and I fight for air. Lucius is at least my age and has been kind to me thus far, but to be forced to marry an old man... Lord Gadsden comes to mind, and I repress a shudder. I wonder if he had been invited that night.

"As the bids rose, the door to the tavern flew open, and in stepped this thirteen-year-old punk with a gun and a shit-eating grin. He held a room full of powerful men at gunpoint, then handed the weapon to me. He gave me a choice, to shoot my way out and come with him, or let the crowd take me." She laughs humorlessly, a dangerous glint in her eye as she fiddles with the trigger of her gun. "I bet you can figure out which I chose."

Amír rises to her feet, not paying mind to the mud crusting her knees. A crack of lightning illuminates her form. Her cape whips around her ankles, and I cannot decide if she looks more formidable or beautiful. Who am I to say she cannot be both?

"All I'm saying is he went through those lengths for a stranger, the least he would do for you is commit treason." She extends her hand to me. "Let's get you home."

I gratefully accept her assistance as my legs wobble like a newborn foal. She offers a thin smile, though she no longer looks quite as cold.

Amír, in some ways, is the same as I am. A child forced to grow up too quickly. At least that much we can understand about one another.

"By the way," she says as we begin our walk, "I never hated you."

I'm not sure what the right words to say are. Are there any words left to say between us at all? Probably not, so I settle for a tight-lipped smile and trail closely behind her into the dark.

My knees shake more with each step as darkness envelopes us. My heart races in my chest, pumping so loud I can barely hear the gunslinger when she tells me we are almost to the horses. I only nod slowly. I can do this. One step at a time.

"Quickly now." She helps to lift me atop my mare before mounting her own. "We need to get you close enough to the palace grounds before the king sends out his search party."

I squeeze my aching legs around the mare's barrel and cluck her forward. My movements are stiff and clumsy, but I swallow my groans as my muscles protest. The memory of my fall earlier this night burns bright in my mind, and my back begins to ache. At least this time I have a saddle and stirrups to sink in to.

Amír rides by my side, constantly checking over her shoulder and in the trees above us. We don't stop once, not even as the reins lather sweat against the horses' necks, and I'm forced to weave my fingers through her mane to hold myself in the saddle. Maybe it is by the grace of the gods that we don't run into any more rebels on the ride. However, the implications of what Rowan could be doing to them, or them to him, forces silent prayers from between my lips. They crystallize in the air.

As dawn sets the sky alight with torturous flames a hulking mass of stone and ivy comes into view. The palace. The sun licks some of the cold from my bones as Amír spins her horse to a halt.

Her flaming red hair whips out behind her, not quite a subdued enough tone to blend into the sky. She was silent the entire duration of the ride, and I figured she must also be exhausted by now.

Despite our earlier conversation, she has returned to her natural aloof and borderline cold demeanor, however, something has changed. I am the one who has changed. Amír is constant and honest to a fault. What I viewed as cold in the past was her blunt nature, her way of protecting herself and others. I had been the fool to think she thought anything extreme of me simply because she refused to placate me with forced pleasantries.

Rowan's second nods stiffly towards the palace, and I understand. I have to make the final stretch alone.

"Run like hell." Is all she says before wheeling her mount back the way we came from.

CHAPTER 23
VEROSA

Before I can even dismount, knights and attendants come pouring from the palace entrance. My gracious steed thankfully doesn't spook, even as I slide from her back to land on my knees and crumple to the ground. Someone calls for a healer as I lay motionless on the gravel road. My legs throb and cramp from the strain of riding through the night. I barely had a moment to sleep and recover from using my magic, let alone the battle and run for my life.

"Verosa!" As someone props me up against the wall, I can see Lucius running towards me. His shirt is only half buttoned, as if he gave up on the top four buttons, and his hair uncharacteristically messy. He sinks to his knees by my side, the stones in the gravel tearing the knees of his trousers. The servants hand me to him as we wait for the healer, and he gently holds me against his chest.

"Thank you, Deungrid. Thank you. Thank you... Oh, gods," the prince murmurs over and over again, half crying into my hair. I suppose news had reached the palace sooner than I had expected.

From the corner of my eye, I can see Blaine and Torin, their shoulders sagging in relief. A glance at their poorly adjusted armor and dark circles under their eyes tells me they were just as worried, but station prohibits them from coming closer. I fight the urge to scream. I want to sink into their arms and tell them all that has happened. I want Rowan here, safe and out of harm's way for even just one second. I want everyone to stop staring at me like I am some foreign object just so they can go speculate what the poor princess must have endured. They wouldn't understand even half of it.

Slowly, Lucius rises to his feet, carrying me with him as the healer arrives.

"I'd like to go to my room, please," I finally find the strength to say. The healer looks apprehensive at first, but one glare from Lucius has her agreeing. Two more follow behind her, just in case my injuries are too much for one healer to bear. I want to tell them they need not worry for me, that I was seen by a doctor, not a healer, and that my wounds would mend themselves with time, but my strength fails me as the world fades to darkness.

When I awake, I am in my own bed, changed into a comfortable gown and laying beneath my blankets. At my side a pile of chestnut curls scatter across my bed, and a hand is clutched in mine.

"Tanja," I murmur. "Tanja." Her name falls from my lips easily, and she stirs from her nap. She blinks the sleep from her eyes then bolts upright once she sees that I am awake.

"Vera!" she sobs, tossing herself across my lap. "I thought you were dead. They told us you were probably dead, and I just couldn't... I couldn't..."

Her chest rises and falls against my own, scattering my heart's broken pieces as she cries loudly. Shame curls around the mangled remains of my consciousness. All this time, fear whispered in my ear that Tanja was nothing more than a servant whose friendship was bought by my crown. That she had never cared for me, not truly.

Yet here she is, kissing my arms and weeping as if I am a miracle. To her, my life is a miracle.

I choke on my words as I wrap my arms around her shaking form and allow myself to hold her for the first time. My friend, who has always been here, waiting for me to see it. I bury my face in her curls and let my breast muffle the sounds of her tears as we cling to each other.

I don't know how long we lay like that before a soft knock comes at the door. Tanja sits up slowly and wipes her eyes before answering.

"The princess is not taking any visitors right now."

"The princess can kiss my ass after that scare." Torin laughs and brushes past Tanja. The maid eyes him indignantly with a scoff but does not kick him out. Blaine follows in closely behind, dressed only in a thin tunic and pants. His hair is ruffled, and his shoulders curve inwards as he approaches my bed.

"What happened?" he says softly, as if afraid to break our fragile peace. Any anger I still hold towards him melts instantly, and I hold out a hand. He takes one, and Torin takes my other. Tanja sits at the foot of my bed, massaging my sore calves as they await an explanation.

"We were attacked on the way back from the Falls, Rebels who wanted to murder me. Rowan killed them all, and I..." My voice trails off and Torin lets me lean against his shoulder for support. "I killed one. Raiko and the others, they were all killed. Rowan and I split up so he could draw them away."

A hush falls over the room as my hands begin to tremble again. In the relief of being home and seeing all their faces, I almost forgot the sins I committed last night. Then I notice the closed windows and the silent halls.

I frown. "What time is it?"

My three friends exchange heavy glances, but it is Blaine who speaks. His voice is surprisingly soft and low as he allows his gaze to finally raise to mine.

"Around midnight. Vera, you've been asleep for two days."

It feels as if my bed has been pulled out from under me, and I lay gasping on the stone floor. Two days? How is that possible?

"You were exhausted. The healers did all they could for your superficial wounds, but they said there was a deep weariness in your soul that they couldn't touch. Not without..."

"Magic." I finish for Tanja. I squeeze the bridge of my nose between my thumb and forefinger. "So they did use healers."

"We did all we could, but it was the king's orders." Torin's shoulders slump and he rests his head on mine. A low fury broils in my gut. My wounds were not severe. They could have used regular medics.

Healers are people like me, people gifted by the divine, but rather than shoot light from their hands, they have the ability to heal. However, I'm learning that all magic, light and dark, comes with a cost. To heal someone, a healer must absorb the pain of the wound themselves. Invisible pain torments them for however long the natural healing process of the wound would have been. Sometimes they die from sheer shock of the pain.

When I was little, I thought healers were saints. I couldn't imagine inflicting pain upon myself just so another wouldn't have to bear it. Then I learned the ugly truth. The healers were more slaves than saints. By the age of fifteen, all healers are required by law to report to the palace and be dispersed across the kingdom for their abilities. To refuse or hide one's ability is considered treason and punishable by death.

"My wounds weren't even that severe! I am pureblood, I have accelerated healing. They could have only called for a medic." I fling myself back against my pillows, disgusted by the relief I'd felt when I awoke to my back no longer aching. "Where's Rowan?"

That same hush falls over the room. My heart stops in my chest.

"Where is Rowan?" I repeat, frantic now. Tanja moves Torin to come sit at my side and wraps her willowy fingers around my wrist.

"Rowan hasn't been found yet."

"That's not possible. He would've come by now."

"Vera."

"No!" I whirl towards the three of them, their faces the perfect mix of shock and sympathy. "He is alive. You've seen what he can do. He's alive."

I yank my arm from Tanja. The maid schools her countenance into cool indifference as she folds her hands.

"Lower your voice before the wrong person hears. Rowan has not been found yet, but a note was left for you by a woman. Presumably the Noiteron's assassin?" I stare agape at the young woman, who laughs drily. "Did you really think I wouldn't find out? I knew who Rowan was the moment I laid eyes on him. And that date the night of your betrothal was all an excuse to buy you time to escape."

I'm sure I must be the perfect imitation of a koi fish, similar to the ones that swim in the pond below my window. My jaw goes slack, and my eyebrows raise simultaneously. Tanja only smirks.

"So let me get this straight. You all can find out almost anything in this palace, and I, heir to the throne, know fucking nothing."

Tanja smiles sweetly. "This is why you should always be kind to the help. You have your armies, but we have the ultimate power. Invisibility. We hear and know everything."

My mouth runs dry. Laei. I am so naive.

"Does this mean all the other servants know what I've been doing. Who Rowan is?"

"No. Lucky for you, you've got the princess' Lady in Waiting, the Captain of the Guard, and his assistant," Torin protests his title, but Tanja continues anyway, "keeping any rumors from people's mouths and ears. As far as servant hierarchy goes, we are gods, so you don't need to worry."

A low laugh drifts in on the evening breeze. My bedroom door swings open silently, and a tall figure walks in cloaked by darkness.

"Don't forget the entirety of the Nightwalkers at your disposal." Rowan's smirk is evident even in the shadows. "You've made yourself a powerful inner circle, Verosa."

I study his form as he walks. No limp or stumble as he carries himself with his usual powerful stride. A hunter constantly on the prowl. I can see no visible wounds on him, and his rolled-up sleeves show no new lacerations as well. I sigh in relief, then push myself off the bed.

Rowan smiles softly, as if expecting an embrace. His jaw slackens as my fist drives right into his gut.

"Two days, Rowan? You stayed away for two days!" I hiss, not caring that I sway where I stand.

"Ver, let's get you back to bed."

"No." I push hard against his chest. "No, not until you offer some explanation for all of this. I thought you were dead."

Rowan chuckles, but there is no humor in his voice, only this lingering tinge of exhaustion. "Then you understand how I felt when I heard from Kya that you hadn't woken up in that time." He steps forward slowly, and I swallow hard. "I couldn't get in. Someone was always by your side, whether it be Lucius, the king, or a maid. I had to wait for an opening, but trust me, I was outside your window every night just waiting and blaming myself."

The king? No one had told me that my father had come to visit. He's never come to my side while ill or injured, he didn't even after the incident with Irene. I had been closer to death then than I am now.

My fists fall to rest by my side. Rowan steps forward, prying my fingers open and massaging my palms until I release the tension entirely. Tanja and Torin watch from my bedside with curious yet knowing eyes. Blaine keeps his gaze on the floor.

"It's not your fault," I whisper.

"Like hell it isn't."

My head snaps back to the source of the voice. Blaine stands now, his fists shaking with barely controlled fury. His shoulders square, and his posture stiffens. His face contorts into pure rage and hatred as he beholds the mercenary king, so much so I find myself shifting my weight to stand between them.

"If you hadn't had insisted on taking her to that place alone, then she wouldn't have been in danger. No, let me rephrase that," Blaine seethes with such all-consuming darkness. "If you hadn't had taken advantage of her, no. If you hadn't had even met her in the first place, none of this would have happened."

I startle with shock. "Blaine..."

"She wouldn't have had to stain her hands. She wouldn't have had to kill someone."

I suppress a gasp of surprise and indignation as Blaine speaks. I know he has never liked Rowan, nor my solution to my betrothal but this... this is pure hatred written across his face as he stares between us both.

Rowan snorts. "Oh, I see what this is. Someone doesn't like that Vera isn't under his thumb anymore. That she doesn't need him to defend her."

"More like how you've turned her into a murderer!"

Murderer.

The word drives a blade through my heart. I fight the urge to keel over and vomit. Murderer. That is what I am now. It is what I have been for a long time.

Tanja gasps, and her eyes narrow to slits. She grabs her skirts as if to stand when Torin grabs her by the elbow and shakes his head. Blaine watches this encounter, and his face softens.

"I didn't mean that." His voice lowers into a plea. "Vera, please. I didn't mean it like that."

I take a shuddering sigh. Deep down I know he would never view me that way. It is Rowan he sees as the monster, the one who has stolen and corrupted the woman he loves. But it doesn't matter who the sword is aimed at if the blade is double sided.

Rowan peers down at me with concern but doesn't say anything else. For once he swallows his pride and bites his tongue. He eyes undress my vulnerability and beg me to say something.

Finally, after a long pause, I look up and glare in Blaine's direction. My voice is cold as iron as I speak, and the other four flinch. "How do you think they fixed your leg?"

CHAPTER 24

ROWAN

Vera looks up, her eyes sorrowful and red-rimmed. My heart gives an audible crack at the sight of it. Torin holds down the Lady in Waiting, who looks ready to smash the captain's face in. I can't say I blame her as I barely restrain my own fury.

"How do you think they fixed your leg?"

Verosa's response takes all of us aback, with Torin going as far as to clutch at his chest. Blaine's face quickly falls.

"What?"

"How do you think they fixed your leg?"

"Ver-"

"*How?*" She is standing now, her fists shaking silently at her side. A part of my conscious pulls, saying I shouldn't be here to witness this. That this is between the pureblood and the captain, and yet, one look at her pale and gaunt face has my heels firmly planted on the cold stone floor.

"You know..." His voice barely goes above a whisper. "You know I don't remember any of it."

"Well, I do." Her own voice matches his, grief and pain strung on every chord of her sweet tone. "You needed a miracle. You needed magic: blood. *Pure blood.*"

I have seen men pray to gods they don't believe in when faced with death and women defending their broken lovers from an army with nothing but their own fists. I've seen children begging on street corners while others pick pockets in feeble attempts to live for one more godforsaken day. I have been that child. I have been the murderer and the lover. I have been death and the judgement, but I have never seen a man shatter quite like Blaine does.

His legs begin to wobble, healthy and injured alike. His grey eyes suddenly seem pale, the color of a cloudy sky rather than forged iron. Vera's own eyes stare at her feet, guilt wracking her delicate features. The firm lines of her mouth pull together, and she blinks rapidly. No more tears fall.

The moment feels holy as we bask in the horror of this revelation. My heart races in anticipation of the words that I know will come next.

"Cut me."

No.

"I need you to do it."

No.

"I trust you."

I take ahold of her hand and flip her palm to face skywards, then hiss at the sight of the long scar running the length of it. Tanja grips the side of the bed.

Vera stares sorrowfully at the scar. Enraptured by it, even. "I did it. I cut myself, I wouldn't let anyone else do it. I watched as the healer spread it over your leg, over the bones jutting through your already rotting flesh."

She pauses a moment to gather herself.

"I watched him tip it between your lips. And then I watched as the soldiers cut him in two, just below the waist." Her voice breaks. "Just enough left of him for an open casket."

Somewhere in the distance, a church bell chimes. It chimes seven times. Vera raises her hand, as if to cross two fingers across her chest but stops. Whether deliberately or because she lacks the strength, I don't know.

"I-"

"Do you want to know what's worse? I watched you open your eyes,

I watched you wonder why there was so much blood, and I had to lie and say it was your own. Then I watched you take your first steps a few weeks later, and you had a limp. A month later, and the limp persisted." She cuts him off, swaying. We both make to grab for her, but she rights herself without our assistance and steadies her furious gaze on Blaine once more.

"And do you know what I thought? I thought 'where can I find another healer? Maybe it wasn't enough.' And maybe if I had let you run me dry, you'd be fine, and I didn't care if they'd kill the next healer, and the next after that, and then the next. It took meeting with five healers, in secret, learning each time that even a miracle wouldn't ever let you walk without pain. I realized I wasn't enough. Seeing you in pain every day reminds me that no matter how much I sully my hands, I can't save you."

Blaine has the decency to look shocked, confused, sorrowful, and maybe even a tinge of fear resides in his heart. An awe of respect coats his mannerisms as well as he studies Vera. He looks as if he sees her for the first time.

"I didn't know." Is the poetry that stumbles from between his lips, a sorry excuse or plea to innocence at best. Vera looks like she can't decide whether to laugh or cry, so she just presses her lips together.

"Just because I didn't do it with my own hands that time doesn't mean I didn't know what it meant to kill. I made the choice to save *you*, knowing it would kill *him*. The only difference this time is that I held the knife. I felt him die."

Outside the window, thunder rumbles lowly, as if the earth, too, is mourning the new bodies to be buried under her skin. The flame in the oil lamp flickers, and Tanja stands to make sure the window is securely locked shut. The sounds of laughter floats through the hallway outside the closed door until it fades, leaving only silence.

"I wear both his blood and the healer's. The innocent and the guilty." As if a switch is flipped, Vera's eyes darken, and her voice lowers to a growl. "Guess which one I killed for you versus him?"

Drip.

Torin turns to the window to search for any signs of rain, but Tanja's eyes go right to Vera's hands. I trace her gaze to see blood pooling beneath her fingertips as she drives her fingernails into her shaking fists.

"Hey, hey." I gently take her hand and open her fingers. The blood drips onto my own, leaving a stream of gold across my heart line. "Ver. Vera, stop."

Another clap of thunder rocks the castle, and Vera blinks. Her eyes clear and widen, and she's quick to try and brush off the blood on her dress. Tanja catches her hand and wraps it in cloth before she has the chance.

"Fingers and hands always bleed so much," the maid says soothingly. "Let's take care of it, okay?"

In a daze, Vera nods and follows her friend back to bed. The blonde knight pulls back the covers of her bed for her to lay in, then hands her a cup of water. Ripples form in the glass as soon as it passes from his hands to hers. Blaine stays rooted where he stands.

"I think you should go." Torin gently lays a hand on the captain's shoulder, kind yet commanding. His body stiffens, but he nods silently, noting that no resentment taints the words. He spares her one more look, a silent apology, before he limps from the room. His uneven footsteps echo through the hallway.

Vera sips from the glass quietly. The only sound that fills the room are her small sips and the soft patter of rain.

"It's the cold rainy season now," Torin notes, and Tanja nods. I only continue to watch Vera take small sip after sip. Her hands stop shaking, and she raises her chin.

"Another face to haunt me I suppose," she murmurs.

The pureblood speaks low and sweet, but the voice is distant as if not her own. She gazes in my direction, but her stare seems to go through me and out the door from which the captain just left. The darkness that was in her voice, that pure malice, is gone now. However, the chill that it brought remains in the room still.

Tanja approaches her friend, gentle hands guiding the blankets up to Vera's chin and taking the cup from her.

"Rest, Vera. You're still in shock."

Vera doesn't answer verbally, just nods and lets her eyelids flutter shut. Torin claps my shoulder as he exits, and I take that as my sign to leave as well.

Before I slip back into shadows, I step forward towards her. My light. Her freckles form constellations across the bridge of her nose and high cheekbone and remind me of the beauty of the lights she created. The beauty she creates. Cautiously I lower my lips to her forehead then step away to let the miracle rest.

The maid, Tanja, watches me curiously as I step away. Her aura matches Vera's in ways I can't explain. There's the same lingering sense of power and ferocity, but also a gentle and playful kindness that masks a heavy sense of dread.

"Why is your face pinched like that?" she tuts, her hands on her hips. I laugh. It is easy to imagine her and Vera running through the palace and causing all sorts of mischief.

"Because," I whisper, "I think she's a bit too much like me."

As I leave, I secretly slip the note that Tanja mentioned off of Vera's desk and open it once alone.

Rowan,

Gold is hard to keep around Adil, sometimes it falls into the wrong pockets. It is even harder to keep surrounded by nobles and the high born. But you know that already, don't you? Wish your pureblood the happiest of engagements for me. I hope to see you at the wedding.

By the way, be sure to remind Verosa to lock her windows.

Sincerely,

Mavis

My lips pull back in a snarl as I crumple the parchment in my fist. The night sky is inviting, the darkness willing to cloak my sins. To allow me my hunt. Out there, somewhere in the dark under those stars, is Mavis, still sprinting to stay ahead of me.

I lean out the window and survey the palace grounds one last time before I leap. Verosa should rest tonight, but my work has just begun.

CHAPTER 25

VEROSA

Nearly a month has passed since my return from Ialenia Falls now, and I am a month closer to my wedding as well. Florists visit the palace every month in preparation, as well as chefs from around the kingdom, all vying for the honor of serving the throne at my wedding.

In the corner of the room, Tanja tries and fails to suppress her giggles as the seamstress tailors my wedding dress. The woman glares at her all the while, no doubt imagining using my friend as a pincushion.

"Is there anything less frilly? Maybe we could take away a bit of the sleeve and neckline?" I strangle out the best I can. The collar of the dress stretches all the way to my chin, stiff and fanned. Looking in the mirror, I resemble more of a peacock than a bride. The sleeves are just as horrendous. They puff out larger than my torso and cover half of my arms, creating a heinous contrast with the form-fitted gown they're attached to.

The seamstress sighs heavily and adds another pin around my waistline. "This was what the king ordered. It is the latest fashion in Tesslari."

"Of course, it is."

Tanja can't take it anymore and bursts out laughing. Her beautiful face pinches together, and her eyes squeeze shut as she mocks my misery. The seamstress angrily jabs another pin a bit too close to my waistline now. If Tanja doesn't stop, I fear I may be too bloodied to go on with the wedding. Mentally, I beg her to keep laughing.

"If holding your tongue is so hard, young lady, then I suggest you wait outside while I finish with the princess."

Tanja solemnly closes her mouth, and her face quickly becomes red from withholding her giggles. I have to look away before I also begin to laugh and risk running myself through with one of her needles.

The seamstress, content now with the silence, continues to preen when the door creaks open. Torin enters with a young knight I recognize from a few months ago. He had escorted me to my last lesson with Miss Eida. His flaming hair is impossible to forget.

"Good... ack! Mei Reinhavich, you look..."

"Radiant?"

"A bit like those birds your mother used to keep." Torin frowns, and the young knight by his side bites his lip. The seamstress' face becomes bright red in an instant, and she throws the pins to the floor.

"If you cannot hold your tongue, then leave the room! I am here by orders of the king," she hisses through clenched teeth.

"So am I. He requests Princess Verosa in the throne room as soon as this fitting is finished." Torin nudges the knight's side, and the redhead brandishes a parchment with the king's official seal on it. The flustered woman accepts the letter and skims through its contents before sighing heavily.

"We are finished for today," she says, groaning. She takes to rubbing at the growing vein in her forehead while she helps me slip out of the dress.

Torin and the blushing knight excuse themselves, but not before Torin elbows Tanja and squawks like a bird, sending her into another bout of laughter. The seamstress all but throws her out of the room moments later.

"Was it that awful?" I groan once in the hallway. Tanja snorts and links her arm through mine.

"It was the highlight of my week! Thank you for your sacrifice."

We walk towards the throne room, a lightness in our step just like it was months ago. Before the engagement, before the Nightwalkers, before my magic. The sunlight warms us despite our layers and the cold breeze blowing through the hall. Winter is officially in full swing in Krycolis, and the farmers suspect we will see snow soon enough.

I shiver and try to push that thought from my mind.

"Tanja," a maid I recognize, Ruby, purrs in passing. Her skirts swish around her ankles as she exaggerates the sway of her hips in passing. She pauses a moment to bow low, and I groan when I see where my friend's eyes trail. "Mai Reinhavich."

I nod and Tanja smirks wickedly. "Ruby."

Once they maid is out of sight, I nudge Tanja with my shoulder. "I thought you said that date was just an excuse?"

"Oh, Vera, darling, it was much more than an excuse. The maids here are very good with-"

"Polishing silverware, is how you were going to finish that sentence, I presume?" Torin quips as he appears beside us, the young knight now lost.

"Among other things."

"Torin, who was that knight?" I ask, desperate to change the topic.

"His name is Seb. Pretty young but devoted." Torin notes offhandedly before turning his attention back to Tanja.

"So is there any reason why you are tagging along to this meeting?"

"Because I'm Vera's favorite, obviously."

Torin gasps. "What? Vera tell her that's not true." I only laugh in response, causing the blonde knight to grip at his heart dramatically. "I can't believe you'd rather spend time with Tanja instead of me!"

The young woman bumps him with her hip and a snicker. "Go lick your wounds somewhere else."

The two of them continue to bicker until we stand before the throne room door. A feeling of familiarity washes over me, but I push the doors open and enter. Tanja and Torin squeeze my arms as they let go, and the door shuts heavily behind me.

It takes my eyes a moment to adjust to the dim light of the throne room. When they do, I notice that my father sits alone, no guards or servants to attend him. His throne is polished and shimmering with pure gold, a monstrosity that had to be made on the spot, for it is too heavy to lift or transport. His clothes are pristine, and his velvet cloak curls around his shoulders like a cat.

His face is weary as I approach. New lines have formed on his forehead, and deep purple circles reside beneath his pale blue eyes. Every time I see him, he looks worse, as if his body is deteriorating rapidly even as he sits on that golden monstrosity.

"Verosa."

"Father." I curtsy low and slow, dipping my head with respect. My father and I have never been close, though I suppose having a loving family just isn't possible as royalty. He tuts his approval and motions for me to rise.

"I am sure you know why I have called you here."

I swallow thickly. "No, Father. I do not."

Ophelus tilts his head to the side curiously. The crown doesn't shift once, even as he stands and steps forward. At this point, I would not be surprised if it has sunken into his skull. I've never seen him without it.

"Come." He motions for me to walk beside him. "We must talk."

I oblige the monarch, daring to step closer to him than I have in a while. He nods in satisfaction, and we walk over to a window. Above the window is a tapestry depicting the birth on light. We both bow our heads in reverence.

"Love is a fickle thing. It longs and leaves without warning. There comes a time when tough choices have to be made. The line must be drawn in the sand. You must decide how far you are willing to go for them."

"If this is about my marriage, Father, I am making an effort." I protest but lower my voice when he turns on me. His face is almost sorrowful, with his brows furrowing further and his lips forming a thin line. He places a weathered hand upon my shoulder.

"Blaine has challenged Lucius to a duel for your hand."

With those few words, I feel the world fall out from beneath my feet. Impossible. It should be an impossible idea. Unless...

"How is that possible?" I speak slowly to keep my voice even. "Blaine is only Captain of the Guard, and Lucius is heir to the throne of two kingdoms through this marriage. Law decrees that only one of equal status to the betrothed may challenge him to a duel."

"Unless given specific permission by the king," Ophelus finishes the bit of law I had forgotten to mention. "I saw no harm in it. Our alliance with Tesslari states that if the betrothal falls through due to cultural influence or customs, the marriage can be canceled without threat to the alliance. This way, Captain Koar can redeem himself after his *accident*."

Fury rises with the bile in my throat when my father mentions and slights Blaine's leg. How dare he consider death the better alternative to an honorable man living with a limp? He speaks like he is broken or damaged due to the injuries he suffered in the war, defending this kingdom. Defending my father... and defending me.

Ophelus notices my disgust and frowns.

"I thought you'd be more pleased. You could potentially not have to marry a stranger after all."

And potentially lose my best friend in the process.

If Blaine wins, Lucius dies. The thought does not quite sit well with me. Truth be told, I was once attracted to Lucius and his pretty words and am beginning to consider him my friend. Despite my abhorrence for arranged marriages, particularly my own, the image of him lying dead in the dust sends chills down my spine and sends gooseflesh skittering across my skin.

But if Lucius wins, Blaine dies.

I nearly double over at the thought. I thought he had died when he left. I am just starting to get him back, territorial bullshit and all, and I can't lose him. I won't lose him. If the fight turns south, I will protect him, even if it means interfering and killing Lucius myself.

Either way, I marry a man I did not choose. Two people will die at the dual, the only certain death being mine. My life dies the moment one of them slips a ring onto my finger. Yes, Blaine would be preferred over Lucius, considering our history and friendship, neither of them is the king I imagine at my side. If Rowan and I had met in another life, I would have made him my king, but simple dreams are all the comfort royalty can afford.

"Why are you telling me this?"

I hadn't intended for the question to be hard to answer. Father looks at me with his mouth open as if preparing to answer, then he softens his features and closes his lips.

"Why? Why..." he asks the question not with aggression, but more of a wistful sadness to himself. "Because I hold no affection for you. I look at you, and all I feel is guilt."

This declaration shouldn't hurt. I have known for a long time now that there was no one who loved me. My father is distant. Irene was cruel. I expect nothing from him anymore under the conditions that I cannot be hurt by them anymore.

And yet, to hear him say it. To hear him say he never even held the slightest bit of love for me in his heart, his daughter. The wickedest blade I've ever known is love, and it rams through my ribs into my still bleeding heart. If I pull it out now, I will bleed to death, but it is no use. My death saw me long ago.

The sweet tang of blood coats my mouth. I've bitten off part of my cheek.

Ophelus continues with no regard to my affliction. "I have done many things I should regret and know I will do many more that I won't. This is all I can offer you."

He stops speaking to stare out the window. I wait a moment before I realize he won't be continuing this conversation. Plastering a saccharine smile on my face, I curtsy and bend deep at the waist.

"Don't worry, father, I understand. For I, too, will do many things I won't regret." Without waiting for him to dismiss me, I stalk towards the double doors. My footsteps click against the cold tile, a deep, howling of wind filling my ears until I feel as if I'm suffocating.

Torin and Tanja's faces are pale as I exit. Someone must have told them.

"Take me to see him," I snap hotly. Tanja flinches and bows her head.

"We can't do that, Mai Reinhavich."

Torin steps in and places a soft hand on my elbow. "It's against the royal decree. Once a duel has been accepted, the maiden being dueled for is prohibited from seeing either competitor before the event. This was placed so she couldn't use magic, dark or light, to give her favored opponent an edge to the competition." The blonde sighs heavily. "It's an archaic rule. I can't believe that idiot. The last duel was..."

"Finneas Iales for Aiko Denize's hand," I murmur in recognition. Torin's eyes widen with questions but shakes them off.

I feel fury and heat pool through my core. He 'saw no harm in it.' Their deaths have no hold of guilt or concern over him. They mean nothing to him. We mean nothing to him.

Fingers lace themself across my wrist. "Not here," Rowan murmurs in my ear. "You're starting to glow, love."

I lower my gaze to my wrist, where his hand is covering the faint glow of my veins. A pounding headache works its way through my temples, though I note it is not as severe as it was the first time.

"Get me out of here." I plead to no one in particular. All three of them share knowing glances before Torin nods his head in the direction of the stables.

"Follow me."

Tanja fastens my cloak tighter around my shoulders as we follow Torin closely. She eyes my glowing veins and squinting eyes with only worry, no signs of fear or confusion. I nearly laugh. Of course, she would know already. Either Rowan told her, or she sorted it out herself. I wouldn't be surprised by either. Tanja is the smartest person I know, though she guards that secret fiercely beneath a bubbly personality.

The blonde knight pulls open the doors to the stables. Thankfully, it is empty. He lights an oil lamp and guides us around a bend towards the back of the stables. As we walk, I find less stalls occupied until we come to the far corner, where I see a familiar black head bob out the opening of his stall.

"Hi, Vestíg." A small laugh burbles from between my lips, though it sends splitting pain through my head. Rowan's fingers find mine and squeeze. Tanja takes my other hand, and the pain lessens.

"No one comes back here anymore. They're all too terrified of him, so we should be unbothered."

I step forward with a frown. "No one has claimed him?"

"The Tesslari delegates said he didn't come with them, and he's not one of ours. He just appeared out of nowhere. Not even the other horses like him."

Rowan bristles beside me. Now that is something we both can understand.

Slowly, I let light trickle from my fingertips, and I concentrate on allowing it to flow from me in a mist on its own rather than concentrated streams or enabled by some other earthly substance. I open my mouth to repeat the words I've taken to memorizing when Tanja stops me.

"Picture the meaning in your mind," she corrects. "Words are just tools to enable you. If you want to fully release your power, you can't rely on others, only the well of magic within yourself. Use your mind as a funnel, not your tongue."

She drops her hand from where it had been, correcting my form moments before when she catches our gawking stares.

"What?"

"How do you know all of that?" Rowan asks suspiciously. He eyes trace over her form, then linger on her wrists and eyes. A sharp jab of jealousy strikes my center despite knowing Tanja has her eyes set on someone else. My friend only shrugs.

"You weren't the first to see signs of her power. I did my research for when this day would come," she says before she stands back. Her eyes look into mine, and she nods.

The wind stills around us, and even Vestíg halts his pawing as if in reverence. I allow my jealousy to fade into that white heat pooling in my stomach. Allow it to work its way through my blood to my outstretched palm. Skeins of light slither through my veins, setting my skin aglow. Torin stifles a surprised yelp as my hand grows hot and begins to faintly illuminate.

Small wisps of light shoot from my fingertips before enveloping my palm in a blaze. The more I concentrate on this energy flowing through me, the less I can feel the pain that burned under my skin only minutes before. I hone my focus on the cool sensation spreading through my limbs, so stark in contrast to the blazing white light I hold in my hands. However, it doesn't burn like it looks like it should. Instead, it feels sweet, like a long sought-after relief. I allow my shoulders to relax and hum contently, suddenly deciding to push it further.

I allow the light to gravitate upwards, then explode into thousands of sparkling pieces that hover in the air. One lands on the stallion's nose, and he snorts, but his gaze never leaves the glow. Almost like he is entranced by the light.

With every broken beat of my heart, I allow the light to grow. The strength coursing beneath my skin is intoxicating and begs for release. I allow it.

I hold no affection for you.

A sputtering ember glows brighter.

When you rot to hell, I'll be waiting.

The ember flickers into a long tendril of power that weaves itself up my arm until it licks the nape of my neck and curls under my chin.

You've turned her into a murderer.

The final chord of restraint holding me back from the edge of full release snaps, and I teeter over the precipice. Its mouth opens wide in welcoming, its warm breath fanning my face. I breathe deeply and prepare when someone pulls me back.

"Not too much," Rowan warns.

The memory of panic and the scent of charred flesh and blood on my hands jolts through my senses. The lights fall immediately. Vestíg whinnies lowly, then resumes his thrashing.

"I think that's enough for tonight. You'll need to save your strength for tomorrow anyway."

Tomorrow. The duel is tomorrow.

The rock feels solid underneath my feet again as Tanja speaks. I look down to notice her hand is still intwined with mine, while Rowan had let go the moment I began my light show. She smiles warmly and squeezes twice.

Fatigue washes over me suddenly, and I nod in agreement.

"There's much to be done."

CHAPTER 26
VEROSA

S tarlight flickers across the arching ceilings of my bedroom, its dim glow reflecting across my skin with pale yellow luminance. With a simple lifting of my finger, they swirl and converge into a single beam, which streams through the jewels of the crown on my desk, sending a sprawling myriad of colors throughout the room. I snap, and they separate again, bursting into their own miniature solar systems.

I'd been practicing since Tanja shut the door last night, not bothering with sleep, though it calls desperately to me. My silken pillows beckon me to rest my head, if even just for a moment, but I shake the notion from my mind.

Though it has only been a month since I began using my powers daily, they no longer drain me like they did back at the Falls. My muscles still ache, and my limbs grow weary, but it is now bearable. The dark sanctuary of sleep doesn't consume me like it used to. It feels almost like learning to spar and wield a weapon again. My muscles then had not been prepared to even hold a blade, let alone use one, but now they've grown thick and corded. The weapon is an extension of my arm and the light one of my soul.

If only this power was more than a cheap party trick, I think with a scowl. All the books I've read and stories I've heard have pointed me towards this power, and yet all I've been able to do is conjure a few light beams and sparkles in secrecy.

Before dawn has even fully awoken, there's a soft knock at my door. Without a second thought, the lights wink out simultaneously, leaving me alone in the dark. The soft patter of slippered feet on stone give away the maids' entry before their oil lamp can. Ruby steps forward first with a deep curtsy before she extends her hand for mine.

I know Tanja is expected to make an appearance at the duel today, so she herself must be getting ready, and yet I find myself yearning for the comfort of her companionship as Ruby leads me towards my tub. The maids are gentle, almost reverential, as they sop my arms with soap that smells of cheap wine. I feel like a prized pony trussed up for a trot around the plaza.

"The king has left a dress for you." Ruby speaks slowly. I could scoff. Of course, he did.

The scarlet fabric pools around my feet, licking at my ankles whenever I walk. The fine fabric is embroidered with pure spun gold, and I don't miss the message Ophelus is trying to convey.

Someone will die today, and I will be the one to wear their blood.

Just as Ruby finishes applying the last of the cosmetics to my face, Tanja barrels through the doors into my chambers. Her fine dress, not maid's uniform, is crumpled, and her makeup is smudged with poorly corrected tear stains. I doubt I look much better myself.

"You look pale. Do you feel faint?"

"No, just worried."

Tanja laughs nervously. "That just might be the understatement of the year."

She extends her hand for me to take, but I hesitate. The moment I walk out these doors and into that hallway, there will be maids gossiping, knights praying, and guests loitering and placing bets. When I walk out these doors, I sign someone's death warrant.

I inhale sharply and place my hand in hers. Her face is a mask of horror as she offers a shaky squeeze.

"He'll be okay," she murmurs. I nod, though I'm quite certain she's trying to convince herself more than me.

"Where's Torin?" I ask, desperate to change the conversation.

Tanja bites her cheek. "He's with Blaine. As his second, he is needed by the arena at the duel, and if Blaine loses, then he is to take over the position of Captain of the Guard."

My stomach drops. Torin never mentioned this. He had spent too much time trying to console her. Meanwhile, all that horror and responsibility has been weighing on his shoulders... I swallow the bile that threatens to rise in my throat.

Footsteps halt before me, and I nearly bump face-first into Rowan. His hand is out in a moment, but I steady myself first. For once, he is the last person I want to see. The guilt of my quickening heartbeat lays heavy in contrast to the knowledge that one man is going to die today, and it's all my fault.

Tanja dips her chin knowingly and makes an excuse to find her seat.

"Are you okay?" Then he laughs nervously. "Dumb question. Of course, you aren't okay."

I sigh heavily. "Is it selfish to weigh their lives against each other in relation to my own? Because, on one hand, I would be guilty about Lucius' death forever, but Blaine's would break me. On the other hand, I can't imagine marrying either of them."

"Oh? Is there someone else in mind then?"

"We are walking into someone's death sentence, and you want to flirt right now?"

Rowan rubs at the back of his neck. "Sorry, thought it would help lighten the mood."

"The only things that could do that would be some *leeche* and the postponement of this duel." I scoff. Rowan shrugs as if making a mental note of this and pats my hand. Torin approaches us, his face disturbingly pale and grim. He wears a fine-pressed coat, probably his only good coat, and thick trousers tucked into his riding boots. He looks dressed for a celebration with the countenance of a funeral guest, though I suppose that's all a duel really is. One massive celebration of a poor soul's death.

I can't imagine Finneas participating in these barbaric rituals, then not regretting it. Moreover, I cannot imagine the fear and anguish Aiko must have felt. She at least had the luxury of hatred towards one of the duelers. She stood to suffer heartache or love. I am doomed to feel loss either way, though one, I fear, may kill me.

"Are you alright, Torin?" I lay a soft hand upon his forearm. "Do you need to sit a moment?"

The knight shakes his head. "The duel is about to start. You must see to your seats," he adds, "and say your prayers to whatever god you worship." Rowan stiffens at my side but says nothing as Torin walks back the way he came from, anxiously wringing his hands.

"Where is your seat? I'll walk you." Rowan looks at his feet guiltily, and I realize. "You're not staying are you?"

"I can't. I've got to go clean up some loose ends." This is the only explanation he offers. The rejection burns my face as I purse my lips to avoid saying anything else. By loose ends, he probably means Mavis. It is always Mavis.

"I see." I whisper tightly.

"Vera, wait." He lowers his voice as he speaks in my ear. "I am going to check that Lucius hasn't tampered with the duel. About a month ago, he offered me a proposition. He asked me to spy on Blaine and report back to him. He thought you still had feelings for him, so I've been feeding him false information and receiving favors as payment. That's how you've had freer rein to leave the palace. I wouldn't put it past him to tamper with the weaponry or bribe a guard to let him take a cheap shot."

Pure silence filters through the castle halls, instilling a chill that has nothing to do with the harsh winter. This cold permeates my bones, my heart. I can feel my eyes crystallize and my breath fogs before me.

He played me. Lucius played me from the first moment I met him. My ego had persuaded my heart to open, plied by his honeyed words and flattering compliments. He is exactly how I feared he would be. Selfish and only concerned with owning me through whatever means.

"How dare he," I seethe. Anger. Good, anger is good. Anger hides foolish things like horror and heartbreak. Lucius told me who he was from day one. I have been the fool who saw something different. "And how could you?"

Rowan flinches as I had stabbed him. "I didn't tell him anything that was real, Ver."

"How could you not tell me!" I hiss underneath my breath. "You knew for a month, don't tell me there wasn't time."

"There wasn't the right time," Rowan corrects. "Look at you now. You're angry and probably thinking of doing something rash. I couldn't make a move until he did."

"Get out of my sight."

Rowan stalls, as if waiting for some hidden message in my words. A plea to stay, a cry for help. My heart grows colder, and I spin on my heel towards the sound of cheering.

"He will live, Verosa," Rowan says softly as I stalk away. "Make sure he lives."

CHAPTER 27
VEROSA

I find Tanja seated on a small wooden chair behind the three thrones on a dais overlooking our arena. Usually, these stands would be filled with spectators waiting to watch the latest joust, or even a play, but today they mutter softly, waiting for blood.

I find my way to my seat, the second of the gold-plated thrones, seated to my father's left. The throne to his right remains empty in reverence to Irene. The lost queen who met a bitter and unfortunate end.

To her people, Irene was a saint. A pious woman who prayed each day and magnanimously gave to the poor as if they were her own family. She was a prize given to the king to honor an alliance between Krycolis and the Tesslari empire, the very alliance I must make concrete through my marriage. They said it was the evil will of the dark god that she passed, and holy unfitting for a woman like her to be torn apart by wolves. None of them know the truth. Not the truth behind who Irene really was, or her death. But I do. I saw the body. She was not mauled to death on an excursion to give to the poor.

My mother was murdered.

My father only nods to acknowledge my existence and takes another sip from his champagne flute. I accept mine from the server with a small thanks, but I don't take a sip. My stomach churns, and I fight the urge to double over.

The trumpets blare. The rabble grows quiet, then explodes as the two opponents step into the arena. The dust rises to swirl about their heels, their chosen armor clunking together as they walk to opposite sides.

Blaine salutes the king, then his gaze drifts to me. The moment our eyes meet, there's a soft resignation in his face. A silent apology. He turns away, and I fight the urge to keel over.

Lucius faces the crowd, offering dazzling smiles and chivalrous bows to the noble ladies. His crimson cape flutters softly behind him, the sunlight catching on the golden embroidery. He looks every part the dashing hero of this story. If we had met under different circumstances, maybe he could have been.

Blaine stands at the opposite end the arena, away from any potential adoring fans. I had prayed that the nobles would favor him. He is a Krycolian who was willing to sacrifice his life on the front lines of the war, and by the gods, there must be someone willing to root for the underdog. As it would turn out, I am wrong.

The spectators gravitate towards Lucius, his empty words and false pleasantries. A façade, he had called it months ago. He had warned me from the start. I am starting to wonder where the mask ends and his true face begins.

The crowd is buzzing with electric energy. They sit on the edges of their seat, men, women, and children alike. All blessed, of course, courtesy of our palace's prejudiced system. It's been nearly twenty years since the last duel, and the people are itching to experience one for themselves.

Behind me, Tanja begins to pray, and Torin steps into the arena.

"The challenge is laid out as such. Captain Koar of Krycolis has challenged Prince Lucius Vangar of the Tesslari Empire to a duel for the hand of Princess Verosa Elyce of Krycolis, as sanctioned by King Ophelus Elyce of Krycolis." Torin speaks loudly as he addresses the crowd. His voice doesn't convey his fear, though I note the slight tremor that could be easily disguised as strain from shouting.

"The ancient laws state that whoever leaves this arena alive is the rightful betrothed of the one whom this duel was initiated for. All forms of weaponry and tactic are permissible save for any with relation to dark magic, including but not limited to cursed blades, curses, magical items, or concentrated dark magic." He turns to the contestants with a bow. "With Deungrid overseeing this duel and my word to be true, let the duel commence at the twelfth strike."

As if waiting for its cue, the bell tower begins to crow, its booming notes stretching over the expanse of the kingdom. On any other day, this toll would proclaim it noon. Today, all it spells is death. Someone will die before the next toll.

I look to the crowd, scanning for a certain face. I spot her easily.

Blaine's mother sits, a formidable and lovely form stark against the cheering cowards surrounding her. It is not her rich skin tone, or the intricate red swirls similar to Kya's that lace around her elegant neck that sets Navi Koar apart from the crowd. It is her powerful aura that makes the weaker men flinch when they make eye contact and makes others hush their whispers as she passes. She sits patient in the crowd, her face passive and calculating as she watches her son.

Blaine's eyes flit to hers. Her chin dips in a slight nod. He mimics the gesture, then lifts his sword.

Lucius mouths something I can't quite make out, and Blaine's brows furrow. Within an instant, their swords clash in a cacophonous song that makes my ears ring. Lucius takes the offensive, driving Blaine back with sharp, stabbing motions. His style is unorthodox, as if he's been raised by the spear rather than sword. Blaine blocks his latest onslaught with the flat of his sword and takes a quick step forward to take over the offensive.

Blaine's motions are the opposite of my fiancé's. His sword strikes in wide arcs and fluid motions as if the weapon is merely an extension of his arm. He slices upwards towards Lucius' throat, and the Westerner dodges just barely, but not quick enough. A single drop of blood drips from the shallow cut on his cheek. The crowd gasps. Blaine has drawn first blood.

Lucius snarls lowly, and I scoff. Blaine should have slit his throat.

The dark thought sends gooseflesh sprawling across my arms, and I tuck in closer to my cloak. I shouldn't have these thoughts, and I shouldn't be enticed by them.

But I am.

The thought of Lucius' blood spilling whispers to me like a clandestine lover, hushed murmurs of soothing words. The gentle caress of karma as the one he once viewed as an object holds the dagger that steals his life. The thought is almost too delicious to ignore.

Lucius charges in a flurry of motions, and Blaine quickly loses the upper hand. Where Lucius' footwork is graceful and coordinated, Blaine struggles to keep up and stumbles. For a moment, they are a perfect match, and their battle becomes a dance. Where Lucius will advance, Blaine will counter. When Blaine feigns left, he strikes right. They move in harmony, placing small wounds that gradually grow in both number and size for a while, until Lucius manages to strike Blaine's hand.

The captain's sword clatters to the ground, golden flecked blood speckled across its hilt and handle. Blaine looks up in horror to dodge, but it's too late. Defenseless and cornered, he squares his shoulders and braces to meet death.

Tanja inhales sharply with a small whimper from behind me, and my father hums contemplatively. As if this is nothing more than an unexpected move in a game.

That burning echoes in my veins again, and it longs to be unleashed.

Lucius raises his blade.

The crowd holds their breath, and I reach deep within that well of power in my core. I draw it out. I command it.

Move.

Lucius cries out as a strong flash of light bounces off his sword into his eyes, temporarily blinding him. It's not much, but it gives Blaine time to scramble for his sword and make a stab at Lucius.

The Tesslarian recovers quicker than I'd hoped and is there to deflect the blow, though it cuts deeply into his arm. His left arm hangs limply by his side, but it is no more a dead weight to him than his sword as he barrels forward. I prepare to risk unleashing another bolt of light as Lucius prepares to stab, but he does the unspeakable.

Lucius drops to slide in the dirt on his hip, slashing a wide arc down

Blaine's face on his way down. However, the true horror comes as I watch him jut his foot out and hook it around Blaine's disfigured leg, twisting it with a cruel snap. He screams in pain and falls as Lucius rises.

"Get up." I plead. "Gods, get up."

No cheap light trick will save him now. I barter with the gods as tears prick the corner of my vision. Lucius prowls forward and raises his sword. His smirk etches deep lines in his cheeks and pulls at the raised edges of his laceration, drawing forth fresh blood.

"Get up. Please just get up."

Blaine does not rise.

Lucius prepares to plunge the sword into his chest cavity, but he pauses.

Every nerve quivers with rage and terror as Lucius turns to face me. That triumphant smile on his face quickly vanishes when he catches my steely glare. Something unspoken passes between us. May it be desperation, a threat, or perhaps a plea, Lucius understands. This moment is the line drawn in the sand. I hold his gaze for a moment before he drops to a knee, bowing his head.

"For my love." He proclaims. "I spare his life."

An uproar begins in the crowd, and my father leans forward to inspect the scene.

"Interesting," he says.

Behind me, Tanja begins to weep with great ragged breaths. Her voice is scratchy as she praises the gods for their mercy. But that is not what this is.

I could laugh. Out of pure rage or relief, I don't know. Blaine would live, but his honor...

How much has he sacrificed for me now, and how long will I continue to let him? He will live in agony so long as I am married to the man who very well should have killed him.

The realization sends me reeling in agony.

In sparing Blaine, Lucius was sending me a warning. This is not mercy, but a challenge.

The healers begin to pour forth. I watch in horror as they load Blaine onto one of their stretchers to inspect the damage. Deep cuts lace his arms, and his leg is curled tightly to his chest; blood dribbles from a slice across his face. It barely missed his eye.

The noblewomen coo about Lucius' handsome mercy, the majority of the men nod their agreement. A man of honor would make a fine king. Though some disagree, saying his grace is weakness, and this was a disrespect to custom.

Our knights will not so much as look at him, damn the consequences for what they may be. I know they will remember this day when he comes into power, that Lucius had taken one of them, the best of them, and degraded them to the point of filth. They see through his mercy; they see the demon rotting beneath that handsome facade just as I do.

Blaine moans on the stretcher. That leg...

I move to go to him, to rush past my expectant fiancé. Let the nobles talk. Let them all rot. I don't care. I just need to get to him.

A startled cry escapes my lips when my father's fingers dig deep into my forearm. Bruises form under his fingertips already.

"You would do well to remember your company," Ophelus warns, still facing ahead, his face giving away nothing, "and your place."

I stagger back to my seat upon the dais, stumbling over the flowing folds of my gown and cloak. The red fabric pools at my feet like blood. With the golden embroidery, it might as well be Blaine's blood I'm steeped in. Like I am not already.

Five thin crescent arcs line my mottled flesh, a drop of blood forming in the corner of one. I fold a slip of red silk over it. Princesses don't bleed, and they sure as hell don't bleed golden.

Torin clears his throat to announce his presence and drops to a knee before the dais.

"Mei Reihn. Mei Reinhavich." He croons with that bastard's smile of his. "Prince Lucius requests her highness."

The king dismisses him with a subtle wave of his hand. Torin murmurs his thanks and many blessings to the king and his offspring, may his reign and life be long, and all that other bullshit he chokes on. He rises and extends his arm, the blooming sunlight catching his face. I force my countenance into a state of neutrality, like I know his is. Cool and quiet rage lays under that mask. It does for us both.

As we step from the dais and approach the arena, his grip tightens only slightly.

"If you don't gut him like a pig, I will." His voice is a low growl, the sound of gravel grinding on concrete. I know he means it. So I just nod, not trusting my voice to not betray me.

I grip his arm fiercely, needing his comfort to brace for the horror ahead. While Lucius has come out victorious, that doesn't mean that Blaine hadn't landed any of his own brutal blows. Crimson blood laced with gold drips from his lips, a nasty bruise garnishing his prominent brow. His eyes glaze over a bit as he catches sight of me, his too white teeth sparkling through his bloody smile. Torin drops my arm with a grunt, no sign of respect or acknowledgment towards Lucius.

"My love." He bows deep at the waist, catching hold of my hand. He moves to kiss the back of it when I lift his face up towards mine. Gingerly, with deliberately painful care, I blot his lips with my handkerchief, a large enough spectacle to leave the nobles cooing. Leaning forward as if to kiss his cheek, I whisper, "You don't know how red my ledger is, all for that man. If you've undone it all..." I pause to fold a chaste kiss into his grimy skin, nearly gagging at the feel and taste. "There'll be hell to pay."

Lucius's smile nearly falters, but it remains plastered to his face. "We will talk later." He lowers his voice to whisper in my ear. "Go to your bastard, maybe then you'll be grateful I showed you *both* such mercy."

The threat does nothing to quell my rage, and my fists itch to smash his face in, but I won't allow it. I won't allow him to win.

With a deep bow, I smile sweetly. "Be grateful I'm showing you mine."

Torin grunts approvingly and, with a deep scowl, extends his arm to me once again. He steers us away from the arena and the vying eyes of the nobles. They all wait, curious to see if I will go to him or not. Torin's hand closes over my shaking arm.

"Don't give them the satisfaction."

I notice now where he is steering us. Blaine will have been taken to the knight's infirmary rather than the royal health bay. There is a direct passage from the arena to the infirmary, but if I go to him now, the nobles will talk. Not only would it tarnish my reputation but Blaine's as well.

Well, whatever is left of it.

The wicked bite of winter nips at any exposed skin as we walk even in the warmed halls. The light radiance of a torch brings small comfort whenever we pass one, but in its absence, the cold stings with greater urgency. My heart quickens, and my eyes begin to sting. Torin notices with a sideways glance and gently nudges my shoulder.

"He's going to be okay."

I force my cold and cracking lips into a small smile. Torin came long after the events of that night, and he was the one who found me is laying broken on a shoddy cot.

The passageway becomes cooler with every step we take towards the knight's quarters. As if winter is mocking my plight, the darkness creeps in, beckoning and sinister. The low sounds of moaning echoes through the halls, pain and agony striking against the stones.

A healer stumbles from the open door at the end of the corridor, her face a sickly shade of green, and her legs faltering beneath her. She lifts her gaze to meet ours and attempts a bow, but her buckling legs refuse, and she stumbles towards the floor.

"Careful!" Torin reaches, his hands outstretched, but I am quicker. She crumbles as my arms lace around her middle, carrying the brunt of her weight and the impact. My knees sting as they slam into the cold stone, its rough edges biting into and tearing my skin. Blood drips down my legs, and I bite my lip to avoid remarking on the small hurt.

"Mai Reinhavich, please don't concern yourself with the likes of me." The healer attempts to brush out of my hold, but I grip her tighter. She's so light, too light.

Sweat beads along her hairline, causing her dark curls to stick flat against her face. Her lips are pale, and I can easily wrap one of my small hands around her entire forearm.

"None of this." I hand her to Torin. "Make sure she finds her way to a physician, and put the cost of treatment on my tab, as well as the cost of any other healers who are unwell."

Torin nods, and I spin to leave when a shaking hand grabs at my cloak. The healer's arm quivers from the act of holding it out, but small determination lights her eyes.

"We did not heal him because we were told to. We healed him because he is one of us," she speaks slowly, as if tasting the treason on each word. The blonde knight holding her blinks slowly as his eyes begin to mist over, and he dips his chin in respect.

Healers are nothing but workhorses in the eyes of the king, and to all others, it would appear to be the same towards his heir at well, but at this moment, an understanding passes between us. A knowing. The knowledge that should I ask at any moment, they would turn on their king because they know who was there when it mattered. That I am one of them.

"And you are one of mine." I breathe, then turn back to Torin. "Call in an outside physician if you must, but no word of this gets to the king."

The knight nods, not even a moment of conflict showing on his handsome face as he stalks back down the darkened corridor. With them gone, I turn now to face the open door and walk towards the horror that surely awaits me.

CHAPTER 28
VEROSA

Blood splatters across the walls as dozens of injured soldiers are piled into one cramped room. A healer screams as he touches a man whose blood has been poisoned by a cursed blade. He lets his eyes drift back and flutter closed. The healer, a boy no older than I am, falls to the ground. He does not rise.

Tanja grips my hand tighter, steering me away from the boy.

"No one is attending to him," I protest, looking over my shoulder to where his body still lays. "I can help."

"Ver, no!" Tanja hisses. "Just keep your head down and try to ignore it. You can't help him."

But I can, and I should, but I let her pull me away with a prayer. By the time I look over my shoulder again, the boy is gone, replaced by another heap of bleeding soldiers.

The room is as much of a battlefield as the mountains they fought in beyond the palace walls. Men are screaming, healers are fighting for their lives to keep them at bay, and all I can do is watch from my own secluded viewpoint.

A weary physician bumps into my shoulder hard enough to send me reeling towards the floor. The stone cuts my hand, and a thin line of golden blood trickles out from my palm. Dripping onto my wrist. When

I look up, my eyes meet another one of the wounded's. His eyes are nothing more than hollow sockets, and his arm is halfway off from his shoulder. A frenzied healer is trying to tie it in a sling with one hand, her other arm hanging loosely by her side, bent at a horrible angle. The scent of blood fills my nose, and I struggle to keep down my bile, but nonetheless, I begin to crawl towards him.

I lift my cupped and bleeding palm to his lips right as Tanja finds me again. Her shriek is drowned out by the moans of the injured and dying, and I can only feel her as she tackles me back to the ground from behind. She tears her skirts frantically and uses the fabric to bind my wound and clean the rest.

"Vera, you can't, they'll swarm you!" Her voice is low and shaking, and her eyes glistening with unshed tears.

"But they're dying."

"That's why they're so desperate. If you show them even one drop of your miracle, they'll rip you apart with their bare hands to save themselves, and no guard could ever protect you. You can't."

I pause for a moment, my gaze wandering to those around me. People who I could save. Then I feel Tanja's pleading stare boring holes into my spine and sigh.

"We need to get to Blaine."

Blaine, who I haven't seen in two years. Blaine, who swore he would return alive. I can still remember the pressure of his lips on mine, the desperation I could taste on them mixed with the salt of my own tears. Can feel the shade of the tree we had to hide behind to say our goodbyes. He smiled so sweetly, nothing but joy on his face, before he sprinted to catch up to the other soldiers saying their goodbyes.

I also remember the lonely nights, rereading his letters he sent from the battlefront. I clutch the most recent one tightly in my hand despite having memorized its contents.

The worst has come to pass. You will see me soon, my love. I will leave a light on.

I woke up this morning with a lightness in my heart that I haven't felt in nearly two years, back before he left to fight in this damned war. I can sense that light fading now as I watch the healers collapse and men die on cramped tables. What type of condition is Blaine in to have landed himself in a room full of dying men?

A hard knot coils in my stomach.

Then I spot it. A mop of dark curly hair, still the exact same as if I'd ran my fingers through it moments before, not two years ago. A grin splits across my face. My light even in places as dark as these. He's come home.

"Tanja look, it's him! It's…"

Tanja stands deathly still, her hand flying to cover her mouth as she chokes down silent sobs. Her shoulders curve inward and shake as silver tears snake down her pretty face. My heart stops for a moment as I watch her reaction.

"Tanja?" A gut-wrenching cry is the only response I receive.

My feet move on their own accord, flying over severed limbs, bloody rags, and stone without losing my footing once. My breathing slows as time suddenly stops. The scent of blood burns my nose, and I begin to choke, but nothing matters. Nothing matters except for him.

Blaine. My love. My light.

My wounded.

Several healers crowd around him, some dropping to the floor, screaming in agony the moment his skin touches theirs. I push past the ones who have fallen to look upon his face, and the world falls out from beneath my feet.

His skin is a sickly shade of grey with sweat coating it in a grimy sheen. His breathes come out in short puffs as his chest rises and falls to keep up with the infection. I trace the blood on his body downwards to his leg.

Gods, his leg.

Pristine, white bones protrude from his gored flesh, chunks of skin and meat still clinging to it. Yellow liquid runs from the wound, congealing in clumps along his dark skin to stain it hues of greens.

Who could have done this to him? Who could bear to do this? Who could…

Sunlit smiles and running from the palace guards flash through my mind. All those times we hid in the stables from Ms. Eida or tried on the crowns and swords in the royal treasury.

Moments that can slip away in a second. Moments that mean nothing if his heart ceases to beat. Moments of a life I can't bear to live if he's not living with me.

"Blaine." I try to clutch for his hand, but someone wraps their arms around my waist. The guards. They've found me.

"No, Blaine! Wake up, wake up!" His eyes remain closed as more hands grab for my arms, my legs.

The scream that tears loose form my throat is guttural as I claw and scrape myself forward on nothing but my fingernails to get to him. The skin beneath my nails tear and leave bloody gold smears on the already crimson-stained floor. I choke through sobs to reach him, to hold him. To watch him open his eyes with laugh and a smile and tell me we are fine. He is fine.

"LET GO OF ME!"

My fingers brush against his, and his silver eyes flutter open as if on command. As if he heard that I need someone to save me. His lips almost curve into a smile before he looks down towards his leg.

And he screams.

The shock I felt then isn't unsimilar to the one I feel now as I watch the healers gather around him, his leg twisted cruelly beneath him. He bites down tightly on a belt as an aiding physician resets it with a splint, and the available healers attend to the smaller hurts that litter his body.

Rage boils beneath my skin as I think of Lucius and his smile as he held the power to skewer one of the most precious things in this life. And for what, petty revenge or jealousy? Or was it something deeper?

I fight the bile back down my throat and decide to make myself useful instead. I pick at the scab on my arm, and when no one is looking, I drop a few droplets of blood into a cup of water and onto a damp rag. Quietly, I pass it to the physician, who tips it between Blaine's lips, and I take to dabbing at his facial laceration with the rag. The wound slowly begins to knit itself closed, and Blaine opens his eyes.

"Hey, it's okay. Just rest," I coo, but he grabs my wrist and sits up, much to the ire of his physician.

"You shouldn't be here," he protests. "Someone, see the princess out."

"Just lay back down, you're fine. Everything is going to be okay, just let me take care of you."

"Just leave." Cold shock douses over my spine and sends a chill through my body.

"What are you talking about? Stop being ridiculous and lay down, I'm going to fix this."

I try to take the rag again, but his grip is tight on my wrist, and I am forced to watch helpless as it falls from my grasp. As if on cue, Torin appears in the doorway again and places his hand on my shoulder.

"Ver, I think we should give him some time."

I scoff. The last thing we need is time. For all I know, Lucius could change his mind and come murder him here right now. No, what we need is a plan.

"Torin."

"Yes?"

"Get her out of here."

The blonde knight looks over at me with such sympathy that it takes me a moment before I realize what's happening. Blaine releases my wrist right as Torin grabs ahold of my midsection and begins to pull me towards the door.

"Torin, stop!" I feel those treacherous, *helpless* tears stream down my face again.

"Blaine, don't you dare. *Don't you dare!*"

The door is shut in my face and locked before I can even put up a fight. Somewhere on the other side, I can sense him slipping away.

The first time he awoke, there was still hope in his eyes before he slipped away into pain. There was love masking fear. Today there is only cold nothingness and resignation. The Blaine I thought I knew, the one I thought I was starting to get back, is gone. If he had died today, I could have found solace in the memory of his love. Now all there is left to haunt me is the image of hollow eyes and the sinking feeling that all of this is my fault.

Torin leans heavily against the door next to me, and I narrow my eyes.

"So much for loyalty." I spit.

Hurt flashes across his face before he drags a hand down it. Then he laughs humorlessly in a tone I've never heard him use before. Every muscle in my body tenses.

"Honestly? You never know when to quit, do you?" The wood of the door creaks as it bears the brunt of his head, which lolls back against it. His tongue runs over his dry and cracked lips before he narrows in on me. My every sense is telling me to run or beg, but my feet remain rooted to the stone.

"You are the last person he wants to see right now, and honestly? I don't blame him. You fucked his life over in so many ways, can't you just leave him alone?"

If my heart can break into any more pieces than it already has, then Torin has just shattered it beyond repair. I stagger back as if stabbed and grab for something to steady myself on. When no stronghold finds my hand, I settle for falling against the floor and praying for the stone to accept my sacrifice.

"That's not fair."

Dammit why won't my lip stop quivering? Why can I never seem to find the right words, the right ways to make things right? Why do I always make things worse? Why, why, why, why?

"*Because you're nothing.*" A female voice whispers in the back of my head. "*You've always been nothing but a pawn in a game much larger than your life. You are insignificant. You can't save your friends; you can't even save yourself.*"

Torin blinks, and his face softens.

"No, it's not. I'm sorry."

"*Worthless.*"

Somewhere in reality, the wind brushes against my skin, but I no longer feel its bite. Something darker calls from within my core, and I answer.

Rising from the stone, I dust myself off. The knight looks at me strangely, but even his voice is lost to the echoes of my resolution as I storm down the halls. My red cloak billows behind me.

There's someone I need to find.

CHAPTER 29
VEROSA

Lucius is waiting in the courtyard just as I expected him to be, his form thinly veiled by the shadows of an overarching tree. The healers commissioned by the king fixed his face nicely. Anyone passing by would guess he has just stepped out from a business lunch rather than a duel to the death.

"I was beginning to wonder if you'd come at all, or if I'd have to seek you out myself." His lips curve upwards in a small grin. A searing pain splits through my core. How easy it had been to trust him. It isn't hard to see how when he smiles like that.

"You make it sound like I had a choice."

The prince's face falls immediately. "You always have a choice, Verosa. I am just an extension of you. If you were to tell me to run myself through on my own blade, I would do it!"

The sight of him groveling on his knees does not strike me as much as I had hoped it would. He does not look small. He appears larger than before. His soft tears slip into the cracks of the mask he wears, slowly chipping away at the cheap paint. No longer a demure prince, but a cunning manipulator capable of swaying an entire kingdom. It's nearly a shame, both that he thinks he can fool be twice and that he could be a powerful ally if he didn't choose to be my enemy.

"Drop the pretense. I just have one thing to ask you before I rid my hands of you."

"And what might that be?"

"Why didn't you kill him?"

"Because I love you."

I scoff. "Save the bullshit for someone who might believe it."

I can see now how easy it had been for him to win my trust and affection. How desperate I was for someone, anyone, to understand. I had been thrown into a political exchange where those in power viewed me as nothing more than a collateral to their plans, and there was no one who could stop it. I thought my best friend and the only one I'd ever truly loved had abandoned me when I needed him most, and I was trapped in a home by parents who never held any form of affection for me. All he had to do was say the right words, promise me freedom and choice, and I would be his.

Unfortunately for him, I am not the same girl I was when he met me. I grew to be cunning and strong, and I've found people who care for me on even footing. There is no power struggle with the Nightwalkers, no strings being pulled to prop me up before them. They do not own me, nor do they try to.

I can hear the prince running behind me as I walk away. How irksome it must be for him to have me slip through his fingers. How annoying it must be that I don't need him anymore.

"You want to know what I think of you so badly?" he roars in a fury. "I think you're a blazing fire that I can't get close to no matter how desperately I want to. You're an intolerable brat with a wicked tongue and flighty senses. I have this feeling that our whole lives together, I'll be pulling carpets over scorch marks because you can't control your temper for the sake of diplomacy. And yet you're kind and have run yourself ragged for the sake of others. You make a place for yourself at every table. You're the spitting image of everything I wish I was and know I cannot be. You're burning me alive, and I could care less. I want you to engulf me whole."

The soft breeze blows across his reddened face and brushes the stray hairs from his eyes. The noble prince protecting and proclaiming. He might as well have been pulled straight from a fairytale.

My jaw visibly slackens. I inhale deeply and ball my fists at my side before I dare to even turn towards him. His face is open and waiting as he assumes he can pacify my rage with pretty words. That churning sensation in my stomach returns.

"Are you out of your godsdamned mind? What makes you think I want you to think of me like that? Did you think that just because I agreed to *try* and be cordial that meant 'take me, I'm helplessly in love with you', or are you just deluded enough to think that I'm an easy target?"

Lucius stumbles, "P-pardon?"

"Pardon yourself when you're king, you fucking scumbag." I jab my finger into his chest for emphasis with each word. "Because, by the gods above, I am going to make sure you become king. And when you are the most powerful man commanding the most powerful empire, you will feel true terror. You will sleep with one eye open knowing I'm right there, just waiting, no, just *dying* to kill you in the most awful way you can imagine. You wanted my love? You should have thought about that before you tried to kill my friend."

In an instant, his aura shifts. His smile becomes a cold smirk, and his hair falls in front of his eyes to shadow his face. His shoulder square, and he looks towards me under the dip of his chin as he rises to his feet.

Taking a deep breath, I allow my feet to spread wide and shift my weight into a fighting stance. Just in case. Lucius notices with no displeasure. If anything, this is the reaction he wants.

"You have the King of Mercenaries at your back, and suddenly you grow a spine," he sneers.

I shrug nonchalantly. "It helps, I suppose." I figured Lucius knew who Rowan was the moment the mercenary revealed Lucius's proposition to spy on Blaine. Lucius probably planted another spy somewhere to find out the truth while he tested Rowan's real loyalties and what he could possibly offer to a princess. I'm sure he audited our lessons in the library as well.

Nonetheless, I can't let him know he has the upper hand. He's only one step from figuring out my real intentions. If I don't discover his first, then I'll never be free of him. I have to find Rowan, make a new plan, and potentially move up our exodus.

"If you couldn't tell already, our agreement is off."

Lucius places a hand over his heart and feigns a gasp. "Devastating."

Focus. I need to focus on anything other than the tantalizing thought of blooding my fists on his face.

My heels are pressed firmly into the ground, allowing every vibration of the earth to resonate up through my shins. As Lucius shifts, I can sense the slight disturbance in the air and how it has to shift to make room for him. The sun's radiant heat dances across my face in rhythm to the swaying of the tree branches and the wind. It is all connected. The sun, the earth, the air, the magic, and me. I am rooted to it all, and Lucius is nothing. He is nothing in the face of my plans. Just another jealous man who seeks to possess that which he can never have, that which he never will have.

My footsteps reverberate through the loose soil, recently upturned by the strong winter wind. It feels like snow.

"I didn't kill him because I want you to remember that I hold power over you. Anything and everything you hold dear is mine to command. I can take it at any moment." Lucius bares his teeth in this egregious act of fury. "You can keep on your petty lessons with your mercenary, but at the end of the day, I can take his life whenever I please, and it will be my bed you have to retire to."

Deep breathes. I am a well of infinite power and patience.

"I own you Verosa, you'd do well to remember that."

Well, that was a nice thought while it lasted.

I turn with deliberate and painstaking stillness as I fix my gaze upon his trembling form. Trembling not with fear, but with anger. Pure rage at the thought that I could defy him. That I dare to defy him still.

I curtsy low and rise slowly with a lovely smile painted on my face. The pose of a perfect princess, the role he wishes for me to play. As I watch him shake, I realize that I've unsettled him more than pacified.

"Princess Verosa. It's a pleasure to *finally* meet you, Prince Lucius."

The joy I felt when seeing Lucius' face redden and drop is lost by the time I return to my chambers. Instead, what is left is only the crushing emptiness of my heart as the memory of today's events flood my senses. To think it all happened on today of all days too...

The cold air bites my naked flesh as my cloak and gown fall from my shoulders. I had dismissed all the maids earlier, so with no one to help me, I sink into the cold bathtub alone. When I raise a now grime and blood-free arm to the light, the skin is smooth. No crescent-shaped marks mar my pale skin, nor is there any skin missing from where the stone floors tore through my knees this afternoon.

My healing abilities were probably Irene's favorite part about me.

The fire is burning low when I re-enter my chambers, and Tanja is nowhere to be seen. I suppose she must be with Blaine and Torin; they probably have no qualms over seeing her like they do me. The thought is unsettling, but I suppose I deserve it.

My silk sheets are cold, and the large bed only serves to remind me of my loneliness. I imagine tonight wouldn't be so terribly dreadful if there were another form pressing into the comforter.

My fingers splay across the pillow beside me, the candlelight creating ghastly shadows across the walls. The wooden frame of the bed creaks as I roll onto my side and tuck my knees to my chest. I grip the blanket with white knuckles as I force my eyes to shut.

"Happy birthday, mom," I whisper as sleep claims my conscious. "I hope you're rotting in Hell."

At some point in the night, I feel someone's lips atop my forehead before the sound of their footsteps echo down the hallway. Still half asleep, I roll onto my back without a second thought.

Dawn offers a gentle caress of light some hours later, and I sit up with a stretch. Paper flutters from my lap. Looking down, I recognize Blaine's messy scrawl and signature.

Tanja rushes in as my eyes scan the last line. A large tear plops from the bridge of my nose onto the parchment, marring the ink. Tanja's tear-streaked face confirms what I find to be true in this letter.

Blaine is gone, and he is not coming back.

CHAPTER 30

ROWAN

It has been three days, and Vera still has not returned from her search. The whole palace is still whispering with stories of clandestine affairs and the scream that tore the palace in two three days ago.

The front door of the compound swings open, the steady pattering of rain growing into a thunderous stream as Amír stomps back into our home, Kya close on her heels.

"Anything?"

Kya shakes her head while Amír wrings her braid out. She takes Kya's cloak and hangs it by the fire to dry as she takes to unzipping her boots. "No one has heard anything from her or even caught a glimpse of someone who fits that description. Looks like she's making full use of the lessons we taught her."

Amír's glare as she speaks is honed and pointed in my direction. As if all of this is my fault. I sigh heavily and pinch the bridge of my nose. Kya's shoulders droop.

"Maybe she saw her chance and finally ran? That is what we were training her for, after all."

"Or Mavis got her." Amír voices what none of us dare to say.

"And what of the captain?" I cut her off, not allowing myself to entertain that thought. "Has anyone seen Blaine?"

"Now that is something I do have some news on." My second rises and fishes a parchment from her cloak. A map with a few drunken scrawls across it.

"There have been a few sightings of him. Some commoners have been housing him as he hops from town to town, making his way towards the border. They all were hoping for the next great love story and pity him. Within the next few days, he should be here." Amír points towards a second circle, this one more elegant and less scrawling.

"Plant someone we trust there. Tell them to report back to me if they find anything."

The gunslinger groans, but nonetheless slings her wet cloak back on and stomps out into the rain. The wind slams the door behind her. Behind me, Derrín, who arrived home this morning, whistles lowly.

"Why are we going through this trouble for a captain? I mean, I get Vera. She's one of us. But why him?"

The mechanic takes to picking at the scabs lining his fingers as he speaks. Without a machine to fiddle with, he's left restless. Kya slaps his hands away and dismisses herself to grab some gauze to wrap his fingers with.

"He's important to her."

"So? You've never given a shit before."

"Didn't he also threaten to kill you?" Kya corroborates as she reenters the room. With nimble fingers that rival her brother's the assassin begins to wrap his scabs, and then his fingertips when he refuses to stop picking at the gauze.

"It'll scar," she tuts.

"We are mercenaries. We already have scars." Derrín deadpans.

Their bickering fills the compound, which feels more empty than usual lately. The air feels heavy, as if the thought of never seeing Vera again crushes all oxygen from my lungs. Never seeing her smile, hearing her laugh, the smug look on her face as she thinks of something especially witty. It is all too much.

What is worse though? The thought that Mavis doesn't have her, and that she chose to stay away on her lonesome? If Mavis or the Rebellion have her, then there is no force on this earth that can stop me from getting her back. I will tear this world apart to find her. But if she chose to stay away on her own... I won't be another person who tries to control her. I will have to let her go.

"Hey, not that you want to think about this, but what are you going to do about your own plan if we can't find Vera?"

I turn to face Derrín slowly, not missing the cautious wariness in his voice. The fear that I will do something drastic.

"You don't have anything to worry about," I groan as I run my hand through my hair. "I already have found an alternate way into the palace. Even if she never comes back, I know how to get in."

Kya frowns. "Then why haven't you killed him yet?"

"Gods, I have to spell everything out for you."

I barely have time to dodge one of Kya's blades with a yelp. She raises an eyebrow in challenging humor.

"If I kill him now, then who gets caught in the crossfire?"

Kya swears softly. "So you're going to break her out then kill him?"

"I'm going to break her out *and* kill him," I smile, "all in the same night."

Vera and I planned everything out weeks ago. The king is planning an engagement ball for his daughter within the next month since she has been secretly engaged to some foreign nobleman. It will be the perfect occasion to sneak away. When the king announces the engagement, Vera will slip out to meet Kya and Amír at the balcony overlooking the royal gardens. While she disappears into the night, I will use the commotion to kill my father.

Kya frowns. "What will we do then? You know they'll come looking for you, for one of two reasons you've probably thought about. Do you really think you'll be able to hide right under their noses?"

I pause for a moment. All these years, I've thought of one thing and one thing only. My mother and getting her to safety. Taking her somewhere she doesn't have to live in fear of my father finding us, where I can provide for her in ways more savory than being a weapon for hire.

Somewhere that Vera and I can be just a boy and girl. Somewhere we can breathe. Where we can live.

"No," I admit. "I won't be able to live in the shadows forever. That night will be the last night you see me."

Silence.

Derrín slumps in his seat, and Kya drops her espa. It clatters to the floor, doing nothing to slice the tension in the room.

"Amír will be in charge and-"

"No."

I blink. "No?"

"Where you go, we go. You got that, mister?" Kya seethes, tears pricking at the corners of her eyes. "You are our family. We have no one here that cares for us or we care for. We will follow you to the end of the earth and back."

"The end of the earth is far away."

"Then so be it."

The front door slams open. "I hope you all weren't making any drastic plans without the other two members of your party."

Amír stalks in, completely drenched through and shivering, with Vera following close behind her. I am by her side in an instant, checking for any sign of injury or illness. She sneezes softly, but she appears to be unharmed apart from that.

"Where have you been?"

The pureblood diverts her gaze to the floor. "You already know the answer to that."

I can't ignore the streak of jealousy that grips at my back, clinging like a shadow. She has been out in this weather for three days, searching for him.

I groan inwardly. As much as it makes my stomach coil, I can't hold her at fault. There was a time before me where he was her everything, and even if their relationship is not romantic anymore, it is easy to see that she still values his companionship greatly.

"Did you find him?"

Verosa shakes her head, sending a soft spray of water droplets flying around her face like a halo. The droplets catch the firelight, sending a short streak of flame dancing through the sky.

"I am sure he will show up. He might just need time to process everything that has happened."

"But what if he doesn't? What then?"

My hand reaches out on its own accord as if to cup her cheek, her breath pausing. In anticipation maybe, but something small and dark says it's fear.

She's afraid of you, the voice taunts. *They all are. They should be.* I let it linger a mere centimeter from her skin. Skin that I imagine is so soft that if I dared touch it, it might break. If she heard me say that, she'd probably give me a bruise that would last a month. I should know by now she's not delicate. And yet I want to hold and protect her as if she is.

"Yes?" Her lip quivers with anticipation, her words coming out as more of a sigh than a question. Her eyes are already halfway closed, her constellation of freckles nearly covered by a hazy blush. How easy it would be to just close this space between us.

I should have said, *Stay. I want you to stay. Don't go back to that hellhole, stay with me. Let me be yours, and I promise I'll take you everywhere you've ever wanted to go. Let me free you. Stay with me.*

"The palace has been in an uproar. You'd better head back before they send out another search party." I say instead. Her eyes snap open in an instant, and she steps back away from me. Silver lines her deep blue eyes, and I pretend not to see the hurt in them.

"Oh," she says, her voice much shriller and more strained than before. It plucks at my heart strings and makes my long to reach for her again, but I restrain myself. "I'll see you tomorrow then."

"I should walk you back. It's late." I try, but she holds her hands up in front of her, her cloak hood already pulled up to hide most of her face.

"No, no, I'm fine. I got here on my own." She pauses and turns to show her face graced with a devious smile. "An uproar, you say? I like the sound of that." Without another word, she spins on her heels and leaves. The howling wind closes the door for her, and the scent of wisteria follows it. With a heavy sigh, I force myself to acknowledge the other gawking presence in the room.

"Follow her."

"On it, boss." Kya whispers, stepping out from the shadows to the door where Vera once was.

I've never been a religious man; it goes against my very existence. If the gods are real, I'm sure they've already turned their back on me. The hybrid bastard in love with a pureblood. The very thought makes me laugh, but it sounds cynical even to my ears. If the gods are real, I'm sure now that they must have a very sick sense of humor.

I've never thought about prayer before, not until recently, that is. Mother used to have me pray at night when I was a child, but those were always half empty words. Prayers for safety, prayers for father, wherever he was, for the sick, for forgiveness for sins committed and sins yet to be done. I said the words as I was supposed to, but I wouldn't call recitation prayer. But Verosa makes me want to scrape my knees in a pew and beg for something better. To make me better. If the Laei are real, she must be their proof of existence. Nothing else could ever be as devastatingly beautiful as her.

The door barely creaks when Kya returns, her red makeup slightly smudged with the rain. Without a word, she sets to untying her boot laces and leaving her long espas sitting on the table. There is no blood decorating their slender sheen.

"She's home safe if you were wondering." My friend groans as she wrings water from her socks, a knowing look highlighting those striking amber eyes.

"I know. I sent you."

"Flattery will get you everywhere." She smirks. "But not with me."

I try to laugh, but the sound that comes out is wearier and more strained than I intended, and my assassin eyes me from the corner of her gaze.

"You know, you probably should have told her that we know where Blaine will be."

"Then she would have rushed headfirst into danger again."

"But Rowan." Kya's voice is soft, but there is a sharp edge beneath her words. "If she's going to be one of us she's going to have to do that daily. You can't protect her forever, not to mention that I don't think she needs your protection anymore. You trained her to take care of herself. At some point, you have to let her actually do that, or she'll grow to resent you too. People like that, who have had others make their choices for them their whole lives, they don't want sheltering."

"So what are you saying?"

It is hard to hide the frustration building within me. Is it so wrong to want to protect her?

"Just be careful your protection doesn't turn into possession. Start by telling her the truth." Kya lays a gentle hand on my shoulder. She glances over her shoulder once more, this time towards the growing pile of letters scattered across my desk, all signed with a single M. Without a word, she slinks off to wherever Amír is, leaving me alone with smothering memories and the chill of winter.

CHAPTER 31
VEROSA

Rowan wasn't joking when he said the palace was in an uproar. I barely managed to sneak back through my window without being spotted, and Tanja's scream when she found me in my bed did nothing to help the matter at hand.

"So where were you again?" Lucius groans, pinching at the bridge of his nose. My father listens closely, sitting on the large throne to the other man's right. Torin, my father's new Captain of the Guard, stands at attention to the king's right. His eyes harbor dark circles beneath them, plucking at the guilt in my chest.

"I was on the palace grounds the entire time," I lie. "I would go for a ride during the day and slip into my room when no one was there. I would leave again before the rest of the palace awoke and spend my days thinking."

"And you mean to tell me you did all of this while not one guard ever saw you enter or leave the stables, let alone your room?"

"Try not to sound so shocked. You were here the day I eluded half the royal guard and jumped from a window, right?"

"Verosa, this isn't funny." If Ophelus notes my pointed glares and sharp words directed towards my fiancé, he doesn't say anything.

"I am not trying to be funny, Mai Reihn." I sigh deeply. "Have you cared to think that while my fiancé's popularity has only grown, my reputation has taken a hit? Not to mention I lost someone who I have been close with since childhood. All I desired was some time to think and process alone. I don't think I did anything wrong."

The king says nothing but inhales deeply. Lucius glowers and flinches at the mention of Blaine. Good. Let him feel a fraction of the hurt I do.

Torin clears his throat loudly. "Mei Reihn, if I may impose."

Ophelus nods. "You may."

"What if Princess Verosa reports her whereabouts to me daily, and then I can report back to you if she leaves the palace. This way, the princess is free to mourn in private, but we do not cause another commotion similar to the one we just experienced. If she's not where she claims, then I will take whatever punishment you see fit in her stead."

Ophelus takes a moment to consider this proposition, while I flash warning signals telepathically to the captain. In return, I receive a look that screams 'shut up and listen.'

"Very well then. Captain, escort the princess back to her room."

I make note of the way Lucius shifts closer to the throne as he isn't asked to leave. His hand rests surely across the hilt of his sword that he now keeps sheathed at his hip constantly. Like he is waiting for some imminent threat. I shudder to think what it might feel like to be on the other end of that blade with such a man wielding it.

My father nods his head, and the doors click shut behind us. The silence feels rather like an anticlimactic resolution to the undoubtedly tense conversation happing behind those solid oak doors.

"I wish you wouldn't have done that," I whisper, allowing him to escort me through the hall. "Is this some sick lesson of yours that you're trying to teach me?"

"And what lesson would that be?"

The passing guards dip their head in reverence. I brush it off, but Torin stiffens as if it is still unexpected. He nods towards them as we continue our walk. The sunlight catches on the golden threaded tapestries, seemingly bringing their stories to life.

"I don't know, that I shouldn't sneak out anymore maybe. Or you're just trying to make me feel guilty."

Torin stops and turns towards me, the shadows no longer concealing his weary face. His eyes are red and puffy, and his shoulders curve inwards as if too exhausted to carry the weight of the armor he wears.

"I just put my life on the line for you, and that's where your mind jumps to?"

"No, I'm sorry, that was wrong of me." I sigh. Blaine's disappearance has worn heavy on all of us, and it would be foolish of me to think that it hurt me the most. Torin was immediately shot to the position of Captain of the Guard, a title Blaine long since coveted but conceded when he left, and all of Blaine's previous duties have been piled on his shoulders. He still grins and jokes with us, but we can all tell that he never wanted this.

"Has the workload been hard?" I remember the permanent purple circles that adorned Blaine's under eye every day as I note the faint beginnings of a bag under Torin's. The captain shrugs and shakes his head.

"Nothing too awful. It's mostly been trying to reorganize our troops and prepare security for someone's upcoming birthday party." He play-fully nudges my shoulder, which almost sends me reeling given his new armor. "Ophelus wants guards stationed at any possible entrance and exit given the recent rebellion uprisings."

I frown. "Are they getting worse?"

Torin sighs and runs his hand along his face, a habit he seems to have picked up from Rowan. "Well, word got out that the target of their recent attack was the princess of Krycolis." He catches my panicked glance. "Don't worry, we've kept it from the public. Your little outing confirmed that you are indeed a pureblood, which has only whetted the blade of their desire to kill you and have another assume the throne."

"I just don't understand. Why do they want to kill me so badly? What have I done to them?"

The captain runs his tongue over his dry lips as if trying to taste the right thing to say. He mulls it over for a moment before he speaks again.

"It's not you, per say. More so what you represent, not to mention the laws your grandfather established."

I swear softly. The Raonkin Ban. A law which prohibits anyone of cursed descent to hold any official position, title, large plot of land, or entrance to the palace. Discrimination at its finest.

"As if your great-great-whatever-uncle banning their mages from practicing magic wasn't bad enough, now there's discriminatory laws put in place which affects the cursed's quality of life. The final straw was when that crooked duke gained permission to hunt them for sport all those years ago, but now they have an heir to the throne who supposedly has the purest blood of the thing they hate most. You're a perfect culmination of everything that is ruining their lives."

"Thank you for summing that up so kindly." I deadpan.

By the time we reach my room, four new guards have been stationed outside the door. A glance out the window confirms my suspicions that at least a dozen more have been stationed outside my window as well. I click my tongue against the roof of my mouth. They've finally learned.

"I guess there isn't any hope that I could have these guards removed?"

Torin grimaces sympathetically. "Not a chance. Unfortunately, I do need the king to believe I am qualified for this job, and to do that, you need to be where you say you are at all times. These guys are here to make sure of that."

The wooden door creaks as I open it, and I frown. Once inside the room, I place my ear against the splintering wood and knock, only for it to reverberate back through my senses. Shit. Someone replaced my door with lighter wood while I was gone. They can hear my every word outside.

Tanja approaches me and bows towards Torin before he is gone as well. She presses a willowy finger to her lips and juts her chin in the direction of the bathing chambers.

"Mai Reinhavich, by the Laei you smell *heinous*! Quick, to the tub with you." My lady in waiting exclaims rather loudly. I roll my eyes as the heavy chamber door snicks closed behind us.

"Was that part necessary?" I groan. Tanja smirks devilishly.

"This is the only room they won't dare enter, and the only door they didn't replace. Besides, I wasn't exaggerating, you do smell dreadful. Get in the tub."

"I could have your head for that."

"I'm sure you could, my little tyrant." She taps a single finger against my nose with a laugh before excusing herself to grab something from my room. Self-consciously, I lift my cloak and take a sniff.

I gag immediately.

Ever so carefully, I slip out of my riding boots, followed by cloak, trousers, and blouse before comfortably sinking into the warm bathtub. Tanja reenters moments later with a parchment carefully concealed in her hands.

"Torin wrote this out. You might want to warn the others," she says as she unfurls highly descriptive notes on the new guard rotation.

She gives me a moment to read through the parchment before I stuff it under a loose stone. She shifts from foot to foot, fiddling with her skirt.

"Did you find anything?" Her voice is quiet despite the thick door and stone walls between us and the guard.

"No." I sink lower into the water to avoid her pressing gaze. "I just can't believe he would leave without saying anything."

Tanja's hands pause, and she inhales sharply. Dread settles in my gut before she even parts her lips.

"He didn't say anything to you?"

"No, he didn't say anything. By the Laei, he wouldn't even let me into the room. I always knew he must hate me, but this... Did he tell you he was going to leave?"

Tanja swallows thickly. "And Torin... Ver, we thought you knew."

Those three nights out alone, searching for him in the dark. Trying to bring him home. Everyone knew he was leaving. They got to say their goodbyes and make peace. Everyone except for me, the one person who needed that closure most.

The water droplets trickle down my forearm as I brace my hands on either side of the tub. My back pops as I turn to face her, an unsettling sound that has Tanja's face blanching.

"And you just didn't care? He's gone, and you let him?"

The woman's face molds into an expression of confusion and mingling irritation.

"Let him? We didn't think you'd care that much."

"And why wouldn't I care?"

"Well, apart from the obvious fact that Rowan is courting you, because you're doing the same thing soon."

My knuckles turn white as I grip the lip of the basin. The water has since grown cold. Dark stringy hairs stick to my forehead and slightly obscure my sight, but there is no mistaking the growing anger on Tanja's face. The hurt behind her words.

"That's different."

"How?" Cold. Sharp. All things I'm so unfamiliar with finding in her voice.

"Because I'm coming back for you all!" I contest, wrapping myself in a thick towel as the winter chill begins to settle in my bones. "We are going to make a place for us where we are safe and comfortable, then I am coming back for you all."

"Vera, has it ever crossed your mind that we *aren't* coming with you?"

"What?"

"We have families here-"

"You don't have a family. They're all dead." The words leave my mouth before I can even register the flash of hurt across her face. That hurt turns into anger, and Tanja reaches into the folds of her gown before raising her hand. I flinch.

When I open my eyes, a mix of horror and disgust is evident on the woman's face as she holds up a ring. It is simple yet elegant enough, with a small sapphire resting in the center of the golden band.

"I am engaged." Tanja speaks slow and low. "Ruby proposed a month ago. I can't name any other kingdom on this continent whose king would allow two women to be wed. I won't leave Krycolis knowing I could be killed elsewhere for love. Not to mention that Ruby has family here; Torin has family here. This is our home. Forgive us for not being so willing to run away from the land that raised us."

Her words register like a backhanded slap across my heart. Not because she's right, but because I never knew. Never asked. Never cared.

I expected her to drop everything and follow me as if I am all she has. The truth is far clearer. Tanja and Torin have people that love them. All I have is them.

"Congratulations," I croak, the air suddenly thick and refusing to enter my lungs. Laei, I really am the worst.

"Gee, thanks, you sound enthused." She bites back. In all my years of knowing her she never once so much as raised her voice against me, never did more than roll her eyes and bite her cheek. She had cultivated the patience of a god, and a creation of equal evil has finally broken it. My selfishness has towed the fine veil between forgiveness and spite for years, and now I've stumbled into spite.

Tanja tosses a towel my way. "You'd better get dressed. The guard rotation is in an hour. It'll be your only chance until morning to get out of here."

She slams the door before I can even find a semblance of an apology, leaving me alone in the cold tub in an even colder room.

I take my time methodically buckling every strap across my thigh, using this activity as a form of meditation.

This garter slips on here, and this buckle pins here. *Snap.*

This dagger settles here. Feel its cold weight. Don't cry.

Lace your boots. Don't shift too much weight onto that stone, it creaks. Snap. Don't cry.

The guards rotate exactly when Torin said they would, leaving the smallest period of time to slip out. Without any hesitation, I slip into the night, letting the darkness consume my form. My fear mingles with relief.

Good, you deserve to feel that piercing pain. You deserve to look over your shoulder. You deserve all of this.

For once, I don't reprimand my mind.

Kya greets me at the door with a smile as she leads me back to our sparring area. I try to offer my own, but I know it must look more like a grimace. As much as I can see that the assassin wants to push, she doesn't.

My motions are sloppy tonight. While recently I've been able to match Kya punch for punch, and occasionally overtake her, I miss nearly every hit tonight. Doubt filters into my mind like a crack in a damn.

Sensing a switch in mood, Kya rethinks her approach, becoming more offensive and not holding back. I allow each hit to land and bruise my skin. My body is too tired to even care about the pain.

"Come on!" she shouts. "Get angry!"

No response. She huffs, red in the face.

"Fucking say something. Don't just lay there and push everyone away."

"I'm not pushing anyone away!"

"Prove it."

Something within me snaps, and I block her next assault as I rise to my feet. Kya grins, her red makeup making her look more feline than usual. She beckons me forward with two fingers, and I launch myself her way.

I can feel the heat under my skin rising. That familiar pressure builds to the point of pain. Gritting my teeth, I push it down. Angry, hot tears slip from the corners of my eyes before I can stop them.

"Get out of your head. Everything is an energy, use it productively." She pants between sharp breaths. She has told me this before. Anger is an energy I can use. Happiness, anxiety, sadness, it is all an energy that can fuel me if I don't let it overtake me first.

The only issue now is I didn't check my emotions quick enough.

I hone my focus on my rage and pain as I throw punch after punch. Kya's hits land less frequently as I focus on blocking and dodging with enough ferocity to consider my defense more offensive at this point.

Lucius and his threats. My father and his spiraling madness. Rowan and his secrets and obsession with Mavis. Blaine and his disappearance.

Kya stumbles and just barely misses a far too heavy-handed assault.

Is he even still in Krycolis, or did he flee to some relatives in Vari? Is he safe? Does his leg hurt from riding for so long? Does he know where to find help? Is he dead?

Dead. He could be dead.

"Vera, enough." Kya hisses as she barely manages to block another blow.

Dead. So many dead.

Kya falls, rolling to the side.

Their blood coats my hands, their screams fill my ears. Dead and it's all my fault. I need out.

Let me out. Let me out. Let me out let me out let me out let me-

"VERA!"

Kya screams as my balled fists fly open and light explodes into the room. I hear a sizzle as the light burns her eyes and the hairs on her arms. The torches on the wall flicker in response, dancing towards my power in respect.

My friend lands a few feet from me, her palms driving into her eyes.

"...see. I can't see," she howls. Kya lifts her chin to display milky white eyes with pure silver streaking down her cheeks. I glance down at my hands in horror as I realize what I've done.

I blinded her.

My hands shake, the veins beneath my skin still glowing. Rowan and Amír rush into the room, Derrín close at their heels.

"Kya!" Her voice is filled with pure undiluted terror as she sprints to the Vari woman's side. In an instant, she spins towards where I stand shaking in the corner. "What did you do?"

Any trace of understanding in the woman's face is gone, leaving only lingering hurt and burning rage. Something tells me that even if we were surrounded by enemies and this was the outcome, Amír's furious gaze would still find mine.

Her voice is venomous as she cradles the sobbing Kya to her chest, and Rowan looks my way in questioning. My knees begin to buckle. He didn't think that I tried to hurt her?

"Ver, what happened?"

When I find no answer, I take a step forward then stumble. Kya's usually amber eyes are a pure white and still streaming blood. Rowan spins on me, repeating himself with a biting tone.

"I-I don't know. We were just sparring, and then... I lost control."

"That light. That was you?" The assassin whirls towards the sound of my voice. "You were light."

Her voice contains more hurt and wonder than it does anger. Fear is triumphant over every other tone she displays, and the gunslinger at her side snarls. Every broken piece of my heart shatters beyond repair within my chest. I did this.

Just like how I pushed Blaine to his death. How I've broken Torin's smile and shoved Tanja into the dark. I have killed everything good in my life.

This gift is no Blessing. The gods were wrong. It is a curse.

Amír faces both Rowan and me as she seethes, "Would anyone care to enlighten us?"

The irony of her statement is not lost on me.

Rowan runs his hand through his hair, his usually handsome face contorted with barely concealed anger and confusion. I have dug him a hole that he doesn't know how to get out of, which, obviously, is a first for both of us. He looks over his shoulder towards me, tossing a look that says *do you want to tell them or should I?*

Please.

He dips his chin in understanding. He never pushes, never asks for more than I am willing to give. I don't dare to open my mouth right now, lest I choke on my own lies. It is the cowards way out, I know.

Vera the coward, always running away.

Rowan's brows pinch together, and his shoulders square as he tells them everything. Periodically, he looks back making sure he isn't telling more than I am comfortable with. He makes a clear distinction standing between us. If things go south, it is me he will protect.

With every word, Amír's piercing glare narrows until it seems sharp enough to puncture through my skull. The anger that she radiates heats the room. Kya and Rowan may interpret her fury as only on Kya's behalf, but the truth settles heavily in my bones.

The gunslinger raises a brow in challenge. *More secrets, princess?*

I can't begin to fathom the depths of the apology that they deserve. I press my lips into a hard line and let Rowan speak.

She loves her, she's acting this way because she loves her, I have to remind myself. But that is not the only reason. Amír functions based on a single principle: truth. Meanwhile, I've been using truth as a tool, something malleable to suit my interests as of late. I can't fault her for hating me for it, not when it is something I hate about myself too.

Silence. It takes a moment for me to realize that Rowan has stopped talking and all eyes are now on me. Even Kya's milky ones seem to have focused in my direction, as if sensing where I am. I wouldn't be surprised if she does have some sixth sense like this. She's a woman of many skills and secrets.

"You've been lying to us." It is Kya who speaks first, her voice small. Amír brushes the drying blood from her face, the silver smearing in stark contrast across her dark skin.

"I haven't," I plead, resisting the urge to fall to my knees. "I'm still me."

"You didn't tell us. You kept a secret. That's the same thing." Her voice cracks, and her face twists into disgust. The sight burns through my skin, and those broken pieces of my heart harden to form a wall.

"You're one to talk about secrets. Hypocritical when you think about how I know nothing about you."

"Trust is earned. You haven't earned shit," Amír hisses through clenched teeth. Good, let them hate me. Hate is better than pity or disgust.

"Haven't I? You haven't given me a chance to prove myself to be anything more than a burden. I saved your life, I bled for you. I've risked everything to be here. But no, nothing I do is good enough for any of you."

Shut up, I mentally plead. You're going to ruin everything, just shut up.

Amír's eyes form slits, and she opens her mouth, presumably to tell everyone what a fraud I am. Go ahead then, ruin me.

But Kya touches her arm, and she softens immediately. It's easy to see now that this woman would do anything for her. I can see Amír tearing Varium apart with her bare hands if Kya would let her, just for a spark of retribution for whatever secret trauma her lover went through. Whatever it is that I am not allowed to know.

"Vera, that's enough." The one voice I have been waiting to hear finally speaks. The one I know will slice through the final strand holding my heart to my conscience.

Rowan's conflicted countenance threatens to break me. To see the way he's now angling towards the two Nightwalkers. I can see it so clearly in his gaze, and my breath catches in my throat. What the fuck is wrong with me?

"You should go," he says softly. His hand grazes my elbow gently, saying *you hurt me, but I don't hate you.* He wants me to know things aren't over, but he has drawn the line in the sand. If I hurt them, I hurt him. I nod slowly. I've wounded myself more than them, and I am not the only one who knows it.

Silently I slip out the door, waiting for the darkness to swallow me whole.

CHAPTER 32
VEROSA

Winter prowls the stone corridors of the inner palace, winding its way through the crevices left untouched. The howling wind batters the shuttered windows and threatens to smash them all to splinters if not let in. At all hours of the night, the gentle flurry and scratching of shoes upon the stone echo through these halls as the maids and servants prepare to board up a newly broken window.

Initially, the guards' rotations lessened. Too many were coming in with such severe frostbite that limbs were being lost, toes dislodging themselves while still in their boots. It was too much, even for my father to ignore.

Winter has also been too much for Lucius, thankfully, as I have seen less and less of him as the blizzard preservers. I had warned him months ago in a heat storm that all of Krycolis' weather is severe. Severe heat flooded our borders when he arrived, a taste of hell compared to Tesslari's temperate paradise. Now his Hell has frozen over.

Our most recent storm resulted in a blizzard that froze the hinges of our doors, leaving us trapped within the palace. Everyone but me. I could get out if I wanted, but I've been trapped elsewhere. Memories flash through my mind.

243

White eyes.

Blood. Blood in her eyes.

White snow.

Blood in the-

The door to my room slams opens and closes within the span of a second. Tanja steps inside, a knight following close behind carrying a pile of firewood. Tanja stands tall, pointing towards the simmering fireplace in the corner of my room. The dying light from the embers catch on her ring, the sapphire's blue hues welcomingly accepting the amber flashes. She wears it daily now, not bothering to hide it. It confirms a suspicion I've had growing in my gut. She was hiding it only from me.

The knight nods and places the wood in the fire, stoking it until the flames rise and consume the logs again. He bows in my direction, keeping his head down before leaving quickly, acting as though he might catch the plague.

Tanja settles by the fire, keeping her distance. It's been over a week now, and we still haven't spoken. Torin stops by when he can, offering small smiles and hushed words to Tanja before he has to rush back to duty. All of us underestimated how much Blaine had to do and how well he had balanced his work and finding time for us. It took me far too long to realize those dark circles I teased him about were not from his work. They were from me. Making time for me.

And now I've lost him. I've lost the Nightwalkers. I'm losing Torin. I won't lose Tanja too.

"Tanja." I whisper, my throat scratching. "What do you want? From life, I mean."

She doesn't lift her gaze from the floor. Instead, she twists a chestnut curl around her finger and bites her lip.

"My job is to protect you. To serve you, Mai Reinhavich."

"I asked what you want, not what your job is. And I'm asking as your friend." I say that last part quietly, praying to the gods above that she still considers me as such, even if I don't deserve it. Every lingering second past my proclamation hangs heavy in the air. Slowly, that dread sinks into my skin. My bones. I haven't been able to leave this bed in three days, and now I fear I never will.

Until Tanja rises with a faraway look, her face finally turning in the shade towards mine. She steps lightly, as if dancing through my room. Her skirts flit around her ankles, her apron shifting with them while her silk slippers tap across the stone.

"I want to marry the woman I love, watch her smile for the rest of our lives. I want to go somewhere peaceful, maybe a small house in the hills by the ocean. I want a dog, maybe a cat and some horses if we can afford it. A simple life." I bite my cheek at the tears that threaten to fall. I notice in this beautiful tapestry of a story she's woven, I have no place. I am a bright blue thread that got woven in with the reds and golds.

"And," she hums softly, "I want my best friend to come visit. I want her to go and live her dreams without fear. I want her to come back and tell me stories of all the amazing places she's been, and maybe bring me along for an adventure someday. I want to live to be an old woman knowing I did everything I could to protect her and let her live happily. I want you to be free, Vera."

She doesn't stumble over her words, weaving lilac around my blue, allowing me a place in her fantasy. A single tear drips down my face, and she's there to brush it away as she sinks down into the bed next to me. I don't need to ask to know that she's forgiven me, and I weep as she holds me.

"I just feel alone," I whisper into her shoulder. "The Nightwalkers hate me, Torin's been quiet lately, and Blaine's just gone. I hurt you. I feel like everyone I love disappears, and the harder I try to hold onto them, the further away they slip."

Tanja runs her fingers through my hair smoothly and hushes me. Her deep breaths lull my erratic heart into comfort, and she presses a soft kiss on top of my head.

"Sometimes it's the things we hold onto the tightest that run away the quickest, but if I've learned anything in my years of knowing you it's that you have a way of making things right. You make a mistake, and you fix it."

"But right now I feel like the mistake."

"Take a moment to feel sad, then get back to work." She shrugs nonchalantly before wrapping her willowy arms around my shoulders. "But you'll never be alone, sweet Ver, because I'm always going to be here. Maybe not here in this bed or with my arms around you, but I'll be here." She presses her hand flat across my heart. Any other day, I could quip how cheesy that is or jokingly accuse her of copping a feel. Not today. Not here while that heart feels so empty.

I sniffle lightly. "Promise you won't disappear?"

"I promise."

I disentangle my body from hers. She doesn't say anything else, letting the power of her words rest in the air. She had told me once that the stars remember everything. That they will remember our names long after the earth does. They will welcome us home someday and envelope us in all our loving memories.

"I have to tell you something."

My sweet Tanja stills, her golden eyes reading my face before I even open my mouth. Tiny tendrils of light snake under my skin, brightening with my heightening anxiety. Tanja says nothing as I speak, recounting my faults and blinding my friend. I tell her how Rowan came to see me three days ago, just to tell me her sight had returned, but Amír will not allow me back until Kya says it is alright. Kya has already said she doesn't wish to hinder my training, but I haven't found it in my cowards' heart to return just yet.

The young woman nods, her hair forming a halo around her heart-shaped face. Her grip on my hands tightens slightly.

"You know what you need to do."

My gaze hardens with my resolution. "Yes, I do."

The darkness envelopes my form but doesn't cling to my skin like it does Rowan's. This probably has to do with my faintly glowing skin. If I weren't sneaking out in a blizzard, this would be a gift, however, I am more of a glowing beacon for our few guards we left stationed outside. My white cloak billows in the sky, lifting slightly to show my glowing face. I tuck against a snow pile, my chin ducked as a guard passes by. I ignore the cold bite of the substance, and the even sharper bite of the memories that surface.

I fucking hate the snow.

Winter curls up my neck, trailing kisses like impending death as I carefully pick my way through the forest. The compound slowly drifts into view, nothing more than a snow-covered mound in the night. A small beam of light tells me where the door is, and I brush it off to knock. When no one answers, I take a seat on the top step, careful to light and angle my lantern towards the dark. Light enough to alert me of dangers, but not enough to alert anyone of me.

The wooden porch creaks under steps that I know could be silent if the assassin wished them to be. Kya stands at the door, wrapped in a luxurious fur coat.

"I didn't expect to find a princess lurking in the dark." She spits my title like an insult, but I'm too tired to care. Too tired of fighting with her.

"You're up," I say tenderly, like a wolf showing its belly. It's more of a question than a statement anyway. Kya seems to notice, and her shoulders cave inwards a bit as she comes to sit next to me on the stairs.

"My mother birthed three children, none of whom could sleep through the night."

A test, to see if I would bite and what I would reveal of myself for a taste of her past. A game Rowan and I played not too long ago, a secret for a secret. To give and get, a balance in our friendship, or a test to see if we have one at all.

"I didn't know I had powers until recently. I've been practicing daily, but even now it's still so new to me. I'm terrified that if I mess up, I'm going to hurt someone again." I lean back against the stairs and allow my face to gaze upon the stars. "My mother did everything she could to hide me. Who I was, what I knew. I didn't realize my blood was different from everyone else's until Blaine skinned his knee one day, and I realized mine didn't have any red in it. I think if it had been up to her, she never would have told me at all. It was just another thing that could have given her power over me. My best guess is that she knew I had magic and did everything she could to hide it from me, even after she died."

"Your mother?"

I scoff. "It feels wrong to even call her that."

Kya tilts her head and shuffles slightly closer. I've given some, but not enough. Not enough to sway her.

"When I was eight, I was told never to go into Mother's study. Not even the king was allowed in without expressed permission," I start, the hairs on my arms starting to stand up at the memory. "But you tell a child who has gotten everything they've ever wanted 'no' for the first time, and that curiosity... it eats away at you. So I waited until it was dark, and I was sure she was asleep, and I snuck in. What I saw... I can't forget."

The cool night breeze picks up, brushing my hair away from the nape of my neck and sending a shiver down my spine. Kya watches with unnatural stillness, the assassin's facade masking any sign of my friend.

"What did you see?"

I take a deep breath, steeling myself against the truth before I whisper, "Death. I couldn't see it until I hit it. The smell was awful. I don't know what magic was used to stop it from leaving that room, but I nearly ran out if not for what I saw. A hand, slender and young, holding a slip of paper. She had a sapphire ring around her finger."

I break off into a dry heave, remembering the festering flesh and dried blood. The blood stains on the legs of the desk, the dark spells pinned to the wall, the charts and circles on a map. There was even an eyeball sitting in a jar upon the desk that I could've sworn swiveled to stare at me.

"I... I knew her. It was my nanny's hand. She had decided to 'retire.' Then the door clicked shut behind me and locked. No one was there. I had to jump from the window to get out and hang on to the ivy vines that clung to the palace walls, but it had snowed all week, and the vines froze. And I slipped. I hit a tree on the way down and broke my leg. Irene, my mother, found me moments later and told me I had to wait for someone else to come find me as punishment for going into her study. I laid there on the ground in the cold winter all night, hearing the distant howls from the forest and snapping of branches. I just waited for something to come from the dark, or for the cold to take me first. By the time the guards found me, my eyes had frozen open, and I had frost forming on my lips. The evening snow had covered most of my body. They thought I was dead."

I laugh bitterly.

"I might as well have been. My father didn't look the least bit shocked or worried when he saw me, and Irene, of course, never came. I had severe hypothermia and had to stay in the med bay for two weeks before I regained my strength, and it took much longer for the leg to heal. Irene wouldn't allow healers to see me. But that wasn't the worst of it. I kept thinking of that room, how the door shut on its own, and how Irene knew where I was. I developed a fear of the dark, to the point where I couldn't sleep and couldn't be in a dark room without hearing those howls again. To this day, I sleep with an oil lamp on."

"Did anyone come to see you?"

"Only Blaine and Tanja. Blaine was with the party that found me that morning, as walking the grounds was the only training he was allowed due to his age. He came by every day with sweets, my favorite tarts, molten chocolate, and some books that he would read to me. He was the only one that I told what happened that night. I eventually told him about what I saw in the study too, but not until I was nearly sixteen and Irene had been dead for many years."

Kya considers this, finally noting the oil lamp at my feet and how I've positioned myself close enough to the door to be back inside within seconds. Her features twist in anger, that aloof act finally dropping. She speaks with a low and soft voice.

"Derrín and I, we had an older sister. When the *Stryga* came and sacked our house, they found us three, Derrín and I were both ten, hiding behind her. She was fourteen." Kya takes in a shuddering breath. "They put us on a ship with a hundred or so other prisoners. Some were Vari like us, others were Nevan, Tesslarian, Krycolian. The only thing we had in common was our blood."

A sick pit lowers itself into my stomach and only worsens when I stare down at those blood-red swirls painted on her golden skin.

"We were unloaded onto an island in the middle of the night and told to run. It wasn't until we saw the armed noblemen that we knew why were there. They hunted us like dogs. It was weeks of hiding and fighting for our lives. It was all a game to them. Derrín made weapons, and my sister and I killed. We did what we must until Derrín finally had enough time to build an escape raft, but we were too late." Her hand clenches the thin fabric of her skirt, and I tentatively brush my own across it. She stiffens, then uncurls her fingers to interlace them with mine. "My sister stayed behind to hold them off so Derrín and I could escape. I knew then, as I saw her laying in the bloody sand, those palms hand painted every day like my own, that I would fight. I would fight dirty and wage war on them all. I would get Derrín out of there first, and then I would return."

Her free hand traces slow and purposeful strokes across the crimson pattern before holding our intertwined hands up in front of my eyes. Begging me to look. To understand.

"Her palms were painted because she was gentle. She wanted to heal, to help people. And they took her and broke her until she couldn't help herself. When I came of age, I decided I would go back. I would take everything from them like they took everything from me. I don't care if I need to get elbow deep in blood to do it, I am going to break them until they beg for death and then some. That is my greatest desire."

Silence envelopes us for a moment, only the sweet susurration of the wind weaving between us rang out. Even it is too loud.

Then I take her hands and pressed them to my chest, let them feel my heartbeat. A heart that beats because she had saved it and me long before any of that.

"When you bring them to their knees and have them beg for hell, you will have the full support of the Queen of Krycolis," I promise, holding her tighter now. Neither of us mention that I will be forsaking that title. I don't need it to help her wreak hell.

Her amber eyes lock on mine, acknowledging the pain there, and I stare right back. I've never seen her without the paint on her eyelids, on her face. She looks human, all that rage slipped away to unveil nothing but sorrow. My dear friend Kya in her most basic form. A girl who loves so deeply that it will fill her own broken heart.

"What was her name?" I gently brush my nail across her pinky finger.

"Her name was Natara."

I smile softly. "Tell me about her."

CHAPTER 33

ROWAN

The blizzard finally stops at some point in the night. By morning, the sun finally peaks through the thick clouds that swirl around our kingdom. The gentle light sets the snow aglow with golden shimmer, and maybe I hate the view a little less.

Kya woke before me, crawling out of her bed at dawn to stretch and work out on her own. She offers for me to join, but fear settles in my stomach as I look at her amber gaze. I don't think I will be able to spar with her for a while.

After lying in bed for another half hour, I finally rise. My back pops with each stretch and motion I make as I slowly pad towards the kitchen. I find a pot of water already boiling, and the rich scent of freshly brewed coffee wafts to my nostrils.

Amír must notice my drool because she pushes a cup my way, and Kya is quick to doctor it with quite a large amount of sugar and cream.

"You don't seem like a black coffee kind of person." She smiles as she pushes the cup the rest of the way into my hands. I stand still a moment, savoring the feeling of its warmth in my hands. When I take a sip, I can feel my eyes roll into the back of my head.

"By the Laei, this is good," I say while Kya giggles.

"It's how Amír takes hers too."

The heavenly drink threatens to make its debut through my nose as I fight a snort at that statement and the glare the gunslinger sends towards her girlfriend. Kya doesn't shrink from it like any other person would. Instead, she blushes and whispers something in her ear. They quickly become enraptured in their own world, and a growing smile fights its way to my lips.

The familiar scent of citrus and leather mixed with soap hits my senses. That smile widens into a full-blown grin as I feel Rowan step behind me.

Rowan inhales deeply as he rests his chin on my shoulder and wraps his arms around my waist. "Glad to see you two made up."

"Good morning, and yes, though you'd know that already since you were hiding behind the door during our whole conversation." I give him a pointed glance from beneath my eyelashes. "It's not polite to eavesdrop."

I use the word whole sparingly, given that he only made his way to the door after I had revealed myself as the princess to Kya. If he had heard that bit then this morning's conversation would be taking an entirely different path.

The mercenary presses a slow kiss to my temple. "Your senses, dare I say, might be better than mine."

"I learned from the best."

Amír gags from her spot on a stool. "Gods, you can't even eat in this house anymore."

I raise an eyebrow and drop my gaze towards her now puffy lips, flushed cheeks, and the slight stain on the side of her mouth. She holds my stare, refusing to be embarrassed. Moreover, she raises her own gaze, daring me to make a comment. I huff in defeat and turn my attention back to my cup, offering Rowan a sip. He takes a small one and cringes. I assume it is too sweet for him when he grabs an extra spoon of sugar and mixes it into the drink. When he takes a second sip, his eyebrows unfurl, and his shoulders droop.

"Now *that's* how you make a coffee."

I laugh and make myself a new cup with my preferred alterations. "I didn't take you for someone with a sweet tooth. You look like you'd only eat jerky and raw eggs with a side of whiskey neat." Rowan's lips quirk upwards.

"You've been reading too many of those novels. Sorry to disappoint, sweetheart."

"Eggs?" Derrín mumbles sleepily, stumbling into the room. His eyes are still heavy lidded, and the ragged state of his bandaged fingers tell me what he's been doing all night. Kya's quick eyes notice the same thing.

She speaks softly. "Amír can make some, won't you, love? Derrín, come sit and let me fix those wraps up." Neither of them argue. Derrín slides into the spot that Amír leaves vacant while the gunslinger grabs a pan. She holds the handle as if wielding a weapon, flipping it once, then twice to measure the weight. With deft hands, she cracks an egg over the lip, and the sound of sizzling fills the room.

Kya finishes applying an ointment on his nimble fingers while Derrín attempts to sip from his mug without lifting it from the table. When he is unsuccessful, he rests his head on the table beside it and splays his scarred fingers across the fine wooden table.

I notice now how fine everything in here is. The coffee, the sugar, the furniture. Usually, I am only here at night when the occasional oil lamp lights the room. Even then, I rarely occupy any room other than the one where we spar, and up until last night, I hadn't realized they had rooms here. I realized as I laid in Kya's bed last night the true weight of the risk Rowan had taken on me. This isn't just their main stronghold; this is their home. The thought causes tears to prick the corners of my eyes, but I rub at them with the back of my hand. No more tears tonight.

My eyes flit around the room, foreign to me. In the center rests a large wooden table, the top showcasing hundreds of rings, proving it must have been hewn from a thousand-year-old tree. We all rest here now, my elbows propped up on its glossy surface.

In the far corner, there are two plush chairs, velvet cushions lining their surface. The red makes me smile. I know exactly who picked those out.

Along the wall is a long rack of weaponry, mostly pistols, though they look as if they have not been used in years. Decoration, I presume. To both the left and right, there are a series of doors. The one on the left leads to the main hall where I usually enter, and from there, there are two more doors that lead either to the spar room or the study. Returning my gaze to the walls in these rooms, I trace the outline of four doors to the right. I came from the middle one this morning, learning the one directly to the right was Kya's. Derrín just came from the one on the left, leaving only the farthest of us.

Before my mind can wander, Amír slides a plate of eggs and toast before me. She doles out the rest of the plates and settles beside Rowan. He accepts it gratefully, eating slowly. Kya smacks Derrín's shoulder as he shoves the eggs on his bread and tries to shovel the full thing in his mouth. He chokes. Amír laughs.

A warmth fills my chest. Is this what it is like to have a family? They had forgiven me so easily, welcomed me back into their home based on nothing more than faith. I clasp my hands together and raise my chin to the sky. I pray and promise I will protect this little peace and earn this love.

To kill, to die. It's all the same. This is to live.

And oh, how short the peace lasts.

Kya disappears early in the afternoon. Rowan sends her first to the palace to check with Tanja and Torin to make sure my tracks have been covered, then on a recon mission to gather intel on Mavis' whereabouts. She's been slowly encroaching on their territory, sending men as threats. Threatening what, I don't know.

"Is she trying to prove that her dick is bigger than yours?" I jest. Rowan tries a small smile, but it's creased with fear and irritation.

Night encroaches just as quickly, and the snow begins again just as the sun goes down. I tense a bit at the first pattering of the snow against the window, even more so when a distant howl pierces the air. Rowan reaches out to hold my hand, and Amír stands to light another lamp. It appears that the whole compound heard my confession last night, but I can't bring myself to be upset about it. It is three times fewer that I have to relive that night.

The front door slams open, and I hear soft swearing as Derrín steps in from the snow. He treks through the room, wet and red in the face, before stepping into his room. He bows his head goodnight, and then the door snicks shut.

Rowan shakes his head, his golden hair splaying around his face in a way that reminds me of a dog. We settle into the two velvet chairs, Amír choosing to stand and lean against the wall.

Finally forced to confront the fourth presence in the room, I turn my face towards the shadows. Kya steps forth, crimsons silks swirling around her knees, silver-tinged blood dripping from her twin espas. Amír's eyes trail up and down her form, scanning for any injuries. When she finds none, she offers a deft nod.

"Was it-"

"A trap? No, we were a step ahead for once." The Vari woman sighs heavily, sinking into the dilapidated couch. "Mavis is moving South, past Belam, even. That's as much as I could get from anyone before things got tight."

Drip. I clutch at my stomach, swallowing back my bile as I watch the blood drip from the blades. Kya gaze drifts to my face before she wipes the espas on her skirt and sheathes them both. I can't help but note how the blood disappears amongst the silk.

"Minor casualties, no deaths to report."

A golden green breeze whispers through the curtains, brushing across my ankles and sending a shiver up my spine. So casually we speak of such matters now, barely a hint of remorse highlighting our voices.

"Good. We leave at first light."

"Leave? For where?" Rowan doesn't spare a second glance, or even acknowledge my question, as he spins on his heel to leave. His spurs click against the tile floors. Amír scoffs.

"To find wherever Mavis is going, as per usual." His second in command's voice chases him from the room. "One of these days, you're going to get yourself killed. Get all of us killed!" I shoot her a nasty look that she returns before chasing Rowan into the snow.

I find him standing in the courtyard outside, the shadows clinging to him as they usually do. I unfurl my fingers towards his, catching the moonlight in my scarred palm.

"Do you ever contemplate the gods?"

His back remains turned to me as he considers his response.

"Just as much as nature contemplates the poet."

I tut my tongue and wrap my fingers around his wrist. Feeling his pulse. It quickens under my light grip, and a smile graces my lips. It fades as soon as I see the weariness on his face. He's letting his guard down for once.

"You and your riddles," I murmur, tracing a pattern on the inside of his arm with my fingernails. He shivers slightly but says nothing. His pinched brows and taut muscles speak for his firm mouth.

Am I going too far?

I kiss his shoulder. *Not at all.*

He relaxes slightly under my touch. *Will you stand by me?*

I prop my chin on his chest and stare into his eyes, my nose brushing against his collarbone. The rest of the tension in his body melts as his heartbeat syncs with mine.

Always.

CHAPTER 34

ROWAN

Vera focuses intently on a single buckle of her boots that refused to snap into place. She swears at it to the high sun and back as she realizes the problem. She'd forgotten to dry them after her trek in the snow, and the bulky clasp has rusted.

"Fuck!" she shouts, now red in the face and fuming. She tosses her hands in the air and glares at her boots for the obvious offense.

"Language. Laei, maybe Rowan's been a bad influence." Derrín stares pointedly at me now, as if it's my fault. It probably is. Nonetheless, I stick my tongue out at him with a childish sneer. He returns the gesture, and Amír rolls her eyes.

"Does everyone understand what they're doing?" She flips her gun in her hand, and old habit. She grows impatient as we throw out vulgar gestures towards each other.

"Yes, Mom." Derrín jests, pulling out a tool from his pocket. Kya planted the listening devices that Derrín had made all throughout the tavern they will be scoping later today. Derrín will wait outside, and if something important is heard, he will vibrate a device in Kya or Vera's pocket. If something dangerous is heard, he will buzz Amír's device twice. I will be heading on my own elsewhere.

"Just to be clear, this tavern isn't that one from Belam, right?" Vera shifts from foot to foot, biting her lip. I hold back a smile as I force my face into a neutral countenance.

"Why? Did you get drunk and flirt with the bartender or something?"

Silence.

"*Oh gods*, you did!"

Vera's face flushes scarlet, and the shade is dark enough to cover her freckles. "Just shut up and go already!" she screeches, shoving me hard in the chest. My laughter chases her out the door as she buries her face in her hands. Kya pats her shoulder and whispers soothing words through a grin that Vera can't see. I pull my hood up and step out into the snow.

Belam. The seediest town of the East. On the outside, it often appears to be one of those poorer western cities, where the nobles can pretend they give a damn. But where there are far too few prying eyes...

I would say it is a miracle Vera survived as long as she did in this city, but the true miracle is that anyone can survive and flourish in this environment. Despite things such as contaminated drinking water, low income, and the uptake in crime, Belam's inhabitants seem to be doing just fine as long as they keep their head down.

I pull my hood closer to my face in a sorry attempt to conceal my identity. Belam is Mavis' territory. To be me or anyone associated with me walking in these streets is a sure death warrant.

The oil I coated my hair with is slick and sticking to my forehead, no doubt leaving behind black residue on the powders we've covered my face with. Any trace of my distinctive features is covered, save for my eyes.

The cold rain has ceased for a few days now, though sometimes some small flurries of snowflakes slip through. The air is heavy, and dark clouds hang low in the sky. Any day now, we are due for a snowstorm.

My mount squirms beneath me. Even she seems to detest the city, or maybe she senses that we are not welcome here. I swing my leg over the saddle and dismount in one fluid motion. My feet barely make a sound as they land in the dirt outside of the most infamous tavern in Belam.

Ryson's is as claustrophobic as I remember it being the last time I was here, pretending to have my brains beaten in and saving damsels in distress. I keep my head low as I enter, only nodding subtly at my informant as he exits. I spot my personal target within an instant, drunk out of his mind and slurring at the bar. I recognize the owner entertaining him, offering refills on drinks and occasionally smiling at a group of patrons.

With a heavy sigh, I approach the former captain and lay a hand on his shoulder.

"Don't you think you've had enough, Blaine?"

Blaine swivels in his chair to look up at me, his hand never leaving his glass. His usually steely eyes have been softened by the alcohol, and he squints with his mouth open.

"Do I knows ya?"

For the love of the gods, he is drunk out of his mind.

"Okay, now I really know you've had too much. Come on, we've got to get you home," I grumble, not entirely thrilled to be doing this. *You're doing this for Vera,* I remind myself.

My muscles groan in protest as I try to pull Blaine from his spot atop the stool without causing a scene, but the ex-captain remains firmly rooted in his spot. Despite my struggles, not a single drop of *leeche* spills. My mouth gapes open in shock. This man is incredibly strong when intoxicated.

"Thees es ma home now." He giggles a bit, his eyebrows wiggling. He touches my arm friendly enough. "Oh, strong," He mumbles to himself before he continues sipping on his beverage.

Gods, I hope he remembers this when he's sober.

The tavern owner approaches with a knowing grin. He laughs a bit at the sorry excuse of a captain, then turns his attention towards me. There's a friendliness in his gaze, hiding a wary edge beneath the facade.

"Are you a friend?"

I look at Blaine and try to hide my cringe. "Something of the sort, yeah."

The man sighs wearily, prominent frown lines etch themselves across his forehead as he lets his guard slip. He pours a third glass of *leeche* and motions for me to take a seat. I oblige, feigning small sips from the cup.

"We've had a lot of them recently. Knights from the palace, that is." Woden takes a large swig as he scans the room. "We don't know how they got here or what happened to them. At first, we joked that they'd just been brained a bit too hard in practice and tossed out, but then it became clear that something more sinister is happening behind those white walls."

I try to keep my voice even and low as I lean in. "What do you mean?"

"Are you going to finish that?' When I shake my head, the man finishes off the rest of my drink as well and sets the glasses aside. "Knights started coming in with more gruesome injuries. They started small, like a lost finger or toe. Then it shifted. They were coming in with burn marks, missing eyes and limbs, sometimes they'd stagger in still bleeding with a gaping hole in their side and a smile on their face."

"Smiling?"

"This one here," he motions to Blaine, "is the most sound of mind out of all the one's we've had. Normally they come in thinking they're enjoying an off day at the palace, or training with some friends. They all smile as if nothing is wrong, even if they're crawling to get through the doorway. I feed them, give them something to drink, but I can't house them all. Times are tough. They wander out of here, and within the next few days, there's a rotting body somewhere in the streets."

The hairs on the back of my neck begin to raise as Woden pushes his stool back. The seat screams terribly as it runs along the stone floors, and a few patrons shoot hurried glares our way. The Nevan man is quick to disarm them with a charming smile and a wave before his countenance switches back to that of a man who has seen far too much.

"Anyways, I'm glad you got here when you did. I'd hate for your friend to share their fate. You're the first to come collect any of them, anyway."

"Really? No friends or family?"

"None. Though we've got a group that goes out and gets them. We look for families, but most of the time, they're already long dead, or the boys are orphans with no one to miss 'em. So we bury their bodies, give them a ceremony if we can, and continue about our day waiting for the next one."

"Good man," I hum. Blaine's eyelids begin to droop, and his grip on his drink loosens. He slumps against my arm, weary and morose. Without that armor he always wore, he looks less intimidating and large than before. In this light, he holds a romantic beauty about him, from his chiseled physique, dark curls, and angular face to the way he carries himself. He might as well be an old god; it's no wonder Vera fell for him.

"Come on, Ver's been losing her mind searching for you."

"She's better off without me. Now she can wear that crown."

I stare at him in bewilderment while Woden turns to take care of another patron of the tavern. "What in the gods' names are you talking about?"

"Can't be together here. I leave, she stays." He snorts. "S'oh well. Right person, wrong life."

Blaine's head hits the table with a heavy thud. I groan. Nothing like a deadweight on a seven-mile trek back in the snow. I loop my arm under his shoulders, hauling him from the seat. When I fish into my pocket and try to flip Woden a gold coin, he holds up his hands in refusal.

"Just get that man home safe. That's enough payment for me."

I nod my head in respect, reminding myself to remember his name as I haul Blaine towards the door. As we walk, a small parchment falls from his sleeve. I prop him against the wall to bend and retrieve it, and my heart stops cold when I recognize the cursive scrawl across the page.

Tell your Vera it's not nice to break and discard her toys. I was more than happy to keep him safe for her. But next time I catch you in my city, I will nail your dick to the walls.

Your Love,

M.

I suck a sharp breath between my teeth and glance over my shoulder. No one notices anything amiss, so I continue walking and throw Blaine over the back of the horse. I mount in front of him, grunting when his dead weight hits my back. My mare pins her ears as well, and I rub her neck fondly.

"'I love her." Blaine whispers in my ear.

I grit my teeth. "I know."

CHAPTER 35
VEROSA

Tanja is the perfect picture of graceful elegance as she twirls in my room, the length of her golden gown shimmering in the candlelight with each swish around her ankles. Her makeup is done in matching shades of metallic gold, causing her to glow in an ethereal light. She moves like sunlight through the room, each of her movements fluid and enchanting.

Aiko smiles as she watches, her handiwork with a makeup brush being put on full display as Tanja beams. She had requested weeks ago to be allowed the honor of preparing me for my birthday ball, and I agreed on one condition. Tanja is also to be dressed and pampered like a noble lady and will attend the ball as Aiko and Finneas' ward. The older woman joyfully agreed and came earlier this evening to help us prepare.

She hums softly as she paints a peach shade across my lips, pausing every once and a while to correct a smudge or dab more color onto the brush. She worked meticulously on my hair before, going through great pains to perfectly pile every curl atop my head, with only a few to frame my face. She sewed diamonds into the updo, causing small rainbows to flicker around my face each time the light struck them. She uses that same painstaking cautiousness as she dabs crushed crystals against my eyelids across my nose and soft cheekbones. She doesn't coat my face with powders of heavy paints like the king requested. She maps my face with her art, but in the end, I still look like me, just a more ethereal version of me.

"How are you feeling?" Aiko takes a step back and sets the brush down on my vanity, allowing me to admire the work she's put into my face.

"Not as nervous as I thought I'd be," I answer honestly. Maybe It's the fact that I know I leave tonight and can finally be free of this place, or that my friends are with me, but I am not afraid. If anything, I feel as if a great weight has been lifted from my shoulders. After tonight, I am free for the first time in my life.

"Well, that's good. You look lovely." Aiko's face is soft and sweet, but her smile doesn't reach her eyes. There's that same pain lingering there that I saw the night we first met. The night I accidentally called her Mom.

"Are you alright?"

"Yes, I am fine." Aiko touches my arm softly. "This time of year is always tough. I lost my daughter twenty years ago around this time. Being allowed the honor of assisting you today... well, it's just bringing back a lot of memories." The sly fox's blue eyes become misty with unshed tears. My own heart breaks for her, and a bit of jealousy slips in as well. To have a mother who loves you so much is something I could never relate to.

Before I can offer any condolences or remarks, Aiko claps her hands together and smiles brightly again. "Oh, I almost forgot! I have a surprise."

Tanja has settled down enough that the word 'surprise' piques her interest, and she bounds on over towards us and takes to perching on my shoulder. I tug my robe closer to my body and laugh at the way her eyes light up in anticipation. The older woman also notices with a hearty laugh. She reaches down and pulls out a basket from which she removes a long piece of sparkling fabric.

I gasp as I recognize the dress from Finneas' story. The dress he thought made her look like dawn itself, and how quickly he fell in love with her. The dress has been kept in perfect condition, despite over twenty years having passed.

"Aiko, I can't."

"Please, at least try it on." The woman pleads, placing the fabric in my hand. I hold it gently as if carrying a sacred relic. Her stare bores into my skin, and I relent.

The material is smooth as I slip from my robe into the gown. The outside is encrusted with thousands of glittering crystals, but the inside is pure silk that is soft against my skin. Each way I move sends small reflections of light scattering, and my very skin seems to glow when covered with the fabric. The draping sleeves fall perfectly off my shoulder, and the gown fits every curve and hollow of my body as if it had been waiting for me to wear it.

Tanja squeals with delight as Aiko finishes lacing the back up with gentle hands. With the utmost careful caress, she spins me by my shoulders so that I can see myself in the mirror.

Tanja steps closer, her fingers interlacing with mine.

"Dawn and her morning sun," Aiko whispers. "You both look lovely."

I'm not quite sure what overcomes me, whether it be the emotion of leaving or the magnitude of this kind of gift, but I rush forward to crush the woman in a hug.

"Thank you," I whisper. "I wish my mother had loved me half as much as you do your daughter. I will always be grateful to you." Aiko's face flushes, but she returns my embrace. I can make out her heart beating steadily through the velvet fabric of her gown. Its rhythm is a comfort, even as I pull away and Tanja grabs my hand in her own.

"Enjoy the ball, Verosa."

I grin as Tanja drags me away with little decorum. I used to loathe these events and dread them whenever the day finally arrived, but now the prospect of tonight is something I look forward to. After all, it is Tanja's first ball.

"Are you excited?" I whisper giddily as we duck in a corridor to avoid the patrolling knights. I didn't exactly tell my father about Tanja's attendance, though I doubt he will care. He has been rather absent lately. I often find him wandering in the gardens silently with his face to the sun, or mumbling to himself in the corridors in words I can't quite make out. In any case, it appears someone else will have to take the throne soon enough.

"I think so. I can't tell if I feel like I'm going to throw up tonight's dinner is because of nerves or excitement." Tanja blushes. "Perhaps it's the thrill of knowing the king could put my head on the chopping block for this."

I laugh and nudge at her shoulder gently. "That's not going to happen. Tonight I just wanted the rest of the world to see us the same way as I do. As equals." She beams brightly. Even without the gown, she could outshine the morning sun. Her stained lips curve upwards just as a knock comes at the door.

"Oh, I almost forgot, I have one more surprise." I wiggle my eyebrows suggestively. Tanja gasps and shoves her ring in my face.

"This better not be a courtesan, Vera, I'm an engaged woman." She giggles through her words, unable to keep a complete face.

Especially as Aiko blushes with a mischievous grin and says, "And darling, I'm a married woman. Eye candy never hurts."

I laugh while Tanja's face flushes bright red. She's much more excitable than usual today. Timid doesn't feel like the right word for Tanja - ever. But today something inward has shifted.

My friend practically glows as her fiancé walks through the door. Ruby's usual uniform replaced with a red velvet gown that drapes across her every curve. She smiles broadly as Tanja's face drops into an expression of pure awe. Silver tears brim in her eyes. Ruby is art, and Tanja is the scholar who has spent her whole life looking for the perfect painting.

Thank you, she mouths. Aiko approaches me from behind, squeezing my elbow with a proud smile. She knows how much this night means to me and how badly I'd like it to just be me and my friends, but it wouldn't be the perfect night if Tanja wasn't smiling the way she is now.

"Do you think the king will let us have a joint execution?" Tanja asks, linking her arm through mine. Ruby elbows her softly in the ribs, and my friend pretends to keel over into my side. "I am mortally wounded!"

"Don't worry, I'll make sure he kills me first so you have a chance to escape." I laugh. Aiko shakes her head softly, then accepts my extended hand. My personal army of four. With our heads held high, we march out of my room and towards the ballroom.

"Nervous yet?" Aiko asks in a hushed tone. A passing soldier bows, and she pretends to whisper a piece of gossip in my ear. I press my lips together and frown, obviously considering her words and rumors. He rushes off immediately.

"Just a bit sad." I put it plainly then shrug. "It's all bittersweet."

"That's fair. Womanhood, marriage, a mass exodus," she whispers that last part, "these are all big things. Just hold your head high, it'll be alright."

It'll be alright.

I try to echo the simple sentiment in my mind as those grand double doors approach. The tapestries beside them billow with the soft breeze of the open window, causing the woven dragons to come to life.

Spring only lasts a few weeks in Krycolis before it bows to more severe heats. The first warmth of life bloomed this morning, making today our first official day of the season. The crowing nobles cheered in the streets, clinking glasses, and sharing *dolceron*. They claimed it is a sign of a prosperous marriage between our future queen and king.

The warm air caresses my face, the fear of winter long since melted with the snow. I take the weather as my own sign. A heralding of a new life, the gods insisting they won't smite me for my cowardice. It lifts an invisible weight from my back, and I roll my shoulders out. I nod to the guards, and with a deep groan, those heavy doors open.

Tanja squeezes my hand. Into the lion's den.

CHAPTER 36

ROWAN

"You are being a child." Emilie crosses her arms over her chest, buried deep in a plush velvet chair. Kya sits in the seat next to her, not caring to hide her smug smirk.

"I couldn't agree more, Emilie." My mother smiles towards the assassin, a mischievous light in her eyes. I fight my growing irritation. Secrets have always been my strong suit. Secrets keep men like me alive. However, secrets from my mother? My weakness.

"What's the worst that happens? Vera gets cold feet?"

I fail at killing my father, your ex-lover.

The big secret she doesn't know. If she did, she would try to stop me, and I can't have that image weighing on my mind if I am to succeed tonight.

Amír and I have spent months planning the assassination, even the smallest flicker of guilt could unravel it all. During my time in the palace, it has been easy to map guard patterns, especially with the disappearance of some of the soldiers. Vera told me that they had just been sent home to recover due to frostbite after the last blizzard, but Woden's words form a pit in my conscience. Something else is happening. Something that Vera doesn't know about.

If all goes well, it won't be her concern after tonight. I corresponded with Torin two days ago, so to my knowledge, he is both unaware and unharmed. Once Vera is out of the palace, I will have to warn him.

"Is Rowan missing game night?"

Ah, there he is. My second secret.

Blaine stumbles into the room, an empty bottle of *leeche* in his hand as he falls against the kitchen table. If he notices our stares, he doesn't say anything, just sits on the floor.

"Have you been drinking?" I growl, despite the evidence that he waves in my face. The disgraced captain hiccups then falls flat on his back, holding the bottle in the air.

"Waiter!'

"I'm going to pretend you said water." My mother hums softly, refilling his glass with water. "Here you are, captain, our finest bottle of liquor."

Blaine kicks his feet out happily, sloppily chugging the drink. Emilie smiles softly and pats his head, then whispers for Kya to go hide the rest of our alcohol for the night. She speaks softly to Blaine, who we learned will only listen to her. If I try to take his drink or even look his way he just shouts "man-whore" and drinks more.

"Are you sure you will be okay with him tonight?" I ask. I hate leaving her to clean up my messes, especially when I know firsthand how hard it can be to look after the Vari man. My mother only smiles as if to say she's seen worse, no doubt from me, and shoos me out the door.

"If you bring her here tonight, let me say hi to her first."

I laugh despite my mother's underlying tone. "I promise I will."

Amír and Derrín briefly look up from their game of chess to wish me good luck before Derrín moves his queen to overtake Amír's king. The gunslinger swears and playfully wipes the board. A few of the pieces slam into our packed bags.

I try not to feel anything for the place I know I am leaving for the last time. My own bag is hidden along the inner palace wall, and we will leave Krycolis straight from the ball. My mother knows we are moving in an attempt to help Vera escape and is more than happy to do it. My heart clenches.

When Verosa, Kya, and Amír meet up with the rest of us, Blaine will be there. Her first time seeing him in over a month. After I returned from

HAYDN HUBBARD

Belam, I hid him in my room, hoping he would remain unconscious until Vera returned from their mission.

Secrets. All these secrets.

We all saw how Verosa reacted to being kept in the dark about Kya's past, and that was for a girl she'd only known for a few months. When she finds out I've hidden the boy she's known her whole life, she may hate me.

My steps stumble as the thought strikes my heart. All the air exits my lungs in a single breath. *It's fine,* I remind myself, I have my whole life to earn her forgiveness.

Still, the notes in my pocket and dagger hidden in my boot burn holes through my skin. They cry for blood, and I am not one to disappoint. My father can stare into my eyes, my mother's eyes, as he dies and know he was his own downfall.

The palace is littered with extravagant items of decoration. Soft flowers blooming along the trellises, diamonds trickling from the high arching ceiling among more blooms like a soft rainfall. Gold lines every inch of the palace. Dancing lights and bubbling glasses of champagne are in abundance.

I raise my chin as I show my invitation, granted to me by Lucius. A thank you, he had said, for keeping an eye on Vera.

It is Lucius who finds me once I enter the walls of the inner palace. His silver suit shifts in the lighting, catching every gilded flicker of the light. He beams broadly when he sees me, and I force the same countenance onto my less than willing face. He clasps my hand tighter than he has in the past. His eyes seem to narrow when I appear unaffected, and he drops his vice grip.

"I'm so glad you could make it tonight." He speaks slowly, but his voice never dips from his friendly tone. "It will be a night to remember."

"That I am sure of."

Lucius flinches slightly at my ease. Sweat crawls up the back of my neck, and I force myself to breath. He has figured out, as I always knew he would, that Blaine was never his rival. I am. His intentions for inviting me tonight must be less than cordial. I shift on my feet and allow the soft spring breeze to cool my neck. I don't have time for his foolish word games, I have things to do.

"Have you seen my fiancé, by any chance?"

I stiffen. "I haven't seen her since our lesson yesterday." It isn't a lie. I did see Vera last night at a lesson. A lesson where she learned how to slip out of binding ropes. I contemplate telling Lucius this for a brief moment, savoring in the image of his face turning puce with rage as the implications.

"Interesting. I suppose she hasn't told you yet. Oh well, saves the surprise for later." Lucius twists a new ring on his finger then clasps my shoulder. "See you inside, friend."

I shrug his hand off and charge ahead. With nimble fingers, I slip the mask on my face and tie it into place. Supposedly the princess' one request was that this ball be a masquerade. How cliche. How helpful.

Because my father doesn't need to see my face, only my eyes as I drive my dagger through his heart and into the back of his throne. I quicken my pace to the ballroom.

Tonight I get my revenge.

Tonight I will kill the king.

CHAPTER 37
VEROSA

Torin stands at the base of the stairs, his usually unkempt blonde hair slicked back into a distinguished look. His characteristic grin is plastered on his face, though his form is rigid, and we can both tell he is itching to lean against the railing as we descend. I allow Tanja to step down first. Her steps are graceful and cautious, but her chin is held high. As the light catches on her gold mask, the swirls of whispering reaches my ears. Speculations on whether she's a foreign princess, or perhaps a priestess of Deun. The former is more prayed for than the latter, given her beauty and the priestesses' vow of celibacy.

Ruby descends next, and I quietly follow behind her, allowing the guests to turn their focus towards her while I slip in unnoticed and unannounced. Somewhere within the hordes of people is Rowan, who still has not put two and two together about my identity. It will stay that way until after tonight. Once I am free of this wretched place, I will tell him the truth. Once we are both free and he can't be charged with treason for assisting in my escape.

The scent of champagne and *dolceron* wafts through the air, a gentle caress against the olfactory senses of the patrons. My heels clink softly against the ballroom floor. A light tittering to my left, a sweet whisper to my right.

The weight of hundreds of gazes falls heavy atop my shoulders, pressing on my worries. I had hoped the splendor of Tanja's entrance would take longer to wear off, but the potent stares of the party goers warn me that their attention has now shifted to me.

"If you were hoping to go unnoticed, you should have at least tried to look a bit less stunning." Torin winks as he extends his other arm my way. Tanja rolls her eyes with a knowing look.

"Vera couldn't look bad if she tried."

"That is a lie. You should see me in the mornings," I protest, but Tanja just leans over to pinch my arm.

"I *do* see you in the mornings. Every day, in fact. Stop being modest for once, and accept the compliment."

My gaze flits around the room, taking in every exit and guard by habit now. The ballroom has been decorated beautifully, in a way that I actually would have done myself. Small blooms of white flowers trail up every column, and small lights intermix with the foliage. These flowers also drop from the ceiling, brushing against our chandeliers every so often with that gentle spring breeze.

The tables on the outskirts of the hall have been covered with thin lace and piled high with *dolceron* and other pastries. Rich meats lay at the center of longer tables that rest by the entrance to our courtyard. Masked servants in all white flit from patron to patron, carrying tall flutes of champagne and hors d'oeuvres. Their identical masks are supposed to be a symbol of unity, though their soulless eyes are more unnerving than anything.

A dais rests raised above the dance floor at the far end of the hall, raising my father above everyone else. He ignores my presence, per my request. He believes it is to raise suspense for my unveiling, hence the masks all attendees wear. Little does he know I intend to be long gone by then.

Aiko excuses herself to find her husband while the four of us rest near one of the large columns near the courtyard. Within a moment, the orchestra ends their song and begins another one. Ruby whisks Tanja to the dance floor while I take small sips of champagne.

"Are the masked servants creepy to you too, or am I just discovering something about myself?" Torin whispers in my ear, having to bend slightly at the waist to do so. He grins as I choke on my first sip of champagne.

"Creepy, yes, but it could be a bit of both." I grin over the lip of my glass as I wash down my cough with another sip. The bubbles warm my stomach, and my muscles begin to release. I can't afford to get even the slightest bit drunk tonight, but I can still enjoy myself.

Torin gazes over my shoulder and stiffens, his grin dropping immediately.

"Good evening, Verosa." The one voice I've been dreading hearing speaks smoothly from behind me. "Torin."

The second reason for the masks: to give me a chance to remain undetected by my fiancé.

"Lucius," I purr, turning on my heel to face him. He stands tall in a smooth silver suit, the fabric shifting in color as it catches the light. I have been unaware that a color such as this could exist in any fabric, but Lucius does always seem to know more than I do. Everything except for one. His mask takes the form of a serpent, the scales glimmering in the light, seemingly in tune with his fine clothes.

"May I have this dance?" The dreaded question. I grit my teeth and nod, allowing him to take my hand. Torin's scowl is visible even below the mask, and he shoots a look my way that says *scream if you need me*.

I smirk back. *Lucius will be screaming before I do.*

Lucius lets my hand fall from his as we find our way to the center of the quartz floor. He bows deeply. I follow the movement with a low curtsy before raising my arm. One of his hands takes ahold of mine while the other finds the small of my back. He steps forward, his chest brushing against mine.

We take the first steps in sync, never breaking the other's gaze. I am sure mine is filled with loathing; his is filled with challenge. To anyone else, it must seem to be passion. The music evolves into a crescendo, and the tempo shifts upwards. Quickly, I slam my heel on his foot.

"Oops. I'm not much of a dancer." Much to Lucius's credit, he doesn't flinch.

"I understand you're upset with me." I scoff. That just might be the understatement of the year. "I know my words were abrasive, and I apologize for that. You must know they do not reflect my true thoughts."

"You don't need to waste your words on me."

"I do." He pauses to spin me outwards the pull my body back close to his. "I care for you, Verosa, I want you to be happy."

"If you care so much about my happiness, then you should have let him kill you," I seethe with the fury of a broken heart torn anew. I should be enjoying my twentieth birthday with my Blaine by my side, laughing and talking with Torin and Tanja. Not Lucius, who doesn't give a damn about any of them, not even me. What's worse? The fact that I still care, and I still wish that the lies Lucius fed me were true. I wish he was still the same person I met.

I can see his heart breaking behind his regal facade, the same way mine is now crumbling. In another life this could have been a nice dance. Perhaps he could have been my friend. I suppose now we will never know.

"I miss the way you used to look at me," he breathes, his voice barely above a whisper. A single tear drips underneath my mask and onto my cheek, and with painstaking slowness, he leans forward to kiss it away. "Happy birthday, Verosa. Enjoy the party."

He disappears into the swirling dancers, leaving me to stand alone in the midst of the ballroom. Embarrassment and anger heat my face as I notice the gawking whispers and stares of the other dancers. Shaking the guilt from my head, I take a step back to exit the dance floor when a hand lands on the small of my back.

My head rests comfortable on Rowan's chest as I tilt it back to eye him. He smiles down, his gaze wistful and in awe.

"The dance isn't over yet, milady." He spins me around, his hand never leaving my back.

All guilt and anger dispels from my heart immediately, as it always does when he is near. It is as if his aura is so light, so loving, that no darkness can find me here.

With a lightness in my heart, I place my hand in his and curtsy deeply. My skirts billow out across the dance floor like starlight sprawling across the night sky. Rowan's lips are slightly parted as I rise, but he quickly closes them with a smirk as the music intensifies. I place my hand on his shoulder with equal cunning before we step into the dance.

My eyes unknowingly dart to the other patrons. Their eyes are narrowed behind their masks, all focusing on me. I don't need to read their lips to know what they're saying. About me. About him. He's the hero, and I'm the whore.

Rowan's grip shifts from my back to my waist, tightening with every extra inch of skin he claims. His lips caress the outer shell of my ear as he leans forward to whisper.

"I'm growing rather jealous of the attention you're giving to everyone else." Heat creeps up the back of my neck. His hand releases my waist, allowing me to circle around him, the hem of my skirt swishing softly against his dark suit. When I return, he grips me hastily, careful not to apply too much pressure.

"Can't you see them whispering?"

"Not when all I see is you." I look up, dazed, to notice a small tinge of color on his cheeks. Rowan, the Mercenary King, is blushing because of me. "The most beautiful woman in this kingdom with two handsome men at her beck and call. It's jealousy, love."

I bite my lip, my heart now racing for another reason. His words have a sharp satiric undertone, but his face is soft and genuine. The thought emboldens me to lean forward right as the tempo increases. From the corner of my eye, I can see Lucius and my father watching from the dais. Lucius's face is pinched in poorly concealed anger. My father isn't even looking at me. No, he's staring right at Rowan.

The dance soon tugs my attention back to the Noiteron. Small beads of sweat prick along his brow, our steps moving in an elegant frenzy. We spin past the other partygoers, my gown brushing against the other women's, leaving stardust on their silk. Light exudes from my every movement until I'm glowing, though it can be blamed on a trick of the light. In a moment, Rowan sweeps me up in his arms, lifting me above his head while he pivots. I toss my head back and laugh, my heart growing lighter by the second.

As my feet brush the ground again, I still feel weightless, Rowan's arms wrapped firmly around my waist, holding me as I tip backwards.

My impromptu move has my hair grazing the ground and blood rushing to my head, but Rowan supports me through the dip. I never fear the fall.

The song ends as he pulls me back upright, and I use the moment to whisper in his ear "Meet me in the hallway past the band." His hand squeezes my hip softly to let me know he heard me, then he releases his grip with a bow. I echo his sentiments before whisking off towards the outskirts of the ballroom again. Torin greets me with a knowing smirk, but my gaze easily drifts from him to my father. Ophelus stands as if in a trance, his gaze following Rowan. Before he can go to him, the mercenary slips behind the harpist and out into the hall. The king sits, but his gaze lingers, faraway.

When I manage to sneak past the guards, the moon has already raised high in the sky. Any moment now, Kya and Amír will have snuck past the guards and laid our distraction. Within the hour, I will finally be free of this place.

The thought chases my feet from the floor as I sprint down the hall, the sounds of the party fading with each step. All the air leaves my lungs as I round the corner, and a familiar pair of arms wrap around my midsection. My hands fly to my mouth to suppress my laughter as Rowan lifts me into the air. I throw my head back, basking in the safety of his grip and the feeling of flight.

My feet touch the ground all too soon, and Rowan looks down at me with a sly grin. Before he can part his lips to utter some sarcastic quip, I grab him by the wrist and drag him down the corridor after me.

"Come on, there's something I want to show you."

The mercenary follows silently, our footsteps not making a sound. It was a perk of my months in stealth training, and years on his part. He follows me through each winding turn we take, a maze of hallways designed to confuse any intruders. Each passage varies in width and height, some ending in dead ends, others splitting in two. I expertly pick my way through each, my path already memorized years ago.

We finally reach a hall with no lights; I step into the hall. Rowan steps close behind me, splaying his fingers across my stomach and pulling me close to his chest. I smile, then pull forth light from that well within my soul. A mist appears above us, rising to illuminate the room with a dim glow. Not enough to alert anyone of our presence, but enough that the panic gripping my chest eases. The magic hardly feels draining anymore; rather, each time I release a burst of light, energy flows through my veins. My skin electrifies, enhanced by Rowan's fingertips kneading delicate patterns into my abdomen.

I spin and toss my arms out to the side. "Tada! Welcome to our hidden tapestry room."

Behind me rests a large room that most would recognize as the palace's first ballroom. By now the architecture is crumbling, some mold growing in the crevices where the floor had cracked from one too many dances. Spiraling up the walls are thousands upon thousands of tapestries. Some fray at the edges or are missing full chunks of pattern, while others remain perfectly intact.

"I thought it would have a more formal name." Rowan raises an eyebrow, feigning being unimpressed. "Like super-secret hidden tapestry room." His straight nose scrunches, mimicking my own expression. I use it as an invitation to drag him away from the door towards the first piece of art.

"Irene hated these tapestries, probably because I loved them so much. These stories were my escape from whatever hell she had concocted that day. I'd wander the halls staring at them, losing myself in the world they presented." I laugh softly. "She had them all moved here, and the doors barred when she found out. But no locks could keep me out." I wiggle my eyebrows suggestively, and Rowan bites back a laugh.

We pause in front of one of my favorites, an older piece depicting a knight and a princess, the villainous dragon laying slain in the background. I both hated and loved the way the blood coated the knight's sword when I was younger, but now I lay those conflicting feelings to rest.

"When I was a kid, I loved the idea of some knight coming in and saving me from my mother. I wished life was simple like that, but as I got older, I wished I was the one holding the sword. I wished I could save myself and save the knight from the struggle of killing the dragon."

I had thought Blaine was that knight. I thought he was the one to save me, but I realized too late I needed to save myself so I wouldn't need to save him as well. Now I've lost my knight. In some ways, the dragon won.

Rowan clears his throat. "I have another idea. What if the princess and the knight saved each other?" He shoots me a crooked grin. "Maybe the knight was really a murderous bastard who wouldn't get out of his own head, and the princess needed a way out of her life. Maybe he freed her from the dragon, but she freed him from his."

A wild, uncontrollable grin threatens to split my face in half as Rowan speaks. I watch his every mannerism, his pinched brows, crooked lifting of his mouth, and the bobbing of his Adam's apple as he swallows.

"I like that."

We flit around the abandoned ballroom, Rowan following me from tapestry to tapestry. He listens thoughtfully, his eyes picking apart the story behind them from my expression alone before I even speak. Still, he listens to my ramblings, occasionally offering his own amendments.

Finally, we reach one torn in half. A queen holding a spiked crown, silver and gold dripping from her eyes. The blind queen. No one knows of this one, as Irene had it destroyed in a rage, but I found it and carried it here. The relief I felt knowing that someone other than had viewed her as the villain woven within the threads. The artist had been hung publicly for treason for this depiction.

"The King's Queen." Rowan reads the threads along the bottom and inhales sharply. I don't need to speak for him to know how I feel, how I am begging him to see. I bite my cheek to avoid from spilling my secrets and apologies right here and now. The thought of seeing him hung in the same square as that artist is all that keeps me from confessing.

"Wait, if all the tapestries were torn down, then why are there some still hanging in the halls? Unless..."

"The king allowed me to select and hang whatever tapestries I chose after my mother's passing. I considered it an apology for him witnessing my abuse for years and never stopping it. I was supposed to be under his protection, and he failed."

Rowan's jaw clicks as it clenches, and I flinch knowing I've hit an unknown nerve.

I swallow thickly, suddenly feeling shyer than I've felt in my whole life. I find myself barely breathing as I lift my heated gaze to his. The mercenary's eyes darken, and my heart rate spikes.

"Did you mean it?" I breathe. "When you said I was beautiful?"

The air between us thickens, only the sound of my heartbeat fills me ears. The world slips away as Rowan steps forward, his hands landing on my hips. My embarrassment fades as his predatory gaze is replaced by something softer. His powerful aura envelopes me immediately, creating this untouchable halo of comfort. We are the only two in this world, the only thing that matters is his touch and how it responds to mine.

He swipes his tongue over his bottom lip. "We are in a room full of the most stunning artwork this kingdom has seen, and yet I can't tear my eyes off of you." One of his hands reaches up to cup my cheek and I lean into the touch. "You are beyond beautiful."

Maybe it is the champagne bubbles floating from my stomach to my head, or the relief that I haven't been imagining everything between us. Perhaps it is the thought that despite how broken and small I am, someone can still see me. For whatever reason in this wide universe, I lean forward on my toes and press my lips against his.

Rowan doesn't wait a second before pulling me flush against him, his one arm wrapped around my midsection while his other hand holds my face to his. I respond with equal enthusiasm, throwing my arms around his neck and pulling him down closer to me. My spine curves into his touch. His body melds into mine as if this is how we were always supposed to be, long lost puzzle pieces finally merging. Two bodies, twin souls.

His mouth curves into a smile as his lips chase mine. "You taste like alcohol," he whispers between kisses. I blush in embarrassment and try to pull away with a small sorry, but he holds me close, our lips colliding again. His tongue sweeps the roof of my mouth before he pulls back again with a sly grin.

"Never apologize." He kisses my palm. "Now you taste like me."

I smack his chest lightly, and he laughs, a full, hearty sound that has desire and love building in my gut like a wildfire. If he sees my blush, he doesn't comment on in, just murmurs for me to hold still. With careful hands, he brushes stray hairs from my face, tucking them behind my ear. I watch mesmerized as he licks the pad of his thumb then uses it to fix my smudged lip stain. I look up at him, his face still locked in firm concentration when he notices my stare. He smiles.

"What?"

"I love you."

Rowan runs his hand through his hair, his lips still puffy and slightly parted. I take a step closer, my chest now pressing against his. I can feel how frantically his heart is beating as I trace a finger up his forearm. He captures it and holds it against his sternum.

"You love me?"

"I love you." I repeat, willing to say it as many times as necessary. "You don't have to say it back. I understand." Rowan jolts as if I've stabbed him. My brows knit together in confusion. What had I said wrong? Rowan must notice my frown because he shifts to grip my chin, using his index finger to tilt my gaze to his.

"Fuck no, that's not it," he swears vehemently. "I love you Vera, I promise."

A smile stretches across my face as his words reach my ears. Coyly, I bat my eyelashes, feigning innocence as I allow myself to push further against him. "Oh, then what is it?" Rowan clenches his jaw and squares his shoulders.

"You need to stop saying shit that makes me want to kiss you again," he warns. "It is hard enough to control myself as it is when you look at me like that." His tone is serious, but I know he would stop the moment I asked him. He would halt everything immediately and step away if I asked. My comfort comes before any of his desires, and it always has to him. But tonight I'm feeling emboldened and tired of waiting in the comfort of the familiar. Tonight I want him.

"Maybe that's exactly why I'm saying things, doing things..." I sway my hips softly, my arms locked behind my back as I lean forward ever so slightly. The minuscule motion sends his eyes darkening and his shoulders tensing. He pauses only for a second before murmuring "fuck it" and closes the small space between us.

CHAPTER 38
VEROSA

I don't remember why I waited so long for this, nor can I remember much as Rowan attaches his lips to mine again. His motions are painstakingly calculated as he shifts his hand from my waist to my thigh, bringing my leg to hook around the back of his knee. His other hand rests buried deep within my hair, pulling me closer still to him. I don't fight it, allowing him to envelope all my senses. All I can see is his darkening eyes. All I can smell is citrus and leather. All I taste and hear and feel is him. I want it to stay this way forever.

His fingers press into my soft skin through the fabric of my gown, leaving fingertip-sized marks by now, I'm sure. I appreciate the pressure and tilt my head back as his lips leave mine to mark my jaw, trailing soft kisses down to the base of my neck. My fingers dig into his broad shoulders as I gasp.

Electricity shoots through my spine every time his skin makes contact with mine. Every time he murmurs something against my throat. The action is dizzying, and I hold tighter to him in an attempt to ground myself. His dark chuckle vibrates through my own throat, and I squeeze my eyes shut.

"Don't you dare leave a mark. We have to see your mother tonight."

"No promises."

Desire like nothing I've ever felt pools in my gut, stealing all the air from my lungs in one breath. Rowan pauses to scan my face, attentive and caring as always, before pressing another kiss to the corner of my mouth.

I sigh against it. He's holding me like I'm the most precious thing in this world, and if he were to tell me I am, I would believe him after this. It's just kissing, and I don't want it to lead to anything more for now, but I feel as if I could conquer anything. I don't need to fear the fall any longer because I know Rowan will be there waiting to catch me.

Suddenly, the door to the tapestry room slams open, and a masked patron screeches.

"By the Laei, we are in public." Torin mocks a gasp, pressing his palm to his chest as if he is about to faint.

"Torin!"

"Next time try behind the training grounds at this hour. Secluded, dark, dangerous...sexy." He winks as my face burns. Rowan makes a sound somewhere between a laugh and a growl, obviously not too pleased to be interrupted. His hand withdraws from my waist, and allows me to smooth my dress and hair out. He interjects at odd moments, pushing my hands away and fixing my unkept hair or smudged rogue.

I ignore the pang of jealousy that invades my core when I notice how experienced he seems to be at this. It isn't fair, I know, especially considering my history with the former Captain of the Guard.

Torin watches with an amused expression. I would find comfort in it if I couldn't see the weariness it hides. He's running off of fumes, and soon enough, I fear he will combust.

"Anyways, thanks for the show." The captain's face falls. "The king requests your presence, Verosa."

Immediately all the lights I had lit fall, the world darkening. Rowan swears and reaches for me in the dark, but I barely feel his touch as I hear the distant striking of the clock. I am supposed to be on the other side of this wall with Amír and Kya right now, already making my way towards the port between the Krycolian and Nevan border.

Rowan leans forward, his lips brushing against my ear. "What does the king want with you?" His concern and anger are both evident as they commingle in his tone. My hands begin to shake at my side. This is the moment I had been hoping to avoid. The moment where the truth comes to light.

I rise on my toes and press a soft kiss against his jaw, unable to reach his cheek at this angle. Brushing a stray hair from his eyes I force myself to be still. *Breathe.*

"Everything will make sense after this," I whisper. "Set your distraction, we will leave right after this."

Without so much as a backwards glance, I accept Torin's arm. I know if I look at Rowan now, I will crumble and run, and everything we have worked for will fall apart. Rowan lets me go with a silent promise. *I trust you. I love you.*

The thought sends a wild flurry into to my stomach despite my anxieties. Kya and Amír will have to wait, the plan will adapt. They will need to trust me.

I suppress a smile. The image of Kya pushing her lover to the point of panic, causing Amír to storm the ballroom, pistol aimed at my fiancé. The ballroom will burst into chaos, but it will be no different from any other mission. Kya and Amír will carve through the ballroom, toss me a sword as we make our escape. I can see my father's shock, as well as Lucius's.

Torin nudges my side, bringing me from my daydream. "You happy about something?"

"Shut up." I rest my head on his shoulder one last time. "Happy, sad. It's all so temporary. I wish I could go back to last summer when everything was simple." *When there was one more of us.*

Torin stiffens as he always does whenever Blaine is mentioned. He had known Blaine was leaving all along, and yet he let him go knowing how much he would have to take on. How much it would hurt. Torin had always been a better friend than I am, and loyalty has always been his fatal flaw. The weight of his station is slowly crushing him, and I fear that one day I will return, and there will be nothing left of the friend I had.

"I think he would want you to be happy. No, I know he does. He never fell out of love with you, you know. He just went through so much. War changes people. The feelings stayed, but the expression changed. Plus, your mother being the one to ship him off didn't help." The surprise of Torin finally speaking on the matter is only overshadowed by the shock of one other thing.

"My mother what?"

Torin blanches. Clearly, he has let a palace secret slip. He licks his lips and lowers his voice.

"Blaine's deployment was sped up by your mother when she learned of your feelings for him. He was never supposed to be on the front lines either. Speculation says she threatened the captain with a curse that when he was of age, he was to send him off. You were only nine at the time."

My mother was a cruel woman, that much was given. She would have let me die in the snow to prove a point. She once whipped my legs raw to the point where my nanny had to throw herself over me. She went missing the next week. She would withhold my meals before balls and celebrations. But this...

She damned a boy's future and life over a childish crush. He was eleven when she made this choice. I knew she was responsible for Blaine being sent to war, but not how early she had begun her plotting. I cannot even fathom the depths of evil in her soul. Even from Hell she torments me.

"I hate her," I whisper, my eyes burning as I press them closed. "I hate her so much."

Torin says nothing, having known me long enough to read between the lies. If Irene had been from anywhere else, then this marriage wouldn't be looming over my head. Had she never whipped me, my nanny wouldn't have died, and Tanja would still have a mother. Had she never seen Blaine, he never would have gone to war, that part of him never would have died, and I wouldn't have had the chance to kill the rest of him. So many have died, when does it end?

Never. All of this, all the pain and loss, it is all because of her.

We reach the ballroom all too soon, slipping in silently among the crowd as if we had never left. We weave through masked patrons who have begun to sway under the effect of the alcohol. We slip behind the band, playing the final few chords of a slow ballad, covering our hushed conversation.

My friend squeezes my arm. "Ready to go change history?" he jests. "The disappearance of Crown Princess Verosa. One night a future queen, the next gone without a trace. A shadow in the wind." He adds the last bit for dramatic effect, and I let laughter slip from between my lips.

"We've had so many 'disappearances' these past few years, I doubt anyone will notice mine."

"Rewrite the story then." He shrugs. "Make them remember you."

The squire standing beside my father clears his throat. All eyes turn towards where I stand, and I realize it is time. Time to face the truth and the consequences of my actions that I've been running from.

"Show time," I whisper with a final look. A goodbye.

Torin nods sympathetically, his mouth set in a firm line. I don't pretend to not see the slight glisten of his moistening eyes. I bite my cheek as I descend the dais, my father staring down in approval. Lucius stands by his side, his hand outstretched to help me up the final steps. Traitorously, I take it, the movement feeling every bit like a betrayal.

The entire ballroom is silent save for the clicking of my heels on the dais as I take my spot beside my fiancé. My skin grows clammy as my hand continues to rest in his. I hope he hates sweat.

The nobles whisper to themselves, and I catch snippets of it.

'That's the princess?'

'Wasn't she dancing with that blonde man?'

'She looks like her mother.'

'Isn't that Lady Iales' gown?'

'...disgrace...'

'What would the Queen think?'

My heart stops at the mention of my mother, but I shake her piercing gaze from my head. From the front of the crowd, Aiko finds my attention and motions a rising and falling action with her hands. *Breathe.* At the same time, her own face looks pale, and I could say the same to her.

I know I appear calm and collected, my mask still covering the majority of my face. But my heart races. Amír and Kya should be waiting in the garden by now, and Rowan is supposed to be setting our distraction. I should be with them, not standing here surrounded by people who look like they would willingly skin me alive.

My eyes scan the crowds for a familiar mercenary as my father begins his speech. My search is interrupted by a cough to my left. Ophelus raises his eyebrows at whatever he said that I had clearly missed.

"He wants me to remove your mask." Lucius whispers, his fingers already stretching towards the back of my head. I flinch perceptibly and raise my hands. My fingers tangle in my dark hair as I search for the satin ribbon holding the gilded mask to my face. I catch onto the silky band and pull, releasing my mask and revealing my secret to the one my gaze searches for.

Inhale. Exhale.

Before my own unmasking, it seemed like a good idea to have everyone in attendance wear masks, but now, with hundreds of masked blondes standing before me, I begin to question that decision. Still, I know I could pick him apart from a crowd of thousands even with the mask, it is just an excuse for the obvious. Rowan isn't here.

I need to leave. Now. As I begin to step forward to descend the dais, I catch on to the squire's words at about the same time Lucius' hand rests on my waist.

"On this hour in two days' time, Crown Princess Verosa Elyce of the Kingdom Krycolis will be wed to Crown Prince Lucius Vangar of the Tesslari Empire in a union between lands. All hail the future Emperor and Empress."

Confusion slows my reflexes as I hear those final words. Father had told me we would be forming an alliance with Tesslari, not merging. I had been promised the title of Queen, not Empress. It is at that moment that Lucius' grip tightens as he pulls me closer. He murmurs something along the lines of 'I'm sorry' before he crashes his lips against mine.

The nobles cheering drowns out my protests. My eyes widen in shock as he holds me tightly against him, his grip a vice as I attempt to squirm out of it. His lips are rough as they capture mine, and I can do nothing but stand still, attempting to press my own lips firmly together. When he pries my mouth open with his tongue, I finally snap, biting down hard. Without so much as a wince, my fiancé releases me, an apologetic look on his face passing for only a moment. I gasp for breath, anger spiking my gut. My skin heats. I have to leave before I light this whole ballroom up.

As the applause sounds, I continue my search for Rowan when I finally see him.

I find him sprinting for the exit.

All the air leaves the room, the many faces blurring together. He had told me his distraction was in the ballroom, there is no reason for him to be running away. Except for one thing. He is going to leave without me.

My face crumples, and I fist my skirts in my hands. Lucius reaches for me but it is too late; I am already leaping from the dais and sprinting towards the hallway where Rowan just exited. The crowd gasps but parts for me as I run after Rowan. My light, my death, my love.

My lungs burn, and my legs groan in protest as I sprint down the corridors. One of my heels snaps with a resounding crack. I ignore it, kicking both shoes off to continue my sprint.

Dark hairs flit around my face, in my eyes, as the doorway I look for comes into view. The breeze calls my name, wicking the sweat from my brow.

I spot him the moment I step onto the balcony. Rowan stands with his back to me, his back and shoulder muscles flexing underneath his black tunic. His coat lay discarded across the railing. I approach slowly, choosing to step on stones I know won't creak. Silently I approach him, waiting a pace away.

Breathe. Inhale. Exhale. *You knew the truth would come out eventually. Yes, this outcome is not ideal, but it won't break you. He is upset, he is allowed to be.*

I square my shoulders and bite my lip. Despite my best attempts to soothe my fears, I already can feel it. Something between us has shifted, cracked. Nothing will be the same after tonight.

I inhale sharply. "Rowan?"

CHAPTER 39

ROWAN

Crown Princess Verosa Elyce of Krycolis. How had I not seen it before? It had been staring me in my face all along. The arranged marriages aligned, the way she was able to have access to the guards' stations any time they changed. The way she flinched when someone called her princess.

The biggest hint? Irene. Her mother's name was Irene, and she had told me as such. She had failed to mention she was the late Queen Irene. It is why her mother had the power to tear down all the tapestries without repercussion and why no one could protect Verosa from her mother. Anyone who tried wound up dead.

All this time I've been fighting alongside, training, bantering, and falling in love with my sister. *Half*-sister, but still a blood relative.

Air. I need air.

Whirling on my heel, I weave through the halls until I find the balcony Vera was supposed to escape from an hour ago. An escape window we missed because I was too busy kissing her in an abandoned hallway.

Disgust crawls up my throat in the form of bile, and I dry heave over the railing. My muscles tense and constrict as my mind reels. I loved her. Gods, I'd fallen for the one person I cannot love.

I clench the lip of the balcony railing with white knuckles. This is why I never should have gotten involved. I should have cleaned up that job in Belam quicker, or better yet, never traversed the borders of that god-forsaken city. I should've stuck to my rules. Never stop. Never slow. Never care.

I breathe deeply. I have to leave now. Verosa can escape on her own if she still wishes to, though I doubt she will, given her new title as future empress. I begin to hoist myself over the railing when a soft voice calls out, halting me where I stand.

"Rowan?"

Shit.

I spin on my heel to find the source of my turmoil. The reason my heart used to beat and now refuses to without splintering further. The one I love and hate the most for this war within me.

Verosa frowns, her eyes pricked with tears. I can see the smudges of makeup beneath her eyes from where she has rubbed them raw. Despite what she may think, I hold no anger towards her for keeping her identity from me; after all, I did the same. No, the only one I harbor loathing for is myself.

"I can explain." She begins stepping forward. I step back.

Her face falters, and I pinch my eyes closed in disgust. I can't bear to look at her any longer. The rapid echo of my beating heart, those soft lips I kissed, what I'd dared to dream on my own. Sister. She is my sister by blood, and I loved her in ways you don't love your family. The very thought causes my grip to tighten on the lip of the balcony, bile threatening to rise and burn my throat.

"I didn't mean to hurt you or lie to you. I was trying to protect you." She swallows, her guilty tears flowing freely down her face now. "If my father somehow caught us and learned you were helping me escape, it would be treason. Keeping you in the dark was the only way I could save you."

I run my hand over my face. This is spiraling out of control too quickly. I've got to get out of here before my last tether of control snaps.

"I need to leave," I tell her honestly. "You can leave now too, thanks to that stunt, but you aren't coming with me. You can't come with me."

"I don't know what you're talking about." She takes a step forward, her hand reaching for mine. I jump backwards until I am standing on the ledge. Hurt flickers across her expression.

"I came here for one thing, Verosa, not this," I groan, rubbing my hand over my face. "I came here to kill our father."

Her eyes widen. "Our?"

My own emerald gaze narrows and locks onto hers. She looks so small, so fragile from this height. Anything I thought I knew about her shatters before my eyes. For a moment, I debate throwing myself from this balcony. How sick and twisted those false gods are to pluck at my fate like this. How dare they blacken my soul.

"My mother was Ophelus' lover. I am his son, which makes you-"

"Don't finish that sentence." Silver lines her eyes and mars the delicate handiwork of Aiko. "This is insane. Rowan, you are ill, you need to come down from there so we can get you help."

She doesn't lunge for me this time, knowing already that I am quicker. Instead, she falls to her knees, begging. The sight makes my stomach churn. She should be on her knees for no man, no gods. What's worse? The longer I look at her, the more I want to believe her words, but I know the truth.

My fists shake at my side. I've loved Verosa fiercer than I have anyone in my life. At first, I didn't dare to let myself think past tomorrow, let alone dream of any pleasant future. I knew I would work until I died, and I would die young. I wouldn't die until my mother was safe, but after that, what was there worth being careful for?

Then she came, and for the first time, I feared for someone's safety. Someone's safety that was attached to mine. I had to be cautious for her sake, and slowly, my walls crumbled. She let me dream of a life other than this one. I was drawn to her, fire to fire, as if we had been cut from the same cloth. I realize with a sickening clench that perhaps we truly had been.

"Please." The whisper leaves her lips in a soft breath. A plea.

Verosa will never allow me to leave her. She will hunt me with more fervor than she did Blaine. She will follow me to the ends of the earth to rectify whatever mistake she thinks has been made. She needs to believe I will be better without her, then she will be safe.

Then you don't have to live with your sins. Weak. What did I warn you of?

That feminine voice I hadn't heard in so long returns.

I force my countenance to stone.

"We should have stayed strangers." I watch her face break, and for the first time in my life, I choose to run.

Vera's screams pierce through my skin and imbeds itself within the caverns of my mind, echoing over and over to the point of madness as I leap from the balcony. I beg the darkness that cloaks me to mask the sounds of her bone-shattering screams. All the air is lost from my lungs, and I let my tears fall and wet my skin.

For the first time in months, I feel that void creeping back in where her light used to reside. Now I am nothing but an empty shell of darkness. The shadow has come home.

CHAPTER 40
VEROSA

"Again." I huff through short puffs of air. My sword hands heavy at my side, my shoulders and arms burning with exertion. Torin only sighs and nods, sending another wave of soldiers my way. This time there are seven.

The first charges forward with a shout, his hollering voice piercing against my senses. I grimace as I easily deflect his blow then disarm him. If his combat strategy was to both alert me of his presence while rupturing my ear drum, then his mission was successful.

The next knights come in a team of three. I bare my teeth at the challenge and dig my heels into the sand of the training arena. The first one, a small blonde who slightly resembles Torin, makes a clean swipe for my knees. The blow is harder to block. I settle for leaping over the blade then smashing it to the ground on my descent. The knight cries out as the sword is pulled from his grip, and the other two attack simultaneously. One aims for my throat, the other my midsection. I leap back, slamming my heel on the hilt of the fallen sword and propel it into the air. Once the second weapon is in my hand, I engage both of the men, just now breaking a sweat.

The pair work well together, their blows synchronized and each aiming for a lethal point. They act like Kya and Derrín. The thought causes me to falter for just a moment, and one of their blows nicks my arm. The poor soldier looks ready to leap into the grave himself.

With a low growl, I set upon them both with unleashed fury until both lay on the ground, disarmed with a sword tip pointed at the base of their throats.

The remaining four soldiers lower their weapons and set off to run laps around the training grounds instead. In full armor. In the heat of the day. That was the alternative option offered to them this morning when I requested sparring partners.

I'm unsure of whether I should be worried that none of our soldiers can hold a torch to the way Kya fights. Most of these men have trained their whole lives in the palace and have seen battle, while I have only been training a few months with a mercenary and an assassin.

"Next." My muscles scream for rest, but I refuse. I lift my sword again, prepared to face my next onslaught of attacks. Torin steps forward, lowering my blade from his face with one finger.

"That's all for today, Vera. You've worn yourself out and-"

"I have not!"

"And," he says with a pointed look, "I have no more knights to offer you. You thoroughly tore through them all."

I frown when I feel that hollow sense of despair begin to resurface. I force myself to push it down and furrow my eyebrows.

"That's all? We should have more than this."

Torin's face says it all. He knows, but he doesn't have answers. Krycolis used to boast thousands of skilled knights, and our numbers have noticeably dwindled far too low. Our remaining knights are predominantly inexperienced, the only senior knight being Torin, if you can even call him that at twenty-two years of age.

"I've been getting reports from some outside sources." My heart clenches. Rowan. He doesn't even have to say it. "They're finding some of our men. Dead."

A chill rattles my bones despite the spring sun and the sweat slicking my skin. The question must be in my eyes because Torin shakes his head. *He is not one of them.* His dark roots are growing out, his blonde hair now scattered it the base with a rich brown color. He jokes about how maybe he will go red next and find Blaine just to see the shock on his face.

"They're all orphans or have no one who loves them. No one to come looking for them."

"Where are they finding them? We need to bury them, search for anyone."

Torin shakes his head. "The king dismisses me. He says he has no proof, and since the reports are coming from Belam and Adil, there are very few nobles or high-ranking knights who give a damn."

I suck on my teeth and inhale sharply. They think it's all false, too blinded by the fact that those who actually care are cursed. "Perhaps if we send someone who is blessed to make the report?"

"And wait for a body to just show up?" The captain raises an eyebrow, and I grind my teeth until my jaw clicks in strain. The wedding is tomorrow. Rowan thinks he is my brother, meaning my father had an affair. My mother was murdered. Blaine is gone. Dead bodies of soldiers are showing up in cursed cities. The connection is staring me in the face, and yet I cannot see it.

I pinch the bridge of my nose between my thumb and forefinger, a habit I picked up from Rowan. I slap my hand against my leg, glaring at the offending fingers. Torin watches sadly before draping an arm around my shoulder.

"I have much to do as it is. The king took no concern over our knights' dead bodies showing up but took the time to task me in finding that damned black stallion."

I gasp. "Vestíg is missing?" Now that I think about it, I haven't seen the dark horse in quite some time. He can usually be found at the center chaos in the stables or the courtyard. It has been quiet lately. Too quiet.

"Disappeared a few nights ago. Stall was locked, but the horse was gone. I thought we'd all rejoice, but no. Apparently, I need to track him down before he murders someone in a village or something." Torin cracks a wry smile.

"Come on." He offers me his arm. "Let's get you cleaned up, or that cut will get infected and postpone your wedding! We can't have the bride bleeding on her wedding day."

I stare into his eyes before, handing him my concealed dagger and deadpan. "Please cut every surface of my skin then.'

"It can't be that bad..." He trails off with a cringe, knowing damn well it is in fact 'that bad.' Tomorrow I am set to wed the man who destroyed my best friend's honor, kissed me forcefully, and has trapped me to him through this false alliance. He also doesn't give a damn about consequences as long as he gets what he wants. Lucky for me, I'm what he wants for now.

I lower my voice as we trek through the halls towards my chambers. The guards posted around my door have lessened now given our shortage of soldiers, but still, my paranoia is relentless. "You know I still plan on leaving before morning, right?"

Torin presses his lips together and nods. "And you know I still don't think it is a good idea given the state you've been in since the ball." *Since Rowan left you.*

Rowan is wrong, he has to be. Emilie is blessed, and so is my father, but he is a hybrid. I don't think Emilie would lie to him about his parentage, so he must be going through some breakdown, maybe from stress?

Or he needed an easy out once he knew who you were. Maybe he made a mistake. That small voice whispers in the back of my head. I force myself to shove it down, but a small fraction remains.

"I am fine. This was always the plan. I'll get to the port and book passage somewhere far from here. I'll make a life for myself then send word when I'm established."

"Under the name Marie," Torin recalls. My heart splinters.

"Yes."

He tuts his tongue but says nothing as we approach my door. My eyes gleam with tears as I notice the sun setting lower in the sky. We'd spent all day together, and it doesn't feel like enough. He sniffles lightly and offers a smile before opening his arms.

Wordlessly, I toss my arms around his neck, letting him hold my head to his chest and muffle my sobs. The hallways are empty, so I don't worry about others seeing us. He may not have been in my life as long as Tanja or Blaine, but parting with him threatens to break me just as much.

"You do what you have to do. Go where you want to go." His laughter rattles through my ribcage. "Write your story. If you ever need any help, know you'll always have an ally in Krycolis."

I knew leaving would hurt. I didn't know it would hurt this much.

Torin lets go first, placing a small kiss atop my head. Before he leaves, he holds both of my hands in one of his then kneels with his chin tucked to his chest.

"Until we meet again, my greedy princess," he jests, then rises with his signature smile. I try to engrave every detail of it in my mind as he walks away. The slight bounce in his step, his bleach blonde hair. The way he used to smile more when it was the four of us and how he clutches his belly when he laughs.

Tanja opens the door behind me, silently tucking me into her arms and leading me into the room. She unbraids my hair and lets me wash myself up before I slink back into the bedroom.

Beneath my pillowy mattress, I've stuffed my weaponry and provisions for when I leave. The plan is that Tanja will stay here tonight under the guise of helping me prepare for my wedding night. I will slip out right before the first brush of morning, and when the palace wakes, Tanja will alert the king that someone has stolen the princess in the night.

We went back and forth on that detail for a while but decided against saying I just disappeared. If they believe my enemies have stolen me, the guards will trace their patterns rather than mine, and I will have a greater chance of making it to the port before they realize I am long gone.

Tanja lay in her long nightgown atop my bed, fiddling with her ring. I slip in softly beside her, my hair still tangled and dripping down my back. I hold out my hand, and she places the jewelry in my palm. It burns cool against my skin, heavier than I thought it would be. The simple gold band matches her eyes while the blue sapphire matches Ruby's. I place the ring delicately on her finger.

"It's lovely."

Tanja hums, taking an ornately engraved brush from my nightstand and smooths my hair. The bristles tickle my scalp, and I lean back into her touch.

"Everything is ready for tomorrow." She speaks lowly, then pauses, straining to listen. Without warning, she raises her voice with a mischievous glint in her eyes. "So when Lucius enters your chambers, you should take his *giant, veinous-*"

A soft 'eep' and the clinking of chainmail echoes outside my door as the maids and guards scurry off, not quite wanting to hear this about their future leaders. Tanja grins evilly and winks at my blush.

"-ego and crush it by not showing up." She pokes at my side. "Get your mind out of the moat, Vera."

She laughs as I push her over lightly while cringing and fanning at myself. Now that I know what it's like to have his disgusting tongue in my mouth, I don't need that image as fuel for my nightmares.

Tanja settles herself under my covers, her chestnut curls splayed out across my pillow like molten gold, each amber shade reflecting in the candlelight. She looks every part the image of a goddess. She holds out her arms, and I crawl into them, our limbs entangling as if we never have to part. As if this might not be the last time I ever see her.

"I wish I could be here for your wedding," I whisper. Tanja brushes her nose against mine.

"Maybe we will do a destination wedding. Get married legally here and hold the ceremony wherever you wind up."

"You'd do that?"

My friend hums and burrows in closer, her arm draped across my waist in some form of half hug. My body aches in response to the grief of knowing this is the last night like this.

"Of course. You're like my sister, Ver. I can't get married without my maid of honor."

Tanja's face tells me she doesn't expect a response, not that I have one to offer, anyway. My throat constricts as I swallow a small sob. To think there was once a time I doubted if she'd stand by myself without the crown. Here I am, the night I walk away from it all, and she still chooses me.

My voice cracks as I finally speak, and I can't find it in my heart to care. "I wish you would come with me, but I know that would be just as bad as someone forcing me to stay here."

"Aw, you're growing up." Tanja teases, but I can see the well of emotions blooming from within her as well. She bites her tongue and dips her cheek as the first few tears slip through. We cling to each other tighter, dreading the rise of the sun.

"Hey, I love you."

Tanja laughs. "Yeah, I know."

For the first time in my life, I wish that night would last forever. Somewhere from within the dark, Tanja rests her head on the crook of my neck. "I love you too, Ver."

Despite the ache in my chest and the tears wetting my cheeks, I feel oddly at peace. The pain of leaving the only place I've known and those I love rips my soul to shred, but this place can never be for me again. I need to live my life for the first time in twenty years.

I've made my peace with all but one now. The one who hated this idea the most. The one who I fell out of love with at the wrong time.

Some time in the quiet dark, I slip off to sleep.

My room feels strange as I awake, foreign in some way. The large canopy bed is empty, though the impression of a person's body is tucked close to mine in the sheets. When I sit up, I notice the oil lamp burning on my bedside table, which is not where I left it before I fell asleep.

I should feel alarmed, I should be confused. I should be anything but calm, yet I'm quite content and at ease. A figure steps out from the shadows, and I grin in recognition.

Blaine sits on the edge of my bed, his face pinched with light worry as it always is whenever I am involved. He pats my knee as he sits with this look that says prepare for a verbal smackdown.

"Do I get to know what I've done wrong before you set into me?"

"Take a guess."

I hum and place a finger on my chin as if in deep contemplation. Blaine swears under his breath, but I see the laughter he is trying so hard to conceal. I am too happy to see him to care.

"Is it because I didn't miss you enough? Because I promise I've missed you this much." I say throwing my arms out like a child. Blaine shakes his head, his loose dark curls falling into his eyes. Carelessly, I brush them away. "Is it because I fell out of love with you?"

"That's not your fault. It's because you're guilty and stubborn."

"Excuse me?"

"You're insufferable-"

"Oh, shut up Blaine, as if I haven't heard that before." Anger burns in my blood. He disappears without any warning, and the first thing he does is tell me off? I nearly scoff. I suppose some things never change despite my praying that they would.

"You're loud and have no respect for authority." He continues despite my driveling protests. "You're entitled, spoiled, and a downright disagreeable person. But you stick to your beliefs and won't let anyone belittle you. You push everyone around you to be better because you see the best in everyone."

"And look where that got me," I mumble into my pillow, cringing at how pathetic this all is. I chose this path for myself. This is the first choice I've made for myself in years, and it is the one threatening to tear me apart.

"Your kind heart will hurt you, but it will only hurt worse if you guard it."

"And you'd know, wouldn't you?" It isn't an accusation or laced with spite like I had intended. Instead, it's a gentle dawn, an understanding I'd been reaching for since he returned from war. Here, Blaine was warning me not as my personal guard or even my friend, but as my first love who never stopped loving. Now I play the role of the scorned and the scornful at the same time. And he stays.

Blaine leans forward a bit, brushing his weathered hand across my own and running his thumb over my palm. He frowns at the calluses and scars that have formed since the last time he held it, the lines of a story he is no longer a part of.

"If you only listen to one thing I've ever told you, let it be this." Every word is low and strained, as if it pains him to part with this truth. "My biggest regret in life is believing that it would hurt us both less if I shut you out, that my burden was mine to bear alone. Don't choose your pride over him."

Somehow, I feel like we are no longer talking about Rowan, but a story yet to be closed. A single tear drips down my face, and he's quick to brush it away. I dip my chin. It's pathetic. I am crying over another man I was never going to be able to be with anyway. A man I'll never see again.

"I'm sorry, Blaine."

It's true. I am sorry for not fighting harder for us, or at least trying to see past the shields he put up. I am sorry for not protecting him from Irene and for being at fault for all the turmoil in his life. I am sorry for not loving him in the way he wishes to be loved.

His eyes are soft again and hold the same joy they did all those years ago when he looks at me. We both know how to close this epilogue.

"Say it."

My peace I've searched for is within my grasp, I just need to be brave enough to reach out and take it. I swallow thickly.

"I let you go."

His shoulders relax, as if some burden has been lifted from them. His lips curve upwards in the kindest of smiles. "Thank you."

When I awaken, I find the room is dark, and Tanja is curled into my side. With the back of my hand, I wipe at the tears that have begun to dry on my cheeks and pull the covers up to her chin.

I sense the attack before I see it. The rustling of a cloth being tugged loose from a bag or sack reaches me first. I reach for my dagger, but the scent hits my nose first, and I know it is too late. The scent of concentrated Etherbane floods my senses as the damp rag comes to rest over my nose and mouth, then the world goes dark.

CHAPTER 41

ROWAN

No one spoke to me once we returned to the compound last night. I didn't offer any explanation as we unpacked our bags, nor did I say anything when they asked where Vera was. My mother and Blaine had already dozed off on the velvet seats together, a storybook open in her lap.

No one spoke to me when I woke up late for the first time since I entered this unsavory business, nor as I sat down and stared emptily at my cup of black coffee.

No one other than my mother.

"I thought she was different," I can hear her murmur to Kya in the corner. "Something must have happened. Has he said anything?" The assassin shakes her head softly, worry clouding her features as she helps guide her to the table. Some days she gets dizzy, and she touches the scar at her hairline. My stomach churns. Just another thing to thank my father for. I don't care to tell her I get matching headaches on occasion.

"Don't bother, Mother, she isn't coming back. She chose to stay on her own." I cringe at the lie but play it off by swallowing the bitter drink before me. Kya coughs not so subtly and tilts her head towards the door into our common space. Amír and Derrín follow behind her silently, but Emilie's heated gaze never strays from my impassive face.

"My son. My love. My light." My mother croons before her soft smile turns to a steely glare. "I raised you to be better than this. Where is she, truly?" Her words pierce my skin, but I attempt to brush it off. Silently, I stalk from the room into my study. My three Nightwalkers sit stoically, waiting for the impending storm. My mother trails me in a fury, her short steps a cacophonous thunderstorm in her wake.

"I just don't understand." Emilie folds her hands under her arms as she glares at me. "Whatever spat you two had clearly isn't as important as your relationship. One of these days, you're going to need to swallow your pride before it swallows you, Rowan!"

"This isn't a matter of pride, Mother!"

"Then what is it?"

"She's my sister!" I nearly choke on the words, bile rising in my throat. "Verosa is my sister. She is the princess and the king's daughter. She may not be full blood, but some of our blood is shared and..." I gag and keel over, pressing the back of hand over my mouth in an attempt not to spew my coffee across the floor. I imagine it would somehow taste even worse the second time around.

Kya gasps. Derrín whistles lowly. Amír swears.

My mother just sighs heavily.

"By the Laei, you got my looks but your father's brains."

"What?" I scoff. My mother looks like she wants to shake my shoulders until my brains return to my skull. Instead, she settles for a deep breath and presses her palms together. When she speaks again, her voice is soft, placating. As if I am just a boy again.

"Rowan, what is your father?" When I only glare at her in confusion, she expands the thought further. "What color is his blood, love?"

"He's cursed." Obviously, I get my golden blood from her. My mother smiles in a rather grating way. I can taste the condescension from here.

"And what is Vera? Remind me again."

Oh.

Oh, no.

The realization must be evident across my face because Mother begins to laugh.

"This isn't funny, Mother. I thought I'd..."

"What? Kissed your sister?" She continues to laugh until it turns into a dry cough, then settles herself into a rickety chair in the corner. Her breaths come out in short puffs, but her eyes are shining against her red cheeks. "You've got this wonderful brain, son. I need you to use it."

My muscles groan in protest as I lower myself into the chair beside her. "I'm so glad I can be of amusement to you. But if Vera isn't Ophelus' daughter, then who is her father? Does the king know that the queen had an affair?"

My mother's face suddenly turns solemn. The air shifts into cool tones as if matching her mood. Something in the room feels... tense and unwelcoming. As if the walls remember.

"The queen was barren." As if this shock is not enough, Emilie does not wait for another beat before dropping her next bomb. "That is why she tried to kill you."

There is silence is the compound. Even Derrín refuses to fidget or breath. It is as if the very earth beneath my boots refuses to even shift lest it disturb the fragile statement that hangs in the air.

Emilie... Mother suddenly looks so old, so weary. However, no weakness can be traced in her stance, her aura. She is still as strong as the woman who took me and ran from the only love she'd known over ten years ago.

Yet another revelation hangs heavy over my head. A sharpened blade waiting to drop.

"Then Vera was..."

"Kidnapped, most likely as an infant. Yes."

A thousand thoughts swirl in my head. Who are her parents? Was she aware of her past, is that why she wanted to run away? Is that why Ophelus could sell her off so easily?

Then the worst one: I left her there every day with her kidnappers. I left her there last night, screaming on a balcony in the arms of someone who coveted her. Who had forced his tongue down her throat despite her obvious disgust. Who doesn't give a shit about her.

All the horrid tales I heard of Irene and Vera's abuse at her hand. All those scars crisscrossing across the back of her legs, the way she freezes at the darkness or the first sign of snow. Her aversion to blood...

"Rowan." My mother grips my arm suddenly. "Do not blame your-self. This is not on you. All of it is Irene's fault."

I never knew I could hate someone I never met until now. My fists clench until my nails bite blood from the flesh. Gold and silver swirl together. My mother and my father. Even their blood is discernible within my veins, and as much as I try to avoid it, I know he is just as much of me as she is. My own self-loathing grows.

"No, it's his," I growl, my lips curling in a snarl. "He did this to you, to us." *To her*, I add silently.

Emilie shakes her head sadly. As if there is so much behind her eyes she can't bear to hold it all in unto herself.

"I'm not here to place the guilty verdict for whatever judgement you have going through that head of yours right now. Just give me a moment to explain, please," She begs. I think back to the last time someone begged me for something. Verosa, begging me to stay. Then I had ran and hid like a coward. I will not make the same mistake twice.

I sit on the chair beside her and clench my jaw. Seeing the resigna-tion in my eyes, Emilie sighs. Her shoulders droop and cave in as she folds her hands. And when she opens her mouth, I finally listen.

CHAPTER 42

EMILIE

A young Emilie squinted as she tried to tie two green ribbons into her hair without stretching the swell of her pregnancy belly. The motion caused a sharp pain to stretch through the lower portion of her spine. The emerald satin slipped through her fingers to the floor, and she didn't need to try to know she couldn't bend over.

She glared down at her offending stomach.

"You'd better inherit your father's charm, or you're going to get into so much trouble someday." She poked at the swell, smiling at the returning kick. Her son was already causing trouble before he was even born. The thought brought a smile to her lips. She loved him so much already.

Soft footsteps came from behind her as her lover bent to retrieve the discarded slip of fabric. He held the ribbons between two fingers with a knowing smirk.

"Need a hand, love?" He smiled even as she crossed her arms over her swell.

"I have everything under control."

"Mhm." He hummed as he set to work braiding her hair back, tying it with the ribbons until a crown formed above her brow. Leaning forward to press a kiss to her temple, he hummed against the warmth of her skin. Someday he would replace this crown with one of diamonds and pearls. Once Irene was gone.

Emilie didn't know any of this, of course. When they met as children, all she knew was he wore fancy, funny clothes, spoke far too formally, and his hands were too soft to not be noble. He had lied and told her his father was a merchant, and now as young adults, that was why he was away so often, only able to visit once every few weeks. He had missed most of her pregnancy, and she knew he felt bad. She never pressed him over it, nor the fact that they had yet to be married. She knew their relationship transcended the conformities of their kingdom, and she had never minded one bit.

She never had any reason to suspect anything different until a few years later, when their son Rowan was now eleven, and a knock came at their door. Emilie ushered Rowan into their bedroom and told him to not come out until she said so.

It had been nearly ten years since Aiko and Finneas' daughter was kidnapped, and she never took chances anymore. She didn't know much about Ophelus' line of work, but she knew he made enough that Rowan would be worth a hefty ransom.

However, when she opened the door, it was not armed burglars that stood there, but a woman. She had sleek black hair and distinct Tesslari features. Her narrow eyes were accentuated with the faintest brush of ink, and her pink lips quivered with muffled sobs. Without wasting a moment, Emilie welcomed her into their home, offering her tea and the only blanket she owned that didn't have any holes.

"What troubles you?" the blonde woman cooed. The other woman eyed her, noting every detail. Emilie's pretty frame, her friendly face, and gorgeous eyes. Where she was thin and sharp, Emilie was curvy and soft. The blonde exuded warmth that enveloped even her cold skin. Loathing wrapped its iron tendrils around her throat and squeezed.

"They told me I could find you here." She spoke softly, and her throat constricted at the strain of doing so. "Said you could help. You see, I love my husband so very much, and I just learned he has been cheating on me for years. Sleeping with another woman."

Dread settled into Emilie's stomach, but her compassion caused her to shove it away as she offered a sympathetic smile. "I am so sorry."

"Turns out he had a bastard with the woman." Emilie flinched at the word, knowing Rowan was just a room over. "Where is he?"

Her dread solidified into outright fear then. Her chair scraped then slammed to the ground as she stood up. The other woman smiled as if she had said nothing wrong.

"You see, my husband is a very important man who has sullied our name by sleeping with the common filth. You might know him." Emilie backed subconsciously towards the cabinet to her right. Where a single pistol laid buried under moth-eaten sweaters. Somewhere that smelled so bad even Rowan's curiosity wouldn't allow him to enter.

Please don't come out, Rowan, she mentally pleaded while the other woman advanced.

"You might know him." Emilie nearly dropped to her knees. "The king of Krycolis."

There were no gods that could save her now, not as Queen Irene stared her down with the most lethal of glares. This was the culmination of her worst fears. This is the one person in the kingdom who could kill her baby, and no one would care. It wasn't even Ophelus' betrayal that stabbed through her heart, but the fact that he was the one person who could save them, and he wasn't there.

None of that mattered now. All that mattered was Rowan and that he lived. Bastard or not, he had some claim to the throne now, and that would be his protection. Not even the queen could touch him if Ophelus found him first. She had to distract Irene, buy him time. Even if it killed her.

In a heartbeat, she lunged for the cabinet and threw it open. Her fingertips grazed the barrel of the gun, but Irene was quicker. The queen's weight pushed down onto her back as she wrenched the pistol from her grip.

"You do realize, Emilie, that you just committed treason? Raising a weapon against your queen- tsk. I'll have no choice but to kill you now." Her crimson lips curved upwards in a wicked grin. "After I kill your son."

Slowly, she heard the creak of a door opening. She didn't dare to hope as she realized Hell had come to her home.

"Mom?" Rowan's blonde head peaked out from behind the door, a toy sword resting in his small hands. Irene's weight lifted from Emilie's back as the queen prowled forward. Rowan raised his sword, unfaltering as the villainess strode towards him.

"ROWAN, RUN!" Emilie screamed. Her vision was blurred, impaired by the knock to the floor, but still, she scrambled to her feet. Rowan stood his ground. Just as Irene's hands were about to wrap around his throat, Emilie lunged and tackled her to the floor.

"Mommy's bleeding!" Rowan's words barely breached her ears as Emilie fought to hang on to consciousness and the fighting queen.

"You bitch!" Irene seethed. "I'll kill you! I'll hang his head by his entrails while you watch, then I'll slit your fucking throat!"

Fear for her life meant nothing to her anymore. The pain in her head was nothing. Rowan was everything. She fought with new strength, yet Irene managed to pin her to the wall. A hidden dagger poked from her waistband, and she reached for it right as the front door banged open.

"IRENE!" Ophelus bellowed, such fury coating his mannerisms. A broken sob escaped from between her lips. Rowan was safe. Ophelus would protect him. Her head lolled back, and she managed to catch a glimpse of his face, only for her breath to catch in her throat.

Ophelus' face was not his own. His lips were pulled back into a furious snarl, and dark black skeins flowed underneath his skin.

Emilie knew he was cursed. She never cared. But this... Ophelus was a pureblood, and he was spiraling out of control. Silver blood streamed from his nose and eyes, and he stood eerily still. Irene, however, cried out in pain. Golden blood spilled from her ears, and her face began to turn a hellish shade of purple. Ophelus was crushing her from the inside out.

Emilie crawled away in horror towards Rowan, tucking his head into her chest and covering his ears.

Irene was blessed, there was no way for Ophelus to kill her. Not without using dark magic. Not without losing his mind.

"Ophelus, please. Stop," she begged, her fingers slowly reaching for her gun. Her beloved didn't even look her way, just narrowed his gaze on his wife, who lay writhing on the ground. She held Rowan closer to her chest as the queen began to scream silently. Her mouth dropped open as she choked on her blood, and her eyes rolled back. Emilie stood with Rowan in her arms, cocking her pistol. Rowan's wooden sword clattered to the floor.

The king's attention snapped to them.

His eyes softened, the first sign of him she'd seen all day. "Emilie-"

"*Don't*," she warned, raising the pistol to her chest. "Don't come any closer. King or not, I'll put a bullet in your head."

"I was saving you," he begged. Tears dripped down her cheeks, mingling with her blood. She whispered for Rowan to close his eyes and cover his ears. He nodded, but his gaze was dazed and unfocused. Then she noticed the blood on his hairline. The blast of Ophelus' magic had hit him too, his body too weak to be in the presence of such powerful magic. She didn't need to look to know that the queen was dead.

"And you've killed yourself. You've killed us. You killed her!" She couldn't help the way her voice cracked. She loved him. By the gods she loved him. But she loved her son more. "That magic, it will kill what is left of you. For your son, please..."

Ophelus' gaze darkened again. "You will not take him from me. I need you."

He took a step forward. And with a broken heart, Emilie fired the pistol.

Ophelus roared as the bullet lodged itself in his thigh, pure silver blood pouring from the wound. She wasted no time sprinting out the door and mounting their only horse. She urged the gelding into a gallop while a storm brewed overhead.

"EMILIE!" Ophelus' howling chased them from the village. "EMILIE!"

The earth shook with the first earthquake of the season.

Emilie, Emilie, Emilie, Emilie, Emilie, Emilie, Emilie, Emilie.

Rowan let his head hit her shoulder as his eyes slipped closed. Something etched deep in his soul, the only knowledge of that day that his memory would not take from him.

They were shadows and would be so long as his father lived.

CHAPTER 43
VEROSA

I don't know how long I was out for. No windows or glint of light offer any hint of what time it is, but I know where I am. They haven't taken me from the palace yet, just moved me to one of our towers.

The Etherbane muddles my brain, lending hand to my confusion. Who would be so bold as to kidnap the crown princess and hold her hostage in her home? The rebels? No, they would have killed me already.

I drag myself towards the wall, only to be tugged backwards. A heavy clinking noise draws my attention to the wall. I notice now that my wrists are bound by a simple rope that has already begun to rub my skin raw, but a chain of some dark material attaches my restraints to the floor.

Wincing at the raw bruising across my skin, I try to slip my wrists out from the binds. It's a simple knot, but it holds effectively as the fraying bits bite into my skin, eliciting a small cry from my lips.

The noise draws the attention of two figures standing by the door. Both are covered in armor made of the same dark material as my chains. I question for a moment why they'd bother with just rope for my wrists when I note a distinctive smell. I swear. It isn't blood coating the binds, but Etherbane. I clench my teeth. These fuckers are continuously drugging me. At these watered-down levels, the worst it can do is make me ill and tamper my powers, but hours of this will kill me. I don't know how long I've been out for, an overdose can be imminent.

The guards advance, followed by an overbearing sense of darkness that wears down my senses. I nearly collapse to the floor, gasping without the strength of my pure blood to protect me. I recognize the feeling within a second, dread filling my gut.

Dark magic.

My dread rises to suffocating levels as a third person steps from the shadows behind his guards.

I cry out as my father stares down at me with a mixture of aloofness and disgust. He clicks the door shut behind him and steps towards a mound in the center of the room. He flips open a book that I recognize from that one night ten years ago. It is one from Mother's study.

Ophelus rests it atop the mound, which I realize is an altar. Bile rises in my throat as he cuts his palm. Pure blood flows out. Pure *silver* blood.

From between the bars of my cell, I can see a fourth figure step out from the shadows and bite my tongue to stop myself from crying out once more. Lucius' eyes are bloodshot, appearing like he hasn't slept in many days, but his signature dazzling grin still rests atop his face. It drops when he sees me.

"What is she... oh." His face grows pale in realization as I struggle against my bonds, the ropes drawing golden blood. Frayed fragments of the rope material is imbedded within my broken flesh, clumping with my sticky blood. I swear as I try to slip out of them again, only to rub my already open wounds raw. What was that trick Rowan had taught me? I wish I had paid more attention.

"One of pure blood must wet the flames of past sin," my father recites. The recitation's origin is unfamiliar to me, but one line stands clear. Pure blood. Pureblood. My own blood runs cold in my veins.

"But it doesn't make sense. She'd be mixed, you're not-" Lucius grasps for straws. Was he trying to save me? No, foolish thought. He doesn't care who he hurts to get what he wants.

But mixed? How would I be mixed if...

Rowan.

Emilie is blessed. Rowan is a hybrid. If Ophelus is truly Rowan's father, then...

My father is cursed, and I am not his daughter.

"I don't know where Irene found the baby." Ophelus waves his hand dismissively, not bothering to unpack that at all or meet my eye.

I don't know where Irene found the baby. All my life, he knew I wasn't his. Irene wasn't my mother. The thought almost makes me sob with joy when sorrow grips at the edges of my heart. I was someone else's, someone who probably spent their lifetime searching for me. Someone who wanted to love me. I think back to Aiko and Finneas, their warm smiles and outstretched arms. The deep sorrow imbedded in her deep and serene eyes. I could have been loved by someone like them.

Another arrow of thought pierces my heart. Rowan and me. We aren't related. Does he know? I want to chide myself for thinking that. I'm about to be served upon a silver platter to create some godforsaken monster, and all I can think about is him? The boy who left. The boy who held my heart and broke it. The boy who apparently is not my brother. Well, if I'm going to die a sacrifice, at least I know I wasn't an incestuous one.

"Bring her," Ophelus finally commands, handing my fiancé a polished obsidian dagger. It glints and sparks with lilac magic, and it would have been beautiful if I hadn't had known it sought my heart. His Adam's apple bobs as he swallows hard, his forehead glistening with new beads of sweat. He accepts the dagger surely with shaking hands, before beginning towards me.

"Wait, if you kill me, you'll never find Rowan!" Ophelus' eyes widen as I swallow thickly. He raises a gnarled hand; his fingertips stained a dark inky shade. Lucius halts, and I take it as my cue to speak. "Only I know where he is. He told me before he left the palace grounds. You need me to find your son and Emilie."

The king's gaze focuses for just a moment before returning to its previous glassy state. "Emilie," he repeats, rolling the name around on his tongue. "Emilie." Lucius pauses as if unsure whether to continue, the dagger sitting idle in his hands. The guards standing by the door don't move, and I wonder if they are even breathing. Even alive.

"He plans on leaving. He and Emilie are going to leave the continent together, then you'll never see your son or wife again."

"My wife is dead." Ophelus smiles cruelly as he takes me in fully this time. Perhaps he is noticing for the first time that I share Irene's same dark hair and blue eyes. "I killed her."

My heart stumbles, and I feel my leverage falter. I always knew that he had lied about my mother's death. The whole kingdom believed she was mauled to death by wolves, and it was believable seeing as her fingers had been chewed off and her eyes ripped from their sockets. But I knew the truth because I had seen the body. The same dark presence that I feel pressing on me now was present then, almost as if it was originating from inside her rotting body. That hadn't been that far-fetched either, given the type of woman that she was.

Yet I had seen the marks that damned her. The bruises and morphed terror on her face. The dried blood that dribbled from her ears and lips. That coated her teeth. Wolves go for soft spots; the eyes were a plausible alibi. But wolves eat organs, they don't crush them.

I knew immediately it was murder, and a death at the hands of dark magic no less. However, there haven't been any factions of dark mages in years, not since the late king's father killed them all. The rebellion is as close as we have gotten to these factions and yet no dark magic arose.

Until now.

"Your love," I amend. "You will never see your son or your love again. Not if you kill me."

It is Lucius who speaks next, his voice surprisingly strong despite our recent discoveries. "Ophelus, my king. She could be lying. If you want to find them, you need a pureblood. Sacrifice is the only surefire way." He searches my face for any sign of understanding. "I wish there was another way."

The way he speaks forces me to believe him, that he truly does wish he could save me. Just not enough to give up whatever end goal he has in mind. I scoff. He was never trying to save me. Within that twisted head of his, he has been weighing the cost to benefit of our every word exchanged, deciding whether there was information I held over him. Power I held over him.

Furiously, I try to pull from that well of power from within me. I focus on pushing a steady stream of light from the warm glow emitted by the torches and searing a cavity into his chest. My magic sputters against the Etherbane still coursing through my blood, eventually dimming to the point of invisibility. I curse in frustration. Powerless and trapped. I will need to rely on my training to break out.

Watching my failed attempt at a deadly light show, Ophelus makes his decision.

"Bring her here."

I suck in a sharp breath as my fiancé advances once more. That dark blade in his hand sings once it reaches my proximity, and that dark power pushes against my senses once more. I inhale sharply, preparing for the performance of my life. I bite my lip hard enough to sting, and tears spring to my eyes.

"Don't come near me." The sob escapes my throat before I can stop it, raw and unhinged. It comes from somewhere deeper than I had access to. It comes from a girl far too familiar with betrayal and abandonment. Somewhere deeper still underneath it all is fury. The burning rage of the mage spited, ancestors murdered. Both of these men kept the truth from me; they surpassed my past.

Ophelus stole me from my home and those who could have loved me. So I will escape then steal his life.

Lucius stands before me down, his dark hair free from its usual slicked back style. Dark circles reside underneath those blood shot eyes, sinking deep into his fair skin. His face softens, his shoulders dropping in sorrow.

"My love, please."

"Don't you dare!" I hiss and bite his hand when he reaches for me. He recoils in shock at the blood drawn as I spit a chunk of his flesh from between my lips. If they want to cage and slaughter me like an animal, then fine. An animal I will become.

Lucius looks to be on the brink of tears at my insinuation. Like he actually cares for me. "You must understand. My mother-"

Understand? He wishes for me to understand him? The sound of rushing water fills my ears, funneling out the rest of his proclamation. In my tapestries and stories, the innocent sacrifice always forgave those who slaughtered her. She chooses the high road of love, and yet, she dies every single time. She smiles in the face of betrayal.

Well, I say, *fuck that.*

When Lucius is close enough, I throw myself forward, my shoulder aimed for his knees. My blow makes contact, sending the dagger flying only to clatter just before me, Lucius an equal distance away.

My wounded wrists scream as I slice the rope free of them, the dank air stinging as my blood drips to the floor. Those violet flames leap towards the sky, licking up each drop before burning brighter than before. The sight is jarring, but I force my focus elsewhere. An empty spot of the floor where Lucius used to lay.

The cool edge of the dark blade presses against my throat as Lucius' labored breathing skitters across the shell of my ear.

"Don't spill a single drop of blood until she's on that altar," Ophelus commands, watching with a void expression. I want to scream at him to care, to act like it hurts even a bit to consider murdering me even if I never was his daughter. Even if I already saw how he smiled speaking of Irene's murder.

Lucius murmurs, lowering the blade just a bit. "He'll bring her back."

His mother. My father has promised to bring his mother back from the dead in exchange for his cooperation.

I can see his shaking grip, the crimson blood laced with golden flecks spewing from his wounded hand. The reality of his words hit me like a bullet through my chest. Could Ophelus really have the power? Would he bring me back once I died, and would I even want that? What would the cost be? I shiver despite the heat of the room. If the cost is an innocent life already, I'm not sure I would want to be brought back.

No, I need time. I turn my gaze towards the shell of my fiancé. There must be something of him left inside.

"You said you loved me, was that a lie too?"

"No." He shakes his head, confused. "But in a world like this, my love for you could never be enough, not compared to my love for her." From the corner of my eye, I see Ophelus stiffen, but think nothing of it as that dagger bares down closer to my exposed throat. He shuffles backwards, forcing me with him.

"Fuck you," I spit, blood dribbling from the corner of my mouth. This dark power in the room, it's too intense. I'll die before the blade even plunges into my heart.

My body burns hot with contained power attempting to break through, and the scent of burning flesh fills the air. Lucius swears but doesn't loosen his grip, even as I feel the boils raising on his skin.

Raising my hands in a desperate measure, I bury my palms against his open eyes and focus on pushing the Etherbane from my blood, forcing it to evacuate my blood through the wounds on my wrist. Then I call for my magic again, this time *demanding* it to surface instead of pleading.

The result is a satisfactory sizzle and screams as I burn through Lucius' eyes, searing through his cornea straight back through the retina and optic nerve. The prince drops to the floor, howling in agony as he clutches at his ruined eyes. I spare him no time as I raise my hands, invigorated and prepared to fight.

Ophelus only sighs and flicks his wrists towards the guards. Dark pressure pushes on my head, forcing me to my knees as my legs refuse to support my weight. The sentries step forward, each placing a hand on my shoulders and elbows, dragging me towards that dark alter.

I lash out, throwing an elbow towards a guard, knocking his helmet clean off his head. His hold doesn't release; rather, my elbow took more damage than he has. I lift my gaze to his face, waiting to see who has betrayed me.

Then I scream.

Raiko's face is all but falling off of his skull. Maggots writhe in his eye sockets, dried blood flecking across the sagging and purple skin. Dark veins stretch up his neck, creating black webs across his rotting skin. His lips sag opens as if he cannot bear to hold his jaw taut anymore.

But Raiko died months ago protecting me from the rebels. This body, it is nothing more than a shell. A host for whatever dark force now resides in his body. A force that my father apparently commands.

Raiko's carcass throws my body onto the alter while the other undead pins me on my back. The midnight stone of the altar does the rest of the work, forcing my flesh to melt with the stone.

The flames spread towards me, specifically my wrist and bleeding lip, where golden blood still drips. My rage made me sloppy, I realize too late. I should have immobilized the guards and never underestimated them. That was one of my first lessons, and I had forgotten it.

"It would have been better if Rowan had killed you," I spat, the stone biting into my back through the thin material of my nightgown. "Now I see why Emilie chose him over you. She hates you; she deserves to hate you."

A cheap blow, and quite a futile attempt to save myself. Ophelus' face only darkens, and he gesticulates a stabbing into his chest then slitting motion across his throat. The dark guards move silently, collecting the blade from the sobbing and blind prince, then returning to the alter.

"No!" I scream. I thrash. I cry and kick and shout and bite, but it does nothing. I am just a counterfeit princess who is in over her head. If Rowan were here- no. Rowan has probably taken his mother and the Nightwalkers *far* away from here by now, trying to forget all about me. Blaine is either dead or has forgotten about me, and by the time Torin and Tanja wake, I will be dead. No one is here to save me this time, and I'm not strong enough to save myself.

I close my eyes in defeat, allowing the darkness to pull me unto it.

"Forgive me." I pray to no one in particular.

Then he strikes.

"NO!"

I see her too late. The force that pushes into my side is stronger than anything I've known, and for a moment, that dark power is completely vanquished, replaced by something warm. Light.

A scream fills the room, something inhuman and dark. The louder it rings out, the more I realize it is not a scream, but a screech.

I roll as I hit the ground beside the altar, the hem of my skirt catching the violet flame. It burns through the fabric to singe my leg, but it's not for the wound that I cry out for. My eyes meet Tanja's, glassy and wide, as she lay atop the altar with the dagger meant for me imbedded deep in her back. The blade slid through her ribs, barely missing her heart. The hilt rests on her back as the jagged tip sticks out between her breasts. She gasps for a moment, but it's a hollow death rattle. Around the blade is thick blood, completely golden throughout.

Terror and despair like nothing I've ever felt before douses my body with a cold shock. How can she... She can't...

"Tanja. Gods, Tanja," I sob, leaping up to pressing my forehead to hers, letting my tears mingle with hers.

"Verosa," she wheezes painfully, gripping my hand as a guard advances. "Vera. *Run.*"

I try to protest, to do anything other than scream as I watch blood identical to my own drip from the fatal wound meant for me. It should be my heart grating against that blade.

Everything begins to make sense all too late.

The last pureblood in the palace died nearly nine years ago, Rowan had said. And she had a daughter.

Tanja.

I press my forehead to hers. I won't leave. I won't run. I cannot live in a world where she's not there, a world where she dies like this.

"*I love you,*" she murmurs, "*So live. Live Vera.*"

I don't have time to respond when the first drop of her precious blood hits the altar. A blinding, violet light sears through the room, throwing me from my feet towards the door. I can hear her scream through the ringing of my ears. I can barely see her anymore, but her last words remain clear in my mind. *Live.* Grabbing a discarded sword that lay to my right, I bolt through the doors. The remaining guard starts to follow me, but Ophelus holds up a single hand, effectively stopping him.

"Let her bleed," I hear him say, then they slit her throat.

I don't dare look back.

I stumble blindly through the palace corridors, slashing blindly at anyone who dares try and stop me. Most of the palace staff look at me in confusion, then terror paralyzes their features when they see the golden blood on my gown and the savage wounds that litter my body.

I want to scream at them, blame them for letting her take that knife. Blame anyone and everyone for letting this happen, anyone but myself. Another sob tears itself loose from my chest when I pass my room. A room where, a few hours ago, Tanja and I had laughed and cried together, preparing for tomorrow. That room looks cold and unfamiliar now, just like the rest of the palace. Had that been the hallway where

Torin and Tanja walked me from my gown fitting? Which way to the knights' quarters, how do I get to that passageway? Why is there so much blood?

The world begins to spin as I find that one rock again, and as if by some miracle, the wall opens just enough for me to get in. I don't care for light as I sprint through the darkness, grief overwhelming my terror. The ground squelches beneath my bare feet, when did I lose my shoes? I see the light ahead, if I can just get to the outer palace, I'll be okay. Rumbling comes from above, and I watch as a chunk of rock falls from the ceiling. I leap ahead to narrowly avoid being crushed to death as the second begins to fall. Whatever Ophelus is doing, it might be powerful enough to bring down the whole castle. The grinding of rock on rock intensifies as I reach the end, the dying beams of sunlight still reaching out for me. But the walls are caving in, I'm not going to make it.

RUN. Tanja's voice rings though my head. *RUN, VERA. RUN. RUN. RUN. RUN. RUN. RUN. RUN!*

With a final leap, I make it out just as the tunnel collapses, and run straight into a familiar redhead, rather, his horse. Seb struggles to hold tight to the reins as I crash into him and his mount, the mare tossing her beautiful head high in the air.

"*Mei Reinhavich*? What's happening "

I clutch at his leg, the world spinning. Information filters through my head too quickly for my brain to comprehend. Palace crumbling. Purple flame. Father not my father. Tanja dead. Tanja...

"Dead. She's dead, she's..."

Seb takes one look from my dismantled state then the crumbling palace before a knowing fear crosses his face. Somehow, he knows just what is coming, and knows well enough to fear it.

"Mei Reinhavich, get out of here. Now." I look up at him in confusion as he dismounts and draws his sword. From the passageway I just exited, I can hear the screams, and something guttural growls as it advances. I look down at the golden trail I left, leading straight to myself. Whatever is in the palace is coming this way, and it is coming for me.

"I'll buy you time." He pushes the reigns into my hands and helps me mount the mare quickly. Gone is the blushing squire who had to chase me through palace halls and escort me to lessons. Determination replaces any fear that had written itself across his face. "If any of us are going to survive, you have to."

I don't ask how he knows what he does, or what he means. Something tells me if he lives, he will seek me out one day to tell me himself.

"Find Torin," I gasp. The knight nods.

"I will. Now go!"

I spin the mare around with a far too rough hand, the bit tugging harshly against her soft mouth. She tosses her neck in complaint but is quick to obey as I urge her into a gallop, leaving the palace far behind. I turn my back to the sun and chase the darkness Eastward.

- CHAPTER 43 –

CHAPTER 44

ROWAN

Silent tears slip down my mother's face as she finishes the memory, pieces of the day coming back to my mind now. My heart aches as if Irene had split it open all those years ago, and my brain is just now telling me to feel the pain.

"Your father loved us more than anything." Her voice breaks as she whispers. "But he died that day. An evil now wears his skin, chasing after your father's final desire."

She doesn't have to say it for me to know what she means. All those times we had to move from town to town, never being able to leave Krycolis for fear of the border guards recognizing us. The king is still searching for us, to 'protect' us, as was his final wish before he died.

Any strength I once prided myself on having crumbles as my throat constricts. He died for us. He died for me.

"I was working with Vera so I could sneak in and kill him," I blurt out. "I was going to kill him, but I was a coward."

Emilie's eyes shine with the very few unshed tears she has left. Her hand rests atop mine, and she squeezes.

"I know. Aiko told me." I laugh softly. Of course, she did. "That would have been a mercy to him, but it would have killed you. You don't have to save everyone. Sometimes you just need to live for you and the ones you love."

"How can you say that? You loved him, you might be the only person who did."

"Love is like anything else. It can die. It can be replaced." She smiles sadly. "Soulmates don't exist, my little *Noiteron*. Love is a choice, and sometimes you have to choose one love over the other."

She grips my arm tightly with her small hands. The corners of her eyes crinkle. Eyes that match my own. Laughter lines in a world like this.

"And I chose you. I will always choose you."

Something Vera said to me infiltrates my mind, the dread seeping in like water in a deep cave. Slowly it seeps through the cracks until it's all consuming.

Maybe you're her new light.

My mother made her choice, now I must make mine. I need to get my light back.

"Kya."

Amír steps through the doorway instead, a knowing smirk playing on her lips. "You don't even have to ask. She left over an hour ago."

I'm already strapping my leathers on and reaching for my sword by the time Amír's lips part for a breath. My mother watches with a knowing, and if I dare say it, *proud* smile.

"I'll be back, Mom," I promise solemnly. "I-"

BANG.

Kya's eyes are wide as she bursts through the door, a tremor of the earth chasing her the rest of the way into the compound. Amír swears loudly. It's not earthquake season.

"What's going on?"

"She's not there."

My heart stops dead in my chest; my mother's eyes drill holes in my back. Verosa. I just left her there, and now she's gone.

"Where is she?" I rush forward gripping my assassin's shoulders, perhaps far too tightly. "Where. Is. She."

"Gone, but Rowan... There was *so much* blood." She swallows thickly. "*Golden* blood."

I never knew it was possible until now to feel the earth fall out from beneath my feet. I left her there. *I left her.*

"I tracked them as far as I could. I overheard one of the maids tell the other that she saw the king and that prince, Lucius, bringing a large number of guards to the tallest tower. No one was allowed to enter, but they saw a weird light and purple flames." Emilie swears softly in recognition. "The maid took off running for the tower, and I followed until they closed the door. I tried to get through but there was this magic, and I heard her call Vera's name and something about a sacrifice but then…"

"But then what." I hardly recognize the icy tone as my own, but my grip weakens on her shoulders in the wake of realization.

"The screaming was terrible. And it sounded like her."

I let the images flit through my mind. Tanja had likely stayed in Verosa's room to console her after I left her. The wedding was going to be tomorrow. My father needed Vera for something… a sacrifice perhaps. My brain struggles to form a complete picture. Where did Lucius fit in? Did he know?

A heavy dread settles in my stomach. Lucius was a crucial part somehow, but Ophelus needed a reason for him to be here, so he offered up Verosa as bait. The alliance is a fraud, and the marriage is a ruse.

So Tanja finds Vera. That's where this story ends… for now.

I release my assassin as I grab one of her espas from her hand. The slender blade allows me to feel even the slightest vibrations of the wind. I grit my teeth. I will feel their hearts stop against this blade. I will feel the air exit their throats as I slit their one oxygen supply. I will murder them all.

Amír steps in front of me. Blocking my path.

"Move," I growl. Kya stands behind me, her hand on her other espa, waiting to intervene. My mother stills, knowing better than to come between my second and me when we are in a disagreement.

"Where are you going?" she challenges, not budging.

"I'm going to get her."

Amír scoffs. "You'll die before you even get past the first sentries."

"Death will wait for me. I'm getting her out of there."

"Rowan." Kya tries softly. "She's *gone.*"

"No, you don't get it. She isn't. She can't be."

"Rowan-"

"Even if she's dead, I'm not leaving her body for those monsters!" I whirl in a fury, panic dulling my senses. "They don't get to imprison her even in death."

The room is silent before Amír strikes. The woman lifts her gun, flipping it to knock the handle across my temple, presumably to knock me out until I come to my 'senses.' She forgets I am the leader for a reason. With the back of my hand, I block the blow, my skin and bones barking in pain upon contact. I push past the pain to take a sweep for her legs and right wrist, disarming her.

Kya leaps forward and blocks the door by swinging her remaining espa my way. She trusts my experience enough to know I will block and that she cannot do much real damage. I raise her other blade, the two slender daggers slamming into each other. The motion shoots pain, and echoes of the strike reverberate up my arms and reside mainly in my elbows. It shocks my system long enough for the assassin to plant her boot on my chest and shove me back towards the wall.

Derrín takes the opportunity to wrap his arms around my legs.

"Oh, for fuck's sake," I growl, shaking out my leg to try to detach the mechanic. He refuses to budge. Amír regains her senses, placing her gun on safety before firmly securing my arms behind my back. Kya guards the door, her second espa reclaimed from my grasp. She raises them both, forming an X over the door even as tears stream down her face.

Vera was their friend too, I remember. They refuse to lose another one all in the same day.

Amír finds her voice first. "Let her go, Rowan." She bites her cheek in a sorry attempt to hide the shake in her voice, and the tears threatening to spill over. She hardens her stare, assuming the role of the strength of our group. "If Vera was used as a sacrifice involving dark magic, we all know there won't be anything of her left. You remember that from Mavis."

No, I won't think that. She can't just be here one minute then gone, not even a whisper to remember her by. I sink to my knees, and much more forgiving arms wrap their arms around my shoulders. My mother's damp cheek presses against my own. We need to run, especially if my father has harnessed dark magic again and is searching for us.

But all I can see is my final shimmer of hope slowly fading away. Too much, this world has taken too much. My Nightwalkers release their hold right as another earthquake sends our home shaking. Another sound rises above this, a sound that stops my barely beating heart.The door begins to rattle on its hinges, and I know now that the gods are dead.

Shadows. We have never been more than shadows all my life, and yet they found us. They have come for her. Haven't they taken enough?

My family parts, defaulting to me as leader again. Kya wipes at her eyes with the backs of her hands as she raises her blades. I motion for Derrín to bring my mother to the back door. I raise my sword before me, preparing to slice through whatever assailant appears.

Then a knock. Soft but sure at the door. Impatient and relentless.

The Laei, I decide, do have a sense of humor. A cruel and wicked sense of humor, I think as I open the door to find Vera staring back at me.

My sword clatters to the ground. This can't be real, she must be an apparition here to haunt me for leaving her. My eyes begin to burn.

She reaches up, her pale and bruised fingers just barely brushing my jawline before she stumbles forward. Within an instant, I have my arms securely wrapped around her shaking frame as I lower us both to the ground. Tear stains streak through the debris and blood littered across her face. My thumb brushes over a bruise. She winces, and fury broils in my chest. I am going to fucking kill them.

Her silken nightgown leaves her shivering in the cool spring morning, the hem torn and bloodied. Some red and gold blood lines her teeth, her mouth, and her gown. The remaining blood is pure gold, and it coats her arms and legs. Her bare feet leave bloody footprints in the entry way. Her indigo eyes stare up at me, wide enough I swear I can see the sockets peeking out behind them.

She coughs, the action rattling her whole body. Black dust spews from between her lips, identical to the debris coating her gown and skin.

Verosa drags a breath through her swollen and bloody lips, then whispers a single fervent word before passing out in my arms.

"Run."

Milton Keynes UK
Ingram Content Group UK Ltd.
UKHW011928271023
431481UK00017B/172/J